RAVE REVIEWS FOR THE DONOVAN NOVELS BY W. MICHAEL GEAR:

"What a ride! Excitement, adventure, and intrigue, all told in W. Michael Gear's vivid, compulsively readable prose. A terrific new science-fiction series; Gear hits a home run right out of the park and all the way to Capella."
— Robert J. Sawyer, Hugo Award-winning author of *Quantum Night*

"A marginal colony on a living world—where human life and human will are tested to the limits. An intriguing and inventive new work from Michael Gear."
— C. J. Cherryh, Hugo Award-winning author of *Downbelow Station*

"Gear kicks off a new sf series by weaving a number of compelling characters into the narrative, including bold heroine Talina Perez and Donovan itself, a planet teeming with danger and delights in turn. The mix of stolen identities, rapacious greed, and treacherous landscape propels the reader forward. . . . Fans of epic space opera, like Rachel Bach's *Fortune's Pawn*, will happily lose themselves in Donovan's orbit."
— *Booklist*

"W. Michael Gear creates a fun and colorful setting on a planet full of interesting fauna and cunning, deadly animals."
— *RT Reviews*

"The novel's prose is as razor-sharp as Donovan's toothy beasts, its characters deftly defined. The enveloping narrative gallops along at a fierce pace."
— *SyFy Wire*

"A thrilling tale of high-stakes survival on an alien planet."
— *Dread Central*

UNRECONCILED

DONOVAN: BOOK FOUR

W. Michael Gear

DAW BOOKS, INC.
DONALD A. WOLLHEIM, FOUNDER
1745 Broadway, New York, NY 10019
ELIZABETH R. WOLLHEIM
SHEILA E. GILBERT
PUBLISHERS
www.dawbooks.com

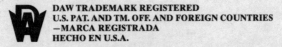

TO MY BEAUTIFUL
KATHLEEN O'NEAL GEAR
WHO HAS FILLED MY LIFE
WITH THE KIND OF MAGICAL LOVE THAT ONLY
EXISTS IN FAIRY TALES.

IRREDENTA

I sit—as I often do—in the observation dome. A transparent bubble, it protrudes from Ashanti's *hull on Deck Three. I look out upon an infinity of stars, see the swirls of nebulae, marvel at patches of dark matter that appear as blemishes upon the composition of light. Gazing at the heavens, I experience the full meaning of awe. To sit here is to dimly, feebly perceive the majesty of Creation. The magnificence of the universe beyond the dome defies comprehension. Reconfirms how small, how absolutely insignificant my existence is.*

A mere mote. Not even a speck upon the face of the deep.

I need but look out at the universe and the words of the Prophets resonate within me. Understanding pervades my soul: I have been chosen.

We *have been chosen.*

Here, in this most unlikely place. Among these most unlikely circumstances.

Only after years of doubt, of faltering faith, do I begin to understand: The universe does not make mistakes. It had to be Ashanti. *It had to be on this spacing. And it had to be us, the Irredenta, who were chosen to initiate such an immense task.*

What we believed to be tragedy, injustice, and horror was nothing more than the universe preparing us for the ultimate revelation. As seemingly insignificant as we might appear, we are the beginning, the spark that shall ignite the flame. Great things come from tiny beginnings. Consider a microRNA. It, too, seems insignificant at first glance. A mere twenty-two base pairs. It can turn a gene on or off, initiating a chain of events that will change an organism, a species, and an entire biome. From the microscopic to the multiverse.

So it is for us.

The Harrowing and Cleansing was necessary to ensure

*that when we were given the Revelation we would under-
stand. The universe had to lock us in Ashanti's belly. Onto
this one miserably cramped deck. It had to confine us to
these few rooms, these short corridors and dim halls. An
entire universe condensed into this compact existence. The
perfect place to break us, to shatter our illusions. Only
through the Harrowing and the Cleansing could we be prepared, made malleable like white-hot iron in a furnace,
purified through heat, and ready to accept Revelation.*

*The Revelation ran counter to all we once believed,
which is the way of illumination. It was the only way we
could learn, could see, and finally accept ultimate Truth:
The universe is conflict. It is polluted and unclean. The
only way it can be purified is by consuming itself and being
reborn. Think of the ancient image of the snake devouring
its own tail.*

*It has fallen to us—to me—to initiate the pulse of rebirth
that will cleanse and renew the universe. And I am desperately afraid that I am unworthy of so great a task.*

*If Deck Three didn't have this observation dome, I
would never have found the strength to endure the burden.
But looking out at the infinite dots of light, the frosting of
stars and galaxies that mottle the endless black, I manage
to carry on.*

The universe doesn't make mistakes.

*If it has chosen me to be its messiah, it is because some-
how, I will prevail.*

*I finger the scars on my arms, remembering the words of
the Prophet Guan Shi. How we were horrified as she took
a knife to her own skin and began to cut herself, saying,
"Pain is purification. It is the path."*

1

Watch began at 06:00 ship's time as *Ashanti* continued its long deceleration into the Capella star system. For Captain Miguel Angel Galluzzi it was anything but another day in the countdown from hell. He strode down the long corridor from his cabin. Every other light panel had been removed years ago to save energy. Didn't matter, he could have walked it blindfolded.

Around him, *Ashanti* hummed, and he could feel the familiar vibrations of a living ship. Could feel the movement of air on his face as he passed one of the ventilators. It surprised him that he could still detect the stale odor of confinement and clogged filters.

It had been seven years, ship's time, since *Ashanti*'s generators had ceased to maintain the fields that inverted symmetry. When they did, the ship had popped back "inside" the universe and found itself in black empty space. Low on fuel, and 0.6 light-years from the Capella system.

Since then he'd lived an eternity—one from which he wasn't certain he'd ever recover. A waking horror without end.

As if perdition began in *Ashanti* and would end there.

Sometimes he wondered if it wouldn't have been better to have overloaded the reactors. Blown the ship into a brilliant miniature sun. Ended it all.

He'd committed crimes against humanity, and in the process, he'd heroically saved his ship. But when one sells his soul to the Devil, the dark one will always have his due.

Galluzzi contemplated that as he passed the Captain's Lounge and hesitated at the hatch for the Astrogation Center, or AC for short. In another day and age, it would have been called the bridge. After the advent of quantum qubit computer operational systems, navigational functions had been completely removed from human control. That didn't mean that people didn't have to monitor systems, that decisions didn't have to be made.

A feeling of excitement—mixed with nervous anxiety—began to burn in his breast. And something he hadn't known for years stirred: hope.

Staring at the featureless hatch, he swallowed in an effort to still the crawling sensation in his stomach. If the conference came off as scheduled, he would be talking to a Corporate Supervisor. For the first time he would have to confess and defend his actions. Didn't matter if they hauled him out and shot him as long as his crew didn't have to pay the price for his decisions.

The sick anxiety in his stomach worsened; that damnable nervous spasm began: his right hand was twitching like a poisoned mouse. He used to function with stone-cold competence under stress. The twitch had manifested in the hard months after they'd popped back "inside" so far from Capella.

Doesn't matter what they do to me. It will all be over soon.

For the last month, his first officer, Edward Turner, had been in contact with the Corporate survey ship, *Vixen*. The messages had been simple photonics, which due to the difference in relativity had been a rather drawn-out affair. This morning, as *Ashanti* came out of its occulted position from behind the system's primary they were finally close enough for a visual conference. Entangled photonic communications would allow them an almost simultaneous transmission.

Galluzzi girded himself. Wouldn't let the others see how fragile and anxious he was. Couldn't let them know how close to tears he felt.

The trembling in his right hand was getting worse. He knotted it into a fist.

Back stiff, composed, he cycled the hatch and stepped into the Astrogation Center to find his officers already in their seats. In the rear, Benj Begay, the forty-five-year-old Corporate Advisor/Observer was seated in one of the two observation chairs. Director of Scientific Research Michaela Hailwood, from the Maritime Unit, sat in the other.

"Good morning," Galluzzi greeted, snapping out a two-fingered salute from his brow. For today he'd worn his dress uniform. It felt good, professional, to be dressed for the part. Not that there were any illusions left when it came to his crew or the scientists. Not after a decade of living in such close quarters. But today, for the first time since inverting symmetry outside of Neptune's orbit, he'd be face-to-face with total strangers. Powerful strangers. And they would judge him.

"You ready?" Begay asked wryly. "I'm so wound up I could almost scream. Half of me wants to get up and dance, another part of me wants to throw up."

"Hard to believe. I know," Galluzzi replied. "But we're still not out of the shit. We've got a couple of months left before we're in Cap III orbit. And there's no telling what's going to happen when we finally inform the Unreconciled that we're closing on the planet."

"Do we have to tell them, Cap?" Second Officer Paul Smart sat at the com console and worked the photonic data.

"Might be better," Turner said, "if we just established orbit first. Shut most of the ship down. Then, when there was nothing left to go wrong, we could let them know."

Begay shifted uneasily. "Just leave them in the dark? Then spring it on them? Surprise! We're here."

Galluzzi, who'd been wrestling with the problem for days, raised a worried brow. "We're in uncharted depths. And remember, it's not our sole decision. There's Supervisor Aguila to consider. She's the Corporate authority here."

"Captain?" Second Officer Turner called, voice tense. "Might have been our sync that's off, but the signal's coming in." He bent to his projected holo data, using his hands and implants to manipulate the photonic gear and refine the signal.

Shit on a shoe. I'm not ready for this.

Galluzzi gritted his teeth, slipped into the command chair. Fought to control his trembling hand. He stared at the communications holo, dark now for a decade. The realization that he was about to face a strange superior sent an eerie chill down his spine.

The image formed up, faces magically appearing as if

out of empty air. Then, under Paul Smart's and the *Vixen* com officer's competent control, the photonics linked and the projection seemed to solidify.

Galluzzi was looking at a raven-haired woman, perhaps in her thirties—though with the benefits of Corporate med, who knew? What would have been a very attractive face was lined with fine white scars. Scars? On a Corporate Supervisor? The piercing blue of her eyes had a laser-like intensity. In her form-fitting black suit, the woman exuded a sense of command, had to be Supervisor Kalico Aguila.

A small brown man sat at her side. Looked Indian, with a round face and flat-mashed nose. His unruly shock of thick black hair—graying at the sides—rose a couple of inches above his head. Curious brown eyes and an amused smile suggested an amicable nature. The biggest incongruity was the man's dress. Like he was some peasant in a homespun brown shirt embroidered with yellow flowers, and a sort of shimmering rainbow-colored cloak hung around his shoulders.

"Do we have sound?" the blue-eyed woman asked.

"We can hear you on our side, Supervisor." Galluzzi fought a tightness in his throat. "I'm Captain Miguel Angel Galluzzi, of The Corporation's *Ashanti*. IS-C-18. Behind me is Corporate Advisor/Observer Benj Begay. Seated to his left is Scientific Director Michaela Hailwood."

"I'm Corporate Supervisor Kalico Aguila, in charge of all Corporate property and activity on Donovan. What you probably know as Capella III. With me is Shig Mosadek, one of the administrators of the independent town of Port Authority."

An independent town? What the hell was that?

An eyebrow lifted, rearranging the woman's scars. "Welcome to Donovan, Captain. From what I gather, you've had a much longer and vexatious journey than you anticipated. I've reviewed your communications with *Vixen*. Somehow, I suspect there's a lot more to your story."

His hand began to jerk spastically. He stuffed it into his belt. Hoped Aguila hadn't noticed. Forced himself to begin damage control. "We've had to make some difficult choices. *Ashanti* wouldn't be here were it not for my crew, ma'am. No matter what, I want it on the record that they have acted with the utmost professionalism under difficult and soul-trying circumstances. We're anxious for the day we can set foot on Donovan."

"I suspect that you will find conditions on Donovan somewhat, shall we say, unique."

Galluzzi felt like he was choking. Okay, get it over with. "Supervisor, we've got our own 'unique' problem. One of the reasons we've been looking forward to this conversation."

Was that a lie, or what?

From behind, Begay said, "Ma'am, as the Corporation's Advisor/Observer, I want you to know that I backed every one of Captain Galluzzi's decisions when it came to the Unreconciled." He paused at her blank look. "Um, the transportees, Supervisor. They also call themselves the Irredenta to signify their difference and isolation from normal human beings."

Galluzzi quickly added, "Given circumstances, we've had to take some rather distasteful and unorthodox actions. While I appreciate the Advisor/Observer's support, ultimately the responsibility is mine, and mine alone. Under no circumstances did my crew do anything but follow orders. They exhibited the most professional—"

The Supervisor cut him short with a raised a hand. "Start at the beginning, Captain."

Like a man condemned, Galluzzi took a deep breath. "After a two-and-a-half-year transit, *Ashanti* popped back into our universe. For the first couple of days, we hadn't a clue as to where we were. Just lost in the black. The reaction among the crew and transportees was dismayed to say the least.

"We didn't have enough fuel to invert symmetry, restart the qubit computers, and run the math backwards in a bid to return to Solar System. Not only that, we were so far out in the empty black, the figures were pretty grim when it came to hydrogen/oxygen scavenging."

"I can well imagine, Captain. Go on."

"After Astrogation Officer Tuulikki finally established our position, it turned out that we were zero-point-six of a light-year from the Capella star system. We made the decision to run for it. Used what was left of the fuel for a burn, fully aware of how long it would take to reach Capella. But we were moving, which increased hydroxy scavenging. Had a couple of months where we weren't sure we were going to make it. At least until we hit the break-even point."

Call that a mild understatement.

Aguila's expression remained inscrutable, and in association with the scars, it suggested that he was dealing with one hard and tough woman.

"Of course, as we got closer to the Capella system, scavenging increased, which increased our thrust. Bootstrapping, you see. Then, two and a half years ago, we reversed thrust. Began the process of deceleration."

"Doesn't sound like anything but prudent and competent spacing, Captain."

"Yes, ma'am. The problem was the transportees. The hydroponics system had an operational life of four years. We were looking at ten. The only way to extend the hydroponics to last ten years was to reduce the demand put upon the system."

Aguila's face might have been carved from cold stone. No trace of emotion showed in her glacial-blue stare.

Galluzzi's heart began to pound. His mouth had gone dry. "I gave first priority to my crew. If they died, the ship died. We survived the cut in rations because we had a command structure. Discipline. A purpose. A bond that went deeper than mere shared humanity. But the transportees . . ."

Aguila's eyes narrowed the least bit, her lips pursed. "Did you euthanize them all?"

Euthanize?

"No, ma'am!" Galluzzi choked down a swallow. "They were panicked. Desperate. They could do the math as well as we could. Enough of them worked in hydroponics that it was common knowledge: Over time, feeding that many people, the vats were going to break down. Didn't matter that we didn't have enough fuel to invert symmetry in an attempt to return to Solar System, some of them decided they were going to seize the ship, space for Solar System. They made a violent try for the AC."

Galluzzi winced, remembering the bodies in the corridors. Blood pooling on the sialon.

"We held the ship, ma'am. Beat them back. They withdrew to Deck Three. Before they could reorganize and try for the command deck again, I had the hatches sealed. Welded. But for that, we'd never have saved *Ashanti*. Or the crew. Or any of the transportees."

"But you saved some?" she asked thoughtfully.

He couldn't stop the shiver that ran through him. Tried to still the memories. His hand was jerking despite being stuffed under his belt. The images that lurked behind his every thought drifted up like vaporous apparitions. To tell it to another person, someone who hadn't lived the horror, left him on the verge of tears.

How did he explain?

"What they did to each other down there? We saw, ma'am. At least in the beginning before they blacked out the cameras. It was . . . It . . ."

He couldn't stop the shakes.

Stop it! You're the captain!

He sucked in a breath, flexed every muscle in his body.

"I take it they turned on each other?" Aguila asked softly.

"With the critical ship's systems isolated from the transportees' deck, *Ashanti* continued to function as best she could. A food ration, insufficient as it was, was delivered to them by conveyor from the hydroponics, air and water circulated. Yes, we isolated the transportees, sealed them into Deck Three, but we gave them every support we could. Those were human beings in there. Families. Men, and women, and children."

"How many are still alive, Captain?"

"Not sure, ma'am. We inverted symmetry off Neptune with four hundred and fifty-two aboard. Eighty-seven were crew. Three hundred and sixty-five transportees, including the Maritime Unit. As of today, I have sixty-three crew. Counting the children born since transit began, there are thirty-two in the Maritime Unit. We estimate the population of the Irredenta at around ninety to a hundred."

"So, they're still sealed in your Deck Three?" Aguila's expression betrayed nothing. She seemed to be taking the news with an almost stoic acceptance. Why?

"Yes, well . . ."

After the "rats" had devoured themselves, they had "evolved" to be such . . . what? How did he describe the Irredenta without sounding like he'd lost his mind?

"Supervisor, we have a voice com still linked to Deck Three, and on occasion messages are passed. The Irredenta— the word refers to a culturally autonomous region existing under foreign control. Well, they don't exactly carry on sophisticated conversations. Mostly it's just propaganda about their Prophets. Their leader is a man named Batuhan. Thinks he's some sort of messiah. They say he interprets for the Prophets, whoever they are. What they send us sounds like raving. Supposed prophecies about what they call the coming 'Annihilation.' Some sort of violent spiritual cleansing of the universe."

"Messiah? Prophets?" Shig Mosadek, who'd sat silently, now asked.

"The Irredenta's leader, this Batuhan, is a fifty-year-old electrical engineer. Trained at the university at Ulaanbaatar, he was contracted on Transluna to install a new solar panel array for one of the outlying research bases on Capella III. Instead, after all the bloodshed, he's ended up as a sort of messianic leader among the Irredenta."

"Messiahs come in all forms," Mosadek replied.

"Sir." Galluzzi fought the urge to pull at his too-tight collar. "If I told you some of the things Batuhan's Irredenta have done down there, you'd call me mad. That human beings could descend to the kind of demonic . . ."

He winced, trying to keep the panic out of his voice. He didn't dare lose it. Not in front of the Supervisor.

Thankfully Benj said, "We're forwarding all the records to *Vixen*. We want you to have plenty of time to review them before we arrive at Capella III."

Aguila had pursed her lips. "What happens if you unseal their deck?"

Benj spoke. "They'd murder us wholesale. Turn us into sacrifices. Cut up and eat our bodies. All in the name of their—"

"Did you say *eat*?" Aguila arched a scarred brow.

Shig had straightened, a gleam of curiosity in his eyes.

Benj's voice strained. "Some sort of belief that the universe must consume itself to be reborn in purity. That's according to Batuhan and his doctrine of holy annihilation. They think they're divine soldiers, chosen to carry their truth into the universe. They see existence as warfare. That the universe was designed to hone the fittest through perpetual self-consuming conflict. According to Batuhan's propaganda, their first trial will be the elimination of all the heretics aboard *Ashanti*. They see the ship as an interstellar womb, and as soon as they burst out of Deck Three, it will be like a birth of rage and fire."

"Fascinating," Shig murmured, his gaze intensifying.

Aguila asked, "Have they said anything about what happens after their arrival at Donovan?"

"Sure," Benj said. "Capella III is supposed to be the home that nurtures their development. Their 'childhood' as they call it. As they mature, the planet is supposed to be the springboard from which they shall spread out into the universe and either convert or destroy anyone who stands in their way."

"How did this happen?" Aguila asked.

Galluzzi winced. "I don't think you can understand until you realize the horror that engulfed Deck Three, ma'am. Like I said, they did the math. Knew that hydroponics could only produce enough to support around two hundred people in the long term. They started with a lottery. Some of the families that were chosen to starve to death didn't think much of the idea. Embarked on a more sanguine means of decreasing the population."

Benj said, "Things got ugly in a hurry down there. Think atrocity and horror and no way out. The ones who survived committed the kind of abominations that defy description. They've been locked away on that deck for close to seven years now . . . lived in the midst of their self-reinforced insanity. They've prepared themselves for the moment of their emergence from Deck Three, and when they do, they expect to initiate a wave of horror that is so terrible it will both consume and regenerate the universe."

Aguila's brow had knit. "What kind of lunacy . . . ?"

Shig placed a mild hand upon the Supervisor's arm. "Unfortunately, depending upon the reality in which one has existed, atrocity might seem the only possible explanation for existence."

Aguila asked, "You think people can make a religion of violence?"

In an oddly calm voice, Shig said, "Human beings can create a religion out of anything. It's hardwired into our genetics. And, when you think about it, it's a lot easier to make a religion out of mayhem than salvation. Let's hold judgment until we see what's on these records *Ashanti* is sending."

Aguila turned her attention to Galluzzi. "And what about you and your crew, Captain?"

Here it came. He ran a hand over the back of his neck. Hated the feel of nervous perspiration. "Supervisor, it's been rough. Most of us who are left, we're hanging on by our fingernails. Not so many suicides these days. We've gotten good at patching ourselves together when we're on the edge of insanity. Would have given up long ago except that we could see the finish line. We knew there was an eventual end to the nightmare and could count down the days. As soon as we have *Ashanti* in orbit around Capella III, it's going to be all I can do to keep my people from storming the shuttles to abandon this ship."

"Yeah, well, Captain, I don't want to rain on your hopes, but you might not find Donovan to be the nirvana you've been led to believe."

"After *Ashanti*? We'll take our chances."

"Unfortunately," she told him dryly, "you will." A pause. "One last question. Is Derek Taglioni on your passenger manifest? Is he, perhaps, still alive?"

"He is, Supervisor. And I daresay, he'll be as delighted as the rest of us to set foot on Cap III."

The Supervisor's smile had taken on a grim set. "Captain, please understand, this is a fragile colony. A dangerous world fraught with perils to life and limb. As the Corporate Supervisor, I will be enforcing all stipulations as set forth in Corporate contracts. We'll give your people time to recover, but we're barely hanging on here ourselves."

"After *Ashanti*, anything would be an improvement."

"Really?" Aguila chuckled. "We have a joke here, we share it with all newcomers: Welcome to Donovan."

2

"What do you think, Shig?" Kalico Aguila asked as her A-7 shuttle dropped into Donovan's gravity well. Through the cabin windows on the command deck she could see the reddish glow as atmospheric friction built.

In the pilot's seat ahead of her, Ensign Juri Makarov monitored the descent.

Shig had been oddly quiet—and more unusual, he'd had a perturbed expression on his usually placid face as he reviewed the hand-held holo that displayed *Ashanti*'s logs. He sat in the seat beside hers on the command deck. Normally, in the shuttle, he reminded her of a schoolboy, fascinated and delighted by everything. As if the shuttle were a new and magical marvel.

He didn't look up as he casually asked, "Who is Derek Taglioni? Why did you ask specifically about him?"

"Derek's a first cousin to Boardmember Miko Taglioni."

"Ah, I see. The Boardmember is your superior and benefactor, as I recall."

"That's a mild way of putting it." To change the subject, she said, "The way you reacted to news about these Irredenta, that's not like you. Seriously, what set you off?"

Shig looked up from the holo display. "You must understand. The human brain is more of an analog rather than a digital organ. It's plastic, and by that, I mean it can be molded, shaped by events. When traumatized, it will struggle to make sense of the violation. Attempt to reconcile and explain the insult. If the trauma is too terrible, the brain will grasp for disparate facts, string together unrelated— even impossible—data to create understanding in the new conditions. Give meaning to everything it has endured."

"Sure. I understand how brain chemistry works. The bizarre things human beings will allow themselves to believe in an effort to cope."

"These were Corporate people," Shig reminded. "Families for the most part. People who were, and I quote, 'well integrated' in the Corporate system. They were educated, affluent, and prosperous families who lived their lives in secure and very comfortable upper-status surroundings. Had nice dwellings. Played by the rules and never suffered deprivation—let alone confronted a serious threat to their wellbeing. Living as they did in the center of the Corporate cocoon, they were coddled and protected. Call them the middle of the bell-shaped curve when it came to living the Corporate dream."

"I'm well aware of the demographic," she replied. "The Board wanted well-balanced families, the kind whose profiles didn't indicate potential trouble when they reached the colony. Families who'd immediately and seamlessly integrate into colonial society."

"Right," Shig agreed. "Kindly folk who'd just do their jobs and expect to be taken care of in return. If they had any overriding passion, it was for their family and raising their kids. Perfect young trade professionals."

Kalico stared out at the curve of Donovan's horizon as the shuttle's pitch changed; g-force pushed her down into her seat. "And then they come out of inverted symmetry. They've just spent two and a half years of ship's time living inside cramped quarters. Their nerves are already frayed when they're told that if they survive the next few months, it might be another seven years before they reach their destination. The hydroponics, designed for a four-year life span, can't support four hundred and fifty people for another seven."

"Things begin to degenerate. They panic. Some try to seize the ship, and Galluzzi seals them into a single deck." Shig rubbed his brow with a nervous hand. "Galluzzi's people recorded the condition of the stripped human bones that came down the chutes for hydroponics reprocessing. My suggestion is that you don't mistake these reports for cozy bedtime reading. At least not if you want a good night's sleep."

"That horrible?"

"The transportees were dying of starvation. Each

corpse represented protein, fat, and life. But what does it mean? How do you justify surviving by eating your companions?" Shig smiled wistfully. "In religious studies, we have a term: sacred abomination. It's when something is so abhorrent and appalling, its very profanity makes its practice sacred. The ultimate reconciliation of opposites."

"What do you mean by abomination?"

"The people locked on that deck were receiving insufficient rations. They were murdering men, women, and children. Their best friends. People they had lived with, laughed with, and knew intimately. Dismembering their bodies, stripping muscle from bones, removing and eating organs. Sometimes even the bones were smashed for marrow. Brains removed from skulls. How did they justify such atrocities? They made it a religious event. A form of communion."

"Dear God."

"And, of course, they understood that sex was the reconciliation of death. Its polar opposite. If you are going to celebrate one, you must pay tribute to the other."

"Maybe I'll skip the reading."

"Suffice it to say that all those cheery, happy, normal, coddled-and-protected families suddenly found themselves trapped in the kind of violent and profane terror that shattered their psyches. The only way to survive atrocity was to commit even greater atrocity. And they did it year after year. Locked in that seeming eternal hell of Deck Three."

She didn't have to know the intimate details to understand, having spent too many hours on *Freelander*. Just the thought of the ghost ship made her stomach turn queasy.

Shig raised a finger. "And into the mix, you must throw agency: Batuhan. The charismatic leader who tells you that it isn't your fault. It's just the way the universe is. You aren't an abomination but a divinely selected agent about to remake reality. Suddenly you are serving a higher calling. Sure, you murdered and ate babies, cut fellow human beings apart and drank their blood, but through that communion they are reborn into purity."

"That's creep-freaked."

"That's the religious mind at work in an attempt to rationalize and condone abject horror," Shig replied. "Or have the lessons taught by *Freelander* eluded you?"

"Believe me, I was half expecting Galluzzi to tell me that, like Captain Orten on *Freelander*, he'd ordered the murder of all the transportees."

"Fascinating, isn't it?" Shig tapped fingers on his chin. "Aboard *Freelander* the crew developed their curious death cult, worshipping the ghosts of the people they murdered and threw into the hydroponics. On *Ashanti*, it's the transportees who are murdering each other, who have developed their own cult. Leaves us wondering if this is random coincidence. Or, with a sample of only two, if there is something about being locked in a starship—faced with starvation, atrocity, and time—that triggers the religious centers of the brain."

"So, what do you think they've become?"

"Smashana Kali."

"Excuse me?"

"I think they have turned themselves into the most terrible manifestations of the Hindu demon-goddess, Kali. The black goddess who is descended from endless time, who decapitates her victims, drinks their blood, and wears the heads of the dead around her neck. By devouring her victims, she purifies them, and the world is reborn."

"And what happens to Kali in Hindu texts?"

"She only ceases her rampage when she steps onto Shiva's chest."

"This is the twenty-second century! And we're talking cannibals? Like some primitive forest tribe?"

"Just because it's the twenty-second century, what makes you think human beings have become a different animal? Because we have The Corporation and space travel? People are still fundamentally nothing more than technologically sophisticated chimpanzees."

"Back in Solar System we could reprogram them at a psychiatric facility." Kalico mused. "Treat the madness."

"We're not in Solar System."

"Shig, you're the professor of religious studies, the proponent of ethical behavior, what do we do with them?"

"I haven't a clue."

3

The captain's lounge aboard *Ashanti* seated six. Located just down the central corridor from Astrogation Control, the lounge was a cramped room jammed against the curve of the Command Deck hull. One of the few perks of "officer's territory," it even had a small galley on the back wall. Not that ten years of ship's time had left many choices except two: tea and ration.

Miguel Galluzzi—cup of said tea in hand—nodded to the rest as he entered, stepped around to the rear, and settled into the worn duraplast of his captain's chair. On the one working holo, an image of Donovan spun against a background of stars.

In their long-accustomed seats, First Officer Turner sat at Galluzzi's right, Benj Begay on his left. Second Officer Smart had the watch, so his chair remained empty. Michaela Hailwood hunched in the seat beside Begay's. Finally, at the far end near the door, Derek Taglioni slumped in his usual place.

Galluzzi took their measure. Begay was descended from Native American stock. He was forty-five now, kept his hair in a bun tied tightly at the back of his head. His dark eyes were thoughtful as he fingered the line of his blocky chin.

Turner, who stood six-foot-five, was now in his fifties. A faint English accent still lurked in the man's speech. Galluzzi couldn't be sure, but Turner's washed-out blue eyes seemed to grow paler by the year. Like all good spacers, he kept his head shaved.

Galluzzi's gaze lingered on Michaela Hailwood, forty-seven. The lanky black-skinned woman had been born in Apogee Station. A curious origin for someone who would become chairperson of the Department of Oceanography at Tubingen University on Transluna. She headed the group of scientists dispatched aboard *Ashanti* to establish the first research station for the study of Capella III's oceans.

Still slumped in his chair, Derek Taglioni had laced his fingers together. The man's genetically engineered yellow-green eyes fixed on Galluzzi. Turns out that designers of fine haute couture on Transluna didn't tailor their snazzy garments for longevity; Taglioni's exotic clothing no longer looked natty and sharp. Derek, Dek for short, might have been in his mid-thirties, but given the medical benefits of being a Taglioni, who knew? Today his sandy-blond hair was combed over. The guy looked classic; his chiseled jaw even featured a dimple in the chin.

In the beginning—being a Taglioni—Dek had been a real self-inflated prig. Imperious. Demanding. But something about survival, about realizing that no amount of power or wealth made him any more valuable than a lowly hydroponics tech, Class III, had wrought remarkable changes in his personality and approach to life. The condescending arrogance had begun to break down during the transit. For years he'd even shaved his head like crew. But during those long months when it looked like they were all going to die? That's when something fundamental had changed in Taglioni.

Amazing what kind of man can evolve when he's knocked off his high horse and face-first into the shit.

Galluzzi stared down into his cup of tea. Not like the real thing, mind you, but a green liquid made from boiled spinach, algae, and leaves. Stuff that still grew in hydroponics, though the nutritional content was down considerably from the early days.

They all showed signs of malnutrition.

"What do you think?" Galluzzi asked. He was long past formalities with these people.

Benj, still fingering his chin, said, "Aguila's not like any Corporate Supervisor I ever knew. When I saw the scars, it scared hell out of me. Like she was one of the Unreconciled. Sent a shiver right up my spine."

Michaela placed her long-fingered hands flat on the table. "She didn't bat an eye when we told her we sealed the transportees on Deck Three. Not a single protest. Nothing about what the contractual implications might be, or what it was going to cost The Corporation in litigation."

"Tough lady," Turner said thoughtfully. "Sounds like Cap III has fallen on hard times while we've been in transit. I don't know about the rest of you, but I'm not sure how the crew is going to take this. We've sold them on the belief that when we reach Cap III, it's going to be like a paradise."

Benj chuckled. "Hey, just being out in fresh air, under an open sky, is paradise."

"After what we've been through, you'd think the universe would cut us a break." Galluzzi sipped his tea. Tried to remember what it was supposed to taste like. Nothing had much taste anymore.

Turner shot him a sidelong glance. "I think you just got your break, Miguel. Aguila didn't immediately order you arrested for what we did. I thought she'd take that a whole lot harder."

"Something's not right," Benj added. "We lost two thirds of the transportees, and what's left are man-eating monsters. Drop that kind of bombshell on a Corporate Supervisor? You expect to let loose a shitstorm."

"She almost took it as a foregone conclusion." Galluzzi rubbed his face, thankful that his hand was no longer shaking. Damn, he'd been on the edge. Like the others, he'd expected to be relieved of command, pilloried, maybe even charged with mass murder.

He glanced at Taglioni. Had hoped that if Corporate was going to flush him down the shitter, that Dek would be his only chance. Betting on a Taglioni? It showed how desperate a man could be.

"Think it's some kind of political gambit?" Begay wondered. "You know. The kind of intrigue the Board is into: layers within layers. Maybe we're suddenly pawns in some complex game she's playing. Like she's going to use our failure to keep the transportees alive as a means to destroy some adversary."

Was that it? Galluzzi's stomach began to roil. He felt the first tremors in his hand. "I just wish it was all over."

"Hey, Miguel," Michaela told him, "you're getting

ahead of yourself. We all are. Think, people. There's going to be an inquest. There has to be. You can't just seal three hundred and sixty people into a confined space, let them mutilate and eat each other, and expect to walk away without some sort of questions."

She glanced around the table. "We've known since the beginning that a day of reckoning is coming. In the meantime, we stick together. Let's not forget that by doing what we did, we got the ship to Cap III. And we did it with most of the crew alive. The entire Maritime Unit is not only alive, but with the kids there's a lot more of us than spaced from Solar System."

"Steps had to be taken," Benj agreed. "Remember what it was like? We all agreed that if we made it, we'd stand together. That what they did to one, they'd have to do to all of us."

"Here, here," Turner muttered, watery eyes fixed on infinity.

Benj turned to Taglioni. "Dek? Your word is going to carry the most weight."

Taglioni's lips bent into a thin smile. "You're assuming my family's still in power."

"Aguila asked specifically if you were aboard," Benj reminded.

"That has as many ominous interpretations as it does positive ones, Board politics being what it is."

"Let's wait and see," Galluzzi told them. "If it comes down to it, and there has to be a sacrifice, it is my responsibility."

"You're not doing that holy martyr thing again, are you?" Michaela asked. "We didn't like it the first time you pulled that shit."

He smiled, sipped his tea, looked around at the familiar faces. He'd alternately shunned these people, loved or hated them, sought their company, and periodically despised them. Between them, they had no secrets. Well, maybe but for Taglioni. Not that he hadn't done more than his share, pulled more than his weight, but he'd always kept himself apart. Maintained a distance.

"No martyrdom. It's just that the end, at last, is in sight. Mostly, however, it's because after what we've been through, if they need a sacrifice, I don't give a damn. I'm just . . . tired."

Taglioni was watching him with those piercing yellow-green eyes. Even after all these years, they still sent a shiver up Galluzzi's spine.

There would be a price. There had to be.

4

The tavern in Port Authority was called The Bloody Drink; the moniker dated back to a more sanguine period in the colony's early existence. Most folks just called it Inga's after the proprietor. Inga Lock was a large-boned blonde woman in her forties with thick arms, a no-nonsense disposition, and a talent for brewing, distilling, and producing extraordinary wines from local grains and fruits.

Inga's tavern had originally been housed in one of the midsized utility domes, but as it was the planet's only public house, the crowds had necessitated expansion. Since the dome couldn't be enlarged—and with Donovan being a mining planet—Inga had dug down to create the cavernous stone-floored room that now sported locally made chabachowood tables, benches, chairs, a restaurant, and on the west end, the curving bar from which Inga dispensed her liquid refreshments.

A ramp in the storeroom behind the bar led up to street level and the two-story stone building that housed her distillery, brewery, and winery. The upper floor she rented out to itinerant miners and hunters—called Wild Ones—who might be in town.

On the righthand side of the bar, Security Officer Talina Perez perched atop her usual stool. She wore mud-spattered and smudged quetzal hide: a rainbow-color-shifting leather made from one of the native predators. Next to her knee, her rifle was propped against the bar. Hung from a strap around her neck, a floppy leather hat flattened Tal's raven-black hair against her back.

"Hard day?" Inga asked as she approached with her rolling gait, a bar towel over her shoulder. Talina's glass mug—filled with a thick stout topped by an inch of creamy head—was in Inga's right hand. This she deposited on the scarred wood with a thunk.

"Step Allenovich and I spent the last three days out in the bush, working the breaks leading into the Blood Mountains. Tracked Whitey that far. Storm hit. Winds were too strong for the drones. Had to wait it out. Once we could fly again, we'd lost the sign."

"You look all in."

"I'm eating whatever you got, sucking down a couple of glasses of stout, and then I'm off to sleep for a week."

"You sure it was Whitey? One quetzal pretty much looks like another."

"We managed to get a drone right on top of him. Crippled left front leg? Couple of bullet scars on his hide? Slight limp in his right leg? Gotta be him."

Down in Talina's gut, Demon—piece of shit that he was—hissed in approbation at the mention of Whitey's escape. But then Whitey's molecules where part of what made Demon such an insufferable beast.

Talina could feel Rocket shift on her shoulder—the little quetzal's presence as illusory as Demon's. In the words of Talina's ancient Maya ancestors, she was *Way*. Pronounced "Wh-eye." A spirit-possessed dreamer, transformed, one-out-of-many. Her quetzals were *Wayob*. Dream essences. Spirits who lived within.

"When it comes to Whitey, you'd know. You were the one who shot him up." Inga wiped the bar down with her towel before slapping it over her shoulder. "Food'll be up in a minute."

Tal tossed out a five-SDR coin.

"You're still up two fifty on your account, Tal."

"Put it toward my tab. Day might come, Inga, when I'm caught short."

The big woman snatched up the coin. "Yeah, as if that would ever happen."

"You forget, I have a habit of pissing people off in this town." And, hero to them she might be, but Talina Perez was still a freak, infected as she was with quetzal TriNA.

"This far down the line, Tal, it would take some real doing for you to make it permanent." Inga shot her a wink and retreated down the bar to note the amount on her big board where she kept her accounts.

Talina chuckled under her breath. Inside, she was what

the Maya called *pixom*—of two conflicting souls. In her case, that of killer in opposition to that of protector.

Funny thing, to travel thirty light-years across space in order to discover that her ancient heritage was the only way to make psychological sense of who she had become after quetzal molecules began playing with her brain.

Down the bar, Stepan Allenovich, mud-spattered himself, was calling for whiskey. Three days in the bush hunting quetzal, and the lunatic was going to spend the rest of the night drinking and singing. Then he'd no doubt wander over to Betty Able's brothel where he'd drink some more, pay to screw Solange Flossey, and finally make his way to The Jewel casino. The man was an animal.

Talina sipped her stout, let the rich beer run over her tongue. Damn, she'd missed beer. Three days of hard-scrabble hunting on foot and by air, and that pus-sucking Whitey had put the slip on them again.

"Yes," Demon hissed from behind her stomach.

It only felt like the quetzal lived in her gut. The Port Authority physician, Raya Turnienko, had repeatedly proven to Talina that there was no quetzal hiding out behind her liver. Rather—like the presence of Rocket on her shoulder—that was how the thing manifested. Used transferRNA to communicate with the nerve cells in her brain. Not that Demon was a single quetzal, but existed as a composite made up of the TriNA molecules from a quetzal lineage. Whitey's lineage.

Nor was that the only quetzal TriNA that infested her. The one she called "Rocket," the *Wayob* that perched on her shoulder, was made up of several different quetzals from the Mundo, Briggs, and Rork lineages. Her blood and tissues were thick with the stuff.

One and many at the same time.

Only a Maya shaman would understand.

Talina just wanted the shit out of her body.

"But I'll get you in the end," she promised both Whitey and Demon.

"Or we'll get you."

"Been trying that for the last four years, you piece of shit." She sipped her stout.

Rocket's spectral presence chittered quetzal laughter in her ear. She gave the little twerp a wry smile in reply.

Talina turned to take in the tavern. Inga's was half full: miners, the local trades people, and the weekly rotation from down at Corporate Mine now came trickling in. The few local troublemakers, like Hofer, seemed to be in a convivial mood.

Good. She'd hate to have to go bust heads.

Talina saw Kalico Aguila descending the steps. Beside her, Shig Mosadek was saying something, his hands gesturing in emphasis. Kalico was dressed in her last fancy Supervisor's uniform—the one she was saving for special occasions. That the woman would dress up like . . . Ah, yes. This must be the day she'd taken the shuttle up to *Vixen* to contact *Ashanti*.

Captain Torgussen had delayed *Vixen*'s departure to rendezvous with a particularly intriguing comet in order to allow Aguila to use *Vixen*'s photonic com. By now the survey ship was accelerating hard to catch the comet as it rounded Capella.

Shig, who had also attended, was wearing his locally milled fabric shirt with the squash-blossom flowers Yvette had embroidered on the front. To Talina's knowledge, the comparative religions scholar didn't have anything resembling formal attire in his wardrobe. Shig's only concession to fashion was the quetzal-hide cape he reserved for rainy days.

Talina arched an eyebrow as Aguila turned her way, strode across the fitted stones in the floor, and hitched herself into the elevated chair beside Talina's. Shig clambered onto the stool on Aguila's right.

"What's with the fancy dress? Trying to impress the new folks?" Talina asked.

"Just back from *Vixen*." Aguila had a thoughtful look on her scarred face. "*Ashanti*'s finally close enough that we could have a conference on the photonic com. Talked to the captain, the Corporate Advisor/Observer, and the science director. Not that it's a huge surprise, but the situation on *Ashanti* is a bit grimmer than we'd been led to believe on the text-only long-range com."

"How grim?"

Aguila grinned humorlessly; it rearranged her scars. "Grim enough that I told Shig he's buying the whiskey."

"Couldn't be worse than *Freelander*." Memories of Talina's last time aboard the ghost ship still sent fingers of ice slipping down her backbone. And to think she'd condemned Tamarland Benteen to that eerie and endless hell.

"Maybe not," Shig agreed. "But trouble still. We finally got an explanation for some of the hesitation they've expressed through their messages. They've been ten years in that bucket. Out there in the black for almost seven now. Popped back in more than a half a light-year from Capella."

"Shit. And let me guess. Didn't have the fuel to pop back out?"

Aguila's gaze thinned as she gestured down the bar to Inga. "Miracle and tragedy all in one. The miracle's that they're alive. The tragedy is what they had to do to stay that way for seven years in a ship that couldn't feed them all."

"They murder the transportees like the crew of *Freelander* did?"

"Might just as well have," Kalico told her. "Captain Galluzzi sent his official log to *Vixen*, along with the Observer/Advisor's reports. Shig and I gave them a quick scan. The transportees tried to take the ship. It got bloody. Failed. So Galluzzi had them sealed onto the transportee deck. And left them there."

"Bet they're ready to get the hell out."

Shig glanced at her. "It's just Galluzzi's word, of course, but it may be a bit more complicated than that. If the good captain and the records are to be believed, things turned remarkably brutal among the transportees. Over the last six years they have apparently developed some sort of messianic cult based on the notion of controlled violence and eating one's fellows as a reflection of the universe. At this stage we can only guess at the depth of the belief and its intricacies. If there's good news, it is that there's only about a hundred of them left."

Aguila added, "Just talking about it, Galluzzi broke into a cold sweat. The guy's almost a basket case, and he's scared. Really scared." She shot Shig an evaluative look.

"So much so that he sent me a private com just before we stepped off *Vixen*. Asked me to consider blowing up *Ashanti* as soon as he could get his crew off."

Shig's round face puckered. "That's a bit extreme, even for cannibals, don't you think?"

"Excuse me? Cannibals?" Talina asked.

Kalico gave her a dead stare. "Think locked on Deck Three with insufficient food. It's eat your neighbor or be eaten by him. One or the other."

"Oh, shit."

"Blowing up the ship would solve some of Galluzzi's problems," Shig mused.

"Hey?" Talina asked. "What about the cargo? *Ashanti*'s holds must be full of things we need. Equipment. Parts. Seeds, maybe cacao, or cotton, or who knows what? And unlike *Freelander* it wasn't lost in space for a hundred and twenty-nine years."

Aguila laid a ten-SDR coin out for Inga, saying, "My party tonight. Put whatever's left on my tab."

"Thought I was buying," Shig said. "That was the deal."

"How's the vegetable market these days?" Aguila asked.

"I sold a couple of squash last week," Shig told her proudly.

Shig made most of his income from his garden. One of the most influential men on Donovan, Shig Mosadek was also one of the poorest. He was a third of the triumvirate— the three-person government of Port Authority. Shig was the conscience, the public face, and liaison to the community. Yvette Dushane—a pragmatic woman in her fifties— did the nuts and bolts daily administration and record keeping. Talina Perez served as security chief, enforcer, and protector.

Inga set a whiskey down before Aguila and placed a half-full glass of wine before Shig, saying, "My latest red from those sirah grapes they transplanted from Mundo Base." Then she scooped up the coin, heading back down the bar before reaching up to credit Kalico's account on her big board.

Talina asked, "We're not seriously blowing up a starship, are we?"

"Of course not." Aguila raised her whiskey and swished it around, inhaled, and took a sip. "Oh, that's her new barrel. Much better than last month's."

"So, remind me. That leaves us with how many traumatized maniac religious cannibal nuts?" Talina asked. "A hundred, you say? What are you thinking? Put 'em in the domes in the residential section? Let them rub elbows with us locals until they come back to their senses?"

Shig studied his half glass of wine. "I think that would be a bad idea. At least given what we currently know about them."

"I can't put them up at Corporate Mine," Aguila said. "First, I don't have the dormitory space. Second, we're a pretty tight organization down there these days. If I drop a hundred soft meat into the mix, I'm going to have chaos. And who knows what kind of skills these people have?"

"Not to mention that they eat people. That will go over big in the cafeteria," Shig noted.

"So that brings us back to some of the empty domes in the residential district." Talina shrugged. "If they start to get out of line, it may take a couple of head whacks, but my guess is that between us, we can civilize them."

Shig held up his hand for attention. "I don't think that's wise, let alone an operative plan of action."

"Okay," Talina told him. "Since when is having someone like me, Talbot, or Step coming down on a bit of misbehaving—"

"I took the opportunity to read some of the ravings the Irredenta sent to Captain Galluzzi."

"The irrawho?"

"The Irredenta," Shig told her. "That's what they're calling themselves. That, and they often refer to themselves as the Unreconciled. The words attributed to their Prophets reek of demented religious fanaticism. These people believe that they have passed through a brutal selection, that they have been given absolute truth. That they've been chosen to possess the one true understanding of God and the ultimate reality of the universe. Worse, they've been locked away, isolated, and survived a most terrible winnowing. Events stripped them of their humanity. They committed atrocities, acts that abnegated the kind of people they were before the trauma."

"So what? Donovan is no one's idea of a picnic," Talina retorted.

Shig softly said, "In my view, turning them loose in PA or Corporate Mine would be to unleash a calamity."

"Bit melodramatic, don't you think?" Talina asked.

Shig arched a bushy eyebrow. "After the rise of The Corporation, religious fundamentalism was suppressed, monitored. But think back to your security training. You must have run across historical references to fringe beliefs, fanatical interpretations of scripture. Millenarians. Radical cults. Most were led by charismatic individuals thought of as messiahs by their followers."

"Yeah," Talina said, "but this is Donovan. That kind of silliness doesn't last long here. You know how I'm always joking about the Buddha never existing on Donovan? 'Cause if he'd seated himself under a mundo tree, a nightmare would have eaten him. Same for a self-proclaimed prophet. They all digest the same in a quetzal's gut."

Aguila had been listening; from her expression she'd been accessing her implants, scanning data. Now she said, "I side with Shig. If these people are as indoctrinated to violence and their holy cause as Galluzzi says and their writings indicate, turning them loose in either PA or Corporate Mine would be a major mistake at worst, horrendously destabilizing at best."

Shig dryly asked, "Do you really think that practicing cannibals preaching apocalypse can just move into the dome next door without repercussions?"

"So? Leave them up on the ship?"

Aguila's wary smile rearranged her scars. "We want that ship. We need that ship. I've got a fortune in rare metals, clay, and gemstones in containers up in orbit. You've got shipping containers full of clay and plunder stacked seven-deep around the shuttle field. Maybe *Turalon* arrived on schedule back at Solar System last year. Maybe it didn't. But *Ashanti* is coming in. If we can load her to the gills with wealth, ship her back to Solar System—even if we have to do it on AI—it's another shot at long-term survival."

"We could lock the cannibals up with crazy old Tam Benteen on *Freelander*," Talina mused.

Aguila shook her head. "What? Compromise our only platform for freefall and vacuum manufacturing?"

"You'll have *Ashanti*," Shig pointed out.

"Not if we can convince someone to space her back to Solar System and make us all rich," Aguila added. "Galluzzi really wants me to blow them up."

"Morally unacceptable." Shig declared as he fingered his wineglass. Talina grunted in agreement.

"Which leaves the planet. Maybe they're crazy as the quanta. Maybe in the end, they can't be reconciled with the rest of us. We won't know until we can see for ourselves." Aguila lifted her whiskey, studying the amber fluid in her glass. "Put them down at Mundo Base? Buy it from Mark Talbot's family?"

"Not that they'd sell," Talina said. "And the quetzal lineage down there's really hostile."

"Tyson Station," Shig said. "Way out west. On that mesa top. Five domes. Just right for about a hundred people. Good garden space. Enough cisterns and capacity to handle a population that size."

"Never been there," Aguila said.

Talina sipped her stout. "Might work. Somebody needs to go out there. Check it out."

Aguila shot Shig a sidelong look. "You all right with that? I mean, given your moral imperatives, all that talk about freedom? About government staying out of people's lives? Isn't this a form of playing god? Making these decisions for those people?"

Shig gave a half-hearted shrug. "One of the few tenants of government in a libertarian system is that the state should provide for the common defense. If these people arrived in our skies infected with some contagious disease, we would be within our moral rights to place them in quarantine for the protection of the general population."

"But this is a cult."

Shig's eyebrows lifted. "And what makes you think that zealous adherence to a messianic religious cult isn't just as dangerous as smallpox, rubella, or ebola?"

THE PROPHETS

I sit among the Prophets. The room we placed them in has come to be called The Temple. It used to be a recreation room, the walls surrounded by monitors and VR holo projectors long gone black and now decorated with drawings based upon the holy utterances. In places quotes that have passed the Prophets' lips are written on the walls.

This room, these three holy people, are the repository of Truth.

Their beds are laid out in a triangle, and I sit in the exact center between them.

At the top—in the position of honor—lies Irdan, once a specialist in the use and maintenance of scientific equipment like microscopes and centrifuges. He was the first who was called. As the sacred presence of the universe slowly possessed his body, took his coordination, and began giving him visions, the initial Prophecies passed his lips.

Within days, Callista, young, dark, and insecure, was the second to be called. Her specialty was medical equipment: scanners, imaging machines, and diagnostic equipment. She'd started to stumble, her hands to twitch, as the universe took possession of her.

Not another week had passed before Guan Shi, a plumber by trade, began to drop things. Started to stumble in her walk. Her speech grew slurred, her train of thought inconsistent. By then, we knew the signs of the calling.

As the years have passed, the Prophets have fallen deeper and deeper into the universe. As they have, their voices have become more profound and ever more cryptic. I suppose this makes sense. Like newborn infants, we need to learn the language. A neonate does not immediately comprehend Shakespeare, Mak Shi, or Sophocles.

What worries me as I sit here is that as the Prophets fall deeper into the universe, their health is deteriorating. They *have no control over their bodies and can barely swallow when food is placed on their tongues. But even more ominous, these days I can rarely understand their Prophecy. Statements like, "Waa wass glick faa faa," which Callista has uttered as I sit here, have no meaning to me.*

It begs the question: When the universe chooses a Prophet, does it inevitably suck them down and devour them, much in the same way as we consume the impure? Is their fate the most enviable of all? Or, is it that we—myself in particular—despite being the repository of so many lives and souls, are only capable of limited understanding? Perhaps I cannot learn the language past a certain level of comprehension, similar to a learning-impaired child whose linguistic abilities are forever capped at the age of five?

In the former case, we are reassured, for we have others now—Shimal Kastakourias in particular—who have begun to show the initial signs of incipient Prophesy.

If the latter—which is the nightmare that keeps me awake in the night—then I am unmanned by the possibility that I might not be capable of performing the daunting task for which I've been chosen.

Irdan's legs twitch; his sunken eyes flicker sightlessly as he says something that sounds like, "Thaaweenaah."

In that moment, I fear I am not only unworthy, but too stupid to comprehend the remarkable Truth that Irdan has just shared.

If that is the case, I am a failure.

I hang my head and weep.

5

The Taglionis were one of the few true dynasties in The Corporation. Back in the mid-twenty-first century, when it became apparent that national governments couldn't be trusted with the responsibility of running the planet, the family had been instrumental in the establishment of Corporate control over the world economy.

The algorithms had taken care of the rest. Remarkable what a settling effect comprehensive monitoring and perfect resource distribution had when it came to keeping the populace mollified and compliant. But then the Romans had figured out the rudiments clear back when it was just bread and circuses.

Since the establishment of The Corporation, through adroit skills, a lack of preoccupation with ethics, and no little daring and guile, the Taglioni family had maintained its position on the Board of Directors. And that—in the face of competition from the likes of the Radceks, the Grunnels, the Suhartos, and Xian Chan families—took some doing.

Derek had grown up as a well-connected and influential scion in the midst of the family's treacherous web. Though they'd vied to dominate the power elite, his parents had been outmaneuvered from the start by Miko Taglioni's mother and father: They'd had a lock on the Board.

Nevertheless, Board politics being what it was, Derek and his other cousins had been kept in the wings, waiting, each constantly being groomed in case he or she should be called upon by the family elders to step into the role of Corporate Boardmember should anything happen to Miko and his immediate siblings.

Yet here I am.

Derek stood in the Crew Deck observation dome on *Ashanti*'s port side and stared at the now-familiar swirls and splashes of stars. He kept thinking back. How he'd thrown a petulant tantrum, told Miko that he was tired of being a sidelined ornament. That if he wasn't given his due, he'd make it on his own.

And Miko had laughed in his face.

Hands clasped behind his back, Derek contemplated the interstellar majesty beyond the transparency. This day he wore a secondhand set of coveralls, the elbows and knees patched. Secondhand? And stained from the hydroponics lab? How far the mighty had fallen. At the thought, a dry chuckle broke his lips.

"Something funny?" Miguel Galluzzi asked from behind.

"Didn't hear you come in."

"Just wanted to take a look outside before I call it a day."

Derek shot the captain a sidelong glance as the man took a position beside him. The captain's gaze was fixed on the dot of light just to the right of Capella. He pointed. "That's Cap III. Right there. In plain sight." A pause. "So many times over these last endless years . . . well, I never thought I'd see this day."

"That's what I was chuckling about." Derek rocked on his heels. "I'll remind you that I came on this trip in a fit of pique. If they wouldn't give me what I wanted, I'd show them. I'd ship off for Cap III and make my own way, build my own empire."

Galluzzi gave him a wary glance. "So you've said. From the reports we've seen, Donovan isn't exactly Transluna. They've got less than a thousand people down there. And government is split between Corporate and this Port Authority. It's starting to sound like growing a garden is the most successful thing a man can do dirtside."

"Aguila is the Corporate authority. If there's anything for me, it will be through her."

"I see."

"No, you don't. Miguel, you come from a normal family. The Taglionis? We have a lot more in common with the Irredenta than we do with normal people. It's just that we devour each other in more figurative terms. Looking back at who I was the day I stepped aboard *Ashanti* compared to who I am now? Well . . . I wonder why you didn't step up when I wasn't looking, shoot me in the head, and drop me down the chute to feed the hydroponics."

"Thought about it a time or two," Galluzzi said. "You might think that being a Taglioni is an imposition, but family reputation isn't without its rewards. It kept you alive back when you'd have been of more value to us as nutrients in the hydroponics vats."

Derek stared thoughtfully at the pinpoint of light that was Capella III. "I'm sorry I was such a miserable shit, Miguel. I just . . . well, I'm sorry." He barked an amused laugh. "Pus in a bucket, imagine that. Derek Taglioni just apologized to another human being for being an asshole. Don't let *that* get back to the family."

"You make it sound like a first."

"You may be most assured that it is." Derek lifted his chin. "We're taught to never, ever, under any circumstance, apologize to anyone. To do so would imply that we were at fault. A Taglioni, you see, never makes a mistake."

"That seems a bit unrealistic."

"What does reality have to do with it? I have discovered— to my undying horror over these last seven years—that people can be such self-deluded idiots. Given what we've survived? The choices I've watched you make. It's like having my skin ripped off to leave my naked quivering muscles and nerves exposed to a most painful truth."

"Neither of us will ever be the people we once were. I'm still not sure that something terrible isn't waiting for me when we reach Cap III. There has to be a price paid for what I did."

"You made a choice and saved the ship."

"I condemned three hundred and forty-two innocent men, women, and children to starvation and the survivors to a living hell. I locked them in and left them no alternative than to become monsters in a free-for-all of murder, inhumanity, and suffering."

"I saw the holo. Supervisor Aguila didn't bat an eye when you told her that you'd sealed the transportees in."

"I expected her to order my immediate arrest." A pause. "I think I know why she didn't."

"Oh?"

"There's another ship in orbit around Donovan. She's

called *Freelander.* Something went really wrong when she inverted symmetry. Went someplace 'outside' where time is different. Some effect of relativity. She aged one hundred and twenty-nine years during a two-and-a-half-year transit. *Freelander* was carrying five hundred transportees. When her captain, Jem Orten—a man I knew and admired—figured out that they were marooned in time, he and his crew killed them. Asphyxiated them. Then froze the corpses and added them to the hydroponics over the years as the molecules began to break down."

"Did you ever consider going to that extreme?"

Galluzzi pursed his lips, nodded. "Funny, isn't it? I could seal them up in Deck Three, let them murder each other and become psychotic cannibals, but simple euthanasia was morally reprehensible. I guess, after what happened with *Freelander,* my actions with the Irredenta didn't have quite the same impact they once would have."

"Then maybe Supervisor Aguila has a pragmatic streak to her personality. And who knows? She may actually live up to her reputation."

"Which is?"

"She was one of Miko's protégées," Derek noted. "As of when we spaced, she was the Supervisor of the Transluna district. Met her a couple of times back in Transluna. The circumstances of which I hope she's forgotten. She has a capability ranking of 9.8."

"What does that mean?"

"Means Miko thinks she could go all the way to Board-member. Me? Best rank I ever got was a 7.6. My flaw was always emotional volatility. The kind that would make me lose control. Do something dumb. You know, like throw a temper tantrum and stomp off to join a ship headed for Cap III. Teach the bastards a lesson. Show them all what a real Taglioni could do." A pause. "And you can see how well that worked out."

Galluzzi chuckled. Pointed at the planet, and asked, "So, what are you going to do now?"

"Haven't a clue, Miguel. That old original plan of making planet, throwing my weight around, taking charge of some money-making and high-prestige venture doesn't have the same appeal. Not only that, but the files *Vixen* has sent on Donovan indicate it's not the thriving colony we were told to expect. It never was. Even way back then. Supervisor Clemenceau, who I figured I could manipulate, has been dead for as long as we've been in space."

He stared at the dot of light that was Cap III. As if he could feel it across the distance. Calling to him in a way that bordered on the mystical. As if the planet was in harmony with his blood.

Sheer silliness. But still . . .

"I'm sure Supervisor Aguila, if she's in the Taglioni fold, will find something for you."

"Maybe."

"Why do you say that?"

"I know that you told her I was on board. Since then I haven't heard a word from her."

"So? She's busy. She's a Supervisor in charge of an entire planet."

"You don't understand. I'm a first cousin to Miko, and she's in his stable. Kalico Aguila should have immediately placed a call to my com. Should have offered up her compliments, inquired about my welfare, asked what she could do to be of service. Doesn't matter that we didn't part on the best of terms, such a call is required protocol for a high-ranking member of the Taglioni family."

"I see." The look on Galluzzi's face indicated that he was happy to only have a ship to worry about.

"That she did not immediately initiate contact is about as disturbing as my own reaction."

"And what's that?"

Derek lifted an eyebrow. "Supervisor Aguila is no longer playing the Corporate game. Either that or she's switched allegiances to another Boardmember. But if she had, why would she tip her hand? That doesn't make sense. You don't just telegraph hostile intent to a potential opponent."

"What are you going to do if she's changed sides?"

"That's the second remarkable thing. The miracle of my reaction to Aguila's slight. Hey, I've scrubbed corridors and toilets, worked in hydroponics, bumped elbows and starved with you and your crew, worried from day to day that I was going to die. I've watched the rise of the monsters down in

Deck Three. Spent nights in terror, unable to sleep for fear they would break free and cut my intestines out while I screamed. That *Ashanti* was my tomb. Do you think that after that, I could give a damn over a skipped courtesy call?"

But that still left the question: Now that the impossible appeared to be happening—that they were going to actually live long enough to get off *Ashanti*—what was he going to do once he set foot on Capella III?

And worse, what did it mean when Kalico Aguila wasn't acting the way she should? Derek might not have wanted to play the game, but that didn't mean that Aguila wouldn't still use him as a pawn in a game of her own.

6

The thing about living on Donovan was that it always seemed to take a series of unexpected twists. Just when a person figured he or she had a handle on life, it was only to find oneself zipping off at a ninety-degree angle from the expected path. Traveling in a direction never anticipated— and initially so stunned from the trajectory-altering impact as to be incapable of reacting to the change.

Security Second Mark Talbot's life had taken exactly those kinds of hits. He'd arrived on Donovan as part of Kalico Aguila's Marine detail. He'd backed Lieutenant Spiro's faction of "loyal" marines when Cap Taggart resigned from the Corps. When *Turalon* was about to space, he'd joined fellow marines Shintzu and Garcia for a quick trip into the forest. Just a chance to say they'd been face to face with Donovan's wilderness.

The forest had immediately crushed their aircar. A nightmare had finished off Garcia. Slugs had eaten their way through Shintzu's guts. Talbot had found himself alone; only his armor had saved him on his march across the forest to Mundo Base.

Again his life had been smacked sideways: Within months he was a polygamist married to three women, had a family and responsibilities as a father. Only to lose it all when Mundo Base fell apart, the local quetzals turned against humans, and he and his wives and children had to flee to Port Authority.

In the curious calculus that was survival on Donovan, he'd been there to save Talina Perez's life when a rogue marine would have shot her from ambush.

Since then he'd been a jack of all trades, with his time spent between Corporate Mine and PA. Father, husband, teacher, advisor, and finally, somehow catapulted into the position of Security Second.

He considered that as he studied Talina from the passenger seat. She was piloting the aircar due west over the vastness of endless forest. They'd passed the Briggs River and given him a longing glimpse of the homestead at the head of Black Canyon. His eldest surviving daughter, Kylee, now lived there. A half-human, half-quetzal child who teetered precariously between two different worlds.

And then there was Talina Perez, the woman who had murdered two of his wives' first husbands. A once-despised enemy who had miraculously appeared at his family's moment of greatest need. A quetzal-haunted woman who was now his superior.

They couldn't ask for a better day for flying, with the temperature in the low thirties, sunny, and no chance for rain. The forever forest stretched off to the horizon, a lumpy mat of greens, blues, and every shade in between. Here and there rivers cut winding paths through the verdure, and ridges, bluffs, and hills receded in distant hazy lines toward infinity.

Talina seemed to be in better control of herself today. Working around her was always interesting, but at times the woman was locked in combat with her inner quetzals. Generally, if a comment contained the words "you piece of shit," it was a dead giveaway that quetzal molecules were whispering in her mind.

Talbot had lived with his daughter Kylee and her pet quetzal, Rocket, for long enough to have at least a hazy understanding of the symbiosis. And his wife, Dya, had explained the best hypotheses that she, Turnienko, and the chemist, Cheng, could come up with: That essentially quetzal TriNA was a "smart" molecule that interacted with human brain cells through common transferRNA.

But all it took was a glance at Talina Perez to know it did more than that. The woman's eyes were striking, larger, darker, peculiarly shaped. Then came the planes of her face, the cheekbones sharper, the jawline pointed at the chin. Her muscles were faster, stronger than any human Talbot had ever known, and she moved with fluid grace that reminded him of a prowling lioness.

She scared hell out of half of Port Authority. The other

half treated her with a wary respect—even if they were unsure of who and what she'd become.

"What's up, Mark? You're looking at me like I'm some sort of lab specimen."

How did she do that? He thought he'd been circumspect. "You're quiet today. Not even a single growl under your breath. Demon hasn't been making a pest of himself?"

"This whole *Ashanti* thing. That's got me thinking of ships. Which reminds me of *Vixen*. Which makes me think of Weisbacher. Kalico was up there. I noticed that she artfully didn't mention if she'd seen the good doctor."

"Which made you think of Trish," he finished. Mark turned, squinted out at the forest. Here and there he could pick out more turquoise patches in the various shades of green. Some sort of unknown aquajade species? They passed the first of the curious ping-pong-paddle trees in their circular clearings. "It's been over two years, Tal."

Talina frowned. "Seems like yesterday. Still don't know what I'd do if I walked around a corner in PA and came face to face with him." A pause. "Think I'm responsible enough to keep from blowing a hole through his sorry hide?"

"Kylee still calls him Dortmund Short Mind. Says he's the biggest waste of skin she's ever known." Talbot gestured amusement. "Of course, her total exposure to humanity can be numbered in the low tens." He paused. "I'm sorry Trish isn't here. I know what she meant to you."

"Six of one, half dozen of the other, Mark. The kid had that innate sense of place that comes from growing up here. She was rock-solid when it came to a tight situation in the bush. A dead shot with a rifle. If she had a fault, it was that she was young. Made the kind of dumb mistakes young people make. Still needed to completely find her feet. Hated herself for letting Benteen scare her."

"Benteen would have killed her."

"Yeah. Maybe. The thing is, she always figured she'd die in the bush. Quetzal, bem, some skewer, or maybe mobbers."

"Odd that you'd say that. I was just thinking about the way life on Donovan changes in an instant."

She shot him an evaluative glance from the corner of her eye. "You're as good as Trish, you know."

"I'll take that as a compliment."

"Better in a lot of ways. You know more about the bush. More mature. Tougher down in your core. Like Trish, I know you've got my back. You proved that when you shot Chavez. You don't have that gut-level handle on Port Authority yet, but you're learning."

"Trish grew up with those people. To most I'm still a stranger, and as the town's only polygamist, something of a curiosity."

"You were Wild Ones, you get more leeway."

Talbot grinned. He hadn't been in Port Authority for more than a couple of months before he became fully cognizant of the fact that he was comfortable in his own skin. Funny thing, that. Knowing exactly who and what you were meant that other people's opinions didn't have nearly the weight they once had.

"What's the story behind this Tyson Station we're going to?"

Talina rested her hand on the wheel, her alien-dark eyes scanning the forest ahead of them. "Tyson's colony was fifth ship. The research base was established on a mesa top way out west. The idea was that, like Mundo down south, it would be a stepping-stone for the exploration of the continent. The site was chosen since it had a different ecology, was considered somewhat defensible from wildlife, and could be easily expanded as the population grew. The big dome, with full basement, contained the cafeteria and kitchen, communications, admin offices, storage, and meeting rooms. Separate domes for the barracks, science labs, shops, and support staff. Last we knew, they had about five acres in farmland. Like everywhere, the bems, brown caps, chokeya, and slugs began to take a toll. There were rumors of other creatures, different from what we know back east.

"Clemenceau demanded that the base be held no matter what. After learning of his much-too-delayed departure, most of the people loaded up and flew back to PA. Five stayed behind, trying to finish up a few last projects."

"What happened to them?"

"When we finally got around to sending a car out a couple of months later, we found three skeletons. No trace of the other two. Not even a pile of quetzal crap."

"And this is a place for *Ashanti*'s kooks?"

"You've got me, Mark. Hey, Shig's the comparative religions teacher. He's been reviewing all the stuff these Irredenta dropped on *Ashanti*'s crew. Shig's worried." A beat. "Worried? Shig? Those are two words I never thought would collide in a sentence. You know Shig. End of the world coming? Fine. Make a cup of tea, read the *I Ching* and a couple of the Vedas, then smile as sattva fills your last days."

Talbot stared off to the right, caught sight of a flock of flying creatures. Pulling up his binoculars, he made sure they were scarlet fliers and not a deadly swarm of mobbers.

"There it is." Talina pointed ahead.

Mark used his binoculars to inspect the mesa that rose above the forest. The thing reminded him of a fortress jutting out like an extended shoulder below what was obviously a volcanic peak. Amazing what he'd learned about geology since coming to Donovan. Even from here he could tell the sheer sides were either lava or basalt. A few trees clung precariously to the precipitous and rocky slopes. As they approached, he estimated the vertical relief at over two hundred meters. A substantial slow-moving river curled around beneath the southern end of the mesa, the waters a translucent green.

Talina climbed, crested the flat, and leveled out. She made a wide swing around the five domes that stood in a clearing on what looked like bedrock. Many of the early research bases had been established on bedrock. Not as many slugs. People could see the quetzals, bems, and sidewinders coming.

Sheds had been laid out in a row on the western side, the doors closed. A solar array consisting of five panels stood on the south. Three of the panels were still tracking Capella's course across the sky. Between them and the landing field just this side of the domes, he could see the garden.

Talina dropped lower, slowing to a hover. As she used

her quetzal vision to survey the place, Talbot relied on his binoculars. The base gave every appearance of being abandoned. Right down to the thin soil that was devoid of tracks. Pieces of equipment looked rusty and dusty; an old pair of coveralls lay wadded beside one of the doors, tattered and faded. Tarps were frayed by wind, torn loose from their bindings. They'd once protected corroding pieces of equipment that Talbot couldn't identify.

"What do you think?" Talina asked.

"Well, at least a swarm of quetzals didn't come charging out of one of the domes with their collar membranes glowing crimson and their claws out. Can't tell about bems, skewers, the occasional sidewinder, spikes, or whatever the hell else there might be."

She arched an eyebrow, then descended to the landing field on the south side of the domes. Talbot retrieved his rifle as she let the fans spin down.

"How's the charge?" he asked.

"Twenty percent. Smart people would plug into the spare powerpack before stepping out of the aircar."

"I like smart," he suggested, watching her plug the auxiliary cable into the spare powerpack and then check as the indicator flashed back to eighty-nine percent. Nothing went to one hundred, given the age on the batteries.

He stepped out carefully, having had four years of Donovan's hard lessons to keep him from acting irresponsibly. The plants here were terrestrial. Some sort of scrubby low weeds that didn't writhe under his foot the way the native flora did.

Talbot kept his rifle up, safety off, finger on the rest just above the trigger. He cocked his head at the chime, different here. Deeper, with a bass rhythm unlike anything he'd heard before. The air, too, had a different odor, more of a saffron and sage than the more familiar cardamom and cinnamon scent around either Mundo or PA. The breeze had a muggy feel. The air heavier and hot.

Talina on his right, he started for the first dome, scenting the air for any hint of vinegar that would indicate a bem or skewer. Got nothing but the background of vegetation. A small herd of roos burst from behind one of the domes, fleeing like a shot across the flats.

At the first dome, Talina tried the latch, found it unlocked. She let the door swing in, swept the room with her rifle. Talbot followed, covering. Standard security room-clearing procedure. Nothing looked out of place, the chairs were upright, desks slightly dusty, but nothing suspicious. Room by room, they cleared the first dome, then moved on to the next. An hour later, with nothing but a single sidewinder and an infestation of invertebrates in the sheds, Tyson Station appeared to harbor no immediate terrors.

The cisterns were full and overflowing into pipes that drained down to the garden patch. To Talbot's eyes the water looked skuzzy, but that could be addressed without much effort.

"Skeletons were all out in the open," Talina told him as she led the way from the last of the domes. "We didn't know it then, but they were probably killed by mobbers. That, or something we haven't seen yet."

"It's a big planet," Talbot agreed, thinking of the various creatures that had attacked him while he trekked through the forest down south. He could count at least five creatures that weren't on the list of known predators. And that included an oversized cucumber-looking thing.

Talbot followed Talina down to the garden. Located on the southern end of the base, it grew on soils that had washed down from the higher exposed basalt. The place reminded him of a smaller Mundo: lettuce, cabbages, pepper plants, lots of garlic, mint for tea, some tomatoes, broccoli and squash all growing in a riotous mixture.

"What do you think?" Talina asked. "Enough to feed a hundred people?"

"Maybe. They'll need corn and potatoes from PA, some grapes, an apple and cherry tree or two, some blueberry bushes. Now that I get a better look, I make this to be about seven acres. From the height of the surrounding trees, the soil's deep enough the garden could be expanded. Maybe all the way down to the end of the mesa."

Talina nodded, her careful gaze scanning the edge of the forest. "Let's check the solar panels and battery packs. Looks like two aren't working. And if the batteries are shot, that's really going to compound our problems."

Turned out that if there was a weakness to Tyson Station,

it was the power. The motors were burned out on two of the solar towers, and whoever last had been responsible for the batteries had left them untended, only two took a charge, and even then, they only tested at fifty percent.

"We really going to strand nearly a hundred people out here?" Talbot asked.

"We could drop them at Mundo. Maybe hope they'll kill Diamond and Leaper. On the other hand, as much as I've got a grudge against those two quetzals, I'm not sure that dropping the Unreconciled on top of them wouldn't be a crime against quetzaldom."

"It's just hard to get my head around. All right, so they ate other human beings. What kind of sins do people have to commit to leave them totally beyond redemption?"

"I'm not the person to ask, given some of the things I've done. And to members of your family, no less. But here's the thing: I know the sins I've committed. If we can believe Shig's analysis of the Unreconciled, they think everything they've done is in preparation for the coming struggle."

"And you think that putting them out here will keep us all safe?"

"Guess we'll see, huh?" She pursed her lips as she looked around the base. "And maybe they're not the psychotically insane and twisted monsters that everyone thinks they are. I mean, I don't know what really happened on Deck Three, but dropping the Irredenta out here gives us the chance to just see just what kind of trouble they might be."

"Tal, I was trained, wearing combat armor, and I almost didn't make it. You and I both know that no matter what these people did, it's going to be a death sentence for a lot of them."

She turned her alien-dark eyes on him. "Doesn't matter where we put them, people are going to die. How many of your marines, let alone the *Turalon* transportees are still alive? It's just how things are here."

"Yeah. Welcome to Donovan."

Talina had walked to the western side of the escarpment, was staring out at the endless tops of the trees. A tension lined her forehead, pinched her full-lipped mouth.

"What is it?"

Talina hesitated, started to speak, then shook her head. "You feel something out there?"

Talbot let his gaze roam the treetops. "Feel . . . like what?"

Talina turned, grunted. "Probably nothing."

But Talbot noticed that she kept looking back over her shoulder at the thick forest, as if something unseen were nagging at her.

THE CLEANSING

Now, with our internment coming to an end, I can take a moment and look back. Remember the Harrowing and Cleansing, and what it meant for all of us.

I understand now: Had we just been given the Revelation, it would have been rejected out of hand as an insane abomination. We had to be broken down, our illusions about life and morality destroyed. It's an old cliché, but like a field, we had to be prepared before a seed could be planted that would eventually bear fruit.

First was the fear. When Ashanti reinverted to normal space and we understood the full scope of the disaster that had befallen us, we realized that, no matter what, some or all of us were going to starve to death. Trapped. Here, in this ship, in the black immensity of space.

Then came the fight: the attempted mutiny led by Irdan and Brady Shaw. Its failure at the hands of the crew. How could they just have shot human beings down like that? We'd lived with these people for close to three years during the transition. Only to have them murder our leaders in the hallways.

We knew disbelief and rage when we discovered that the hatch had been sealed. That we were not only doomed but trapped in the limited warren that was Deck Three.

What followed was a mind-numbing despair—the kind that left even me weeping, defeated, and broken.

Then the rations were cut.

How clever the universe is. It let us observe the worst in humanity while teaching us the ultimate lesson: Survival is conflict.

Raised within the warm and secure womb of The Corporation, we could not have been more shocked by this rude and disturbing awakening. The depth of the deception we had been living back in Solar System was as traumatic for us as the ensuing starvation. As we wasted away in an agony of hunger, it became clear that altruism was a myth. Everything The Corporation had taught us to believe was a sham and a lie.

We witnessed the base brutality of the human soul.

In the beginning, when the interpersonal violence broke out, we dropped the bodies down the chute. Sent them to the hydroponics.

It was Irdan—who would become the first of the Prophets—who realized that it was a waste. All those calories, the protein, and fats. He was the first to begin the Harrowing.

See the cunning of the universe? Indeed!

Upon the revelation of Irdan's actions—that he had cooked and eaten another human being—most had a feeling of revulsion. Thought the consumption of human flesh was abhorrent. A few sought retribution; Irdan killed them when they came for him. Nor did he leave them to waste, but promptly processed their meat and organs.

The Harrowing was over and the Cleansing began.

With it, so did the beginnings of the Revelation.

I remember the guilt I experienced the first time I ate human flesh. The self-revulsion. At the same time, I relished the sustenance. The relief from the hollow pangs of starvation.

This was meat.

This was life.

I knew it was Sally McKendricks, mother of two, whose meat I was cutting up and chewing.

But that night I slept with a full stomach.

For a time, following that, I was lost. Guilt. Guilt. Guilt. Disgust. A loathing of who I'd become. How low I would sink just to live another day. To keep breathing. To be rid of the hunger pangs.

Irdan—always in the forefront of the universe's will— was the one who told me: "Batuhan, they're not dead. They're inside us. Living through us."

And that night I had the dream, a vision.

Nothing like those bestowed upon the Prophets.

This was just a simple understanding: The universe had

put us in such dire circumstances to serve a purpose: This was *its will.*

If killing and eating another human being was the universe's will, it could not be a crime, an abomination, or a sin.

Consuming another human being was immortality.

7

The increase in gravity was the first indication of the beginning of the end. Security Tech II Vartan Omanian felt it as he rose from Svetlana Pushkin's bed. Cocking his head, he could hear it, feel it through his bare feet. *Ashanti* had changed. The sound and vibration of the ship, the air, even the surrounding sialon hinted of hard acceleration.

Vartan made his way to the toilet, relieved his full bladder, and re-crossed the small room to Svetlana's bed. Nominally, as a member of the Messiah's Will—as the enforcers were called—he slept in the men's dormitory. His rank, as Second Will—or the second in command of Batuhan's enforcers—granted him certain privileges. That included access to available women as long as they weren't ovulating.

Among the Irredenta, the tracking of a woman's cycle was of paramount concern. During those critical days during ovulation, she became the sole property of the Messiah—and if more than one female was fertile at the time, the responsibility of the First Chosen to inseminate.

Those who had objected to the True Vision of the Prophets when it came to women and reproduction had long since become immortal. Vartan had been responsible for most of the disciplinary actions. The one thing the Irredenta couldn't afford was any hint of division or strife. Those who might have doubted, who suffered from a lack of faith, would finally discover Truth in their next existence. After they'd been consumed, purified, and reborn.

Vartan himself had once doubted. Back then. In the beginning. But he had learned, adapted, and as the universe taught, survived.

Privately he wondered if his ex-wife, Shyanne Veda, didn't still doubt. As Second Will, he had her and her few friends watched. With the death of her year-old son a little over a year ago, she'd had a period of recalcitrance and grief, but had acted in no overt manner to demonstrate any apostasy or disbelief in the revelations of the Prophets. Now she doted on six-year-old Fatima, her remaining daughter.

But then, they all had secrets. Private thoughts that each of them desperately hoped the universe wasn't privy to.

We live in fear.

Vartan stopped at the side of the bed, staring down. Svetlana slept on her right side; her long body lay mostly exposed, a twist of sheet around her midriff and left thigh. The swirl of her long brown hair curled behind her head. Her arms were bent, hands tucked next to her lips.

He settled himself on the side of the bed and dialed up the room light to dim. As he did he felt the ever-so-faint change in acceleration. The ship had just kicked it up a bit.

"Hey, wake up."

She shifted onto her back, blinked her brown eyes. "It's been three times already. You're an animal. Let me sleep."

"Ship's boosting. Gravity's changed. I think we're starting the long burn toward Capella III. Listen. Feel."

She did, coming fully awake. Sitting up, she wiggled past him, stood. "I feel heavier."

"*Ashanti* is killing delta vee. It's actually going to happen. Just the way the Prophets said it would."

She studied him, brown eyes pensive, the light casting shadows across the complex patterns of Initiation scars that marked her as the second of the Messiah's four wives. After the Cleansing, she had been one of the first to offer herself to the newly acclaimed Messiah, had borne his first two children, and was waiting to see if she'd conceived the third.

Vartan reached up where she stood before him, ran his fingers along the long scars that marked her body. At his lingering touch, she shivered, closed her eyes, and leaned her head back to let her hair cascade down her back.

"The path of souls," he whispered, tracing down the line of scar that led to the thick mat of her pubic hair. He gave the curly mat a light tug, causing her to stare down at him with irritated eyes.

He softly asked, "Do you really believe that the souls of the dead have followed the same route my fingers just did? That they were reborn inside you?"

She chuckled just as softly. Said, "I could feel it. Both times I conceived with the Messiah. Wasn't anything like a regular orgasm. What began as more of warm honeyed feeling burst through my hips like a brilliant light that filled my uterus. An explosion of life that wracked my entire body."

From her expression, the tone in her voice, he wasn't sure if she was having fun at his expense. Or might have been just parroting the Messiah's lines.

That was the thing about Svetlana. He could never quite know if she believed the revelations of the Prophets, or if she was the penultimate survivor who accurately assessed the situation and sided with the man most likely to prevail.

All of which made his relationship with her so fascinating.

"I see that look," she told him with a grim smile. "You still wonder, don't you? But let me ask you, do *you* really believe? Because I think, like me, you're a survivor."

Another lurch, increasing the sensation of weight.

She looked up, as if she could see through the decks to *Ashanti*'s AC. "It's really going to happen. So, how do you think this will play out, Mr. Policeman?"

Vartan rubbed a hand on the back of his neck. "No matter what the Messiah says or believes, they're not going to welcome us with open arms. To them, we are going to be monsters."

She reached down to lift his chin and stared into his eyes. "We're alive, Vartan. As long as we are, there is hope and opportunity. And many of us are still under Contract. You were trained in law enforcement and security. You know of any law that says eating another human being is illegal?"

"No. But killing them for apostasy or heresy most certainly is." He raised a hand to take hers. "We plead that Galluzzi, by starving us, forced us into the practice. That we could either die or bow to necessity."

"Batuhan and the Prophets insist we're the tools of the universe. The chosen," Svetlana told him. "They believe. And so do most of the rest. After the Harrowing and Cleansing, the Revelations were like a straw floating on a sea of fear and guilt. The desperate not only grabbed onto it with two hands, it's become the only salvation left to keep them afloat."

He nodded.

Still staring into his eyes, she said, "You and I both know who among us might just be playing the game, keeping their heads down until the hatch opens. And when it does, they're going to run right to the Corporation and condemn us all."

"Why are you telling me this now?"

Another lurch of acceleration pulled at his body.

"Figure it out for yourself. Maybe we are the mystical chosen, and the universe will see to our ultimate triumph. Works for me. But when that hatch is finally open, I want to be positive that I, and my children, have a way out."

8

Dan Wirth surveyed his domain. He was lord and master of The Jewel. As night fell on Port Authority, Dan leaned on the bar and chewed a chabacho-wood toothpick. The stuff wasn't really wood, but close enough. The cells, so he'd been told, were a sort of polymer rather than cellulose—whatever the hell that was. Anyway, the wood was different than wood back on Earth.

Science wasn't really Dan's kind of preoccupation. Money was. And he was good at it. He'd made himself the second-richest person on Donovan—second only to Kalico Aguila.

Second.

Once upon a time, that fact had bothered him. He'd plotted various ways of murdering Aguila, seizing her assets, and turning himself into the richest man on the planet.

But then, just because Dan might have been a psychopath didn't mean he was stupid.

Killing Aguila would have meant the collapse of Corporate Mine, because he sure as hell wasn't going to go down and try to run the damn thing. Far better that the cunning slit of a Supervisor spent her time ensuring that fabulous wealth kept pouring out of those holes in the ground.

As long as her miners continued to patronize The Jewel, betting at Dan's tables, drinking his booze, buying his pharma, and paying for sex with his whores, he kept making money.

He had enough trouble maintaining good will with the kind and gentle people in Port Authority. When it came to the Wild Ones who lived out in the bush, prospected and hunted, at least a fella could whack them up alongside the head to get their attention. It was the "upstanding" and "decent" folk that drove Dan to the brink of distracted madness. They had to be treated with kid gloves. It was a full-time job.

The result was that nothing that happened in Port Authority took place without his knowledge, and as it turned out, his blessing.

Thankfully, he had Allison Chomko to carry some of the load. Originally, he'd targeted her because she'd been vulnerable, beautiful, and he'd needed her knowledge of Port Authority. Back in the old days, he'd drugged her. Prostituted her for all the benefit he could get. What he hadn't calculated into the equation was that she might be cutting-edge smart down under all that voluptuous beauty. He should have had a clue, given that both of her parents had been PhDs.

As she had taken over more of the management, become integral to the workings of Dan's little empire, their relationship had become a great deal more complicated. He now wondered when, and under what circumstances, he might be forced to remove her from the equation.

That would be a tricky piece of work. Allison had her backers, including Step Allenovich, Talina Perez, Shig, and even Yvette. Not to mention a lot of the "respectable" women who had once been Ali's friends. These days the righteous bitches might spurn Allison as a whore, but if there were so much as a hint that Dan had murdered her, the hypocritical slits would come after him with a rope.

Even as he thought about her, Ali emerged from the back with Desch Ituri hanging on her arm. The contrast was almost laughable. Ituri stood maybe five-foot four, stocky and black-skinned, with short curly hair and eyes like balls of obsidian. Allison towered over him, stately, elegant, a perfectly shaped Norse goddess of a woman with pale skin and silky silver-blonde hair that hung down her back. Sparkling blue eyes were set in a classic face. Laughter bubbled off of her lips as she reacted to something Ituri said.

Dan watched as they parted; Ituri headed for the door. Every eye in the place was glancing back and forth between Ituri and Allison, and most of them were covetous. No doubt imagining with salacious detail what Ituri had just enjoyed in Allison's bed.

For her part, Allison stopped to deposit something in the cage at the back of the room. First and foremost, Allison was a businesswoman. Dan could count the men she'd sell her sex to on two hands. Whatever Ituri had offered to bed Ali, it must have been worth a small fortune. But then, the man could pay. He was Kalico Aguila's head engineer down at Corporate Mine.

Dan inclined his head graciously as Allison turned his way. She paused only long enough at the tables to share a greeting and smile with the patrons. Called, "Vik! Another whiskey for Lee Halston."

With an almost predatory smile, she sidled up next to where Dan was keeping an eye on the roulette table as Shin Wong called for bets.

Dan asked, "Have a nice time?"

She gave him a conspiratorial wink. "I wouldn't screw him if I didn't. No matter how much plunder he offered."

"So what did he offer?"

"Turquoise. Ever hear of it before?"

"Yeah, I might have. Blue-colored stone, right? What's the big deal?"

"The deal is that Lea Shimodi, that Corporate geologist that works for Aguila, was down on the south continent. Found a big copper deposit. I guess it's a kind of desert down there. Something about it's got to be dry, and there's aluminum involved, and anyhow, the conditions are right for this deep-blue turquoise. The first ever found on Donovan."

"What's it worth?"

"Haven't a clue. It's a chunk the size of my fist. The important thing is that it's the first piece ever found on Donovan. Shimodi wrote it up in her notes. Described it."

"How'd Ituri get it?"

"He made a bet with Shimodi. Some technical thing about the Number One mine down at Corporate. She lost."

Dan flipped his toothpick to the other side of his mouth, delighted to watch as C'ian Gatlin lost an entire stack of chips betting odd on the roulette table.

"Anything else interesting down at the mine?" Dan asked.

Allison twitched her lips in disappointment. "Ituri

made some kind of deal with Aguila to get to come back here. He takes it seriously. He doesn't let slip about anything critical or salacious. Any kind of talk about the mines or the Supervisor is strictly off limits."

"Yeah, too bad. It's like the good Supervisor has stopped all of her leaks over the last year. Did you ask about Kalen Tompzen?"

"No. I didn't want to even hint that we had an interest in him." Allison stopped long enough to greet the bootmaker, Rude Marsdome, and Bernie Monson from the clay pit as the two strode in the door.

As they retreated to the pinochle table, Dan said, "Listen, it's been over a year since we've seen or heard from Kalen. We've had feelers out to the other marines that serve with him. We know he's still alive down there. So my best guess is that she finally figured out that he was our agent. That we had our claws into him."

Dan made a face, gestured with his toothpick. "I gotta hand it to Aguila, if she finally narrowed it down to Kalen, she's put the screws to him. Not that Kalen is the toughest of birds to start with, but she'll have sweated him for everything we had on him."

Allison waved to Fenn Bogarten as the chemist entered, headed back to join the others at the pinochle table. To Dan she said, "Just be glad she didn't order this place off limits after she found out."

"If she wanted to make something of it, she'd have sent Tompzen's corpse, or at least a couple of his body parts our way. That she hasn't speaks volumes."

"At this stage, given time for tempers to cool, perhaps we could make her a deal for Tompzen. Buy him back. Ever since Benteen killed Art Maniken, we've needed a good enforcer." She gave him an amused sidelong glance. "You don't have the same brute touch that Art had. By nature, you're much too subtle."

"I'll mention it the next time I see the wily cunt." Fact was, he did need a good enforcer. Not that he was above slitting a throat now and then, but too many such doings affected his standing in the community. Who the fuck would have ever thought that maintaining a reputation could be such hard-sucking work?

Allison arched a slim eyebrow. "Why don't you let me? Aguila and I don't have the same history that the two of you do. But enough of that. While I was relieving Desch of his built-up stress, what did you learn at the meeting with the triumvirate? That ship really coming in?"

What's your game, Ali? Building an alliance with Aguila? Strengthening your position at my expense?

Dan gestured his dissatisfaction. "Oh, *Ashanti*'s coming in, all right. But she's a mess. Turns out they've been locked in that bucket of air for ten years. Word is that the transportees got out of hand, so the captain, a guy named Galluzzi, welded them in. Bottled them up in their quarters."

"God, that sounds . . ."

"Yeah, gets worse. Shig said that according to the ship's records, they gleefully murdered each other to start with, and ended up eating their dead. Having been sealed in without crayons or color markers, they practiced art on each other with knives. And in the process, they've elevated some guy called Batuhan into a sort of guru messiah who interprets for three babbling prophets. Batuhan's calling for some sort of galactic jihad that's supposed to end in the universe having itself for supper and being reborn in purity like him and all his fawning acolytes."

Allison's lips tightened in distaste. "That for sure?"

"I guess so. Shig's clap-trapping weird over it. Remember Shig? The bipedal Buddha? Never-got-his-balls-in-a-knot Shig? That guy? Well, he's fart-sucking freaked about the transportees." Dan glanced at the palm of his hand where he'd written it down so he wouldn't forget. "They call themselves Irredenta. Means something about being culturally unique in someone else's territory."

"They still scheduled to make planet in a couple of months?"

"Give or take."

"So, what's the plan? Just let a bunch of cut-up cannibals land at the shuttle field?"

"We're thinking of Tyson Station. Supposed to be an abandoned base somewhere out west."

Allison grunted under her breath. "I lived out there for a while. My parents died there while I was in school here in Port Authority. After Clemenceau was no longer in the picture, they were going to close the station down. Mom and Dad stayed behind to finish up some research. They found Mom's skeleton. Never did find what happened to Dad. Not a trace."

"Apparently some of *Ashanti*'s scientists and some of the crew are still sane. Since the ship's Corporate, the cargo manifest has gone to Aguila. She'll share it with the rest of us as soon as she has a chance to go through it. As to what happens to *Ashanti*, that's up in the air. Word is that the crew just want to be dirtside for a while. That for most, ten years in that bucket is enough."

"Aguila going to claim them like she did the *Turalon* deserters?"

"Maybe. I don't know. My take was that Aguila's still figuring this thing out."

"We'd better be figuring, too," Allison mused. "Ship's crew? They're going to be hitting dirt, looking for any kind of diversion, and they're going to be coming here."

"Yeah, all looking for a good time, and the randy marks aren't going to have a cent to their names." He paused. "There's opportunity in that."

She tapped a slender finger on his chest. "But carefully this time, Dan. We don't want a replay of the Tosi Damitiri mess."

Figures you'd bring that up.

Was she trying to piss him off? Remind him of how that had almost turned into a disaster?

Dan nodded, thinking. "You might want to talk to Aguila sooner rather than later regarding Tompzen. Something makes me think we're gonna need a good enforcer. And the thing about Tompzen is that he's proven that he's not squeamish if it comes to a little blood and pain."

9

Ashanti looped around Capella, using the star's gravity to decelerate. As it did the ship's energy fields scooped up the dense solar wind, harvesting hydrogen for the reactors. With fuel to burn, and the generation of one-and-a-half gravities of thrust to slow their velocity in relation to Donovan, *Ashanti* entered the final course corrections on her seemingly eternal voyage.

The ship might have been structurally rated for a 2-g acceleration, but after having been lived in for ten years, many of the constructions, such as ad-hoc shelving, plant stands down in hydroponics, and make-do repairs were not.

For Miguel Galluzzi and his crew, it was a constant scramble to deal with one minor calamity after another. Pumps failed, pipes began to leak, and so far as Galluzzi was concerned, the activity was a godsend. His people were constantly occupied, and they had to be extra careful. Every move had to be planned. He went to the extent of having them employ safety harnesses to go up and down stairways. Even a simple slip or fall at 1.5 g could have dire consequences. No one had time to think about Donovan and what disembarking was going to necessitate.

Of course, Galluzzi's crew weren't the only ones to notice. Every time the captain stepped into the AC, the board was flashing messages from Deck Three.

He checked a few. In among the usual propaganda about the coming end of the universe as he knew it, were demands for information. Unsurprisingly, each came with a threat, that if it were to be unanswered, dire consequences would ensue.

Galluzzi considered that as he stared at the holo of *Freelander* where it was projected over his worktable. He had taken to wondering about the derelict, had spent hours staring at the dead vessel. Had read all of the reports and logs Supervisor Aguila had sent him.

He'd barely survived ten years. How did he get his head around Jem Orten facing what he thought was an eternity lost in nothingness? On *Freelander* they had murdered the transportees. Jem and his first officer had welded themselves into the AC and ultimately used a pistol to blow their brains out.

Just because my actions weren't as extreme, it doesn't absolve me of my failures.

Galluzzi—seated in his captain's chair—was reading through the latest list when Derek Taglioni minced his way into the captain's lounge on carefully placed steps.

"Can't believe my back hurts so much," Taglioni noted. "Makes me wish I'd built up to this. That, or we'd practiced for a couple of hours every day."

Galluzzi glanced up at the bulbous shape of *Freelander* where it was projected from the holos. "Won't be long. Another couple of days. Just about the time you start to adapt, we'll shut down. *Ashanti*'s got the final course plot. It's just a matter of watching the hours count down."

He flicked the image of *Freelander* off and replaced it with a holo of Cap III, Donovan, as he reminded himself to say.

Moving like an old man, Taglioni seated himself in Turner's seat at the nav panel. "Hope the Unreconciled are enjoying it. Wonder what they make of all this?"

Galluzzi tapped the side of his head. "Playing some of their latest demands and threats on my implants now. 'As the fire is to the wood, so are the Irredenta to you and the rest of humanity. You are about to burn, for only as ashes will you finally reap the true reward of being.'

"And here's another: 'You cannot hide the truth. We know we are nearing Capella III. As we emerge from the womb of transformation, it will be to expand upon a wave of blood. Upon it we shall ride, consuming the ignorant, devouring their being, until reborn in blood they shall be made whole and will know illumination.'"

Galluzzi winced. "This one is my favorite: 'The moment of our release is at hand. The universe shall see to this. Upon the instant of our release, you shall know the fulfilling rapture of terror. In it, you shall be reborn and find immortality.'"

"I've heard it all before." Taglioni stared absently at Donovan where it spun before them. "You don't think that just maybe we've got it all wrong, and he's talking in metaphors?"

Galluzzi shot him a chiding look. "Want me to access the photos of the butchered remains they've sent down the chute to hydroponics?" He paused. "And don't forget that we sampled their sewage before it was sent to the tanks. More than enough human myosin II was found in their feces to pretty much discount the notion they were only biting their nails."

"So what does Supervisor Aguila say about all this?"

"She sent a message to the Irredenta that she asked me to forward on for her. It stated that a research station was being made ready for them on Donovan. That upon disembarkation, subject to contract, each individual would be evaluated and suitable employment would be provided."

"She's got to be kidding."

"Whatever else she may turn out to be, she is a Corporate Supervisor, and by making the offer, she's covered all of her contractual obligations. The Irredenta replied in a most colorful way. They informed the Supervisor that they would consume her corpse in a community feast. That the pollution of her existence could only be purified through the concerted action of each and every true believer."

"You forwarded that to the Supervisor?" Taglioni asked. "I'd have loved to have seen the expression on her face."

"My take on Kalico Aguila is that the woman isn't your rank-and-file Corporate Supervisor. A fact you might keep in mind when dealing with her. Her reply, which was radioed in almost immediate return, was 'Please inform them that they're going to have to age me for a couple of weeks since I'm a lot tougher than they realize. And they'd better have an ample helping of salt and pepper on hand.'"

Taglioni smiled at that. "Tell me you didn't send that on to Batuhan and his merry band of man-munching fiends."

"I do have some good sense."

"I've been reading the reports the Donovanians have sent up. What do you make of them?"

Galluzzi fixed him with a measuring glance. "I had to

look up the word 'libertarian.' If there's a total and complete opposite of Corporate, that's it. Dek, that planet down there is a free-for-all. Corporate Mine, for what it's worth, is structured, ordered, and Corporate in nature. A person can know where he or she stands. Where he or she fits.

"Port Authority on the other hand? It's chaos. How do they live? Who takes care of them? What's this market economy they're so taken with? No one's in charge. Just stumble along on your own. Who keeps people from making a mistake? And if they do, they have to take full responsibility for it. No equitable redistribution. No management whatsoever. How do they even make it through a day?"

Taglioni said with smile, "Funny thing. I *dreamed* of that planet last night. Like it was singing to my bones. Call me crazy, but it's like I'm coming home to a place I've never been before. I can't wait to set foot down there and see what chaos feels like. Sounds remarkably liberating and terrifying all at once."

"You're kidding, right? Port Authority exists in defiance of everything your family has believed going all the way back to the founding of The Corporation. And they live behind a fence for shit's sake. Because the wildlife can creep in and eat people. You read that, didn't you? That the gates are locked at sundown. And if we're not inside, that they won't come out looking for us."

Taglioni grinned wider. "I went to one of the rewilding reserves on Earth when I was a kid. Stepped outside at night. Knew that there were lions and tigers out there. That I could be eaten. Liked to have scared myself to death."

"You've seen the holo taken during the *Tempest* expedition? Of Donovan? The first guy to die down on that rock? That thing, the quetzal, eating him alive? And you find that exciting?"

Taglioni nodded, expression turning thoughtful. "Looking back, Miguel, I have trouble remembering who I was the day I stepped on board *Ashanti*. I'm not that Derek Taglioni." He looked down at his hands, spread the fingers, inspected the palms. "I've scrubbed caked shit out of the insides of toilets. Fought to keep from puking while I hung over the ferment tanks to repair the agitators down in hydroponics. Hell, I could qualify for a Ship's Technician Level I rating. I've crawled into raceways, come within a whisker of electrocuting myself. Carried the dead bodies of men and women I considered friends down to hydroponics after they committed suicide. I eat at the common table in the crew's mess. So, compared to that arrogant scumsucking Corporate prick who strolled aboard back in orbit off Neptune, who the hell have I become?"

Galluzzi gave him a slight nod. "Once I would have died before I said this, but perhaps you have become a human being?"

"Makes you wonder, doesn't it? Looking back, I was a sort of monster once. Now I have become human, and down on Deck Three all those perfectly humdrum humans have become monsters. How—on the scales of universal justice—does that balance out?"

Galluzzi stared thoughtfully at the projection of Donovan. "Maybe you'll find an answer on Cap III."

"What about you?"

Galluzzi shook his head. "I don't have a clue. Once the last of those people are down-planet, I wonder if I won't just disintegrate into atoms and fade into nothingness."

The one-and-a-half gravities had been like an endless torture. Locked as they were in the confines of Deck Three, it wasn't like the Irredenta had any avenue open to them but monotonous endurance. It didn't matter that over the years, more and more ration came tumbling out of the conveyor in the mess. These days—eat as much as a person might—he or she just didn't gain flesh.

"Ration" consisted of a cake-like composite of protein, fat, carbohydrate, and glucose injected with synthesized vitamins and recaptured minerals. The stuff was made from algae, plant tissue, and bacteria that grew in reprocessed nutrient-rich water.

From the loose teeth and thinning hair, the frail bones, the slightly sunken eyes, and occasional motor coordination troubles, malnutrition was simply a fact of life. Things might have been better if the ship's physician and medical techs hadn't been killed in the initial rioting.

Vartan stood in the back of what served as the infirmary. His ex-wife, Shyanne Veda—she'd gone back to her maiden name—was treating the scars on one of the little boys who'd undergone Initiation. It didn't matter that the infirmary had some of the best lighting left in the whole of Deck Three; she still had to bend down to inspect the scabs that ran down the little boy's arms and legs.

With a sigh, Shyanne straightened. Shot Vartan a look through weary umber-colored eyes. Like Svetlana, she was another tall, thin woman who crowded six feet. The similarities were enough to make him wonder if he cleaved to a certain type. Thinking back, most of the women in his life had been taller than him.

"'M I okay?" little Pho asked, staring up at Shyanne as if she were an oracle.

Fat chance that, the job already had been taken by the Prophets.

Shyanne gave him a nod. "You're healing. Be careful not to tear the scabs off like you did on your leg. I want you under the UV light for a couple of hours a day. It's the only thing we've got to get that infection under control."

She helped the little boy up off the table, watched him limp stiffly out of the room. Then she glanced at Vartan. "So, Security Officer, what can I do for you?"

"They'll be coming soon."

She crossed her thin arms under the scarified spirals that covered her small breasts, lifted her brows. "Given the shutdown of the ship, the sudden return to normal gravity, that doesn't take a Prophet to figure out."

He turned, glanced to make sure the hallway remained empty. Turning back, he said, "A Supervisor has been in touch."

"I've heard. But not the details. What's it mean, Vart? Incarceration? Psychiatric confinement? Some kind of prison camp? Given the things we did . . ." She lifted a hand, turned away.

"A research base," he told her. "Somewhere out away from the main settlements. That's not common knowledge."

"Then why are you sharing it with me?"

He shrugged. "You're not like the rest. I know that. You don't buy the Prophets and the Universe. But most of them do. It's the only way they can cope."

"Vart," she told him, a distant look in her eyes, "I'm not a fool. I bought in the first time I looked down on a plate and told myself: 'It's eat it, or die.' Understood that if I died, it would be cooked pieces of me on the plate. After that, the rest was easy. Well, all but the shit-sucking Initiation with the all the cutting, the screaming in pain, bleeding, and weeks of agony as the scars healed."

She stared into the distance of memory. "The first time the Messiah came to my bed, I was creep-freaked. But I figured I could lay there while he did his thing. I let my mind go somewhere else. It wasn't like there was anything left of me to lose."

She cocked her head. "And now, after all this time, why the hell do you even care?"

"I've heard that there are a few who are planning to

demand their rights under Contract as soon as the hatch is open. I don't want you to be one of them."

The way she looked at him, the light of her soul might have gone dark. "I told you, I'm in. So far as I'm concerned, we're the chosen. The universe speaks to the Prophets, and the Messiah is their voice. We are the living dead. Through us, they are reborn. Pure."

"Why don't I believe you?"

"Because, Vart, there's little else left to believe."

11

The feeling was surreal. After all that Derek had been through, it had to be the way a convict felt: Like his sentence was finally over. That he'd served his time.

He looked around the small sialon room that had been his cell. The once-stately quarters—with a bed, desk, the separate toilet and shower—had been a most remarkable luxury. Almost sixteen square meters of living space. At times this had been a refuge, and at others a confinement. A place of soul-numbing fear, endless hunger, and desperate hope.

He laid a hand on the wall, feeling the ship's vibrations through the hard material. "*Ashanti*, access please."

"*Hello, Dek,*" the ship's com said. "*What can I do for you?*"

"Nothing. Just wanted to say thanks for keeping us alive and getting us here."

"*You are welcome. Safe travels.*"

It was said with feeling, but then the AI was programmed that way. When all was said and done, the ship's intelligence was incapable of emotion, but still smart enough to evaluate a human's behavior and tone, then respond accordingly.

Dek took a final look at the room, thinking, *Maybe I'm not so different from the Unreconciled. Maybe I was gestated within these walls just to be born as someone different.*

He cracked a parting smile, lifted his two bags and gun case, and stepped out into the familiar corridor. It struck him that he, a Taglioni, was carrying his own luggage—all that remained of the two large trunks of fine clothing, special foods, entertainments, expensive jewelry, and the ornate plates, pitchers, and engraved silverware. Even his family tea service had been traded away to different members of the crew during the long years.

Beyond that he hadn't frittered away the two shipping containers in cargo. One contained his airplane—the one he had intended to use traveling between his holdings. The other had various recreational gadgets, exercise equipment, a home VR theater, interactive furniture, sports equipment for his leisure time, and other indulgences suitable to a Taglioni.

Given what he now knew about Donovan, he was wondering what exactly the use of a squash ball might be, or the value of his self-aware drink caddy.

In his two bags were his com equipment, a couple pair of worn coveralls, a set of utilitarian tools, and a few keepsakes he couldn't abide to part with. The gun case contained his hunting rifle, pistol, bullets, and powerpacks. He was wearing his last, best, formal wear. Shabby as it was.

Walking down the corridor for the last time filled him with a curious remorse. *Ashanti* had brought them through. Carried them across thirty light-years of interstellar space from Solar System. The error that had almost killed them hadn't been the ship's fault. It had been in the math hidden down in the quantum qubit computers in the ship's core. Something that someone back in Solar System had programmed into the complicated statistics that governed inverted symmetry.

When *Ashanti* had popped back inside the universe a half light-year away from her target, she'd still managed to get them to Capella III.

A man couldn't help but have a fondness for a ship like that.

He took the lift down to Deck Four, made his way to the shuttle deck, and stepped into the Number Six hatch area. Passing through the decompression doors, he found Captain Galluzzi at the airlock in conversation with Michaela Hailwood.

"We the first ones here?" Derek asked. "It's not even 15:00 hours."

"Hardly," Michaela told him. "The entire Maritime Unit's already aboard, buckled in. Kids included. Have been for the last fifteen minutes. And that's after they'd been waiting nearly an hour at the airlock. You'd think they were in a hurry to get off."

"Just waiting on you, Dek," Galluzzi told him with a smile.

"Thought there'd be a riot to get on the first shuttle." Derek glanced around at the empty hallway.

"Funny thing," Galluzzi told him. "Yeah, we got some real anxious sorts who can't wait to shuttle down. Set foot on dirt again. But the closer we got, the more people began to waver. It's like they're suddenly unsure. It's a bit intimidating to leave what's comfortable, you know what I mean?"

"Guess I do."

Galluzzi waved toward the lock. "Welcome aboard. Soon as you're strapped in, Ensign Naftali can dog the hatch, uncouple, and see if the shuttle still works."

"What if it doesn't?" Michaela asked, her dark eyes thoughtful.

"Another reason a lot of us aren't in a hurry to leave." Galluzzi gave her a wide grin. "If you explode and burn up on reentry, we'll know to stay aboard."

"Cute," Derek told him. Dropped his bags. Took Galluzzi's hand in a hard shake. Pus and blood, the look in the man's eyes was like that of a suffering martyr. "See you dirtside, Captain."

"Yeah. You, too."

Derek followed Michaela through the lock and into the main shuttle cabin.

"You and I get to ride on the command deck," Michaela told him as he handed over his luggage. "Benefits of status."

He let Tech Third Class Raptu stow his bags and followed Michaela through the hatch into the command deck. He got the right-hand seat in the row of three behind Naftali and copilot Windman's command chairs. Begay, the old, familiar, pensive "don't disturb me" look on his face, was in the left seat. The Advisor might have been meditating given the lines of concentration.

Derek buckled in. Aware of Michaela's curious appraisal as she snapped her harness tight.

"What?"

"Just thinking. About all we've been through. You and me. All of us."

He arched an eyebrow. "Ten years in that bucket of air

is a long time, Micky." He called her his old affectionate name from one of the two periods when they'd been lovers. "I haven't a clue about what awaits us down-planet. Whatever it is, if you need me, let me know."

She glanced away. "It's not like there're many secrets left after all this." A beat. "I'm sorry for the way I . . . Well, I could have been more diplomatic that last time."

"I just wish that things would have worked out better between you and Turner."

"All right, people," Naftali's voice carried from the command chair. "Let's go see a new world."

Thumps could be felt through the deck. Servos whined and hydraulics moaned.

"Hatch is sealed and secure." Raptu's voice announced through the com.

"Begin undocking sequence." Windman's voice couldn't mask the excitement.

A bigger thump shivered the shuttle. "Locking latches free."

Looking through the right-side window, Derek watched the shuttle rise, clear *Ashanti*'s hull, and Capella's bright light spilled through the transparency. As they rose, Derek got a good look at the ship. Could see the occasional pits in the sialon hull, and then they were above it.

Ashanti seemed to glow in Capella's light, radiant. Part of the ship's hull lay in shadow. And behind it the wash of the Milky Way—in a billion stars—gave it a special sort of beauty.

Then the shuttle changed attitude, banked, and the stars—masked by a pattern of black nebulae—took the ship's place.

"I can't believe this is happening," Michaela whispered. "It's really over. We've made it. There were times when I almost gave up."

Derek chewed his lips, the surreal sensation increasing as acceleration pushed him into the seat. As it did, they passed *Freelander* where it hung in orbit. Unlike *Ashanti*, the big ship's hull was dark behind the terminator line. Dek had read the reports, seen the images of the temple of human bones in the cafeteria.

There, but for the grace of God, go I.

The ghost ship seemed to hold his gaze as it cried out to his sense of tragedy and horror. People had committed mass murder, died of old age, gone mad. Now, studying the dark vessel, something wasn't right. The light, it didn't reflect. The sensation was like looking at one of those fifty-percent mirrors that passed half the photons. Which was clap-trapping crazy, of course.

But something about the derelict sent a shiver up his bones.

As if *Freelander* took the trials and tribulations that *Ashanti* endured and magnified the horror tenfold.

With a sense of relief, he felt the first turbulence of atmosphere, watched the reddish haze trace its way across the wings and past his window. A faint roaring filled the cabin, the shuttle bouncing down out of the sky.

They shot over the terminator, looking down on an eerily dark planet. He could barely make out the continents, the seas, and islands.

Dark.

How odd after Earth, Moon, and Mars, all of which were stitched with patterns of light while in their nighttime phases.

As they shot into the sunlight, dropping down, Derek picked out the signature outline of the giant meteor impact crater. The sight of it reminded him of a bite taken out of the continent. Knew it marked the location of the human settlements on Capella III.

G-force threw him into his seat as the shuttle banked out over the ocean, leaving him a view of a sky that seemed to have a deeper blue than Earth's.

The shuttle's nose lifted. The roar grew louder. The ground seemed to rise, as if to smack them. Only to have the shuttle flatten out, almost skimming over the blue waters. Patches of white cloud flashed past the window.

They were over land now, a reddish soil dotted with what looked like trees. And nowhere, to Derek's amazement, could even a speck of civilization be seen.

I belong here.

The planet might have been a magnet, drawing him. A thrill, like a vibration in his bones, had him staring down at the terrain flashing below. The feeling was . . . mystical!

And then they were down, the shuttle dropping on its landing struts. Dust blew out to curl before a wall of stacked shipping containers.

Dust?

"Welcome to Donovan," Naftali called. "If you'd keep your seats until we spool down, we'll have you off as soon as possible."

Derek could hear whistles and cheers coming from the main cabin.

It's real. I'm actually here.

He could feel the gravity. Stronger than on the ship.

As he stepped back into the main cabin, it was to see people in tears. They were hugging each other, crying, smiling. These were mostly the Maritime Unit people and their families. But a few of the crew had managed to snag some of the open seats.

Raptu got the all clear. The crafty tech opened the hatch, lowered the stairs, and raced to the bottom, ostensibly to offer people assistance, thereby getting to claim that he'd been the first from *Ashanti* to set foot on Cap III.

A decade ago, Derek might have had the guy's head. Now he just chuckled as he grabbed up his bags and took the stairs to the ground. At the first contact, the electric thrill in his bones intensified. Could have been his body turning into a tuning fork.

I am home. This is my place.

With the seared clay under his feet, he took a moment to get his bearings. Stacked cargo containers blocked the view in every direction except toward the town. But the scent! Perfumed, a sort of cardamom and sage with a trace of cinnamon. For a moment, he closed his eyes, filled his lungs. Pure bliss.

Benj and Michaela clumped down the stairs, and both sighed in unison as they stepped onto the ground.

As Derek turned his attention in the direction of town, the first thing that struck him was the fence. Fully fifty feet tall, composed of cobbled-together sections of woven, welded, and chain-link wire, it looked like something from a maximum-security prison.

Behind it he could see weathered duraplast domes, peaked roofs that looked somehow medieval, and a collection of people who crowded against the fence. They were calling, waving, obviously happy at the shuttle's arrival.

From a gate came four people who . . .

Derek stared, wondered what he was seeing. Escapees from the circus? A sort of freak show? The notion of old-time pirates came to mind. They were dressed in gaudy, wide-brimmed hats and shimmering, rainbow-hued leather boots, vests, and cloaks. Each wore a shirt of some light fabric embroidered in colorful patterns. Okay, maybe Gypsy clown pirates.

It took him a moment, but Derek picked out the Supervisor, tall, raven-haired, with her scars. Hard to believe this was the same stately beauty he'd coveted in Transluna. The one who had once perched on Miko's arm like an exotic ornament. She walked forward with a swinging stride and stood out only because she wore a black business suit beneath the dancing colors of her prism-colored cloak. Disconcerting was the holstered pistol upon which she rested her right hand.

She picked him out immediately, recognition flashing. And then distaste and barely masked loathing turned to puzzlement as she noticed he was carrying his bags and gun case. Good. Let her stew on that.

Shig Mosadek was the short one with the unruly hair, brown face, and amiable grin. Beside him strode a tall silver-blonde woman with piercing green eyes. She might have been in her fifties, or with the right med, even older. She had a curious, almost mocking smile on her lips.

And finally, the fourth woman was mesmerizing. Thirtyish, maybe five foot six, with long blue-black hair and angular cheekbones unlike anything Derek had ever seen. Then he fixed on her inhuman, almost alien-black eyes. She walked with the same innate grace and flow as a hunting panther. The military-grade rifle slung on her shoulder, the big knife and the use-worn pistol on her pouch-filled belt, added to her look of deadly competence.

Supervisor Aguila stepped ahead, offering her hand as she said, "Advisor/Observer Begay, I'm Supervisor Kalico Aguila of Corporate Mine. To my left is Shig Mosadek, Yvette Dushane, and Security First Talina Perez of Port Authority. Welcome to Donovan."

That she'd deferred to the Advisor/Observer irritated something deep in Derek's chest. Yes, Begay was the senior Corporate official. But to spurn a Taglioni? What was the woman trying to prove? What was her game? What percentage did she play by antagonizing him and throwing down the gauntlet . . .

Stop it. You're not that guy anymore.

Derek fixed on Begay's face, realized that the man looked stricken. On the verge of tears, Begay said, "Thank you, Supervisor. A lot of us, well, we thought we'd never see this day."

Michaela, too, was looking shaken. Her mouth was working, a glitter of incipient tears behind her eyes. At the moment she seemed too overcome for words.

When Aguila finally looked his way, Dek stepped forward, dropped his bags, and offered his hand. "Derek Taglioni, Supervisor. Good to see you again. Allow me to introduce Michaela Hailwood, in charge of the Maritime Unit and our lead scientist."

She ignored his hand, a mere quiver of distaste at the corner of her mouth. A thousand questions lay behind the look she gave him.

He tried not to be distracted by the tracery of scars across her face. Oh, yes. She remembered that last meeting. Her blue gaze seemed to shoot through him like lasers. "Welcome, sir. I hope the vicissitudes of your journey weren't unbearable."

Derek felt an old part of himself bristle at the reserve she tried to keep from her voice. She still loathed him. That brought him no little amusement. And yes, had he stepped down from the shuttle ten years ago . . .

Have I changed so much?

Aguila had shifted her attention to Michaela, saying, "Welcome to Donovan." She had no trouble offering the woman her hand in a firm shake.

Mosadek—a beneficent smile on his lips—said, "I look forward to getting to know you all. Port Authority is delighted to welcome you."

Dek could hear the buildup of people behind him as the Maritime Unit came flooding down the stairs. Children were crying, people wondering at the smell of the air, the feel of sunlight on their skin and ground underfoot. He could hear complaints about the gravity.

Grabbing up his luggage, he stepped off to the side, happy to be out of the limelight.

In a loud voice, the alien-eyed Perez called, "Welcome to Donovan. I'm Security Officer Talina Perez. If you'll all follow me, my associate, Corporal Abu Sassi, has a registration and orientation set up in the cafeteria."

Aguila turned to the crowd. "Please stay close. We don't want anyone to stray off on this side of the fence. Once you are in the cafeteria and have completed orientation, your Corporate status will be determined. Temporary housing will be assigned, and we'll get you fed." A beat. "With *real* food!"

That brought a round of happy cries and applause.

As Perez lined them out, Dek matched Aguila's step, asking, "Is the fence to keep people in, or something out?"

"Out." Aguila shot him a measuring glance. "Sir, forgive me for being blunt, but Donovan is not Solar System, and Port Authority is not Transluna. In the next few moments you are going to hear yourself referred to as 'soft meat,' a 'Skull,' and who knows what else? The terms are not disrespectful, but a reference to your having been aboard a ship. It's a difficult request, but if you would be so kind as to grant the locals a bit of leeway, I would sincerely appreciate it."

Derek tried to decipher the message she was sending him. Obviously, a warning, but not even Miko's woman would dare hint to another Taglioni that he not behave like an ass.

They were nearing the gate, and behind the fence he could see the crowd, all dressed in insane costumes of leather, boots, worn coveralls, and looking like ruffians from a VR fantasy. The number of weapons alone should have sent prickles down his back. Would have, once upon a time. What kind of lunatic gave weapons to the common people? They couldn't be trusted.

Is that what living two decks up from the Unreconciled for all these years has done? It's left me numb to physical threat?

The gate was a big thing, ten meters wide, fifteen tall,

but the smaller "man gate" was set into the side. His Donovanian escort led the way through, and Derek followed them into Port Authority proper.

He returned greetings called from the cheerful Donovanians and delighted in the fact that though they carried them, none were waving guns around. Gravel crunched under his feet. Gravel? Not paved?

The domes to either side appeared old, weathered, streaked with what looked like fungus. Here and there he could see pieces of cannibalized equipment, much of it sitting up on blocks. The sunlight seemed harsher, the sky a deep shade of turquoise that hinted of lapis.

Stopping before the double doors at the cafeteria dome, Aguila said, "Sir, rather than attend the orientation, how about you and I get some things straight on our own?"

"Listen, Supervisor, given our last meeting, I don't blame you for the chilly reception. Just for the record, I'm not here to cause you any grief. Not after what I've been through."

Skepticism filled her laser-blue eyes. "Actually, nothing would delight me more than to leave you on the other side of the fence. But I'll tell you what you need to know to stay alive. Call it the Aguila crash course."

"And where are we going to do that? Your office?"

"Hardly." She barked a laugh. "Follow me. And don't worry about the rest of your luggage. They'll send it to a dome. Two Spot will tell me where."

"This is it." He raised his bags and gun case. "Well, there are a couple of containers in cargo. An airplane. Some other toys. But this is all I've got."

"You're kidding."

"It's all that's left."

For a long moment she tried to dissect him with her cutting gaze. "Whatever game you're—"

"No game. I don't have any left to play."

He watched the others as they passed through the doors into the cafeteria dome. All those expectant faces, men and women, their children. People he'd known so intimately for all those horrifying years. And here and there a crewman. Including Koikosan, with whom he'd worked hydroponics. How had she managed to snag a seat down-planet?

"Long story, Supervisor. Call it a beautiful terror, a wondrous nightmare. A numbing epiphany."

She was giving him that you're-more-disgusting-than-shit-on-my-shoe look again. "Let's just get this over with as painlessly as possible so I can be shut of you."

She led the way down what looked like the main avenue. Domes were interspersed with stone-and-wood buildings of local manufacture. He saw signs proclaiming ASSAY OFFICE, GUNSMITH, GLASSWORKS, and FOUNDRY. The street was empty of traffic. The town's entire population, it appeared, was back at the cafeteria and shuttle field.

"Not even a stray dog," he mused.

"According to the records, dogs rarely lasted more than a couple of months before Donovan got them. The invertebrates took out the cats even faster."

Derek had started to pant. His feet heavy, the two bags like sodden weights. He could feel the strain in his shoulders, wondered if they'd be pulled out of joint. When had he gotten so soft?

Fortunately she led him to a dome a block down. The place looked old; oddly matched benches sat in front of a double door. A faded sign proclaimed: THE BLOODY DRINK.

Derek glanced at it, then at the I'll-take-no-shit-off-you Supervisor as she opened the door.

What the hell have I gotten myself into?

12

Kalico took the chair to the left of Talina's. Indicated that Taglioni seat himself on the stool generally occupied by Shig when he chose to join her. Or sometimes by Step Allenovich, the part-time biologist and security third.

Puffing to catch his breath, a sheen of sweat on his too-pale skin, Taglioni dropped his bags and the expensive gun case on the fitted stone slabs. The guy was way out of shape, and Donovan's gravity was a couple of points higher than that provided by the ship's rotation.

He looked sallow, half-starved, and he probably didn't have a clue that he smelled bad. But then, after ten years in the same ship, they all did. Hard to believe this was the same man as that foul-mouthed maggot back in Transluna.

"What is this place?" Taglioni asked, glancing around at the tables, the benches, the stairway that led up to ground level, and the high dome overhead.

"It's called Inga's. The local tavern. And this is Inga herself." Kalico gestured to the big blonde woman who made her way down the bar. "Do treat her respectfully. Or not, if you want a quick one-way trip up to a grave in the cemetery."

"What'll it be?" Inga demanded in a tone that obviously shocked Taglioni's patrician sensibilities.

Kalico indicated Taglioni. "Meet Derek Taglioni. Fresh in from Solar System. Sir, this is Inga Lock, master brewer, distiller, and winemaker. She's also owner of Donovan's finest and only tavern."

"My pleasure." Inga shook Taglioni's hand. From the guy's expression, it looked like she was crushing his bones. "What'll you have?"

"Um . . ." Taglioni looked suddenly unsure. "It's been so long."

"You name it, we got it."

Kalico asked, "Sir, do you prefer wine or beer or spirits?"

She watched the corners of his mouth quiver. "Something mild, I suppose."

"I recommend the blond ale," Kalico said. "Me? I'll have the new-cask whiskey."

Inga inclined her head. "He on your tab?"

"Yeah. You eaten, sir?"

"Ration this morning," Taglioni replied, a curious insecurity growing behind his eyes.

"Two plates of the lunch special." Kalico added.

"You got it, Supervisor." Slapping her bar towel over her shoulder, Inga went bundling off down her bar, bellowing, "Two lunch specials!" at the top her lungs. As if she'd need to, given that Kalico and Taglioni were the only people in the place.

Kalico considered the man next to her, watched the interplay of emotion behind his too-perfect face. He was still handsome, striking actually, with his yellow-green designer eyes and sandy hair. "I doubt you would recall, but you and I have actually met before, sir. Several times. The last was at a Board reception in the Heiman Hotel. You were rather intoxicated. Knew I was accompanying Miko. Offered your own—"

"Loud, lewd, and vulgar offer of . . . um, companionship." He finished, followed by a crestfallen look and a humorless laugh.

In a weary voice he said, "I am deeply and sincerely apologetic. Not that I remember the totality of the occasion. I'd like to blame my behavior on the liquor or whatever mood-altering substance was dulling my brain. Unfortunately, I can't, knowing that it was the man himself who proved himself a rude boor."

Kalico blinked. Of all the . . . Was this really Derek Taglioni? "You're not exactly what I expected, sir."

In a soft voice, he said, "Can we dispense with this 'sir' thing? At least for the moment."

"Would you prefer that I call you Mr. Taglioni?"

"Most call me Dek."

Dek? Kalico arched an eyebrow. "Okay . . . Dek. An apology from a Taglioni? Whatever game you're playing—"

"I meant what I said. No game. After what I've been through . . . well, I'm just sorry for the way I behaved back then. I mean that."

"Just like that?"

He seemed to fidget, and for an instant, gave her a crafty sidelong glance. "You're not exactly what I was expecting, either. Back on Transluna, you were in the game for keeps. You're . . . let's say, a little different."

"Welcome to Donovan. If you survive here for long, you'll get the humor in that. Start with why you were aboard that bucket of air in the first place."

"You are still in my cousin's service?"

"Miko helped wrangle me this appointment. One of my tasks upon arrival here four years ago was to ascertain your whereabouts and status. Obviously, if *Ashanti* never arrived, neither had you, so I forgot about it."

"Back on Transluna . . . Can we just say I was angry and feeling slighted? In a fit of irrational and puerile rage, I ran away from home. Thought I'd come to Donovan and make a name for myself."

"You say that with a good deal of regret." *Real or faked?*

"*Ashanti* reinverted symmetry and popped back into the universe way off course." Taglioni's lips twitched. "Thought we were lost. Not enough fuel. Surely you've read Miguel's report. He told you the God's awful truth. Damn noble fool thinks he's going to get the ax for what he did to the transportees. Supervisor, I was there. At that time, at that moment, the smartest thing Miguel could have done was seal the transportees into Deck Three."

"No other choice?"

"Looking back with twenty-twenty hindsight, he could have taken the *Freelander* option. But no. No choice." Taglioni shook his head, eyes fixed on some internal hell. "Oh, if he'd let the transportees take the ship, under some freak of fate *Ashanti* might have arrived here under the ship's AI. But it would have been filled with corpses."

"Like *Freelander*."

"Right. All dead. Even with Miguel's actions, it was a close-cut thing. For nearly six months it was nip and tuck as to whether we lived or succumbed to starvation. When it finally became clear that we were going to make it, I weighed eighty-nine pounds." He smiled into infinity. "That sort of thing changes a man."

"What about these others? This Maritime Unit?"

"They got the same ration as the crew and I did. Their director, Michaela Hailwood, she got them out of Deck Three before the shit came down. Kept them together. They're supposed to start the first oceanographic survey of Cap III." Taglioni's brow lined. "It's like three worlds up there in *Ashanti*. There's the Maritime Unit and there's crew. But no one knows the Unreconciled. They're locked away in their own private hell."

"Okay, Dek"—awkward calling him that—"let's step off the record."

"Seriously? Does anyone really go OTR?"

She chuckled at his skepticism. "You haven't lost all of the Taglioni wits. But, yes. We do. On Donovan. What's your call on what to do with the Irredenta?"

"Heard you had someplace where you could isolate them."

"We do."

"Hope it's far away. 'Cause if you're putting them here, inside this fence, I'm shuttling back up to *Ashanti* the moment they're off board."

"See, this is the thing I don't get: If they've been sealed on that deck for seven years, how do you have any idea what kind of people they really are?"

His haunted look was more eloquent than his words. "Because I worked hydroponics. I *saw* the remains that slid down that chute from Deck Three. You putting them here, in Port Authority? I want to be outside that fence when you do. And I'm still beating feet into the hinterlands as fast as I can."

Derek Taglioni worked hydroponics? Was she seriously supposed to believe that? But then, he carried his own bags. Claimed they were all he owned. "As soft meat you wouldn't last a day out there."

"Wouldn't last a day in here with the Unreconciled, either. I'd rather be eaten by your local monsters, thank you."

Inga thumped one of the handblown beer mugs onto the battered chabacho-wood bar in front of Taglioni. It was filled to the rim with golden ale. She set Kalico's whiskey in front of her. "Food's coming up. Good news is that you didn't have any orders in front of you."

And then she was gone.

Kalico lifted her whiskey. "To Donovan."

Watched Derek raise the ale. "To Donovan."

He took a sniff and closed his eyes. Then the man touched the glass to his lips, sucked a small taste. A look of other-worldly transcendence filled his face. Then he took another drink, deeper. Made a moaning sound of ecstasy down in his throat.

Kalico signaled Inga for another ale as he drained his mug and sighed in contentment.

"I remember exactly what you're experiencing," Kalico told him. "And that was after only two years stuck in *Turalon*."

Then came the plates. Hot, steaming, and smelling of crest meat, beans, peppers, and recado with a side of fresh cherries and blueberries. She watched the man eat like it was the fulfillment of dreams.

This was Derek Taglioni. She'd never forget the eyes, the dimple in the chin. But where he'd been arrogant and vile, the guy was now like a pastiche of hard and soft, clever and mellow. It was the damaged-but-strong part of him that intrigued her. Still, she remembered that old Derek Taglioni. The one who'd wanted to "fuck Miko's squeeze inside and out." Was that man truly gone? Or was this just his quetzal side, working under a most convincing camouflage?

Never trust a Taglioni.

When he'd finished, she asked, "What the hell are you doing here? Seriously. With everything you had back in Solar System, you left because of a temper tantrum?"

He ran thin fingers through his sandy-blond hair, a bitter smile on his sculpted lips. Then he turned those yellow-green eyes her way and said, "I was going to prove that they'd misjudged me. That when it came to guts and daring, I could tame an entire world."

"And?"

"Something funny happened during the months when

we didn't know if any of us were going to live out the week . . . if *Ashanti* was going to be our tomb. That man who'd been Derek Taglioni was slowly leeched away. For a while, I thought I could see him go. Sort of like a faint dye, swirling around and disappearing down the drain every time I washed. When I started working hydroponics, I looked carefully in the vats. Tried to see if anything of him was left. All I ever saw was brown goo."

In her ear bud, Kalico heard Two Spot announce: *"The alert is about to sound. This is a drill. Repeat: This is a drill."*

At the wailing siren, Taglioni straightened, looked around. The piercing note rose and fell, an involuntary shiver running through Kalico's flesh and bones.

She said, "That's a quetzal or mobber alert. Now, pay attention. It means that either a quetzal is in the compound, or a flock of mobbers has been spotted flying this way. If it's mobbers, the siren will continue to sound. Your first priority is run like a striped-assed ape to your dome and lock your door."

"I saw images of a quetzal on the holo. What's a mobber?"

She pointed to the scars. "Five of them did this to me in less than twenty seconds. When you hear that siren, don't hesitate. Don't stand around like a gaping idiot. Drop whatever you're doing and run. Flat out. Get under cover, out of sight, where you're supposed to be, and don't come out. And for God's sake, don't try and 'help' the search teams. You'll just get somebody killed. Somebody who's a lot more valuable and important when it comes to keeping people alive than you are." She glared into his eyes. "We clear on that?"

To her surprise, he took her warning without getting his back up. She figured he'd bristle, make some remark about being a Taglioni. Instead, all he said was, "Clear."

"Some things might turn out to be worse than your Irredenta."

"So, you're telling me I might have just left one kind of hell for another?"

"Welcome to Donovan."

At the sound of the two short blasts of the siren, and then the repeat, she said, "That's the all clear. After you hear that, you can come out."

She signaled Inga for a refill of Taglioni's mug. After he'd taken a swallow and had that mellow look on his lean face, she casually asked, "So tell me. Now that you're here, what specifically do you want?"

For couple of seconds Taglioni stared thoughtfully at his beer. A puzzled look grew behind his yellow-green designer eyes. "You know, Supervisor Aguila? I don't have a clue."

She searched his face for any hint of guile. But to her surprise, the guy really seemed to mean it.

She cocked an eyebrow. Was he playing her? After all, she had a real live Taglioni on her hands. Close cousin to Miko. Not the sort she could allow to wander out into the bush and be eaten by a quetzal.

So, what the hell was she supposed to do with him?

Especially when she couldn't get that last image of his leering face out of her head. Leopards, the saying went, didn't change their spots.

13

The pounding was like someone was pumping hydraulic fluid inside Dek's head in a bid to explode his skull. Worse, his mouth was dry, his tongue like a senseless lump. He tried to swallow, gagged when his tongue stuck in the back, managed to conjure enough saliva, and finally got some moisture down his throat.

He blinked, squinted against the light pouring through a square window in the side of a dome. Pus and blood, but that was bright!

Straightening, he pushed back an old-fashioned blanket and sat up. Didn't recognize his surroundings. Where the hell . . . ?

And it came back.

Donovan. Port Authority.

The last thing he remembered was Inga's tavern. Eating another meal of beans, peppers so hot they left him crying and wiping his nose. But the *taste*. The *marvelous* taste. It made it all worth it after years of ration.

And beer.

He remembered beer. Lots of it. Wonderful beer. And then whiskey. Tasty and . . .

His stomach twisted. Tried to squeeze itself inside out. *Easy. Just breathe.*

Somehow, he staggered to the small bathroom, figured out how to operate the sink, and stuck his head under the flow. Then he scooped water into his mouth with cupped hands.

He used the toilet, stepped into the shower, and turned the water on hot. To his surprise, it didn't stop after thirty seconds like the ones on *Ashanti*.

When he stepped out, no vibradry slicked the water from his skin for recycling. Took a moment to realize the old-fashioned towel wasn't a quaint decoration but the real thing. Fascinating. He'd never used a real towel before.

He was wondering if he was supposed to rehang it on the rack when a woman said, "Thought you might like a cup of tea. Mint is the local favorite."

He spun around, startled. The woman stood in the doorway, a cup in her hand. He fixed again on her eyes. So large and dark. The almost inhuman angles of her face gave her an exotic look.

"Talina Perez," he reminded himself. "I remember you from last night. But . . . Damn. It's all a bit fuzzy. Think I'm sick. Maybe some local fever. Head hurts like it's about to split."

She grinned, handed him the cup. "It's called a hangover. Sorry, but no pills. We get over it the old-timey way here." She gestured. "Not that I mind naked men traipsing around my house, but I've laid out a couple of your suits. Me? I'd go for the coveralls."

He stumbled out of the bathroom, caught a hint of the mint tea, and found the temperature just right. He sighed as he let the taste spill over his tongue. "Of all the things I've missed. Taste is the one. Damn! I feel terrible. This is a hangover? That's, like, for the drunken and ignorant masses."

She was watching him through those incredible alien eyes. "I forget that you're a Taglioni, and then you can't help but remind me."

He figured she was probably right about the clothing, so he chose the secondhand overalls. Once dressed, he followed her out to the main room, separated as it was from the utility kitchen by a breakfast bar with four stools.

By the door two rifles were racked. He did a double take. Rifles? In her house? But then, a gun belt with pistol and knife, hung on the couch back.

The smell reoriented all of his thoughts as he climbed onto one of the stools and stared at the plate she set in front of him. He took a moment to inhale the fragrances of real food. "What is this?"

"Breakfast tamales. Reuben Miranda has a farm on the southeast side. He grows the corn and chilis. The meat is from something we call chamois. We have an annatto tree in the greenhouse. Some of the other spices, like turmeric there, come from local herb gardens in the greenhouses. I make my own recado."

Dek picked up the fork and—despite the queasy feeling in his stomach—ate as if it were the last meal in the universe.

She was watching him, seemed to be seeing right through him.

"So, how did I get here? The last thing I remember, the Supervisor passed me off to some big guy for safekeeping. Is that right? And how did I get drunk in the first place?"

A crooked grin bent her lips. "Kalico wanted to know what you were really here for. There's an ancient saying that in wine, there is truth. In beer, with whiskey-shot chasers, there is a window to the soul."

"She got me drunk to discover if I was a threat?"

"In your previous encounters with Kalico, you didn't exactly endear yourself to her."

He toyed with his fork. "She's right to despise me."

"Loathe is probably a more accurate term. She told me that when it came to a choice between suppurative pus and you, she'd take the pus any day."

Dek winced, studied the woman through a pain-slitted eye. "Okay, I probably deserve no better. But why all the suspicion about my motives?"

"The last high-ranking official to arrive by ship was Tamarland Benteen. Yeah, the one from the history books. He tried to take over Port Authority and got a lot of people killed. We're a little gun-shy when it comes to mucky-mucks."

"Mucky-mucks? Is that a . . . what?"

"Means the high and mighty. And the way Kalico tells it, the last time you and she were face to face, you acted like a toilet-sucking prick."

"That was my usual operating parameter back in those days."

"So, what happened?"

"I had to become someone else." He smiled, wished his head would stop hurting. "This hot and spicy food. Is that the best thing for my stomach?"

"Trust me. It is."

He took a long moment to really study her, trying to put his finger on what made her so . . .

"It's quetzal," she said. "I'm part quetzal. Infected with their genetic material. That's what you were wondering, isn't it?"

"I, uh, sorry. I guess I was just—"

"I'm used to it."

"Double sorry then." He forced his thoughts away from the thousand questions that popped into his head. Tried to access com through his implants, but couldn't. "Something's wrong. I can't access the net."

"No net to access. You're on Donovan. It'll take a while, but some people claim they like the silence in their heads once they get used to it."

"That big guy I was drinking whiskey with last night?"

"Step Allenovich. Kalico tasked him with keeping you out of trouble."

"He kept calling me 'Skull.' Referred to me as soft meat."

"You just came off a ship."

Dek took a deep breath, trying to remember. "How did I get here?"

"Step and I alternately walked, dragged, and carried you. Be glad you tossed your guts in the avenue last night. If you hadn't, that hangover would be making you consider a single gunshot to the head as a viable remedy."

"This is your place?"

"Yep."

"You slept on the couch?"

"Yep." She arched a thin brow. "Not the first time."

"So . . . where do I live?"

"You remember Shig from last night?"

"Short guy. One of the Corporate Administrators?"

"Nothing Corporate about him. He's like a third of the government, such as it is. He said that if you'd like, you're welcome to his study. It's a small dome out back of his place. Sits in his garden. Has a charming view of the perimeter fence."

"I can bunk down with the contractees. I don't need anything fancy."

"We're a market economy. Yes, I know you have Corporate credit. Which is meaningless here. We transact business with real currency, plunder, and trade. You'll get a period of grace, but you're going to have to figure out a way to support yourself."

"Like . . . what?"

"What can you do? Hunt? Mine? Farm? Medicine? Security?"

"I can fix things. I like to joke that I could qualify for a Ship's Tech I rating. And there's hydroponics. But you have farms here."

"Well, you've got a couple of days to figure it out." She frowned slightly. "What?"

He realized that he was staring again. "Sorry. I've just never met a woman that was so . . ."

"Go on."

"You seem so competent. Exotic. In control and somehow invincible."

She threw her head back and laughed. "Wow! You should be locked in here with me and the quetzals. It's chaos. Their thoughts popping into my head, one bunch trying to get me killed, another trying to find a bridge with humanity. Their memories get all mixed up with mine. And the physical changes? My face and eyes? I miss the old me."

"I'm new here, so I can tell you that the way you look? Well, you're doing just fine. Remarkable in fact. And before I make a fool of myself, let me say thank you for taking care of me last night."

"You're welcome." She frowned. "Not exactly what I was expecting given the stories I've heard about the vaunted Taglionis."

To change the subject he asked, "So, what happened to Benteen? I remember something about him. He killed one of my great uncles. Assassination."

"He's locked up on board *Freelander*. We needed a jail so we sealed him into the ship's astrogation center. You guys on *Ashanti* aren't the only ones to employ that option. We left him with hydroponics and water recycling. As long as he doesn't screw it up, he could live his life out in there.

You've heard about Schrödinger's cat? He's our Schrödinger's assassin. You don't know if he's alive or dead until you unseal the AC and look inside."

"Screw vacuum. Isn't *Freelander* supposed to be, like a ghost ship, or something?"

"No supposing. You set foot on that bucket of air, and weirdity happens. You see things. Parts of that ship are still tied to wherever it went; it's leaking part of itself back to that place. Every hair on your body will stand on end."

"Thanks, but I had enough of that living with the knowledge that the Unreconciled were eating people, and only a sialon hatch was between me and their next meal."

Again she turned those unusual eyes on his. "We have a saying here. People come to Donovan specifically to leave, to find themselves, or to die. Why have you come?"

He sopped up the last of the bean juice with a tortilla. "Maybe I came to eat your breakfasts. I swear, after ten years of ration and weak spinach tea, I'm in heaven.

"As to the rest, Officer Perez, if those are my only choices, all I can tell you is that I'm not leaving. So that means I'm either going to find myself, or I'm here to die."

═══ CONFRONTATION ═══

I *am like a man balancing upon a precipice. Within hours I am to be face to face with this Supervisor. My stomach flutters, and I want to be sick. Since the Harrowing and Cleansing, this is the first real trial.*

The universe expects me to look into a demon's eyes, and not quail. I am the warrior who must face down evil, ignore its lies and deceit. She cannot see so much as a flicker of weakness, or know the churning anxiety gripping my heart.

I must be invincible. A pillar of belief. Any doubt has to be discarded as a distraction given the great responsibility now looming before me.

"Faith fills the hollows of the soul," Callista whispers. She lies on her bed, curled in a fetal position. Her spasming fingers flutter where they're positioned before her mouth. She's a frail thing, little more than a living skeleton, but today the universe has left her coherent. I assume for my benefit.

"Faith fills the hollows of the soul," I repeat, taking strength from her words.

The anxiety and uncertainty fade.

The other two Prophets, Irdan and Guan Shi, blink vacant eyes, their lips moving soundlessly.

At that moment First Will Petre enters the Temple. He glances uneasily at me. In his hands he carries two containers. One filled with white paste, the other, smaller, with a charcoal-black concoction made from burned cloth.

"They're ready," Petre says.

He places the containers beside the box of jewelry and the blue makeup I keep for my third eye.

"The com device?"

"Inserted through the hole they drilled in the main hatch. As you ordered, I've had your throne carried into the corridor."

I swallow hard, clench my teeth. Petre cannot be allowed to see so much as a crack in my armor. "Send me Svetlana."

He inclines his head and steps out.

"The true life whispers in the flesh," *Callista murmurs.* "Like leaves in a wind. Whispers . . . around in a bowl they go."

I take a deep breath.

Svetlana, my second wife, steps in; her light brown hair is pulled back, her dark eyes wary.

I untie my waist wrapping and let it fall so that I am naked. "Prepare me."

She steps forward. "How, Messiah?"

"This Supervisor, she's the embodiment of evil. She's everything the universe calls on us to defeat. Irdan told me, 'Go forth in white.'"

"In white?"

I point at the container. "White is the color of good, symbolic of purity." *I raise my arms.* "It will be my armor. Paint it all over me."

"You're facing her naked?"

"She will be dressed in finery. Is there any more powerful way to emphasize our differences? I go naked before her, a mark of ultimate humility. Representative of the fact that I am clad only in truth."

Svetlana uses her fingers, rubbing the white paste onto the patterns of scars and over my skin.

When she is finished, I indicate the small jar filled with black grease. "For my eyes and lips. I want this woman to see a living skull. To know that we are the living dead. That I am not facing her alone, but as the repository of all the souls and bodies inside mine."

Svetlana's expression remains grim as she attends to my eyes and lips. I even let her blacken my teeth to enhance the effect.

As she paints, I feel the righteous strength of Revelation swelling within me. I begin to pulse with the universe. One with its purpose.

She finishes by painting the eye in my forehead in bright blue.

When I face her, I see a startled look. A hesitation, and she bows before me, obviously upset.

"Wife?" I ask.

"You are someone else," she whispers. "What next, Messiah?"

"The jewelry," I tell her. "I want to wear as much as I can. The emblems of the dead. Actual mementos of the lives for which we are responsible. The rings, necklaces, and bracelets are the physical presence of those for whom I speak."

I inhale as I feel the dead pulse within me.

As I begin to don the jewelry, it is as if each piece burns against my flesh.

"Yes!" Guan Shi cries from her bed. Her eyes—sharp for once and seeing this world—focus on the polished gold and silver. "Today . . . rises . . . the glory . . . all the sunshine . . ."

Finally I am done.

The universe fills me.

"Let us go and engage the enemy," I say jauntily.

But down deep, I pray I am good enough, strong enough, to carry this off.

Believe, Messiah. You must believe!

14

The shuttle thumped, rocked, and was slammed sideways as the grapples clamped onto it. Not the best docking Talina had ever experienced, but then Ensign Naftali was ten years out of practice.

The ship's voice said, *"You have hard dock. Establishing hard seal."* A pause. *"Hard seal. Welcome aboard."*

Tal glanced over at Shig, who sat in the seat beside her. The man looked absolutely nonplussed. But in the seat beyond, the Corporate chemist and design engineer, Fenn Bogarten, had a slightly amused expression on his tanned face. Kalico Aguila was riding in the copilot's seat.

"Welcome to *Ashanti*," Naftali called over his shoulder. "We have hard dock. Grapples engaged. Hatch has a hard seal. You are welcome to deboard."

Talina unbuckled, almost launched herself as she misjudged the angular acceleration. Shuttle deck didn't have the same circumference as the crew and cargo decks did; the effect was as if she were in seven tenths of a gravity. As a result, she had to mince her way out of the seat, walk carefully from the command deck to the hatch where a crewman gave her a smile and welcomed her aboard.

Tal followed Kalico through the main cabin and into the small airlock. As she exited it was to see a crisply uniformed Captain Miguel Galluzzi. He was in the process of greeting Kalico. And doing so with obvious relief.

In person, the man was smaller than Talina had expected. Looked emaciated. Nevertheless, he greeted her with a smile and an extended hand, saying, "Welcome aboard, Security Officer. *Ashanti* and her crew are delighted to have you."

With her quetzal-enhanced senses, Talina tried not to notice the odor: *Ashanti* stank. Not the musty-and-clinging scent of rot and death like aboard *Freelander*. This was more of a packed-humanity smell of long-unwashed socks, stale sweat, and fetid breath.

"My pleasure, Captain."

She stepped past as Shig shook the captain's hand, followed by Bogarten.

Dogging Kalico's heels, Tal was introduced to First Officer Edward Turner, Second Officer Paul Smart, and finally the A.O. Bekka Tuulikki, all in their dress uniforms. Tuulikki was a pale Nordic woman with steely blue eyes.

The *Ashanti* officers kept looking at Talina as if she were some sort of freak. Or it had been too long since they'd seen a different human face.

As Shig made the round of introductions, he said, "We have a present for you. If you'll have your people attend to it, we've packed the hold with fresh vegetables and fruits from the farms around Port Authority. It should come as a welcome relief in the crew's mess."

At which point Shig offered the captain one of his acorn squashes, proudly announcing, "I picked this from my own garden just this morning. I hope you like it."

"What is it?" Galluzzi asked warily, taking the squash.

Shig, his expression still mild, seemed confused.

Aguila gave the short Indian a crooked smile. "Shig, the captain's a spacer. Hydroponics are for growing yeasts, leafy vegetables, and tubers. My guess is that he's never seen a squash before. Am I right, Captain?"

"So this is a squash!" Galluzzi cried in delight. "What a wonderful gift."

Shig, still his amiable self, said, "I'd be delighted to tell your kitchen staff how to cook it."

"While you show the Supervisor to the conference room and discuss recipes, how about Bogarten and I take a look at the Deck Three situation?" Talina suggested.

"This way," Turner told her, taking the lead.

Something about the ship, the way it smelled. The dingy corridors and sense of despair. It all sent quivers up her spine. Like the thing was a trap—a prison that might close down around her in an instant and crush the soul out of her body.

Her demon quetzal squirmed in her gut.

"Yeah, you piece of shit. Welcome to space."

She figured Demon wasn't going to settle down until she was back dirtside. At least, it had been that way every time she'd been aboard *Freelander*.

"Not right."

Talina grinned to herself. The only thing quetzals hated more than space was deep water.

Turner led her and Bogarten past the hatch and into a curving corridor. The ship's angular acceleration was even weaker here. To her surprise every other light in the corridor had been removed.

"You saving lighting panels?" she asked.

Turner, a thoughtful look on his face, said, "In the beginning we took them out to cut the draw on the electrical system. Every amp we could save was one we didn't have to generate. Could put that much more energy from scavenged hydrogen into the reaction engines. We even tried ditching the cargo ring to reduce mass."

"Why didn't you?" Bogarten asked.

"Couldn't figure out how to detach it without structurally damaging the ship. And without being able to balance the counter-rotation, it would have played hell with stability."

Talina told him, "Well, you may not know it, but that cargo is going to make all of our lives a whole lot better. We're hoping you've got a lot of spare parts and equipment we need. The biggie, however, are the cacao seeds. We're hoping, desperately, that they're still viable, and we can grow the trees."

The lift carried them up a deck, and the radial corridor took them to the transportee ring. Talina was relieved that the ship's rotation left her feeling more firmly planted. Took a while to get used to the difference between gravity and angular acceleration.

Bogarten asked, "Is this the only route to the shuttle deck? Using the lift? Or is there a companionway? Ladders? Something where we can have better control?"

"Companionway's around that bend." Turner pointed. "We can close off the lift. Block the corridor just past the stairs if we have to."

"That or use armed guards." Talina hooked thumbs in her utility belt as she studied the hall.

Bogarten gave them both a wary look. "And you don't think they'd just walk down to the shuttle deck on their own?"

Turner shrugged. "After all this time? Who knows? Maybe. But as for the crew, we've got a say in this, too. We'll feel better if we give them one possible route: a straight shot from Deck Three to the cargo bays and the shuttle. Once they're locked in the shuttle's hold, off the ship, and unloaded dirtside, we're all going to be sleeping a lot better."

"You make them sound like a disease," Talina noted.

"Whatever." Turner didn't argue. "You didn't have to live with them. See the things they did to people before they dropped the fragmented bones into the hydroponics chute."

Turner stopped before what would have originally been the pressure hatch that led into the transportees' section. Sialon was a ceramic composed of silicon, aluminum, oxygen, and carbon that was molded and superheated in vacuum. To say that the hatch was welded was something of a misnomer. Rather it was glued with a thick bead of bonding material.

The machine that stood before the door was a hypersonic drill. Sialon—being harder than any metal—didn't cut. But the atomic bonds would separate under intense heat and the right hyper-frequency vibrations. A four-inch hole had been bored into the door, a remote holo com device having been installed.

"So this is it." Turner told them. "Maybe five temporary bulkheads to install, and we can make an alley that runs all the way to the shuttle. Then it's just a matter of securing the cockpit and command deck so they can't commit mayhem once they're aboard."

"You'd think you were transporting wild animals," Bogarten noted as he used his laser scribe to measure the corridor. Then he went to the companionway, checking out the stairs.

Turner softly whispered, "I guess you'd have to define what's human, and what's animal."

In Talina's ear com, Shig's voice said, *"We're about ready, Tal. If you could meet us in the captain's lounge?"*

"Be right there," Talina and Turner said in unison, apparently getting the same message from ship's com in their implants.

"This way." Turner, again, took the lead, leaving Bogarten to inspect the route back to the shuttle.

The lift deposited them on the Crew Deck. Turner showed her to the small lounge just down from the AC. Inside, Shig and Kalico were already seated. Galluzzi was in the captain's chair in the rear. Turner took what was obviously his seat, and Talina settled for the chair near the door.

"Are we ready?" Galluzzi asked hesitantly. Talina noticed that his right hand was trembling as he rubbed it nervously on his pantleg.

"We're all curious," Kalico told him, a shadow of smile on her lips.

"Supervisor, please. Just be aware that I have no idea what kind of reception we're going to get."

"It's all right, Captain." Kalico lifted a scarred hand. "Proceed."

The image formed up on the holo. A projection of the corridor just behind the sealed pressure hatch on Deck Three. The walls were decorated, painted with skeletons in various poses. It hit Talina that had they been fleshed bodies, the postures would have been erotic.

What really grabbed attention, however, was the naked male seated in an ornately carved chair that blocked most of the hallway. Behind the chair back—two to either side— stood four women.

Talina fixed on the seated man. He slouched, almost insolently. His entire body was painted in blotchy white, as if it had been daubed with clay. It took Talina a moment to realize that what looked like designs covering his skin were intricately patterned scars. Combinations of chevrons, interlocking squares, a Grecian key style, overlapping circles and loops ran down his arms and legs. A series of lines ran down his belly to converge in the man's pubic hair at the root of the penis, and fantastic spirals—centered on his nipples—covered each breast.

Then there was the jewelry. His fingers were thick with rings. A myriad of necklaces hung at his neck, and a row of bracelets ran from wrist to forearm above each hand.

But it was his paste-white face that mesmerized. The cartilaginous part of his nose was missing, leaving a gaping hole split by the septum. The scars on the man's cheeks each created a maze that opened at the corners of his mouth. His eyes were blackened with what looked like kohl to make them dark in contrast to his white-pasted face. And in the middle of his forehead someone had carved the image of a single eye, painted blue and surrounded by a white sclera. The black pupil was like a window to darkness.

Whatever Talina had been expecting, it wasn't this. The guy looked like a character in a VR holo from hell. Even his hair was greased up into a macabre fan that ended in a series of black spikes.

A faint smile bent his black-painted lips. He more whispered than said, "Blood and pain and terror."

"Excuse me?" Kalico asked, leaning forward.

"The holy trinity of birth, but then you wouldn't remember." A pause. "Who are you?"

"I am Corporate Supervisor Kalico Aguila, in charge of all Corporate property and holdings on Donovan. What you'd know as Capella III. To whom am I speaking?"

"The ending and the beginning, the purification, the living repository of the dead and the initiator of life. I am the holy vessel."

"That doesn't answer my question," Kalico barked back.

Talina couldn't take her eyes off the man, kept trying to understand what kind of pain he must have endured to have his body mutilated like that.

"It tells you everything," the man replied.

"So, cut the crap," Kalico snapped. "Whoever you are, you're under contract. That means you answer to me. Now, do you want to . . ."

Shig held up a hand, gently urging Kalico to desist. "If I could rephrase the Supervisor's question, who were you prior to your illumination?"

"The past is a meaningless term. There is only being and becoming."

"Perhaps," Shig said. "It would help us to understand who and what you are if we could know what person you came from. I assume you were once Batuhan."

"That was another existence." He lifted the hand that had been lying on the exotic chair's arm, and part of the arm detached like a scepter. The thing was a couple of feet long, slightly curved, and remarkably carved in relief, the spiraling designs incredibly intricate. It reminded Talina of the ancient ivory carvings done on tusks in East Asia; the delicate relief was too tiny to make out in the holo.

"All right," Kalico continued, clearly annoyed, "So you're Batuhan. I understand that you and your people have had a most difficult passage from Solar System. But you're here. Given that you are under contract, I have the right to—"

"Neither you, nor The Corporation have rights. The Corporation is pollution, and you are its agent. Not that you could know, drowning in ignorance as you are, but you are suffocating, wallowing in self-delusion. Until you are freed from the black and engulfing prison of your lies and unquestioned deceit, you cannot grasp the simplest or faintest sliver of illumination. Let alone understanding."

Talina shot Kalico a sidelong glance. Saw the roiling anger mixing with confusion.

Again, Shig raised his hand to still Kalico's incipient outburst. "Illumination and enlightenment aside, we need to deal with some more pragmatic and immediate concerns. I have read many of your tracts and revelations. You think your current confinement is the universal womb. That you will be born the moment you set foot on Donovan."

"Nothing you can do will stop that," Batuhan said softly.

"Stopping you is not our wish. We are finalizing plans to shuttle you down to the planet. To a place called Tyson Station. There you will find housing, a garden, water, and everything your people will need to survive."

"We know." Batuhan made a shaking gesture with his scepter, baton, or whatever it was.

"You know?" Shig asked amiably.

"Of course. We serve the universe. In order to consume darkness and corruption, the universe will first free us from the confinement of the womb. As it eventually will free us from this planet when we mature from childhood.

Only then can we begin the task of purifying the universe itself." He smiled, exposing dark and vicious-looking teeth. "We are the chosen. Through us will come redemption."

"Heard that before," Kalico snorted.

"Of course you have. We are the culmination of the Kali Yuga, the turning of the katuns, the End of Days, Ragnarok, the monsters who devour the universe. We are the terror. And we are the rapture. Chosen, harrowed, tested, and purified within the womb to redeem the universe."

Kalico asked, "Just how do you plan to redeem us all?"

Batuhan shifted his dark gaze, fixed his intense eyes on hers. "You must be consumed. The three holy Prophets have said so."

"Who are the three holy Prophets?" Shig asked.

"They are here, with us. Irdan, Callista, and Guan Shi. They hear the voice of the universe and shall go with us, lead us through childhood, and their teachings shall be universal."

Shig's face lined with curiosity. "So you are not the Prophet?"

"I am only the beginning and the end. I am the receptacle of souls. The interpreter of Prophecy. The first and last of the eternal graves of the martyrs."

Kalico said, "I don't understand this first and last, this whole graves thing."

Batuhan gave her a pitying look. "It's simple semantics. By consuming the dead, my people and I become the end. The last receptacle for the dead person's physical body and a pathway for his or her soul. Each piece of jewelry is the physical manifestation of a human being who lives within us. The proof of their existence."

He pointed to the mazes on his cheeks. "Thus, we become their living graves, their breathing tombs. They live through us since we are but repositories for their essences. And when my semen impregnates one of my wives, I am the vehicle through which a renewed and pure life is once again born. I plant that purified life to grow in a field fertilized by the essences of the dead who reside within that woman."

Kalico looked stunned.

Talina's stomach turned.

Where he sat, looking enchanted, Shig whispered, "Absolutely fascinating!"

"You see," Batuhan insisted softly, "we are blessed by the universe as the vehicles of immortality."

15

Vartan stood back in the shadows next to Petre Jordan, the Messiah's First Will. Just behind Vartan's shoulder, the Third Will, Tikal Don Simon, had his arms crossed, a sour look on his round Yucatec face.

The four Chosen—the men who originally accepted Batuhan as the Messiah—along with the First Wives who had offered themselves to the Messiah, stood in ranks behind the Throne of Bones.

As the holo that displayed the Corporate officers flickered out, the Messiah chuckled. For a moment he sat there, facing the hatch. His back to them, he waved his intricately carved thigh bone back and forth as though it were a cat's tail. Then, standing, he turned.

Vartan studied the man, saw the cunning in his kohl-darkened eyes, the confusion of polished jewelry. Had to admire his audacity. Not only had he gone to the meeting nude, but they'd made a white paint from finely ground white duraplast. With the black accents on the eyes and lips, along with his hole of a nose, it had given his face a skull-like appearance.

If Vartan remembered anything about the Corporate mindset, it was that they liked things neat. According to plan. Without deviance. They wouldn't have had the first clue about the meaning of the scars as offerings and self-sacrifice, or the pain the Messiah had endured as penance for past sins. Rather, his appearance would have shaken them to the core.

Walking around the throne, the Messiah paced his way down the hall, beckoning for the others to follow him to the cafeteria. There, he waited while the Chosen placed his throne in its traditional spot. Only after he'd seated himself did the rest slip into their chairs.

"Now you know the measure of the opposition." The

Messiah closed his eyes and looked at them, one by one, through the great blue "spirit" eye carved in his forehead.

A shiver always ran down Vartan's spine when that gibbous blue orb was focused on him. As if the "spirit" eye really could see into his soul as the Messiah's physical eyes could not.

"I see worry, hesitation. Some among you are unsure." The Messiah's voice came as a husky whisper.

"Messiah?" Petre asked, bowing his head so deeply that his long white ponytail rode up his back.

"You are my First Will," the Messiah replied. "Speak."

"You know they're going to take precautions. Limit or even deny us access to the crew. After all this time, the moment has come to unleash our wrath, the long-held anger of the dead we host. We've promised—"

"They will indeed plan, devise, and do all in their power to keep us from the *Ashanti* and her crew." The Messiah fingered his long-bone scepter. "The Prophets heard the universe last night and they sang. I heard them, and they allowed me to see." He pointed a finger at the eye in his forehead.

"What did you see?" Petre asked.

"The time is not right to purify the crew. But it will be. When the universe determines we are ready. Look around you, at each other. We're weak. Starved by *their* ration and tea. In the song of the Prophets I heard what their visions had seen. I have been given a glimpse."

"Messiah?" Svetlana asked. "A vision of what?"

"Ah, Second Wife. An infant doesn't run into battle before he can so much as crawl. In this ship, we are nothing more than a fetus. On the planet, at this Tyson Station, we shall become infants. Who then grow into children. Who finally become adults. When adults fight, they win. But only after they've grown, learned the arts of combat."

"Messiah?" Vartan asked with respect.

"Second Will?"

"How, then, do we deal with the evacuation? What do the Prophets wish of us?"

"We will act submissively. Follow the Supervisor's orders. Do as they ask. The Prophets tell me that our goal, and our only goal, is to get to the planet. To a place where The Corporation and its agents no longer control us."

"And then?" Svetlana asked.

"Then we finally come into our own."

Vartan chewed his lips, thinking back to the unending rage they'd lived with after the hatch was sealed. For so many of them, it had been the anger, the promise of retribution against Captain Galluzzi that had kept them alive. Given them purpose in the endless hell of their gopher-warren of a deck.

"Messiah," Petre said. "We have detained five who would betray us. Just as you foresaw. They are bound, awaiting purification and immortality."

"Five?" The Messiah shook his head, exhaled through the ruin of his nose. "The universe provides. This is my Will. Listen. Hear it. Make it so. We have but two days. At the end of them, we shall need our strength. To have fortified our bodies. To do that, we must feast. Each and every one of us must eat, fill our stomachs in anticipation. We are leaving the womb. Being born, and birth requires strength and energy."

Petre reached down and removed the cleaver from its scabbard on his belt. Finely polished steel caught the light, gleamed along the razor edge.

Vartan ground his teeth. Glanced at the Messiah. Beneath the ruined nose, a grin split the man's face. Raising his thigh-bone scepter, he said, "We shall need all of the buckets this time. I don't want a single drop of the blood to be wasted."

ENGAGED

I sit in the observation dome. An odor that one of the Prophets once called mutton-pork—that sweetly cloying and unmistakable scent of cooked human flesh—hangs in the air. The others are still feasting. Preparing for our "birth" as the figurative release from Deck Three will be. I absently run my fingernail down the lines of scars. Think of all the souls that have followed that path to rebirth and immortality. It is for them, for the universe, that I fight.

And the battle is now engaged.

My people do not understand the depth or intricacies of that combat.

After all these years, I have a face for my True Enemy. Since we were confined on Deck Three, I filled the role with Captain Galluzzi. Not that he really was the enemy, being nothing more than the universe's tool, the one it used to create us.

If there was a parallel in human history it might have been Rome and the early Christians. But for Rome, there would have been no Jesus. But for The Corporation and Miguel Galluzzi, there would have been no Irredenta. Pontius Pilate had to play his part in the creation of the Christian messiah, Galluzzi served the same purpose in creating us.

But now I have Kalico Aguila.

The physical embodiment of The Corporation.

The Corporation had to play its role. The Irredenta had to be raised in the midst of its lies, deceit, and inhumanity. Trust me, we'd bought it all, been faithful followers and believers. Never questioned that The Corporation—and all it stood for—served the ultimate good. That it was kind, just, and caring.

Which made the Harrowing and Cleansing epically traumatic. When faced with brutal Truth, it was to discover that The Corporation had deceived us on every level. To *discover that we'd been played for complete fools had been soul numbing.*

So much so, that some never could justify themselves with the Truth.

But they've since been purified and will be reborn with a full and better appreciation for the universe and its fundamental Truths.

When first looking upon Kalico Aguila, I must confess, her scars gave me the slightest bit of hesitation. The woman has undergone an Initiation of her own, made her own sacrifices of pain and blood. I hadn't expected that from a Corporate figurehead. But then, the universe makes no mistakes. The scars are there to warn me: Here is an opponent you must not underestimate. She will try and pervert the Truth. Seek to mislead the Irredenta from the Revelation, the True path, and the teachings of the Prophets.

She will be ruthless.

Praise be to the universe. I am warned.

To do battle with Kalico Aguila, I need my people united. The feast serves not just as a means of eliminating dissension among the ranks, but as a reminder of our unique identity. We are the chosen. We are the living dead. The vehicle through which they shall become immortal.

Staring out at the billions of stars, I am made humble. Aware once again of my failings, my weaknesses, and overwhelmed by the responsibility that has been laid upon my shoulders.

I am Blessed by the knowledge that I am no longer alone. It's not just me, but all the human beings I have incorporated into my flesh and bone. They pulse with my blood, live in each cell of my body. I am they, they are me.

As long as the Irredenta are united, without divisions and rancor, we shall win. The universe, in its wisdom, has prepared us. Marked us as separate.

At the time, I didn't see the genius of the Initiation. I was lost in the moment and trying to comprehend when Guan Shi began to scarify her flesh. I thought it a penance. That the pain and mutilation was a way to atone for guilt and previous sin.

And yes, the terrible agony of scarification is an offering to the universe—each of us sacrificing and suffering at the most personal level. What more intimate and honest sacrifice is there than to proffer from our own bodies?

Accepting that belief, I have given more of myself than any of my people. I can think of no other way to prove my devotion.

And the scars serve the dead. Not only are they a path leading to immortality, they demonstrate the willingness of the pure to suffer on their behalf.

How simple of me to think that's all that the Initiation was.

Only today—face to face with Kalico Aguila—did I realize the universe's true genius: the scars set us apart. The Irredenta will never fit into Corporate society. They separate us from the rest of humanity in a way that can never be bridged. They unite us as a people in a way that no feasts, no shared experiences ever could.

So, now, as we emerge into our inheritance, I am reassured that no failing or inadequacy of my own, no heresy, or doubts on the part of the Irredenta, will cause us to fail.

I pity Kalico Aguila.

She has only The Corporation to serve.

I have been chosen to fight for the universe.

16

When she peered down into the glass of whiskey, Kalico could see no facial features, just an outline of her head and hair against the gleam of the dome overhead.

Inga's was full—the suppertime crowd having trooped in for whatever the kitchen offered. The place felt reassuring; the clank of mugs on chabacho wood, the tinking of silverware on plates, and the jovial calls from the miners and locals somehow came across as jarringly normal after her day on *Ashanti*.

She barely acknowledged Shig as he climbed onto the stool beside hers and flicked a finger Inga's way for his traditional half glass of wine.

Kalico shot him a sidelong glance. "If there was ever a day when I'd expect you to drink a full glass, this is it."

He shifted on the stool, expression thoughtful. "I've canvassed the literature. The Unreconciled are delightfully unique."

"Excuse me?"

"They've taken an entirely novel approach to anthropophagy and mixed it with teleological eschatology."

"Repeat that in a human language, please."

"Religious philosophy has always preoccupied itself with what happens at the end of time. For Christians it's the rapture, the four horsemen, and judgment day. End of Days for the Muslims, or perhaps the return of the Twelfth Imam for the Shia. In Hindu mythology Kali and Shiva destroy the fourth cycle and restart time at the end of the Kali Yuga. Among the Central Americans, it was the turning of the Katun, the great wheel of time. For the Zoroastrians, a monster comes to destroy the world. The Norse thought it would be Ragnarok, the battle of the gods."

"Got it."

Shig gave Inga a smile as she placed his half glass of

wine on the bar before lumbering off to mark it on her board.

"Usually," Shig said, "the end is preceded by an apocalypse. You know, the usual chaos of famines, plagues, warfare, boiling oceans, maybe a meteor, or flood, or wildfires. Cannibalism? Consuming the universe, purifying it through digestion and sexual reproduction? Becoming a living grave for the dead you have consumed? That's remarkably novel and innovative."

"How can you be so jazzed over something that creep-freaked me half out of my skin?"

He gave her a wink, his other eye twinkling with amusement. "When I was young, I was constantly amazed by the workings of the religious mind. It doesn't matter what the tradition, each one depends on some mystical acceptance that defies common sense: an immaculate conception; a great tree that holds up the sky; gods who can change sexes and colors; bringing the dead back to life; emerging from a hole in the earth; or maybe they fell from the sky. No matter how outlandish, people choose to believe this stuff. Can't help it really."

"That's why The Corporation regulated religion as thoroughly as it did. No one has ever figured out whether—when you chalk up the total body count—religions or governments killed more billions or caused greater suffering. When you get into those kinds of numbers, it's a wash. Both are equally dangerous to human life, liberty, prosperity, and happiness."

"The Unreconciled are proof of that." Shig fingered his glass. "I've studied cults like the Aghori Hindus who seek to immerse themselves in corpses as a means of achieving purification. By embracing death and corruption, they seek to attain a state of non-duality. The hope is that it will help them break the eight great bonds that keep the soul from achieving moksha. Um, moksha is the transition into illumination, emancipation, and spiritual fulfillment."

"But not cannibalism?"

"Only by a matter of degree. The Aghori may ingest something derived from a corpse, but in doing so, they're hoping to find their own illumination. Not acting for the benefit of another by eating a whole person in an attempt to purify him or her."

Kalico suppressed a sense of panic. "These were normal, everyday people, Shig. What we saw . . ."

Shig stared thoughtfully at the back bar. "Understand that as bizarre as their beliefs are, those people reflect the horror and despair they lived every day for seven years. The transportees didn't have enough to eat, so they ate each other. To assuage the guilt, they chose to believe they were keeping the dead alive within themselves.

"And the entire time each of them was asking, 'Why did this have to happen to me?' The only thing that made sense was that the universe chose them specifically for the purpose of bringing about its renewal. The reason their ordeal had to be so terrible was because of the grand scope of their coming endeavor: universal purification and renewal. Not only did that assuage survivor's guilt, but it made their actions inevitable and heroic."

"What was with the white makeup? The too-much jewelry? Being buck-assed naked? Is Batuhan out of his fricking mind?"

Shig arched a knowing brow. "Everything he did in that display was calculated. The white color? Symbolic of purity? Accented by the black eyes and mouth? Perhaps to represent a living corpse? And he wanted you to see the scarification, the lines leading to his penis. Death and sex, the ancient dance and balance of life."

"Then what was with the jewelry? He said it was taken from the dead."

"That they might be witness. In place of a name, he wore a possession from the dead."

"You ask me, they were nothing more than a collection of trophies. The kind a serial killer keeps as mementos of his victims."

"Anything but. That man *believes*."

"So, how do we fix them? Reprogram them?"

"You don't. At least, not on Donovan. A psychiatric hospital in Solar System might. For now, this cult of theirs is how they cope. Maybe, in a couple of years, you might start trying to talk sense to them."

She sighed. "Let me guess. You're telling me that offering counsel to them now would be a waste of time because they're too close to it. Bonded by a rite of passage. They'd just see it as an attack and hunker down on the core belief."

"Correct."

"A true believer? Is that why Batuhan had to be such an arrogant prick? It's like he was purposefully picking a fight. Daring me to do my worst. What would possess him to act like such a hard ass?"

"You really don't know?"

"Do I look like I do?"

"It's the only defense he has. Sheer blind faith in himself and his cause. Unwavering, unquestioned. As his makeup symbolized, it's all black and white."

"Come on, even mystics question. Can carry on give-and-take conversations."

"Not when they're scared."

She gave him a disbelieving glare. "Batuhan? Scared?"

"Oh, yes, Supervisor. If you ask me, that's the most frightened man I've ever seen. Shaken, terrified right down to his bones. His nightmare—the terrible fear that haunts his soul—is that he's unworthy, incapable of attaining the task before him."

"Came across as pretty sure of himself and his cause."

Shig's expression turned thoughtful. "Most great mystics are terrified. What they often call 'The Dark Night of the Soul.' Or sometimes, 'The Cloud of Unknowing.' It's the sense of being unworthy of the task God has chosen for them. Think St. John of the Cross, or St. Teresa of Calcutta. The only defense Batuhan has against his gnawing and deep-seated self-doubt is to project a complete, absolute, and unwavering certainty in his cause. The greater his self-insecurity, the more absolute and unbending his public face will be. His greatest fear will be that his mask will slip, that someone will glimpse his terror."

"Shig, seriously, do you think that putting them down out at Tyson Station is the best thing we can do? Even telling them what to watch out for, half of them will be dead within six months."

Shig lifted his glass of wine, touched it to his lips, but she wasn't sure that he actually tasted it.

After he placed it back on the bar, he said, "Supervisor, Donovan is all about making the best decision out of nothing but bad choices. Do you choose what is just, what is moral, or what is correct?"

"God, I hate you sometimes."

"That's why being me is so much fun."

17

Allison Chomko descended the stairs into Inga's and found the tavern doing a good business. The first rotation of *Ashanti*'s crew had come down with the latest shuttle. People had volunteered to personally escort the malnourished and frail crewmen, to ensure that they didn't get into trouble. And, most of all, to be sure that no one got devoured by the local fauna. Donovanians considered it bad luck to be eaten on a person's first night planetside.

She and Dan had been of two minds about allowing the *Ashanti*'s crew into either The Jewel or Betty Able's until it was learned that the Supervisor had provided each spacer a hundred Port Authority SDRs in advance of their Corporate pay back in Solar System.

Granted, it was only thirty crew people, and with only a hundred SDRs to their names it wouldn't be good business to pick them completely clean the first time they set foot in either establishment. The best that could be hoped for was that they'd think kindly of The Jewel or Betty Abel's. That they'd come back sometime when they were flush.

Allison picked out Kalico Aguila seated at the bar next to Talina Perez's chair. Even as she spotted her, a bowl of the house chili was placed in front of the Supervisor. Would have been—in the old days—that Aguila would have had a marine guard to watch her back. That she didn't showed how far the woman had come since that long-ago day she set foot on Donovan surrounded by twenty marines in battle tech who were toting hot weapons.

Allison nodded to and returned calls from patrons, gave a wave to others.

It no longer bothered her that old friends, people like Mellie Nagargina, Friga Dushku, or Amal Oshanti never so much as met her eyes. Losing their respect had been a price she'd had to pay. Odd notion that. Once she'd been one of them. An aspiring wife and mother, a homemaker for Rick. Only to lose him to an accident and then her infant daughter, Jessie, a year later to a quetzal.

So, where would she be if Dan Wirth hadn't sniffed her out with the same acuity as a slug in the mud homed in on a bare foot? Remarried? With another two children? Teaching at the local school? A housewife bustling about her garden, preparing suppers, and ensuring the kids were properly dressed and supervised?

It brought a tired smile to her lips as she walked up to the chair beside Aguila's and slipped onto the cushion.

"Good evening, Supervisor." To Inga, she gave the hand sign for a glass of whiskey.

"Allison Chomko," Aguila said in a flat voice. "To what do I owe the pleasure?"

"At first I thought maybe we'd try girl talk. You know, chat about the weather and gossip about who's doing what. Then I figured fuck it, we'd talk business."

"And just what business did you have in mind?"

"How much do you want for Kalen Tompzen?"

Aguila laid her spoon down, fixed those laser-blue eyes on Allison's as she asked, "You really want to go there?"

"Supervisor, history is what it is. You and Dan had to learn a few things before you could understand what Donovan is all about. There's enough here for everyone, but it takes all of us together." She grinned. "You beat Dan at his own game. Got to admire a woman with that kind of acumen."

"What makes you think I don't hold a grudge?"

"Fine. That's your concern. Mine is business. How much do you want for Tompzen?"

"You assume he's still alive."

"I figure we'd have heard if he wasn't. As for myself, I suspect you've had him doing whatever unpleasant thing you could possibly find or invent. At this stage, he's probably so miserable that an up-close-and-personal encounter with a quetzal might come as a welcome relief compared to the crap he's got to look forward to."

"What do you want with him?"

"He has skills."

"On Dan's orders, he killed three people who worked for me. Threatened my life. I don't forget."

"I'm not asking you to. Twenty thousand?"

Aguila chuckled, returned to her chili.

Allison read the wariness in Inga's eyes as she set the whiskey on the chabacho bar. Allison slid a five-SDR coin across the wood, saying, "Keep the change."

"Hope this batch is better than that last," Allison noted, swirling the amber liquid in the glass and inhaling the aroma.

"It is," Aguila told her.

Allison sipped, swished it around her tongue. "Never had a taste for the stuff until I had to start drinking it as part of the job." She paused. "You were up at the new ship today. You really putting the transportees out at Tyson Station?"

"Believe me, you wouldn't want them here."

"I lived out there for a while when I was a kid. My folks died out there. It's about as far as you can get from anywhere. And these people are soft meat."

Aguila finished off the chili, washed it down with a slug of whiskey, and turned to face Allison. The scars on the woman's face rearranged as she smiled humorlessly. "I got to meet the leader. The guy's sitting naked in a chair carved out of duraplast with human-bone insets. His skin's all cut into fancy scars and he's painted white. He cut his nose off to leave a hole. Says he's a walking grave because he's become a repository for all the people he's eaten. The guy thinks he's a messiah who will lead the universe as it consumes itself. Now, even if he doesn't speak for them all, don't you think we'd better get a handle on who these people are before we let them loose?"

"That bad, huh?"

"Before I came to Donovan, nothing scared me. Then there was *Freelander,* followed by *Vixen,* and now *Ashanti.* Not to mention Donovan itself. Makes you wonder what kind of moron would agree to be locked into a starship, confined in a small space for a minimum of two or three years, popped out of the universe by an energy field, to hopefully pop back in somewhere light-years away. And only then discover they were going to die of starvation or old age in that tiny little tomb?"

"Not all ships end that way."

"No. But too many of them do." Aguila shook her head. "There's something going wrong with the theoretical physics that we don't understand. What's really frustrating is that with the time lag, unless *Turalon* made it back to Solar System, they don't have a clue back there that there's a problem."

"You were high in the ranks. What do you think they'll do when they find out? Stop sending ships?"

"It's a possibility. The Corporation was founded on the principle of limiting risk, controlling business cycles, providing social value through efficient distribution of resources. The biggest aspiration was getting rid of uncertainty and the destabilizing effects of nationalistic governments. Extraction, refinement, manufacturing, production, logistics, distribution, and consumption. All perfectly monitored by AI and ever-evolving algorithms."

"And you think The Corporation will balk over the number of dead aboard *Freelander* and *Ashanti*?"

"You think The Corporation gives a shit about people? Human beings are a renewable resource." Aguila's expression tightened. "It's the cost of the ships versus the potential returns. We'd just damn well better hope that *Turalon* made it back on schedule, and with all of its cargo intact."

Allison took another taste of her whiskey. "Welcome to Donovan. Which means we're on our own. And that brings me back to my purpose: Will you take twenty-five thousand for Tompzen?"

"Wirth getting tired of cutting his own throats these days? By the way, in case you haven't noticed, that's a real nice playmate that you're in bed with."

"Dan is more than capable of keeping the chuckleheads in line and assuring that the marks cover their bets. But that's not always good business. It behooves us to have another person in the position of enforcer. A layer of insulation between the occasional strong-arm tactic and the loftier position to which Dan has aspired in the community."

"Doesn't want to have to build any additional schools to rehabilitate his image, huh?"

"As he says, 'Once was enough.'"

Aguila chuckled. "Fifty thousand."

"Supervisor, you're not thinking this through. A great many of your people from Corporate Mine patronize our establishments. Knowing that we've taken one of your ex-marines as an enforcer reminds them that certain standards of behavior are expected. And that Corporate Mine's interests are aligned with ours when it comes to their welfare."

Aguila's gaze had sharpened. "You're not exactly the woman I thought you'd be."

"Let's just say I had a rough patch a couple of years back. Life didn't deal me the cards I thought it would. When I came out of it, I realized that where I found myself wasn't where I wanted to be. Or who I wanted to be."

"And who are you now?"

"The second-richest woman on the planet. One who can sit here as an equal, dealing with the most powerful and richest. For the moment, we're dickering over the value of a man's life. And no, I don't have aspirations when it comes to your mine or authority. I'll do everything in my power to keep you where you are and successful."

"Why?"

"Because you and your people are making millions down there. As long as you do, Dan and I get to take our cut, and we get to do it without the headaches of administration."

Again, Aguila gave her the probing look. "So you're sitting on all that wealth. What are you going to do with it?"

"Me? I'm young. The day is going to come when The Corporation figures out the problem of the missing ships and the navigational errors inherent in inverting symmetry. When they do, I might send them a couple of shipping containers of the finest gemstones on the planet, buy myself a townhouse in Transluna." A beat. "Or maybe I'll buy Montana, or that island they call Fiji."

"Assuming that in the process, you don't run afoul of the good Mr. Wirth."

Allison took another sip of her whiskey. "You're right. He is a dangerous playmate. There isn't so much as a whisper of empathy, remorse, or regret in his body. The man's as forgiving as a sidewinder. So far I've been smart enough to avoid any conflicts that would incline him to slitting my throat in the middle of the night."

"Who said that only the wildlife was deadly around here?"

"Welcome to Donovan," Allison agreed, clinking her glass against Aguila's.

"All right, twenty-five thousand. And one other thing: Derek Taglioni? He's hands off. Get my meaning? I don't care if he plays the tables, buys a whore every now and then, but that's it. Just simple business. You and Dan don't try and play him because of who he is."

Allison shrugged, wondering just who Derek Taglioni was and why Aguila would be worried. "Done and done."

18

The mine gate on the north end of town was a huge square opening in the fifty-foot-high monstrosity of fence. The size was large enough to pass the haulers coming down from the clay pit. The gate itself rolled on large wheels and cammed into place when closed. Truly a remarkable piece of engineering.

Unlike so many of Dek's kin, he'd spent time during his youth in many of the re-wilded areas on Earth. He had enjoyed the open air, hunted—as only a Taglioni could—and come to relish the out of doors.

Maybe that's why Donovan called to him. He'd been ten years stuck in the confines of *Ashanti*'s few decks. When a person is removed from nature for any length of time, coming back into contact with it is an almost mystical experience.

He extended a hand—a futile attempt to touch the ethereal. Closing his eyes, he let the breeze caress his outstretched fingers.

Better than nothing.

Dek laughed at his folly and raised his face to the partly cloudy sky. He let his gaze rest longingly on the dusty haul road where it vanished into the scrubby trees. The curious scent that he equated with cardamom and a hint of cinnamon tinged with the lightest touch of saffron teased his nostrils.

The sound of the place was just as enchanting with its melodic rising and falling of harmony. Something similar to a symphony that was on the verge of finding the perfect musical score. But each time it was almost there, it would drift off into an atonal direction and have to start all over again. He'd been told that those were the invertebrates—a series of species of winged, shelled, and legged creatures that made up one of the lower trophic levels of Donovan's biome.

"Kind of a treat, huh?" the guard asked. He was a red-haired, brown-skinned man with a large triangular nose and knowing black eyes that stared out from under a shelf of brow ridge.

"I could listen to it for days on end. There's a magic here. Something that echoes in my soul," Dek told the man. Then offered his hand. "Derek Taglioni."

"Wejee Tolland. I'm part of the security detail. I like being posted at the mine gate the best. You see, that's the bush out there. Right close and personal. The other gates, they all let out on farms, the aircar field, the shuttle field. But that's pure Donovan running right up to the fence."

Dek took a long step, planting it firmly beyond the high wire enclosure.

"Uh, sir? I gotta ask you to step back inside."

Dek retreated, asking, "Is there a problem?"

Wejee gave an offhand shrug. "Orders are that we're not supposed to let you—and especially you—get eaten. Of all the gates, the quetzals try this one the most often. Whitey brought two others of his lineage right through here last time we had a major incursion. And that's not counting the bems, spikes, sidewinders, and skewers. Cheng's slug poison is working pretty well, and dry as it is, slugs aren't a major threat. At least not today. But I wouldn't trust it to be out with those soft town shoes of yours, sir. You'd be a heap better off in boots."

A man had to appreciate orders that said he wasn't to be eaten. "Can't set foot outside the gate, huh? Those are Kalico's orders?"

"No, sir. She don't give orders here. That comes from Tal. And if Talina Perez asks me to wrestle a quetzal bare-naked, shoot a hole in the moon, and toss *Freelander* out of orbit with one hand, I'm going to do it."

"I guess you and I see Talina Perez in the same light. Where you from, Wejee?"

"North of Alice Springs in the red center of Australia. Mother made the trip out from the city so I'd be born on the ancestral lands. Family's lived in Sydney for a couple of generations. I'm the first to qualify for deep space. I came here on the seventh ship. Never wanted to go back."

"Worked for Talina the entire time?"

"Yes, sir."

"I'd rather you called me Dek. I wasted too much of my life being called 'sir.'" He turned his gaze out to the bush. What the hell was it? This incredible longing, as though some unseen thing was beckoning him from just beyond that line of trees. After ten years in *Ashanti*, he really wanted to go wander, smell the land. "Who do I talk to about going out there?"

"Talina Perez."

"What *is it* about her? I'm not sure yet, but she may be the most amazing woman I've ever known."

Wejee's grin wrinkled the brown skin around his mouth. "Don't go getting a thing for her, Dek. Half the men in this town cast covetous eyes at Tal. Problem is, she's got quetzals inside her. That, and she'd break any man in two if he riled her the wrong way."

"So, she doesn't have a man in her life?"

"Here's the thing about Tal: I'd die for that woman, and she's saved my skinny Aboriginal ass more than a couple of times. But she's had her share of heartache. Buried her first man, Mitch, when he died from an infection. Cap, the second, got broken up by a quetzal, crippled, and somebody overdosed him. Then there was Trish. As close as Tal was going to come to a daughter. Trish's in a grave up at the cemetery after some soft-meat piece of shit shot her by accident. That was a couple of years back. Since then Tal's been different. Aloof."

"Tell me about these quetzals inside her. I overheard her talking to herself this morning. Not that I don't talk to myself, but this sounded like she was answering questions."

"She say, 'You piece of shit,' on occasion?" At Dek's nod, Wejee said, "Yeah, those are the Whitey quetzals. The ones she calls 'Demon.' Local lineage around here. They've got a blood vendetta against humans."

"Hold on a second. How does she have these creatures inside her?"

"It's the molecules, Dek. We humans got DNA: two strands of nucleic acid. Quetzals got what they call TriNA. Three strands. With three they can encode three times the information for a given length of molecule. I get a little hazy on this, but Cheng, Dya, and Dr. Turnienko, they figure the molecules are intelligent. That they think, or at least process information."

"So Talina has smart molecules running around inside her? And they talk to her?"

"Talk is the wrong word. They communicate through transferRNA, just like in terrestrial cells. Hey, I'm a security guy. You want details? Take the microbiology up with Cheng and Dya Simonov."

"The quetzal molecules don't just interface with her brain, do they? Is that the difference in her eyes and face?"

"She can see into both the UV and IR spectra. Hears way better than any human should. And she may not look it, but she's twice as strong as any man I ever knew."

"How does she deal with it? Must be, well, unsettling at best."

"She had a tough go of it a couple of years back during the Benteen excitement. Then, to lose Trish? That girl was like a daughter to her. Damn near broke her, but somehow, she put it all together, keeps the quetzal part of her separate."

"Hell of a lady."

"Yep."

"Hey! There you are!" a voice called.

Dek turned to see Michaela Hailwood's tall and slender form striding down the avenue; her long legs were clad in some dark fabric; an embroidered shirt was tucked in at the waist. She had one of the quetzal-hide capes over her shoulders.

"New wardrobe? Looks good on you."

"Hell, yes," she told him with a wide grin as she came to a stop; Capella's harsh light glinted in her fuzz of short black hair. Sticking out a hand toward Wejee, she said, "Doctor Michaela Hamilton. Maritime Unit. Glad to meet you."

"Wejee Tolland," he replied with a grin. "What's a maritime unit?"

She gestured east, past the fence. "We're supposed to establish the first research base for the study of Donovan's oceans. We've got a submersible research module aboard *Ashanti*. I've spent all morning with the Supervisor and Dr. Shimodi about where to set up. Looks like it will be on a series of reefs five hundred kilometers out from the coast."

Dek gave her a grin. "That's the best news I've heard all day."

She gave him a wan smile in return. "Hard to believe after all we've been through. But, yeah, we're finally in business. They'll start downloading cargo as soon as the Unreconciled are safely planetside."

Dek made a face. "Glad I don't have to be part of the team that has to clean up Deck Three. Something tells me it's going to be a nightmare."

"You and me both." She looked out the gate. "So that's the storied bush, huh?"

"It is," Wejee told her. "The sound you hear is what we call the chime. It's the invertebrates singing to each other. Not sure if it's something they do to distract predators, or attract mates, or locate food. And since we've figured out about the intelligent molecules, it could even be language for all we know."

"Bugs with language?" Dek wondered.

Wejee shot him a cautioning glance. "Now, Dek, don't go making judgments based on Terrestrial life. On Donovan that can get you killed. Things don't work the same here."

To Michaela, he said, "And we haven't even begun to look at the oceans and rivers. But if an old hand can give you any advice, Doctor Hailwood, you'll live a lot longer out there if you'll take for granted that everything on this planet is trying to kill you."

"We'll be taking care to make sure we don't expose ourselves to any unnecessary risks."

"Good. Take that care, and then take it twice more, if you get my meaning. Nobody has ever died of old age on Donovan."

"I hear you, Wejee. We'll be extra careful."

"Good. But prepare yourself, Doctor. If I'm any kind of a guesser, you're going to lose a couple of people in the first month."

"Isn't that a bit extreme?" Dek wondered.

Wejee's knowing eyes had no give. "Just the opposite, Dek. That's unbridled optimism on my part."

PARTURITION

I sit in the observation dome, knowing it is the last time that I shall do so. This has been my haven. My retreat. I have come to this place when I was drowning in self-doubt. When my faith wavered, and I was frail and terrified that I wasn't worthy of being chosen for such an immense responsibility.

Here, looking out at the universe, I drew sustenance. In this place I was able, somehow, to summon enough courage to meet the challenge. Even if only for one more day. But it carried me through.

As the Prophets had said it would. Back in the beginning, before their language became that of the universe.

I so desperately wish I could appreciate the profundity of their words and utterances. But I fear they've fallen so deeply into the universe, that our frail and stumbling brains can no longer comprehend. This saddens me, for I am desperately envious of the Truths they now understand.

Sometimes they sing.

Used to be they'd sing in a sort of unison, now it's only occasional, and one at a time.

We've tried to record their songs. Learned the words to the early ones. Today we will sing their "ecstasy" song as we leave Deck Three. Depart the womb where we have gestated for these last ten years.

Everything goes back to procreation, be it peoples or individuals. Figurative birth. Literal birth. Life and death.

Sex is the inverse of death. Like Siamese twins, one cannot exist without the other. Opposites crossed. The divine reconciliation of opposites.

The universe laughs.

In the background I can hear the Irredenta. Excitement fills their voices. There is banging, the sound of crates being slid across the sialon deck. The preparations have been going on for hours. Kalico Aguila sent a list of things for them to do. Orders. Bring this, don't bring that. Wear shoes or boots. Hats are necessary. A long list of reasons for the above had been included.

We have no way of knowing what might be true or what might be a lie. Being Corporate, whatever she tells us is probably a lie. What we do know is that the universe has brought us this far. It has taught us that we can only depend upon ourselves and the Prophets.

The universe will provide. We will continue to live with that faith and take with us only what we can carry.

I gave the order based upon something the Prophet Callista said a couple of nights ago. Sounded like, "Taaa whaaa ya c . . . c . . . carree."

Take what you can carry?

So often, I can only guess. But for the most part, the universe has backed my guesses. None, so far, have been proven horribly wrong.

Given that three hundred and forty-two people once lived here, that's a lot of possessions. Why the universe wants us to leave so much behind is beyond me, but it is not my place to question.

Somewhere in the background I hear a crash. Perhaps a shelf has collapsed or been torn down?

Cackling laughter breaks out from one of the children. They're half manic with excitement. Born here, they've never known anything else. Deck Three is their world.

As Ashanti rotates, I see Capella III come into view: a green, blue, and brown globe with white polar caps, its oceans and continents brilliant in the star's light. Within moments the terminator is visible like a black line through the middle of the planet.

Before I sleep again, we will be down there.

I catch a gleam of silver off to the right. Crane my head.

With a smile on my lips, I recognize the shuttle. Watch it close until it slips beyond the observation dome's field of view.

I rise, tilt my head back, and whisper, "Thank you for the strength and vision to do what I must."

I turn. Walk unsteadily out of the dome and into the chaos that is Deck Three. I see old belongings strewn about. Once-precious possessions too large or heavy to be *carried. Not our concern. Let the* Ashanti *crew clean it up. A reminder of their original sin.*

Many of these things will be missed in our new home. But then perhaps that is the lesson we're supposed to take away with us. We will leave here humbly. Wearing nothing that so much as hints of hubris or vanity. As the living graves of the dead and vessels of their immortality, we go as near to naked as we can. No one has ever been born wearing clothes. This is our womb. The hallway to the shuttle shall be our vagina. The shuttle shall deliver us into the sunlight.

When we walk out into a new world, we shall be as infants.

And then the hard work really begins.

19

The amiable ship's voice said, *"Shuttle Corporate One. You are on approach to* Ashanti. *Request permission to take control of your navigational functions prior to docking."*

"Thank you, *Ashanti*. Corporate One prefers to maintain manual control. Please notify us if there is any deviation during our approach." Ensign Juri Makarov replied.

"Roger that, Corporate One."

Where she sat in the right-hand seat behind the pilot, Kalico Aguila smiled to herself. Word was that any able shuttle pilot would decline surrendering control. Docking was about a pilot's only way to show off given the automation that was space travel.

Through the transparency, Kalico watched the A-7 shuttle drop down into *Ashanti*'s docking bay. Ensign Makarov eased them onto the grapples without so much as a quiver.

But then, Makarov had been flying almost constantly since *Turalon*'s arrival more than four years ago.

"We have docking," Ashanti said through the com. *"We have hard seal. Welcome aboard. Captain Galluzzi will meet you at the hatch."*

"Hard dock, hard seal," Makarov confirmed from the pilot's chair.

"Deal with it, you piece of shit," Talina Perez muttered where she sat beside Kalico. The expression on the woman's face was the one she adopted when she and the quetzal presence she called Demon were sparring over control of Talina's limbic system.

"Quetzal's don't like flying?" Kalico asked.

"Hate it," Talina told her, unbuckling. "Good news for us. Means that Whitey and his bunch aren't going to have any desire to commandeer a shuttle, steal a starship, and invert symmetry in a desperate attempt to space back to Earth and invade it."

Kalico stepped free of her seat, head cocked. "Too bad. I'd consider giving them *Freelander* if they ever wanted to give it a try. Might be worth it just to see them attend their first Board meeting. Ultimate predators finding themselves face to face with ultimate predators. Wonder who'd win?"

Tal grinned, glanced at Mark Talbot where he rose from the left seat. The man was dressed in full and battered combat armor, his helmet clipped to his belt. From the seat rack he retrieved his service rifle.

"You ready?" Tal asked, slinging her own rifle.

"Good to go, Tal." Talbot stepped forward, the slight whine of his servos distinct in the shuttle's silence as the turbines spun down.

Sheyela Smith had managed to cobble together a small powerpack that had allowed Talbot to salvage his worn-out armor. The system wasn't military grade, but Talbot and the rest of the marines had their tech back online, at least for the time being. For the most part the remaining marines only wore armor during quetzal and mobber alerts. Today they would wear it to keep the so-called Irredenta in line. After all, there was no telling what kind of surprise the Unreconciled might have cooked up to "celebrate" their release, birth, or whatever.

Tal, dressed in coveralls, her knife and pistol on her utility belt, led the way.

Stepping into the cargo bay, it was to see it set up as a passenger cabin with rows of seats. Kalico gave it a preliminary inspection.

Corporal Abu Sassi and privates Dina Michegan and Katsuro Miso rose from their seats, all dressed in shining combat armor, their helmets clipped to their belts. The rows of seats looked oddly out of place given that the shuttle had been used for shipping cargo into orbit for the past few years instead of as a people hauler.

Kalico took a stance, calling, "All right, people. You've been briefed on the Irredenta. Your mission is to ensure that they are deposited at Tyson Station with the least amount of disruption. Your opinions about them, your reaction to them, is not part of this operation. You will ensure that they board this shuttle, that they are seated, and transported to Tyson without incident. Any last questions?"

Of course there weren't. She, Galluzzi, Bogarten, and Abu Sassi had planned this down to the final resort, which was to gas the entire cabin if things started to get out of control. Separated from the command deck by the hatch—and with the marines in full combat armor with their breathing systems—the Irredenta could be rendered unconscious and harmless.

"Let's do this," Talbot muttered, leading the way to the hatch.

On the other side, Galluzzi waited; the man looked like he had an electrical short in his underwear given how he was bouncing on his feet. The way his right hand twitched reminded her of a spastic mouse.

"Good to see you, Supervisor," he greeted. "Welcome aboard."

"Got the corridors sealed?" Kalico asked, taking the captain's salute.

"They've got one route to take. From their main hatch, right down here and into the shuttle."

"All right." She turned. "Mark, you and Abu Sassi have the enviable job of bringing up the rear to ensure that no one is left behind."

"On it," Abu Sassi said, giving her a salute. Then he and Talbot disappeared into the corridor.

"My people will sweep the entirety of Deck Three as soon as you've spaced, Supervisor." Galluzzi was still fidgeting. "Don't think they'd leave us a lethal going-away gift, but Batuhan comes across as the kind who might carry a grudge. Or at least might want to make a parting statement."

"See to it." She looked around. "I'd hate to have them compromise the ship. It's the only reliable one we've got."

Which was true. *Freelander* was a ghost ship, and *Vixen,* besides only being a survey ship, had a programming flaw that would take her fifty years into the future if she spaced for Solar System. At least *Ashanti* had made the transit to Donovan in the expected two-and-a-half-year time frame. It was the next seven and half years that hadn't been anticipated. They'd just have to take on faith that she'd return home a lot closer than the navigational error that had left her so far from Capella.

That was the thing about life on Donovan. One always had to pick from bad choices.

"F.O. Turner reports all is ready," *Ashanti*'s voice sounded from the speakers.

"Supervisor?" Galluzzi asked in a voice filled with tension.

"Proceed," Kalico told him.

In his com, Galluzzi said, "You have the okay. Open the hatch."

The captain gave her a salute. "Supervisor, I wish you good spacing. I'll see you on the planet after we've secured the ship.".

He turned on his heel, stepping through a hatch, and sealing it behind him.

"I guess that's our cue to lock ourselves in the command deck." Talina turned. "So how about that, Demon? You're about to ride down to the planet with a bunch of human cannibals. Given the way your kind treats their elders, that ought to have you feeling right at home."

Kalico wondered what sort of retort the beast in Talina's gut made to that.

At the command deck hatch, she followed Talina in and watched as Juri Makarov flipped the switch that sent the dogs clicking home to lock the door.

Retreating to her seat, Kalico accessed the holos that interfaced with *Ashanti.* In the image, First Officer Turner dissolved the last of the bonding agent on the Deck Three hatch and beat feet for the secure hatch that led up to Deck Two.

Abu Sassi moved into view; dressed in full armor, he tapped the panel control beside the sialon hatch. Through his helmet, Kalico could hear the whine as the latches retracted.

With a tug, Abu Sassi pulled the hatch open.

Talbot's armored form stepped to the far side, rifle at the ready.

"Attention please," Abu Sassi used his helmet speaker to project it into Deck Three's dim recesses. "Your transportation is ready. Please proceed forward, down the companionway, and to the shuttle."

The familiar drawings on the side of the hallway could

be seen, the skeletons erotically posed. But beyond lay a dark haze.

Kalico waited; each beat of her heart measured her rising tension. Where the hell were the Unreconciled? They'd had ample notice that this was their relocation day.

Unless they were planning something else.

"Supervisor?" Galluzzi's stressed voice asked through com. *"Think we should send someone in?"*

Talina muttered, "You don't think they did us some big favor like committing mass suicide, do you?"

"We're not that lucky." Into com, Kalico said, "Sergeant, send a drone in."

"Yes, ma'am."

She watched as a recon drone detached from Abu Sassi's shoulder; the little flying sensor whirred off down the hall. A separate monitor snapped on, showing the halls bathed in the green-and-shadow glow of IR and UV. The walls were all decorated with images, the effect spookily reminiscent of the scrawlings in *Freelander.*

And there were the people, reflected in visual spectrum and IR heat signatures. All lining up. Just as the drone fixed on them, the parade started forward. Kalico stared in disbelief. Where the hell were their clothes? Men, women, and children—they had only fabric wraps around their waists.

Batuhan was in the lead, followed by four young men who carried his ornately carved chair. Behind them were the four women with babes in arms, and following were three people borne on litters carried by men.

Kalico tried to get a better image of the people being carried. Looked like two women and a man, all three of them emaciated, looking half dead, but their hands were working spastically, their legs kicking and trembling.

Immediately to their rear were the rest of the people, dressed in the skimpy patchwork of clothing. Their hair long and unkempt, they shuffled forward in ranks.

"They're going down dressed like that?" Talina wondered. "To Tyson Station? What do they think it is, a beach?"

As the people passed the hatch, a weird and eerie song burst from their lips. They locked step, walking in time to the rising and falling half-chant. Kalico tried to make out the slurred-sounding words, something about an ecstasy of everlasting life, eternal salvation, and being the living graves of the purified.

At the hatch, Abu Sassi had stepped back. As per orders, he and Talbot had taken positions to either side, standing at attention, rifles at port arms. The pose was to make them look more like an honor guard than a threat. But if the situation went sideways, they could both tap the gas grenades on their hips, use the stun guns on their belts. And if worse came to worst, fall back on the non-lethal rounds in their rifles.

Emerging into the full light of the corridor, Batuhan walked barefoot ahead of his chair. For the exodus he had at least draped his loins in a sheet. Like a king, he strode with back straight, head up, his weird spiky hairdo in a great fan sticking up from his head. The man's skin was still covered with the splotchy white makeup, and the intricate scar patterns on his face and the eye carved on his forehead contrasted with the missing flesh of his nose.

The four young men bearing his chair—though less intricately scarred than Batuhan—had large sections of their bodies scarified; their half-glazed eyes flashed in every direction, taking in the marines. She could see them swallowing hard. One was almost shaking, looked to be on the verge of panic.

Why?

"Sergeant, keep that drone searching." Kalico rubbed her chin. "Check for anything unusual in there. Any odd heat sources. I want the chem sensors to reconfigure for anything explosive."

"Roger that."

She wasn't sure what to watch—the drone or the continuing procession of the Irredenta. The amount and patterning of the scarring, she realized, was different depending upon the person. Batuhan, in the lead, had the most and greatest intricacy. Then the four throne-bearers, then the four women. After that, the amount of scarring dropped, with fewer and fewer designs.

It's a sign of rank.

To her surprise, most of the women were either carrying an infant, or showed some degree of pregnancy where they walked under shouldered burdens. Like the men, they, too, only had a wrap around their hips and went barefoot. And of the children—all of them clad only in breechcloths—none looked to be over the age of six.

The children walked with a bouncing excitement, eyes aglow with the adventure. All of them were skinny little specimens, with hollow guts and too-well-defined ribs. To Kalico's disgust they'd all been scarified, but nothing like their parents. Their hair, with varying measures of effectiveness, had been done up in the fan. Looking closely, Kalico couldn't tell the little boys from the girls.

On the lower screen the drone continued its search, whizzing in and out of rooms, rising and falling as it inspected discarded personal items, old bits of clothing, looked under beds and into gaping closets. The rooms were rife with trash and abandoned belongings. Why were they leaving so much behind? Most of the light panels were dark. Looked like what was left behind in the poorer parts of Earth when a slum was cleared.

Following along at the back of the exodus came young men in their twenties and teens, each bent under the weight of a crate, bundle, or duraplast container. Apparently, they were the porters for the few assembled belongings of the Irredenta.

The drone buzzed, getting her attention. It was in the women's locker room, hovering over a pile of five skeletons. Most of the soft tissue had been halfheartedly stripped off, leaving the still-articulated bones looking red and ill-used. The skulls had been chopped open, the brains extracted.

"What do you make of that?" Talina asked.

"Reminds me of what mobbers do to a person, but they're a lot more efficient when it comes to cleaning the bones."

"You want to do anything about it?" Talina asked.

Kalico shook her head. "Not now. Maybe later, after they're planetside and safely contained at Tyson. There'll be plenty of time to ask questions then."

At the companionway to the shuttle deck, people were filing down. The children, of course, had never encountered stairs. They were having a wonderful time, jumping down, step by step, giggles of laughter rising, smiles bending their scarified cheeks. Their bare feet slapped onto the treads.

"You know the eye carved in Batuhan's forehead?" Talina asked.

"Yeah. That's creep-freaked, isn't it?"

"Just caught the light right. Got a good look," Talina told her. "Those three on the litters, they've got the eyes carved in their foreheads, too. But it's just them. Batuhan and the three on the litters."

Kalico thought back to the interview she'd done with Batuhan. "You think they're the Prophets?"

"Could be. Something's not right about them. And look, there, that young woman." Talina pointed. "See the way she's walking? Like she's got issues with coordination. And she's not the only one."

Tal was right. Something about the woman's coordination was off. Intoxicated? No, this was different. Like impaired motor control. Might have been the result of a brain injury. Kalico kept seeing odd movements, loose steps, curious wobbles of the head. Or a rocking tremor of the hands.

The continued sing-song chanting—the words being distinctly and purposefully slurred—sent a shiver down Kalico's spine. With a gesture, she muted the sound.

"We have a total count of seventy-seven," the com informed.

In the transportee quarters, the drone was continuing its search, only to stop at a collection of shoes in one of the rooms. They'd been piled, maybe a meter high. A carefully built pyramid with the toes pointed outward.

"What's that all about?" Talina wondered. "We told these people they needed shoes. And what are they doing? On top of being damn near buck-ass naked, every mother's son and daughter of them is barefoot."

"Sent them an entire checklist for how to dress, what to expect."

"We dusted Tyson with slug poison, but that's not one hundred percent effective. And stepping on the wrong invertebrate is going to get a lot of them bitten." Talina made a face. "Thing is, it usually only takes once before the lesson is irrevocably learned."

The last of the Irredenta were descending the companionway.

In the shuttle's monitors, Batuhan strode imperiously past Dina Michegan where she stood before the hatch. His chair bearers had to fit the thing through the door and into the limited clearance between the first row of seats. At the hatch to the command deck, Miso snapped to attention, his helmeted head faced forward, but you could bet he was watching everything on the heads-up display inside his helmet.

Batuhan took the chair in the middle of the first row, his bare toes not more than a foot from Private Miso's armored feet.

The chair bearers clambered around, bracing the "throne" awkwardly on the seats immediately behind Batuhan's. People continued to file in; those bearing the litters carefully laid them on the deck where space could be found, thereby blocking the aisles.

As the rest tried to crowd in, bedlam ensued, with people trying to step around the three litters, scrambling over seat backs, and chattering.

But no one, Kalico noticed, crossed in front of Batuhan. The Mongolian tech sat motionless, back straight, head up, eyes forward as if he were a carved statue.

To Kalico's relief, none of the Unreconciled tried the locked hatch. No one brandished anything that looked like a weapon. The sensors picked up nothing that indicated an explosive was hidden on any person or in the various containers, bundles, and baskets.

"Sergeant?" Kalico contacted Abu Sassi. "Looks like we're about loaded. But before we seal the hatch, I need you to take a cargo net back and collect that pyramid of shoes."

"Roger that."

Talina gave off a weary sigh. "So far, so good."

"Yeah," Kalico was rubbing nervous fingers over the backs of her hands. "Why do I have a really bad feeling about this?"

20

The sound of the shuttle lifting off had brought Dek wide awake. His dreams had been filled with forest and the smells of Donovan. In them, he'd been out there beyond the fence. Some intangible temptress—like a siren of old—had danced and beckoned him. Just a fleeting shape among the bushes and scrub. But the harder he pursued, the more elusive the phantom had become.

He blinked, taking in the small and neatly furnished dome. The walls were stacked with books—the old-fashioned bound-paper kind.

Shig had explained to him about the books: "These are old, valued because various preeminent scholars of religion have underlined passages and left notes in the margins. Oh, I have them in the implants." He'd tapped the side of his head. "But when I open to a page in the Vedas, I have the thoughts of Ramanadas, Irrawiri, and Raja Singh right there, written in the margins in their own handwriting."

Dek sat up in the small bed—something called a futon; it folded out from a bench. Not the most comfortable thing he'd ever slept on. Shig had called it "surprisingly restful," and after having spent two nights on the contraption, Dek suspected you never took an ascetic at his word when it came to basic creature comforts.

Within a matter of moments, Dek had attended to his toilet, made the bed, and dressed. He chose the coveralls, figuring he might want to save the last of his "good" clothing.

Stepping out into the day, he was surprised to find Shig bent over the plants in his garden. The short scholar had an old plastic gallon container labelled "mayonnaise" into which he was dropping green beans. Another quart container, by his foot, was already filled with blueberries from the bushes that were growing into the perimeter fence.

"Good morning!" Dek called, blinking in the light.

"Shuttle awaken you?" Shig asked.

"How did I sleep so long?"

"It's the gravity." Shig collected his containers and straightened. "And wholesome food. Not to mention being able to sleep in a proper bed after all those years in a starship."

Best not to tell him about the futon's shortcomings.

"Kind of early for the shuttle to be going up, isn't it?"

Shig shrugged. "They're going to transport the cannibals down to Tyson Station today. Strange, isn't it? As of the moment they step off of the shuttle, they won't be the Irredenta. They'll be their own people in their own place and responsible for governing themselves. Have to come up with a new name, I suppose."

"The Unreconciled." Dek glanced covetously down at the green beans and blueberries. "That's what they told us aboard ship. The Universe had picked them specially, and they would never find reconciliation with the rest of humanity until they had purified it."

Shig's knowing brown gaze had picked up on Dek's preoccupation with the beans and berries. "I suppose that given their history, reconciliation might be beyond hope. But what about you?"

Dek laughed at the thought, heard his stomach gurgle with hunger. Screw him in vacuum, but ever since he'd set foot on the planet, he was always feeling as hungry as he had during those starvation months aboard *Ashanti*.

"Shig, I can reconcile with anyone over anything." His stomach sounded its discontent with greater volume. "Well, but for my nether regions."

The brown man raised his buckets. "I was just on the way to trade these to Inga. I think it's enough that she'd give us both breakfasts. Care to join me?"

As he matched pace, Dek said, "Funny, isn't it? The way a man's life changes. Were you to transport me back to Transluna, to the man I was, you wouldn't recognize me. And seeing me, as I am now, they wouldn't recognize me either. Me then. Me now. Same man? Or two different men? Begs the question: Do we ever really know ourselves? Can we ever define a constant whereby a person can say, 'This is who I am regardless of the environment I'm in or the events I'm experiencing'?"

"The mystics in the Eastern religions would tell you that you cannot know yourself until you break the bonds of samsara and experience moksha. Only then do the scales of illusion fall away, and even the notion of 'self' is discarded because it perpetuates duality."

"How does that work on Donovan?"

They had stepped out into the main avenue, and Shig closed his garden gate. "Talina tells me that had the Buddha ever come to Donovan, he would have seated himself under a mundo tree. That the moment he did, a nightmare would have reached down with its tentacles, impaled him, and yanked him up into the tree to spend the next couple of months devouring him."

"Leaves me thinking Talina will never be a mystic."

Shig gave him a wide grin. "She has a young soul, one balancing between *tamas* and *rajas*. That's darkness and passion in case you were wondering."

"She's a most remarkable woman." He remembered the way her eyes looked, how she moved. "Something about her . . ."

Shig was giving him the eye, a slight lift to his left eyebrow. "She is our warrior. Being a society's warrior sets a person apart. The warrior is the one who is called upon to do the distasteful, to act for the protection of others. But in Talina's case, she has also been chosen by Donovan to be an intermediary. She is a bridge between humanity and the planet. A role that leaves her in even greater isolation. Because of that, she lives in constant fear."

Dek pursed his lips. "I know what that's like."

"Why would you say that?"

"Being a Taglioni means you're always apart. Perpetually worried whether you're worthy of the name. I think I see something Taglioni-like in Talina. Makes me wonder who she would be back in Transluna."

Shig's curious look had intensified as Dek held the door to Inga's; Shig led the way down the long flight of wooden stairs to the tables below. At the bottom, people called greetings, to which Shig replied with waves and cheery responses.

He didn't lead the way to a table, but to the bar stools, taking the one where Supervisor Aguila had sat, and indicating the empty stool to the left.

Dek climbed up, noting, "I sense a definite hierarchy in the seating. You pick this for a reason?"

Shig set his containers on the bar and indicated the empty stool beside him. "That's Talina's. Turn around. Look out at room. That's what she does, resting her elbows on the bar behind her in the process. It's how she looks out at her people."

"Why are you telling me this?"

"Because she can't go back to Transluna. You asked who she'd be back there? She'd be a freak. A human contaminated with Donovanian genetic material. A warrior in a land of neutered and autonomous worker bees. The Corporation would destroy her. You must understand: The kind of people necessary to survive the vicissitudes and dangers of frontiers are not tolerated by the civilized and tamed."

"I see."

"I hear that you want to go out beyond the fence. That you want to learn how to live out there. That you've been asking about the Wild Ones."

At that moment, Inga appeared, hurrying down the bar and looking flustered. "You drinking or eating?"

Shig gave the woman that remarkable beaming smile. "Good to see that business is booming. How are you today?"

"Up to my ass in quetzals. What's in the containers?"

"Green beans. All that were ripe. Oh, and blueberries. Dek and I were wondering if you'd trade us for two breakfast specials?"

Inga shot Dek a who-the-hell-are-you look, lifted both eyebrows, and chuckled. "Yeah, but don't push your luck, Shig. If it were anyone but you . . ."

With that she scooped up the containers and bulled her way back down the bar toward the kitchen.

Dek spread his hands wide. "Yesterday I stood at the fence for what seemed like hours. Wejee puts up with me. Answers my questions. Says I should contact some of the farmers, that they'd trade labor for information. But, yes, I want to get to know the Wild Ones. I've heard of the Briggses, the Philos, the Shu Wans. And then there's the prospectors. I figure I can work while I learn. Pay my way in this clap-trapping crazy free-market economy of yours."

"What would you do to get out there?"

"Anything, Shig. You name it."

"Why?"

"I feel it. Here." Dek touched his breast. "Donovan, I mean. Like it's a sort of presence."

"Odds are that a skewer, a slug, or a sidewinder will get you. Even with a knowledgeable guide. If you had someone like Tip Briggs and Kylee Simonov as mentors, I'd say you still had a seventy percent chance of being killed in the first week."

Dek took a deep breath. "But maybe I wouldn't. What the hell, let me go, Shig. You can order it, can't you?"

Shig's gaze softened, seemed to see right down into Dek's soul. "I might. But say you do go, that you manage to make the deal with Donovan. You understand, don't you? You'll be just like Talina. Donovan will claim you. You'll never be able to go back. No reconciliation with that old Derek Taglioni, let alone your family."

"That man's already gone. I want to know who this new one will be."

"Even if it comes at a price?"

Dek looked at Talina's chair, a symbol of isolation. Smart man, this Shig Mosadek. "Nothing comes without a little pain, Shig."

"I'll remember you said that."

21

With his hands clasped behind him, Miguel Galluzzi stood in the observation dome and watched the Supervisor's A-7 shuttle as it lifted from the bay. Capella's harsh light gleamed on the sialon hull, the craft's aerodynamic delta shining against the dark interstellar background. The sleek vessel turned gracefully, like a thing alive, and began to accelerate.

Within moments it had passed out of sight, leaving only the empty majesty of the galaxy as it glowed in righteous splendor against the black.

Righteous?

Galluzzi snorted to himself, curious about the sudden emptiness that hollowed his core. Surprised at the intensity, he staggered to the side, tears welling in his eyes. His heart began to pound against his breast.

He blinked, jaw quivering.

They are gone.

The notion left him dazed, reeling.

What the hell was this? He'd never experienced the like. This sucking emptiness of body and soul. A vertigo of self—all whirling and disoriented. He swallowed against the sudden nausea, put a hand to his mouth.

For long moments he sat half crouched against the side of the dome. Seemed he could barely get enough to breathe. That everything that he had been was looted away.

They are gone.

From the moment he'd learned of *Ashanti*'s arrival so far off course from Capella, in the wake of his decision to seal Deck Three, he'd lived in guilt, terror, and desperation. Every breath. Every beat of his heart. Each pulse of blood in his veins had been with the knowledge of the horror he'd unleashed upon his transportees.

Now that living shame was gone.

Deck Three was quiet, dark, empty. Halls, decking, and rooms that had shivered in time to the screams of murdered and butchered human beings now lay thick with ominous silence.

Years of desperate yearning to deliver the Unreconciled to their destination—once an almost impossible dream—was now a fact. That terrible weight was lifted. It no longer lurked like a beast on his shoulder, exhaling its fetid stench into his waking thoughts, his nightmares, or deepest fears.

They are gone.

The reality should have left him ebullient. Filled with life and hope. It should have been freedom.

Instead, Galluzzi just huddled against the transparency, his arms tucked tightly against his aching gut.

I just wish I was dead.

Out in the black, the endless patterns of stars mocked him in silence.

22

As the shuttle lifted from *Ashanti*'s bay, Talina kept her attention on the monitors that showed the main cabin. There, just behind that locked hatch, seventy-seven of the Irredenta sat, waiting. Some trembled with anxiety, others chatted in an almost manic fashion with their neighbors. Still others kept singing that oddly atonal, slurred-sounding song. Over and over, as if it were a mantra.

"What do you think?" Kalico asked, her gaze uncertain.

"Reminds me of an anthropology video from the twentieth century, like some sort of long-lost tribe discovered on an isolated island or deep in the jungle."

"Does, doesn't it?"

Talina crossed her arms, feeling herself growing weightless as Makarov changed attitude. At the I'm-falling tickle down in her stomach, Demon, like usual, panicked. The quetzal sent filaments of anxiety through her limbic system. Tried to paralyze her with fear.

Failed.

On her shoulder, Rocket chittered softly.

Back in the main cabin, people who hadn't followed the instructions to buckle in, especially the children, screamed and yipped. Some floated up from their seats. As Makarov applied thrust, acceleration returned to a reassuring 1 g and a concurrent resettling of half-panicked bodies in the back.

"They are not us," Kalico mused. "They have become something other. Different. Alien."

"I wouldn't have believed it. Not after just seven and a half years."

"That can be an eternity, Tal," Kalico noted. "We're off the map. First *Freelander* and then *Ashanti*. The patterns are similar. The crew does their best to save the ship, but in the case of *Freelander* it's the crew who develop the weird death cult. In *Ashanti,* the crew and the Maritime

Unit stay sane, and it's the transportees who become . . . well, this."

Talina's frown incised her forehead. "I think The Corporation needs to rethink deep-space travel. That, or don't pack as many people into the ships. It always comes down to food. Essentially being stuck in a can and making the choice as to who lives and who dies as the hydroponics break down and begin to fail."

Makarov, taking extra care—given the mess of unsecured humans and their luggage—eased them into the atmosphere and juggled the stick as the shuttle hit turbulence.

"Be happy to get this load off," he growled just loud enough for Talina to hear.

"That's a unanimous decision."

Down in her belly, Demon shifted, still teetering on the verge of panic.

To make his point, Makarov took the fast way down, pulling as much as 1.5 gs as he used atmosphere to brake their descent. Then, roaring in a tight circle, he dropped down toward the endless mat of green, blue, and turquoise forest that covered the land west of the Wind Mountains.

With a howling whine, he settled the shuttle over the pad at Tyson Station and eased the big A-7 down onto its landing struts.

"Welcome to Tyson Station," he said into the com, adding with irony: "Please remain seated while we spool down."

"All right, let's get this circus unloaded," Kalico stood, palming the hatch.

Talina followed her out to see a cowed and almost silent crowd. Some of the children were crying, clinging to their ashen-faced mothers. Others looked like they were on the verge of throwing up. But puking what? Raw red meat from the scavenged skeletons back in the women's locker room on Deck Three?

In his seat immediately in front of her, Batuhan was doing his best to appear aloof, but the tension in his face was bunching his scars into an unpleasant grimace. Face to face with the guy, his missing nose, the scars, the weird fake blue eye in the middle of his forehead, it sent creepy crawlies through her bones.

"I'm Security Officer Talina Perez," she told them. "I'm

responsible for your introduction and orientation to Tyson Station. You will disembark, one by one, through the hatch and down the stairs. At the bottom you will proceed to the admin dome. There you will be processed by medical personnel before assembling in the cafeteria. We've got a hot meal prepared the likes of which you haven't had in years. After that, I will tell you what you need to know to survive. Now, Batuhan, if you will follow me."

She turned, not caring if he did or didn't. At the hatch, the ramp lowered and she stepped out into Capella's bright light. Privates Sean Finnegan and Paco Anderssoni, dressed in combat armor, had stretched lines of plastic ribbon to create a lane that led to the doorway of the admin dome.

Talina started down the route, hoping that Batuhan would follow. Not that it mattered in the end. Once the Irredenta were off the shuttle and the hatch was buttoned up, they could run wild all over the place. The marines would evacuate Raya Turnienko, Dya Simonov, and the kitchen staff. Kalico's A-7 would take them back to Port Authority.

If the Irredenta played by the rules, they'd get what help PA and Corporate Mine could give them.

She glanced back, seeing Batuhan plodding along behind her, almost hobbling on his bare feet. Donovan's gravity was having its effect, and the guy didn't look healthy at all. His white-powdered makeup looked even more bizarre given the scars and his kohl-black eyes and lips. She could see into his severed nose to where the turbinate bones were visible.

"Whatever you're planning," he told her through heavy breaths, "it won't work."

"We're not planning anything except to give you a fighting chance."

"We are the universe's chosen."

"Good for you. So, here's the deal: You and your people are malnourished, unaccustomed to the gravity. It'll take you about a month to adapt. We'll help you through that, but if you threaten any of our people, hurt anyone, or try to eat them, we're out of here. You're on your own. No second chances. Get my message?"

"You are only a vehicle," he said. "The universe's way of opening our path to the stars."

"Yeah, right. Well, Donovan's going to have some say about that. In the meantime, those are the ground rules."

He chuckled under his breath. "Of course. We only need to bide our time. In the end the universe will ensure our triumph. Until then, we will only become stronger, more numerous."

"Whatever."

"You don't understand, Security Officer Perez. As time passes, there are going to be more and more of us, all preserved in these bodies, passing through time, existing, being consumed, and continuing along."

"Uh-huh."

"When you look at me, you see a body that once belonged to Batuhan, but on the inside there are a couple hundred of us. Interred in this flesh. Waiting. All those souls, all those bodies. And the day will come when we break free in purity and light."

She kept her expression under control.

He followed her into the dome, and she was able to look back and see his poor acolytes staggering under the weight of the carved duraplast chair. In the light of day, she got a good look at it. The seat had been made out of a desk. Someone had spent a huge amount of time shortening the legs, carving remarkable bas-reliefs that depicted human corpses, skeletons, various bones, phalluses in full erection on the verge of penetrating gaping vulvas, all mixed with spirals, mazes, and geometric designs. The intricately rendered chair back had been carved into artistically intertwined skeletons and might have once been a part of a wall that had been carefully mortised into the chair's frame.

The four manhandled it through the doorway and down the hall in pursuit of Talina and Batuhan.

Not my parade. And thankfully so.

At the end of the hall, Raya Turnienko had set up her station. The lanky Siberian waited on the other side of a table. The woman was tall, slender, with almond eyes in a severe round face.

She greeted Batuhan, saying, "I'm Dr. Turnienko. If you'd extend your hand, this will only take a second."

Batuhan stared at her. Raya stared back, clearly fascinated by his mutilations.

"Just do it," Talina growled. "That, or we're out of here. It's nothing more than a medical sample to see if there's anything we can do to help you and your people."

Batuhan warily extended his ridge-scarred hand. Raya efficiently ran a U-shaped device around the web of his thumb. It snapped and Batuhan jerked his hand back.

Talina said, "After what you've done to yourself, that had to be like a soft scratch. Come on. Let's go feed you."

She led the man into the cafeteria, the place smelling of broccoli, chili, chamois steaks, and freshly baked bread all backed with the scent of mint tea.

Batuhan might have considered himself a walking living graveyard, and the soft part of his nose might be missing, but his ruined face betrayed a deep anticipation as he inhaled. Nor did he waste any time stepping to the table and eagerly accepting the plate that Millicent Graves handed him.

Batuhan missed the horrified look on the woman's face as she gaped at his mutilated face and the rest of his scars. He was too busy staring in disbelief at the food. Seemed to stagger to a table, sinking down to begin shoveling morsels into his mouth.

The bunch with the throne had made it through Raya's blockade, the duraplast chair intact.

Talina gestured to the side of the room. "Set it there. No one here's going to steal the thing."

The three on the litters were brought through next. Their bearers, placed them reverently in a row on one of the tables before taking their turn in the chow line.

As the Irredenta filed through, taking plates, attacking the food, often with fingers given their hurry, Millie asked, "Are they really cannibals?"

"They are." Talina told her. "And as soon as you're finished dishing out plates here, one of the marines is going to hustle you right back onto the shuttle."

"Won't be quick enough for me."

Seeing the last of the young men pass the door, followed by Raya's high sign, Talina stepped to the center of the room.

"Welcome to Donovan. This is Tyson Station. It will be your home from here on out. The term *Irredenta* means a culturally distinct people living under a foreign or culturally incompatible rule. You are no longer Irredenta. This is now yours. For you to rule as you see fit. Welcome home."

Scarred faces turned in her direction.

"Everything you need to survive is here. A farm, water collection and cisterns, shelter. I know you consider yourselves newly born after leaving *Ashanti*. Hold onto that thought. In terms of Donovan, you are infants cast loose in a world you don't understand and where everything will kill you."

She looked around the room, at the scarred faces, heard the crying of the infants. "First rule, no one sets foot outside barefoot. We tried to poison the slugs, but we can't be sure that we got them all. They'll burrow into your foot, divide, and eat you from the inside out.

"Second rule: No one sets foot outside the compound. If you venture into the forest, you'll be dead or dying within a half hour at most. We've left you fencing supplies out back behind the sheds. Until you put the fence up, quetzals, bems, skewers, sidewinders, and fifty other predators can wander in at will and eat you."

"How do we recognize these things?" one of the men who'd followed Batuhan asked.

"We're leaving you a holo." Talina told him. "Study it. I mean that. Your lives will depend on it. In the meantime, we've provided you with a siren for an alarm when predators are inside the compound. You have to train yourselves to immediately find shelter when there's a threat.

"Third rule: And this is the hardest one. You are in mobber territory. These are flying predators who will strip a person down to a skeleton in less than a minute. Your only defense for the time being is to get under cover. Failing that, you must fall flat and *don't* move. Mobbers may have killed the last people here more than a decade ago. Our hope is that they've forgotten that humans are prey since then."

"Just hold still?" someone called. "That's the best we can do?"

From the back of the room, Kalico called, "We can

make you a couple of cannons at Corporate Mine. Provide you with shot shells. But that will take a while."

Talina was actually relieved. The questions were the sort she'd expect from a human audience. "I mean it. Stay close to the domes for the first week or so. Organize expeditions to the farm plot. Keep your eyes open. And wear your shoes. We've brought them from *Ashanti*."

"That was an offering to the ancestors!" one of the throne bearers cried, standing and raising a fist. "Symbolic of the fact that while the immortal could no longer walk on their own, we now walk for them!"

Angry cries of assent filled the room.

"Fine." Talina threw her hands up. "Make your own damn shoes. Personally, I suggest boots." She lifted her right foot up to show them the quetzal-leather that rose to the top of her calf.

"Don't! I repeat: don't try to eat the local vegetation. It will just go through at best, but nine times out of ten, it will poison you dead. The plants here move. Stay away from them. Same with the roots, they will grab hold of you, and if they get a good grip, you're going to regret it."

"The plants move?" someone asked.

"We're leaving you a radio with the frequencies marked for Corporate Mine and Port Authority. You can contact us any time if you have questions. Both Supervisor Aguila, and I and my people, will be happy to send you what advice we have."

"We have the Prophets," a voice chimed up from the back. "They've brought us this far."

Grunts and mild applause came in response, and people turned to look at the three gaunt figures who rested on the litters. They were twitching, being spoonfed—without much success—by a couple of the younger women.

Batuhan was looking pleased, his slight smile bending the maze-patterned scars on his cheeks.

"Disregard my advice if you will, but here's the last and final rule: On Donovan, stupidity is a death sentence."

Around the room, she could see the skeptical expressions. Everyone was looking toward Batuhan or off to the side where the Prophets reposed on their litters.

As if he could sense their reliance on his reaction, Batuhan stood, spread his arms as he faced the room.

In a hollow voice he said, "The universe has brought us this far. It will not let us down now. We are the chosen, the possessors of the Revelation. We are the living dead. We are the ending and the beginning. We shall have no fear."

Whatever that meant.

Talina took a deep breath. Turned to see that Millicent had indeed departed.

Kalico stepped up beside her, saying, "I am Corporate Supervisor Kalico Aguila. I control all of Donovanian Corporate assets and—"

"You are in control of nothing," Batuhan thundered. "You are deceit, darkness, and corruption."

Applause sounded across the room.

Talina couldn't help but drop a hand to her pistol.

"Do you need anything else from me?" Kalico asked the room. "Any concerns under contract that—"

"No," Batuhan told her. "You have served the universe's purpose. For that we thank you."

Kalico's soft laugh was filled with wry irony. "Then, I take it there are no contractual issues. But I need to hear it from the room. Any of the rest of you have a claim under contract?"

"The Messiah speaks for us," one of the women declared hotly.

Kalico turned to Talina. "Then, I guess we're done here."

Talina gave the room one last thoughtful appraisal. "Welcome to Donovan."

Then she turned, following on Kalico's heels as the woman led the way from the room.

As Second Will, Vartan had command of the small detachment that watched the Supervisor's shuttle vanish off to the east; a final gleam of silver flashed as its sound faded away.

He turned, along with the rest, to stare warily around at the remarkable new world in which they found themselves. The hot sun felt like a miracle on his pale skin. How long had it been? Twenty years since he was last on Earth and had seen the sun? And then it had only been for a couple of hours total as he shuttled back and forth between classrooms. Most of his security training had been on Transluna given that his specialty was institutional security for factories, mines, processing plants, and the like.

"Smell that," Tamil Kattan said reverently. The man closed his eyes, head back, sniffing the warm air. "Never smelled nothing like that in my life."

"And listen to the sound. What is that? Like singing." Wonder filled Shimal Kastakourias's voice as the woman turned, staring out past the edge of the escarpment at the tops of the surrounding trees. Hands twitching with the early signs of prophecy, she shifted her feet, used her toes to scrape the loose dirt. "This is . . . a dream. The kind I never had before."

"What do you think, Vart?" Tamil asked. "This is, like, too good to be true. All these buildings. That farm down there. It's our own town."

Vartan squinted around in the bright light, raised a hand to shield his eyes and take in the features of Tyson Station. The domes, the weathered sheds, the solar collectors down on the point.

"It's a prison," he decided. Laughed self-derisively. "No fences, no guards, but it's still a prison."

"The universe will provide," Shimal told him. "The Prophets will guide us."

Tamil was giving him that sidelong look. "You were Corporate security. What did you make of that orientation? That sample the doctor took. All the things that Perez woman said? More Corporate lies?"

Vartan shrugged. "They want tissue samples. Tells them who's really here when they check it against the *Ashanti* records. As to Perez, she was telling the truth. There are dangers here. Why wouldn't there be? It's wilderness, yes? And we all know that guy, Donovan, was killed on this rock way back when."

"The universe will see us through." Shimal repeated the familiar mantra. And, maybe it would. It had gotten them this far.

Even as Vartan tried to absorb his surroundings, the doors from the admin dome opened to spew children, all of them whooping and running on their skinny little legs.

They were staring around as they jumped, pointing up at the sun, shielding their eyes. Some were so recently Initiated that their preliminary scars were still pink lines. Pho was in the back, having just lost the last of his scabs.

Didn't take long, the gravity being what it was, for the exuberant dancing to taper off. It was replaced by wide-eyed exploration as the children fanned out about the complex, looking at this and that. Given that they'd never seen dirt, a sky, or even a plant, they were rapt.

Somebody ought to be keeping an eye on them, Vartan thought as he turned his steps for the admin dome.

Not his job. Petre had assigned him to ensure that Aguila had really left them alone. His next responsibility was a reconnaissance of the domes in order to develop a plan for their security.

Stepping inside, he made his way to the cafeteria, the smell of the food still lingering in the air. Damn! But that had been the most marvelous meal he'd ever eaten. Turned out he'd missed taste, had missed color, and open air, and . . . Well, so much.

His muscles, atrophied from all those years, pulled, and his lower back could feel the strain, but he made his way to the cafeteria, joining the group around the Messiah.

"Second Will, report?"

He nodded respectfully to the Messiah. "She's gone. Disappeared into the east."

"You were trained in security," the Messiah noted, his eyes straying back toward the kitchen with a certain longing. Hell, they were all hungry. "What do you suggest we do next, Second Will?"

"Messiah, first thing, my task is to conduct a complete inspection of this place. Determine the lay of the land. Start an inventory of the station's resources. We've got most of a day. We need to be organized by nightfall. The rest of the Will should assign lodging and duties. And someone has to be detailed to begin the next meal. I see that there are crates of provisions back there."

"First Will?" The Messiah turned to Petre, "Can you do that?"

"Of course," Petre bowed his white-haired head, the ponytail bobbing.

"See to your reconnaissance." The Messiah turned back to Vartan. "Take a small group. I think there's a map back in that pile on the rear table."

"Messiah," Vartan added. "The children . . ."

"Yes?"

"They're running around outside. Unsupervised."

"I have the women and young men attending to the placement of our belongings. If you think that's a problem, detail Shyanne and Marta to keep track of them and make sure they're safe."

Vartan nodded and turned to leave.

"Second Will?" the Messiah called.

Vartan turned back, squirmed as that blue eye in the Messiah's forehead seemed to bore into his soul.

"What do you make of this warning the Supervisor and that Perez woman gave us?"

"I think we should heed each and every one until we can separate the lies from reality here."

The Messiah puckered his black-painted lips, sucked at them for a moment, and nodded. "I agree. While the universe has indeed brought us this far, it doesn't expect us to be fools. Develop whatever security protocols you think necessary."

Vartan fixed on Petre. "You and I should put our heads together and—"

"Deal with Tikal on that. I'm afraid the First Will and his picked team have other priorities," the Messiah said, an absent look in his dark eyes. "He's going to be arranging for our next meeting with the Supervisor. You saw the scars on the woman? That's a sign, a warning from the universe itself. Worry about the wildlife and plants, yes, but ultimately, she might very well turn out to be the death of us."

Vartan kept his expression neutral. Bowed his head again. "Of course, Messiah."

"To defeat her, we must first reassure her. She must believe that we are not a threat. I need Shimal, who understands these things, to cause a malfunction in the solar panels. Something easy to fix that will require the Supervisor to send a party out. One that we can convince that we are humble, grateful, and thankful for our new home."

"Of course, Messiah," Vartan told the man. "I'll see to it immediately."

But as he walked off, he glanced back at the piles of boxes Aguila had left for them. Aguila might be the long-term threat, but he worried about the I'm-not-giving-you-shit tone in Talina Perez's voice as she talked about the dangers surrounding them.

Seemed to Vartan that they'd be better off figuring out how to deal with Tyson's dangers before going to war with Kalico Aguila and the rest of the planet.

Where the Prophets lay on their litters in the back, being tended to by the Chosen, Callista cried out, "Whaaa . . . whaaa . . . shoot."

Watch out?

At the door he shot a look back at the Messiah. *Hope you're right about all of this.*

24

"**N**ever figured I'd see the like of those people." Mark Talbot perched on his chair with a knee up as the Corporate shuttle arced above the clouds where they packed against the eastern side of the Wind Mountains. He glanced over to where Talina and Kalico sat in the row of seats behind the pilot.

Aguila said, "The human brain has given us the keys to the universe, allowed us to travel across thirty light-years, banish all but a tiny number of diseases, colonize distant worlds, and control the laws of physics. Can those human beings really be related to us?"

"The religious mind," Talina mused, gaze unfocused. "It operates on faith. They choose to *believe* the universe has chosen them. They have *faith* it will protect them for its own purposes."

Talbot rapped his fingers on his knee. "This is Donovan. Sometimes I think even the most basic laws of the universe don't apply here. So what's going to happen the first time they figure out that nothing's working the way the Prophets want? And what's with them, anyway? Looked to me like they're spastic."

At that moment, Raya Turnienko leaned in the hatch. Her round face was thoughtful. "Supervisor? Are you in a hurry to get back to Corporate Mine this afternoon?"

"Yeah, one of the first things unloaded from *Ashanti* were a pair of Semex 81-B roto mills. Brand new. We can replace our old, broken-down jury-rigged mucking machines. And besides, Talovich has half of my people building shoring in the Number Three."

The Number Three had seemed like a good idea. Tunnel in from the bottom of the mountain, then the ore could be rolled downhill on tracks all the way to the smelter. What no one had counted on was the shattered rock zone they'd hit about two hundred meters into the adit. The impact-shocked rock was rich with exotic metals, but so unstable as to come tumbling down if it was disturbed by so much as a loud sneeze.

"What have you got, Raya?" Talina asked.

"Preliminary data on the Irredenta. I won't know for certain until I can run some of these data through the lab. Especially their so-called Prophets."

"Anything you can share with us now?"

"Outside of anemia, vitamin deficiency, malnutrition, and atrophy? No. But once we're back in PA, I've got some serious research ahead of me."

"You look pretty grim," Talina noted.

Raya arched her thin eyebrows. "Yeah, they've got the dead inside them. No doubt about it. The problem is, if I'm right, the dead aren't happily going along for the ride."

"Zombies?" Talbot asked, making a face.

Raya didn't rise to the bait. "Actually, pending results of the tests, this could be a whole lot worse. I'll know in a couple of days." She glanced at Kalico. "Want to be there when I figure this out? They are your people, after all."

"Sure."

And then Raya ducked back through the hatch, her concentration locked on her handheld monitor.

25

On the monitor, Miguel Galluzzi watched as the last of the containers dropped into Donovan's atmosphere. In the telemetry, the rectangular box began to tumble, the corners glowing from dull red to orange to fiery as the duraplast heated.

Like the others that had preceded it, they'd accelerated the container, shot it out so that Donovan's gravity would increase its speed for maximum effect when it hit atmosphere. The tumbling container glowed now, streaking through the planet's upper skies, leaving a trail behind.

Didn't take long. Given the velocity, friction disintegrated the container's sides, spilling the contents into the fire. The combustibles, things like clothing, bedding, woods, and plastics, immediately flared into ash. The metals, sialon, and glass all lasted a little longer, tiny streaks of light as they incinerated. The bigger items, furniture and the like, splintered off from the main mass, trailing fire into oblivion.

And then it was gone. Only vapors and tiny particles marking the path of the Unreconciled's last belongings.

Far beneath, dotted with patterns of white cloud, Donovan's ocean gleamed in serene blue, Capella's light adding a golden sheen along the planet's curve.

Galluzzi sighed, turned, and strode down the hallway to the Deck Three hatch. He'd had the crew working in hazard suits as they packed everything loose into sacks. The room fixtures, beds, furniture, the kitchen wares, the tables and chairs, anything that wasn't structurally attached to *Ashanti,* had been packed into the containers. Then, one by one they'd been jettisoned to burn up in Donovan's atmosphere. A symbolic final resting place for anything having to do with the Unreconciled.

At the hatch, Galluzzi pulled on his hazard suit, flipped down the hood, and sealed it. Then he palmed the hatch. As it slid open, billowing gusts of steam and cleanser rolled out.

Stepping inside, Galluzzi sealed the hatch behind him, staring through the clouds of cleanser. The air here was toxic, filled with chemicals, soot, particles, and hot enough to sear a man's lungs, should he inhale.

But along with the Unreconciled's trash and belongings, the filth was gone. The macabre art had been blasted off the walls, partitions had been removed, every surface scoured of as much as five millimeters of material. A combination of fire, chemical, and abrasive had stripped *Ashanti* of every last vestige of the horror that had thrived here.

It is gone from everywhere but my memory.

That, Galluzzi couldn't scour.

As he looked around at the snaking hoses, the pressure machines, and blowtorches, he wondered what The Corporation was going to say about his modifications to Deck Three. Assuming he ever made it home.

Not that it mattered. That was then. This was now. He and the crew wanted every last trace removed. Even the notion of trying to space *Ashanti* with the reminder of Deck Three had been too horrifying to countenance.

Turner, in his trademark hazard suit with a yellow duck emblem on the chest, appeared out of the infernal fog. "Last one burn up?"

"It did. Just like the others. Whatever's left can float down on Donovan now. Food for their fishes."

"Wonder if they even have fishes. Guess Michaela's team will find out."

"Do I hear regret in your voice?"

"Cap, do you believe in temporary insanity?"

Galluzzi waved a gloved hand at the surroundings. "You ask me that? Here? Given what we're doing to the ship?"

Turner's expression through the transparency communicated a wry humor. "I'm thinking that when it came to Michaela, I'm going to be spending a lot of the rest of my life thinking I was an idiot to let that one get away."

"Might not be too late."

Turner's shrug was masked by his bulky suit. He turned

away, saying, "Come on. Let me show you what we've done."

The finer details were masked by the noxious atmosphere, but for Galluzzi, he might have been on another ship. Dark, dingy, Deck Three was transformed. With all the light panels in, most of the walls removed, the kitchen-cafeteria and rec room as one large open space. The cabins and barracks were scoured; the entire deck was foreign, new, pristine.

Galluzzi even liked the rounded effect. The cleansing hadn't left a single sharp corner to be found. The place had a melted look, creamy and open.

"What do you think?" Galluzzi asked.

"It's a miracle," Turner told him. "Got a question: You sleeping better, Cap?"

Galluzzi paused, surprised when he said, "I am. What makes you ask?"

"Crew was talking about it. How the nightmares have been going away. It's like with each day's work, the more we clean down here, the better we're doing. Like a weight lifted off. A terror that's now becoming a really bad memory. Like we're never going to be the same again, but we're all going to make it."

"Yeah, I hear you." Sure. Easy for Turner to say.

Galluzzi stared around through the swirling mist. *Ashanti* was cleared of the physical reminders of the Unreconciled. They were all feeling better, but it wouldn't last. The things that had happened here, the things Miguel Galluzzi was responsible for, those haunting memories would cling to him like the albatross of legend.

Ultimately, *Ashanti* might be cleansed of the corruption, but looking around at the scoured surfaces, it was to see the scar. A scar might be healed tissue, but it also served as an enduring reminder.

Like my ship, I will never outrun my shame.

26

Mark Talbot couldn't believe it. It hadn't been twenty-four hours and he was on his way back to Tyson Station. All he'd had in between was a pleasant evening with his family—a rare night when his two wives, Dya and Su, along with the kids, had been home at the same time. After dealing with the Unreconciled, the evening had been a reminder of the blessings that had befallen him. To be part of a family, to have women who loved him, children to be proud of.

Sure, they had suffered tragedy enough on Donovan, but with the exception of Kylee, they'd come through it. Adjusted. Dya's skills had earned her a valued position as one of the preeminent researchers on Donovan. Her insight into the biology was going to revolutionize humanity's chances for success on the planet. Su was reworking the PA computer systems, her coding abilities allowing for increased data manipulation in the town's single quantum cubit computer.

The kids had finally integrated into the local academy, a transition made somehow easier because Dan Wirth had built a new school. As though everyone moving into the new building had leveled the playing field, hadn't left the Mundo kids feeling as much like outsiders.

Talbot had sprawled on the couch, watching as Damien, Sullee, Tuska, and Taung had led the rest of the children in a game of snap. He'd had one arm around Dya, the other tucking Su close.

This, he had thought, *is the meaning of existence.*

That lingering knowledge had made his lovemaking with Su even more tender and fulfilling than usual—though he had slept that night with nightmares of the Unreconciled, recoiling from tortured dreams in which they stalked his children from the shadows, their eyes burning red in intricately scarred faces.

And what do I wake up to this morning?

Two Spot had called on the com. *"Mark? We've got a plea from Tyson. Something's wrong with the solar generators out there. They're losing their electricity. Kalico wondered if you could take Sheyela Smith out with a squad of armored marines and see what's wrong?"*

So here he was, at the wheel of one of the new airtrucks, scooting along some thousand feet above the rumpled and mounded carpet of forest. Tyson Station was just ahead, a flat mesa jutting out from the broken and tumbled hills that marked the old volcano. He could see the white dots of the domes, the paler green of the agricultural fields to their south. And there, on the point, were the culprit solar collectors.

"All right, people, gear up."

Behind him, privates Paco Anderssoni, Dina Michegan, Wan Xi, Russ Tanner, and Briah Muldare strapped into their combat armor. The sound of the armor clicking into place was like music to Talbot's ears. He could hear the hum of the servos as his former team checked their systems. The *slick-slick* of weapons check meant that rounds were being chambered.

In the rear, Sheyela Smith, a woman in her thirties, called, "Whatever you do, don't let the freaks eat me."

"You're our electrical guru," Dina Michegan told her. "Didn't even need to hear it from the Supervisor. We'll level that shit-sucking station before we let them harm a hair on your head."

"Indispensable," Wan Xi agreed, a smile on his mobber-scarred face.

"Yeah," Muldare agreed. "Second only to Inga, but that's only 'cause while you can keep electrical shit running, you can't brew a keg of IPA that wouldn't gag a slug."

"Hey, guys," Talbot warned, "Kalico wants us to go in, fix the solar, and get the hell out without an incident. Job one is to keep Sheyela safe. Job two is to fix the electricity. Job three is to get out without an incident. In armor, with non-lethal tech, that shouldn't be an impossible mission."

"Yeah, Mark," Anderssoni replied. "Who do you think you're talking to? After all the shit we been through, you're not going to find a tighter squad in the Corps."

Mark turned, grinned, and slapped hands with Anderssoni. Donovan had honed them, shaped them, and compressed them. Cap Taggart, Deb Spiro, and Kalen Tompzen had torn them apart and Donovan glued them back together. What was left of the original twenty marines were closer than family.

God help the Unreconciled if this were a trap.

Mark wheeled the airtruck around, wishing he had the A-7 with Makarov at the helm, but the big bird was in orbit, tied to *Ashanti* for a refit.

He cocked his head, seeing people as he circled the compound. They were all outside, clustered before the domes, waving.

"Looks friendly enough," Muldare noted as she peered down.

"Don't see any weapons," Wan Xi agreed. "Hell, they're half dressed."

"Let's go down and see," Mark told them. "Helmets on, kiddies. Sheyela, the marines will jump down first, form a box. You and I will climb down after them. They'll proceed in a diamond formation to the solar collectors. You and I stay in the middle while the marines use their tech to keep eyes on the man-eaters. Russ?"

"Yo!"

"You're in charge of the airtruck. Keep it secure. We might have to beat feet out of here, so do what you have to. And, Russ, as soon as we hit the dirt, get some drones in the air to keep an eye on things."

"Roger that, Mark."

Talbot set them down on the landing pad, powered down the fans, and asked, "Ready?"

"Yut yut!" came the call from the marines as they opened the door and began dropping to the ground outside.

Talbot climbed down, took Sheyela's toolbox, and helped her to the ground. The Unreconciled were crowding around just beyond the marines, waving, calling excitedly.

"It's just women and kids," Anderssoni muttered.

"Fuck me," Michegan growled uneasily. "I'll never get over those scars. Who'd do that to themselves?"

The crowd parted, a man and woman walking through the press. The man was white-haired, a long ponytail hanging down his back. The scars gave his thin face a pinched look. The woman was tall, maybe late thirties, intricately scarred. Both were naked to the waist, and to Mark's curious relief, they were both wearing shoes.

"I am First Will Petre Jordan," the man introduced. Indicating the woman, he added, "This is Second Wife Svetlana Pushkin."

"Call me Svetlana," the woman added with a smile. "The formal titles really are a bit over the top. On behalf of the Messiah, we want to thank you for coming at such short notice." She glanced askance at the marines in their gleaming armor, rifles at port arms. "The guns and soldiers won't be needed. It's just an electrical problem. Probably something simple. But we don't have anyone left who can fix it."

"The marines are just a formality," Mark told her with a smile. "If you could tell us what the problem is?"

Again, it was Svetlana who extended an arm. "Something down at the collectors. If you'd come this way?"

To the people she added, "I know you all want to talk to the newcomers, and you have a thousand questions, but please, stay back. Maybe, when some of the suspicion has been allayed, we can truly welcome these people to our homes."

Mark felt that warning bell go off. After Batuhan and the first impressions, this was just a little too good to be true.

Nevertheless, Svetlana and Petre started south, leading the way.

"Screw me with a skewer," Sheyela whispered. "So that's a cannibal?"

"Shhh." Mark waved her down.

Svetlana had dropped back, seemed nonchalant as she matched Mark's pace, apparently unconcerned about Muldare artfully staying between them. "So, you're Mark Talbot, right?"

"Yeah. I'm security second for Port Authority."

"I saw you when the Supervisor brought us down. We would have liked to have talked then, gotten to know you all, but you've got to understand, we were scared. After what had been done to us on that ship, we didn't know what to expect."

"Welcome to Donovan."

"Yeah," she shot him a grin. "This is like a paradise."

"One that will kill you before you know you're dead."

"Oh, we're taking precautions."

"Half those women and kids following us are barefoot."

"Mark, you've got to understand, we're still trying to cope. Those kids have never had shoes. Didn't need them in Deck Three. What we endured? Well, it's going to take a while to come to terms with it. We've barely survived a holocaust. Probably be a while before we're normal again."

Amen to that. Aloud Mark said, "We'll do whatever we can to help. Get you a start, at least. I lived on a station like this one down to the south. Everything you need is here. Use the radio. Call if you have questions."

She indicated the marines who tromped along in their armor. "Listen, combat-ready soldiers don't exactly send a reassuring message to our people. I know where the Supervisor is coming from, and I can only guess what that shit-sucker Galluzzi has told you. But if you'd give us a chance . . . well, maybe today can be a first step. You follow what I'm saying?"

"Sure. Just let us get your electricity fixed, and we'll call it a win all the way around."

She shot him a warm smile. "Then we'll consider this the first step. What do you need from us? How can we help?"

"Just let us do our job."

Svetlana crossed her arms under her small breasts and frowned as they passed the agricultural fields. "It won't be easy for us. We're not in the habit of trusting strangers. Any consideration you could show would be helpful."

"One step at a time." He knew the marines were monitoring their tech. Into his com, he asked, "Russ? What do your eyes in the skies see?"

"Not a thing, Mark. You're definitely the center of atten-tion, but it's just a bunch of women and kids, most of the men are working in the fields, harvesting crops. Nothing that looks like a weapon anywhere. Looks to me like they're good."

It took Sheyela five minutes to bypass a fried circuit board. As she closed and latched the access door, she said, "Looks like, old as it is, it just couldn't take the load. They'll be good to go."

As they started back, Mark's com announced, *"Mark? The men from the fields are headed in my direction bearing baskets."*

To Svetlana, he said, "My marine tells me that a bunch of the men are headed for the airtruck."

"Good," she answered. "It's the only thing we could think of."

"Think of what?"

"Fresh food. It may not be that noteworthy or valuable to you, but after years of ration, it's the most valuable thing we have to offer as a way to express our appreciation for your kind help."

Five minutes later, as he piloted the airtruck up from the landing pad, Talbot wondered what had just happened. Behind him, the marines crowded around baskets of green beans.

And yes, he understood the symbolic offering it represented.

So much for salivating cannibals.

Maybe they'd been overreacting to the threat from the beginning?

Vartan stepped up beside Svetlana and Petre as the airtruck sped its way eastward. The sound of its passing had long since faded. Now it was but a dot in the distance, barely visible against the clouds. Then it vanished.

"Well, what do you think?" Vartan asked.

Svetlana shrugged, rubbing nervous hands up and down the scars on her arms. "We could have been more convincing if the marines hadn't been wearing that armor. Talbot was skeptical right up until we gave them those baskets of food."

"That almost broke my heart," Petre said with a sigh. "My mouth watered at the sight. I kept thinking what that lot would have tasted like broiled over a grill."

"You did well," Vartan told Svetlana. "Me, I've never been good at lying. Too much honesty in me, I guess."

"It's not like a lie, Vart," Petre told him. "That's the enemy. Deceivers. We owe them nothing but destruction."

27

The small conference room midway down the hall in the Port Authority hospital was packed. Kalico Aguila sat in the chair just back from the door. Across from her, Talina Perez was listening to something in her head. Given her expression, it must have been Demon. The woman's eyes had that penetrating, almost alien look that reeked of quetzal.

Dya Simonov was using her implants to scroll through a complicated holographic display Kalico couldn't quite make out given her angle at the table.

And in the chair beside her, Lee Cheng was fiddling with some sort of protein that was projected in the air before him. He kept using his fingers to flip the projection this way and that as if studying the protein's geometry.

Mgumbe, Cheng's assistant, sat back in his chair, his fingers crossed. A pensive expression gave his face a sagacious quality. Beside him, Iji Hiro, the Port Authority botanist, was doodling on his tablet.

Raya Turnienko came bursting into the room in a long-legged stride, her lab coat flapping behind. She abruptly pulled out a chair and dropped into it. For all the haste of her entry, she sat for a moment, staring as if at some distance beyond her mental horizon.

"What have you got, Raya?" Dya asked, breaking the woman's almost trancelike stare.

Kalico shifted, curious as to what Raya's big mystery might be. It wasn't like it was a secret that the Unreconciled were cannibals—as tough as that was to comprehend in the twenty-second century.

"Cheng," Raya said, "could you turn the display so that everyone can see it, please?"

He did, and Kalico got a good look at something that resembled a warped oval that had been bent out of shape. At the same time, Cheng said, "Is this it?"

"It is."

Cheng blinked. "No pus-sucking way!"

"Way," Raya replied flatly.

Talina, beating Kalico to the punch, said, "Fascinating conversation. Mind cluing the rest of us in?"

"Kuru," Raya said without emotion. "A disease that vanished in the early twenty-first century. What you are looking at is called a prion. Specifically PrP^{sc}, a misfolded protein that causes a form of transmissible spongiform encephalitis. It's similar to Creutzfeldt-Jakob disease, though kuru has a slightly different etiology. In this case, transmission of the disease is via the consumption of infected tissues found in the human central nervous system. Particularly the brain. Though it can also be found in other bodily fluids."

"Where did they get it?" Talina asked. "I mean, who passed it through screening back in Transluna?"

"Maybe no one," Cheng said with a shrug. "Could just be a chance folding of the protein."

Mgumbe grunted, said, "If they even screen for prions. It's not like a whole host of cannibals are applying to The Corporation for space travel. It should have been extinct."

Raya added, "Even if the prion was present in one of the transportees when he or she boarded *Ashanti,* most people have a genetic resistance against kuru. Paleoanthropologists have proven that our evolution is rife with anthropophagy. That's the fancy word for people eating other people. Like for the last two million years. No matter how hallowed you think your ancestors were, go back far enough, and someone was chowing down on his or her fellow man."

"You're joking," Kalico said.

"Not at all. According to the anthropological literature, cannibalism served four different functions: survival, ritual, political, and pathological.

"Survival speaks for itself: A dead body represents a lot of calories to a starving person. Ritual? As with the Fore people where kuru was first identified, they ate their dead ancestors as a sign of respect. Political cannibalism is what we see in places like the prehistoric American Southwest. There, if you rebelled against the rulers, they'd eat your family in front of you. And, finally, there's pathological, like the psychiatrically disordered who kill, dismember, and eat their friends or lovers. The Unreconciled seem to have incorporated all four functions at once."

Dya said, "Let's get back to the initial infection and why it wasn't detected back at Solar System. Where did this come from?"

Raya cleared her throat. "So whoever the original patient was, he or she might have lived a normal life. Never known the prion was in their system. When he or she died, the disease would have dead-ended.

"But there are two mutations on the 129th location on the PrP gene; if they turn up homozygous recessive, and the individual is exposed to the prion, they will develop the disease."

"How contagious is this?" Talina looked grim, thinking no doubt of her time in contact with the Irredenta.

"You don't want to handle any brain or body tissue from the infected. You don't want to expose yourself to sores on their bodies. Nor do you want to stick yourself with anything contaminated by their blood or body parts. Oh, and if I were you, I'd be very careful if I got a lunch invite from the Irredenta." Raya was back to staring at infinity.

"What about the *Ashanti* crew?" Kalico asked. "Are they in danger?"

Raya said, "Only if they ate infected Irredenta. The standard precautions taken in hydroponics would have been sufficient to protect them."

Dya ran fingers through her blonde locks. "I'll send Galluzzi's people an update. Ensure they take the appropriate measures as they sterilize Deck Three. As to hydroponics, the systems are designed to denature proteins down to their constituent amino acids. The design ensures that microviruses are rendered incapable of transmission, which should similarly denature prions. But be aware, prions are durable, long-lasting, and resistant to most simple sterilizations."

"How do we cure this?" Talina asked. "Some vaccine?"

"You don't," Raya told her. "You saw their prophets. Those must have been the first cases. Their dementia is so advanced they've lost motor control. Remember how they were being fed? The trouble they were having eating? That's because they can't swallow. Their brains are full of lesions, holes, that will kill them within a month, I'd say."

"And their prophecies?" Talina asked.

"The ravings of dementia," Raya told her. "The slurred speech and disjointed words. Mumblings, jumbled utterances. Sometimes they'll break out in laughter, other times, tears. Not the first time in human history that the demented were believed to be oracles, or to have a direct line to God, or whatever."

Raya then added, "And there are others who are in the initial stages. Go back to the holo of the Irredenta leaving *Ashanti*. The ones lacking coordination? The trembling? The ones with odd facial expressions? Those are the early stages. Along with slurred speech. The patient has trouble with basic motor function."

"Slurred speech?" Kalico mused. "Remember that eerie song they were singing?" She paused, putting it together. "I thought it was so odd that they'd pick a chant that mimicked being drunk or drugged. That they'd sing something like that with such enthusiasm. Bet it was one of the prophets who sang it first."

Cheng, always the hard scientist, muttered, "Wait a minute. I mean, sure, things were pretty grim on Deck Three. But we're supposed to believe that when these prophets started going crazy, saying demented things, that all the rest of the survivors just bought into it? I mean, there had to be somebody sane who said, 'Wait a minute, this isn't divine revelation, these guys are going claptrapping insane.'"

"I wouldn't doubt but you're right." Talina was squinting, as if picturing it in her head. "But it's a traumatized population looking for answers. Wouldn't surprise me if good old Batuhan himself wasn't the one to sidle up behind the naysayers and whack them in the head. Probably noted the event by saying, 'And such are the wages of disbelief.'"

"Believe or die?" Mgumbe rubbed his jaw.

"Religion has always flourished as a means of maintaining group identification, solidarity, and harmony." Raya was staring at the prion holo where the oval-shaped protein was displayed, the fold running through its middle.

Kalico asked, "What happens when we tell them it's a prion disease and not divine revelation? These are educated people, professionals, the kind who understand cause and effect in the physical world. It's not like being Unreconciled is the only reality they've ever known. Surely we can appeal to the sane and intelligent among them to give up this crazy belief that they're going to devour and thereby cleanse the universe."

Dya had been thoughtful, tapping her fingers on the tabletop. Now she said, "I suspect you're right. Most of them probably had that underlying skepticism all along. Probably went along with the belief. As long as they were locked away on Deck Three, they were surrounded by reinforcement. What other reality was there?"

Dya lifted a finger. "But say that we show up, having done genetic scans from the samples we took as they got off the shuttle. We tell them: 'These people will develop kuru and die of dementia. The rest of you are immune to the prion. There is no divine revelation. It's just a simple illness.'" She paused. "What happens next?"

"They realize that they've been duped." Cheng shrugged. "Go back to being normal people again. Problem solved."

"Hardly," Dya shot back. She glanced around the table. "They murdered, dismembered, and ate their fellow transportees. These were people they'd known intimately over the years that they were in transit. They committed acts of repulsive abomination. Scarified their bodies. And did you notice? Every woman is either pregnant or breastfeeding a newborn. And, reviewing the preliminary genetics, about half of the children are sired by Batuhan and—with a few exceptions—his four lieutenants."

"So you're saying Batuhan and his Chosen have preferred sexual access to the females?" Cheng leaned forward and frowned.

Dya fixed him with hard blue eyes. "I'm saying that there's no 'normal' for any of these people. Sure, the sane among them are going to understand that what comes out of the prophets' mouths is demented babble. What does that do to their feelings of guilt when they realize it wasn't divine revelation, wasn't the universe telling them it was all right to murder and eat people? Wasn't God telling them to scarify their skin, or to surrender their bodies to Batuhan to sire his children? It was just a disease. Sorry."

"So what do we do about it?" Talina asked.

Kalico rubbed her eyes, a growing sense of distaste down in her gut. "We tell them the truth."

"That might split those people right down the middle," Raya warned. "It's not like they're novices when it comes to murdering each other."

"Can we offer them anything?" Mgumbe asked. "Maybe a chance to relocate the nonbelievers?"

"Put them where?" Talina asked. "Three Falls? Wide Ridge? Rork Springs?"

Dya had turned introspective. "Interesting moral question, isn't it? What do we, as the surviving humans on the planet, owe these people?"

Raya leaned back in her chair. "Someone's going to have to go give the Irredenta the bad news."

"Want to draw straws?" Mgumbe asked.

28

Working outside on the farm, out past the fence, felt like a tonic. The heat from Capella's rays was in the process of baking Dek Taglioni's hide. He'd peeled off his thin jacket and was down to an undershirt. Not only that, but he'd drunk four liters of water from the jar Reuben Miranda had provided.

Nor was the heat his only problem. Every muscle in his body was aching and his joints were creaking. The gravity was sapping every bit of reserve, but he was feeling better. Toughening up by the day.

Nevertheless, he kept shooting glances at the bush, that aqua-and-green-colored band of scrubby trees and low vegetation beyond the edge of the fields. The sensation was eerie, the kind a person got when hidden eyes were watching him. Judging his every action and thought.

Get over it. It's just trees and wilderness. There's no sentience behind it. Donovan's only a planet. Not a consciousness.

"Yeah, right," he whispered under his breath and forced himself back to the task of picking peppers.

The quetzal-hide boots Reuben had loaned him shot rainbows of color along their length with each step he took. He looked like a vagabond, wearing the light claw-shrub-textile pants of local manufacture. A wide-brimmed fiber hat topped his head. And on his hip now rode his Smith & Wesson 3-41 electro-rail pistol. An expensive, engraved, and elegant weapon made with sculpted grips carved from finely figured black walnut. Gold inlay gleamed along the three rails and in the scrollwork on the receiver.

So now, not only did he look like a pirate, he felt like one, too.

Pirate he might be. Nevertheless, he'd picked five whole baskets of peppers and was almost finished with a sixth.

Something about that filled him with an incredible sense of purpose.

This wasn't just work, it was food. Until *Ashanti* had found itself in trouble, he'd never given a second thought to what he ate. Food was just there, ready, whatever he wanted to order, prepared in any way he desired, and provided for his gustatory pleasure. No limits. Not on variety. Not on quantity. Nor had he ever so much as wondered where it came from. How it was produced.

That had all changed when Galluzzi ordered rations cut. When Derek Taglioni had gone to bed hungry. When he'd laid, night after night, tortured by the craving in his belly. Knowing it wouldn't be filled. Not tomorrow. Not the next day, or the day after. He had lived with the knowledge that hydroponics couldn't continue to feed the number of people they had on board. That when the tanks finally broke down far enough, he and everyone around him would starve to death. Didn't matter that he was Derek Taglioni. He was just as condemned as the lowliest ship's tech.

His relationship with food had been forever altered.

Panting in the heat, he blinked sweat from his eyes and reached down to pluck another couple of jalapeño peppers from the bush. These he dropped into the basket Reuben had provided. Feeling crafty, he slipped over to the poblano plant and used his little knife to cut the stems on two large green peppers. They brought his basket up to the brim.

All it would take was another . . .

"Dek?" An irritated call carried over the chime.

He straightened from the row of green plants, seeing Talina Perez as she came striding across the field at a no-nonsense pace. The woman was dressed in a black chamois-hide one-piece that was most likely supposed to be utilitarian but conformed her curves in a most enticing way. Still, there was nothing feminine about the utility belt with its pistol and knife, or the service rifle hung from her shoulder.

He pulled the wide-brimmed straw hat from his head and wiped sweat from his face with a sleeve. Reuben looked up from where he was plucking beans. "Hey, Tal!"

He threw the woman a lazy wave. "You didn't need to come out. I'd 'ave had one of the kids drop off the latest at your dome."

"I'm not here for beans, Reuben." She stopped before Dek, gave him a distasteful appraisal, and then shot Reuben a sidelong squint. "Dek here isn't supposed to leave the compound. You know better than to bring soft meat out past the fence."

Reuben's expression bent into an amused quirk. "Since when are you getting between me and my hired labor? The man asked me for a job."

"And what are you paying him?"

"A tenth part of whatever he picks."

"He's soft meat. And not the kind we can let get eaten by a slug. The guy doesn't know a bem from a toilet plunger."

Dek crossed his arms, feeling that old irritation raising its ugly head. "Hey, I'm right here. That's right. Look me in the eyes. Now, what's the trouble?"

"Do you know the repercussions if something happened to you?"

"I'm not an ornament."

"You're a Taglioni."

"Congratulations. You've read the passenger manifest on *Ashanti*." He raised a hand, cutting off the response that was bubbling up on her lips. "Stop it! That's an order." Turned out he could still summon that old brook-no-nonsense tone of voice.

To Reuben he said, "Thanks for the chance to get outside. If you don't mind, the security officer and I have to clear some things up."

"Yeah, Dek. Take that last basket. We're square." To Talina, Reuben said, "Cut the man a little slack, Tal. He's got grit."

Dek picked up his basket, adding, "I'll get the boots back to you."

"No, you keep them. You're gonna need 'em, and they're too small for my feet as it is."

Tucking his basket of peppers under his arm, Dek started through the rows of crops, Talina matching stride.

"Look at this," he told her, patting the basket. "Aboard

Ashanti I could trade this to someone for a whole month's work scrubbing hydroponics."

She ignored him, snapping, "Do you have a death wish?"

"Not on me right at this moment, but if you're in desperate need of one, you might try the Unreconciled."

"Hey, don't fuck with me!"

"That makes two of us." He shot her a look of warning. "Yes. I got the message the first time Supervisor Aguila gave it to me: Donovan is dangerous. It'll kill me, and I don't have the first clue about what to look out for. So I asked around. With the exception of the Wild Ones and some of the security folks, the farmers know best how to stay alive. They live on *this* side of the fence. And among the farmers, the best are Miranda and Sczui. Some folks said Terry and Sasha Miska, too. I ran into Reuben first. Good man. Said he'd trade a part of the harvest for the labor."

"Yeah, they're good and solid. All of the farmers are." He could hear a little give in her voice. "Well, at least you're armed. You know how to use that thing?"

"I have an implant. Spent a lot of time at the range. Same with the rifle."

"An implant and range time. I am *so* reassured." The sarcasm in her voice was heavy enough to sink a ship.

"Talina, here are the facts: Transluna and Solar System are thirty light-years away. As incomprehensible as it might be for anyone back home to even conceive, on Donovan being a Taglioni—along with a one siddar coin—will get me a beer at Inga's." He lifted his basket of peppers. "This might get me supper and breakfast along with a beer. For the time being, it's all I've got."

She was watching him sidelong through her alien-dark eyes. Walked quietly for a time. Then asked, "What do you want, Dek?"

He stopped, turned, and pointed to the bush where it lay beyond the verdant fields. The aquajade and thornbush were shimmering in the mirage. "I want to learn the things I need to know in order to go out there."

"Why?"

"Because I have to. You see, when I ordered my name

added to *Ashanti*'s manifest, I was coming here to show Miko and the rest of the family that I was a man to be reckoned with. When things got bad on *Ashanti*, when I realized I was going to die, I wanted to die with the knowledge that I'd done everything I could to keep the ship and crew alive. Now that we're here, I want to know and savor Donovan."

"I'm not sure that anyone can 'savor' Donovan. It has its own agenda." A pause. "You know why Aguila has all those scars?"

"Said it was mobbers."

"But for a handy crate, they'd have stripped her down to a skeleton before anyone could have saved her. And that was inside her compound, surrounded by her people, behind her fence. The point I'm trying to make is that Donovan kills nine out of ten people who come here. You ready to accept those kinds of odds?"

Dek shifted his basket. "I am."

"You might talk to Mark Talbot, ask him about the way people die on Donovan. What it's like to be eaten alive from the inside or digested over a couple of months as a nightmare's tentacles wiggle their way through your guts. Nothing about death on Donovan is glorious or noble."

"Who's Briggs?"

That got a start out of her. "Well, that might be Chaco or Madison, or their boy, Flip. He's eighteen, just finishing his studies in minerology and chemistry here in town. Wants to go to work for Kalico down at Corporate Mine. Where did you hear of them?"

"Over a beer. Heard about a lot of people, Wild Ones, who live in the bush. Makes me think they know something the rest of us don't. Like maybe I could go and learn what they know."

"And what would you do with this stuff you'd learn?"

"I'm not sure yet." He glanced back at the distant bush. "But here's the thing: Do you think I'm bonked out if I tell you that I can feel it? Like some sort of summons?" He gestured off toward the west. "It's out there, like a siren's call. I really need to go find it."

She took a deep breath, slowly shook her head. "What is it about me and men who hear Donovan calling?"

"So, there have been others?"

"Yeah."

"Can I talk to them?"

"They're all dead."

THE TERROR

Terror is nothing new. I have known it before, during the Harrowing and Cleansing. In those days I feared my fellows. Lived with the constant knowledge that with even a small shift in alliances, I'd be the next meal. We all spent our days that way. A shared anxiety that made it impossible to sleep. Hard to explain the psychological impact it has to anyone who's never suffered that kind of fear. What it does to a person. How it can wear away at hope and endurance until a part of you screams: "Get it over with! Just kill me!"

There's a worse kind of terror compared to that anything-is-better-than-this fear of one's fellows.

It is the terror of knowing that the whole of the universe is depending upon you. Looking up to you. Expecting you to be perfect, omniscient, and omnipotent.

The realization that you are not any of those things is like acid poured upon the soul. It eats into your every thought, and the fumes bring tears to the eyes—sear through the nose and into the very brain.

I live this terror: I am not good enough. Smart enough.

That knowledge is indeed my personal acid. Not only has it eaten holes in my resolve, in my faith in myself, but I can see it the eyes of those around me.

It is the middle of the night.

I sit alone on my throne of bones, the symbol of our strength as a people.

"You are no longer the Irredenta." The words uttered by that damned Perez woman rattle around inside my head like loose parts. The implications are too disturbing to even consider.

I finger the long-bone scepter, stare at the intricate carvings of people who are struggling up a spiraling ramp. The little figures are no more than a centimeter tall, and perfectly rendered in the slightest detail. Fodor Renz spent a year in the carving of it. Rendered it from the thigh bone of the first woman I ever ate.

Now, I fear it is a mockery.

What is the fate of a false Messiah? One who cannot intercede with the universe on behalf of his people? One who can no longer understand the sacred voices of the Prophets? One whose people are dying all around him?

29

Sunlight amazed Fatima Veda, as did soil, plants, color, and the magical terror of an endless sky. She had just turned six. That wonderful age where awe, fear, and curiosity seesawed back and forth, each constantly giving way to the other. At first, she and the other children had been terrified of the open. The unsettling notion that there were no walls had slowly given way to curiosity.

On Deck Three, the only off-limits had been the temple and the observation dome. Children were not allowed to disturb the Holy Prophets. Otherwise they could go where they wished, play where they wished. Every nook and cranny had been known.

Once the great dome had been explored, the next fascination was the outdoors. A huge, awe-inspiring universe of space, places, sights, and light.

Fatima, at age six, was one of the oldest children. And, because she was, the little ones looked up to her. Shimal, Bess, her mother Shyanne, and the rest of the women had told her she was to help keep the little ones out of trouble.

And she would do that. Just as soon as she decided where they could and could not go. The women were all in the kitchen. Cooking something called vegetables.

Fatima wasn't sure she liked vegetables; ration was what food was supposed to be. Mother had assured her that there was no more ration. How could that be? Ration just was. Instead, in this new place, there were vegetables. That they pulled out of the dirt. Seemed a lot of work when ration just fell off the conveyor.

Fatima stepped outside, raised a hand to block the hot light pouring down from Capella. Hard to think that wasn't a ceiling. Just open space forever overhead.

She blinked around. Amazed at the smells, the moving air, the feel of loose dirt under her feet. She laughed as she scrunched her toes in the stuff. So different from hard and smooth deck. The air sounded magical, the rising of the chime, the breeze in the forest. She giggled in delight.

Everything here was new. She wandered over to the pieces of machinery. Wondered at the purpose of each, and ran her fingers over the steel, duraplast, and sialon, amazed at the shapes of hoses, fittings, and levers. At six, she was old enough to know the machine was supposed to do something. It even had a weathered seat that she climbed up to perch on.

Tired of that, she hopped down, stomped her way across the green plants. She bent down for a closer look. Mother had said they were alive. Like people. Fatima fingered the leaves and stems, pulled one of the stems loose and sniffed and nibbled it.

She made a face at the bitter taste. Tossed the stem away.

A change in the musical chime drew her to the edge of the cliff to stare out at the forest. She tried to imagine the ends of it, couldn't. And looking down brought her heart into her throat. She instinctively stepped back, vertigo causing her to gasp. Long way down! She'd never felt anything like that.

Something red flashed down by the vegetables, and she turned, trotting to see. The thing was pretty, the brightest red she'd ever seen. Something else alive. And it flew, fluttering through the air as it dropped down to snap something up from among the plants.

"A bird!" Fatima cried with glee. Mother had told her about birds. Animals that flew. She'd seen her first animal!

Giddy, she chortled to herself, clapping her hands. Rubbed her shoulders, surprised at how hot the light was making her skin.

One of the pipes running down from the dome dribbled water onto the ground next to the plants. When she stepped in it, her foot sank. Stepping back, she stared in amazement at the impression her foot had made. Stepping forward, she pressed her foot down into the mud again. Felt it squish up between her toes. A sensation like she'd never known. Again and again, she stomped her foot down. Each time she made another track.

Delighted, she stomped her way to the end of the muddy spot.

And with the last jump, a stinging pain made her scream.

She dropped to her butt, pulled her muddy foot around, and stared at the bloody puncture in the sole of her foot. She screamed again as the pain burned its way through her foot.

She'd known pain. She had wailed and screamed during the Initiation. This was as bad. And worse, it was moving.

Moving *inside* her foot!

She tried to stand. Couldn't. Hurt too much!

"Mother!" she screamed.

But the women were inside. Cooking in the kitchen.

The only sound was the rising and falling of the chime, and it seemed to mock her.

30

Talina was sitting on her stool in Inga's; the tavern was full of locals and a few *Ashanti* crew. The rise and fall of conversation echoed from the high dome. The occasional scrape of a bench across the flagstone floor was augmented by Inga bellowing an order to her kitchen.

Talina's gut kept tying itself in a slipknot, and then releasing. Half of it, she was sure, was Demon making a nuisance of himself. The rest was the result of her conversation with Dek Taglioni. Shit on a shoe, what was it about the guy?

So what if he had rich-man's designer eyes and a dimple in his chin?

"The chemicals say you would mate with him."

"Oh, go fuck yourself."

"Quetzals do not fuck."

"Okay, go share spit with yourself."

"Takes three."

"Asshole."

Demon chittered its amusement.

She kept half an ear open to the chatter that rose and fell behind her as the supper crowd came in. The clunking of mugs on chabacho-wood tables was reassuring, as was the sound of people calling to each other. The big news was that the first cargo shuttles bound for PA had landed from *Ashanti*.

Picked out from among the multitude of containers slated for the marine unit, Pamlico Jones and his crew were unloading the first lots of medical supplies, spare parts, farming equipment, and a new set of yard lights ostensibly for the Wide Ridge Research Base up north, but that had been abandoned for ten years. The good news was that Port Authority would have streetlights again. Assuming they could broker a deal with Kalico; this was, after all, Corporate property.

The distant rumble of thunder boomed above the rising din of conversation. Figured. Hot day like today, of course there'd be rain rolling in from the east.

She gave Inga a nod as the woman brought Talina her stout with one hand, whipping the five-SDR coin into her pocket with the other.

"I'm still thinking about what I want for supper."

"If you want the chili, don't wait too long. Don't have that much left."

Which left either chamois steaks or the squash bake.

"Chamois steak with broccoli and cherry pie," she decided.

"You got it!" Inga pivoted on her heel, bellowing the order in the direction of the kitchen.

Talina lifted her stout, took a sip as Shig climbed up onto the stool beside her and slipped his water-spotted cloak from his shoulders.

"Looks like it's going to be a hard rain," he noted. "I checked with Talbot on the way over. He's got everyone on the gates. The *Ashanti* people from the shuttle field are safely inside the compound."

"Good. We can use the moisture. It's been a couple of weeks. I was out in the fields. Things are looking a little dry."

"Indeed, but the Sczuis got their wheat, barley, and rye harvested. Worked out perfectly for them." Shig paused. "Trouble out at the farms today? Heard you had to make a trip out to Reuben's."

"No. Well, maybe. Dek Taglioni was out there, picking peppers for Reuben. I gave specific orders that he wasn't supposed to go outside the gates." She gave him a sidelong glance. "Ko Lang tells me that someone named Shig told him that good old Dek could go work for Reuben for the day."

Shig was giving her his mildly reproving look. "It might seem churlish of me to remind you Dek's a free man, an adult, of sound mind, and seemingly healthy if malnourished body. You have no right to tell him what he can or can't do."

"The guy's a pain in the ass!" she snapped.

Demon hissed down in her gut.

She thought she heard Rocket laughing somewhere in the back of her head.

Shig's knowing gaze fixed on hers. "I see."

"Don't go dropping any of that Buddhist crap on me. I'm not in the mood."

"There is something in his personality that reminds me of Mitch. Some quality of having been tested, of not knowing the answers, but willing to tackle whatever it takes to find them."

"Don't even think of going there."

Shig smiled his thanks as Inga rushed down the bar just long enough to place his half-glass of wine before hurrying back to fill more mugs with beer.

"He's different from Cap. Didn't land with that cocksure, I'm-gonna-kick-asses attitude. But at the same time, he's similar in that he's fascinated just by being here."

"Do you want me to break your jaw?"

"Unlike both of them, Derek Taglioni has a different depth of personality. Mitch never faced the kind of desperate trial Taglioni did. And Cap, of course, had a head start from his training. He didn't have to begin his reevaluation of self until he was faced with disaster."

Talina gave Shig her most evil I'm-going-to-make-you-hurt-like-you-never-thought-you'd-hurt glare. "If you say one more word, I'm knocking you off that chair."

Shig lifted his glass, sipped. He studied the wine, a nice translucent red. Worked it in his mouth. "Very pleasant," he told her as he set the glass down. "I think it has possibilities."

"Glad you can talk about something besides Taglioni."

"What makes you think I was talking about the wine?"

Tal slapped a hand to the battered chabacho bar. "That does it! I'm shooting you through the knee."

Shig stared thoughtfully at the backbar with its glasses and containers of liquor. "History can be a burden. It accumulates. Becomes a weight and a hinderance. In its own way it can become blinding, so that the only thing people see is who you once were. They see you gunning down Pak or Paolo. Eliminating Clemenceau. Burying Mitch. Saving the town from disaster. Facing down Kalico Aguila, and walking out of the forest with Cap. Or they remember you taking down Spiro or standing up for quetzals. Maybe they remember you shooting a shipping crate when you thought it was Sian Hmong. Or single-handedly hunting three quetzals in the rain. They might—"

"Does this have a point?"

"The point is, they might not see Talina Perez."

"Well, duh! Right here. Filling this chair."

Shig's amiable smile bent his lips. "But do they see you, Tal? Or do they only see your history? The legend?"

"Let's just say that I'm too dense for the holy mystical shit. The learning-by-analogy crap. So stop with the hocus pocus, already. What's your point?"

Shig gave her one of his bemused looks. "If you were truly as dense as you attempt to portray yourself, you'd have been turned into quetzal shit years ago."

"Yeah, well, I've come close to ending up that way more times than I like to remember."

Demon made that broken gurgling that quetzals thought sounded like laughter, then hissed, *"Yes."*

"Very well, I shall be as blunt as a boulder." Shig twirled his wineglass on the counter. "When it comes to raw material, Taglioni is as good as I've seen over the years. I think he would be a real asset to Donovan for a lot of reasons. For one, his name, assuming we ever hear from Solar System again. For another, he's got that spark of soul. What should have snuffed it dead aboard *Ashanti* has given it additional illumination. He has the makings of greatness in him. My fear is that he will never be allowed the chance to discover it within himself."

"Why not?"

"He is going to pursue his calling. Follow his Tao where it will take him. And do so in the company of whomever will serve as a guide. Perhaps Rand Cope? Or maybe Bernie Monson?"

"They'll get him killed within a week." A beat. "He was asking about the Briggses today."

"They'd be adequate for the time being, though insufficient for what I think Taglioni's ultimate needs will be."

She gave him a distasteful look. "So, you're playing matchmaker?"

He studied her with an intensity she wasn't used to.

"Tal, over the years, I've developed a certain fond regard for you. In truth, I never figured you'd live this long because of the *tamas* in your soul. Not to mention that you're the tip of our sword. There's not a man, woman, or child in Port Authority who doesn't owe you their lives. Taglioni needs a teacher. I think you need a student, even if you don't recognize that fact."

"I need a student?"

"Since Trish died, you've existed alone. You distance yourself from your people in Security. You only socialize with Kalico when she's up from Corporate Mine, with me, and on rare occasions Yvette when she comes in. Otherwise, your beloved bar stool might as well be on up on Donovan's moon."

"And what would I talk to people about?"

After the silence dragged for a bit, Shig said, "Precisely my point."

31

Fatima's arrival interrupted Vartan's concentration; he'd been going over the inventory of supplies, equipment, and stored items. Jon Burht, the first of the First Chosen, had heard the girl screaming down by the garden.

Burht brought little Fatima in just before dusk. She was bawling, said that something had hurt her foot. And there, inching up her pencil-thin calf, was a lump as big around and as long as Vartan's thumb. Moving. The thing was crawling along under the skin.

"Call Shyanne!" Vartan cried as he tried to soothe the child. "Hey, it's all right. Your mother's coming."

"It hurts!" Fatima declared as tears streaked her cheeks. "I'm scared. I want my mother!"

"Coming. She's coming."

The Messiah, disrupted from his reading, walked over, stared down. "What is it?"

"I don't know," Vartan told him. Lifting the girl's foot, he could see the wound, a bloody puncture where the child's foot was caked with mud. "What was it that they said? Something about slugs?"

"And shoes," Burht reminded. "That we needed to wear shoes."

The Messiah tipped his head back, eyes closed. The blue eye in his forehead continued to stare aimlessly at the light panel overhead. "Perhaps we should."

"It's moving faster," Burht noted.

The Messiah reached down, pressed on the lump moving slowly up Fatima's lower shin.

The girl screamed, and the lump slipped down behind her tibia and fibula, as if hiding. As it did, Fatima shrieked and kicked, as if trying to dislodge the pain.

"*Fatima!*" Shyanne cried, her expression panicked as she raced into the room. "What's happened?"

"Something bit her," the Messiah replied thoughtfully, a curious stirring behind his dark eyes.

"Bit her?" Shyanne bent down, taking her daughter's hand. "Baby? What happened? What bit you?"

"It hurt my foot! It's in my leg! Make it stop, Mother! Please. Just make it stop!"

Vartan ground his teeth. He'd always had a soft spot for Fatima. But for the universe, she might have been his child. Even after the Harrowing and Cleansing, he still had feelings for Shyanne. Couldn't help but remember how it had been before.

His soul ached at the expression on Shyanne's face as her quick hands began to press on the girl's swollen lower leg. As she did, Fatima screamed her pain.

"Sorry, baby. So sorry." Shyanne glanced at the Messiah. "What do I do?"

"You're the vet tech," the Messiah told her. "The closest thing we have to a doctor."

"I'd better call Port Authority," she said through a nervous exhale. "They'll know what to do."

"No." The Messiah's tone left no room for doubt. "That is forbidden. We want nothing from those people. All they intend for us is harm."

Shyanne's brown eyes had taken on that gleam Vartan knew so well. He laid a hand on her shoulder. Felt her flinch as he told her: "Deal with it. You can figure it out on your own. It's just like an infection, right?"

Shyanne blinked, winced as Fatima screamed again.

"Please. Let me call."

"No. I will not tell you again," the Messiah told her. "You are our medical expert. You've seen the materials they left us. What do you think this is?"

"Probably something they call a slug." Shyanne was wavering on her feet, her hand clutching Fatima's. Tears were rimming her eyes.

"A slug," the Messiah said softly. "I thought they poisoned them all."

"Lies!" Burht snapped. "Corporate deceit."

Fatima began to whimper.

Vartan looked down in time to see the lump shift behind the little girl's skinny knee. "It's in the lower thigh now."

Shyanne clamped her eyes closed, both hands holding her daughter's. "They said it could be cut out."

"This is the universe's will," the Messiah said with finality. "This is a lesson to us."

"Get me a knife." Shyanne's voice had that high waver on the verge of hysteria. "I'll need something to sew with. I've got to get that *thing* out of my daughter."

"And risk yourself?" the Messiah asked. "Shyanne, think. Yes, she's your daughter. But you are our only medical person. What if, in trying to save your daughter, it infects you? We can't let that happen. You are too important to us."

Vartan watched the interplay of anger, fear, and worry behind his ex-wife's expression.

Before she could do herself irreparable harm, Vartan spun her around to face him. "I need you to run back to your room. Read everything you can find on these slugs. That Perez woman left the notes. Once you do, we'll know how to proceed. So go now. There's not a moment to lose. Find the answer for sure."

Shyanne shot him a look of disbelief.

"Yes," the Messiah agreed. "Go read the notes. See if there's anything mentioned besides surgery. Hurry!"

Vartan, praying, watched Shyanne hesitate, saw the skepticism, but the woman nodded. Bent down. "Baby, I'll be right back with the cure."

Shyanne left at a run. Almost bowled First Will Petre off his feet as he met her at the door.

Vartan wiped sweat from his forehead. "Maybe it won't be as bad—"

"Take her to one of the back rooms," the Messiah ordered. "I read the section on slugs. They are probably dividing inside the girl's leg as we speak. I want Fatima quarantined."

To Petre, he said, "Your job, First Will, is to keep Shyanne away from her daughter. Whatever it takes. But remember, as our only medical person, she's not to be too badly harmed."

Vartan fought down his urge to protest. Glanced at the

agony reflected in the little girl's face. This was going to break Shyanne's heart. It was already breaking his. "Yes, Messiah."

As he reached down and gathered up the writhing little girl, he heard the Messiah say, "And no one goes outside barefoot from here on."

As Vartan carried the whimpering little girl down one of the dim hallways, he couldn't help but wonder.

If they lost the children, they lost everything.

32

A roiling muddle of thoughts filled Miguel Galluzzi's head as the shuttle's pitch changed, g-force pressing him down in the copilot's seat as Ensign Naftali placed them on approach to Port Authority.

Ahead the blue expanse of Donovan's ocean was broken by the continental mass; the old impact crater made it look like a bite had been taken out of the coast. They were shooting through clouds now. Flashes of cumulus that momentarily blotted the view.

Galluzzi might have been an old space dog—and he had to maintain his decorum—but inside he bubbled with excitement. This, after all, was the culmination of everything. The entire purpose of space flight. He was living the dream that had filled human imagination all the way back to the moment the first hominin looked up at the stars and wondered.

For that one moment, it didn't matter that *Ashanti*'s voyage here had been disastrous. If anything, knowing how close they'd all come to dying made this arrival even more fulfilling.

To get to this point, Galluzzi had crossed thirty light-years of space, lived for nearly three years "outside" of the universe. Brought his ship, the survivors, and cargo to this distant world.

G-force increased as the shuttle cupped air, the roar of it loud through the hull. Then the nose dropped, Naftali caressing the thrusters as he crossed the coast, put them into a glide over a vegetation-dotted landscape, the colors oddly vivid compared with Earth.

The shuttle slowed into a hover, and Naftali eased it down. Galluzzi caught sight of another A-7 parked off to the side of a stack of shipping containers. Then a billow of dust spewed out, and the shuttle settled onto its landing skids.

"Welcome to Donovan, Captain," Naftali told him as he spooled the thrusters down.

Galluzzi could feel the change through his seat. Planetary gravity. So different from the angular acceleration that served as a surrogate aboard ship.

I am on a distant world.

For a moment he wanted to giggle, to shake his fists with delight. Didn't, of course. He was the captain. Captains didn't do those sorts of things.

Even if they had survived the kind of spacing he had.

Rising, he emerged from the command deck hatch and crossed aft through the cargo-packed main cabin to where Windman opened the aft ramp and let it drop.

The acrid smell left by the thrusters gave way to fresh air as Galluzzi minced his steps down the ramp. Gravity, after all these years, was a tricky thing. He could feel the strain in his muscles.

And then he was out in the light, blinking, aware of the air on his skin and its incredible perfumed scent. The direct heat from Capella was a marvel, the light so bright it hurt his eyes. In wonder, he extended his hand to the breeze, feeling it trickle over his fingers. Eyes closed, he leaned his head back to the sunlight; for a moment, with breath going in and out of his lungs, he savored the miracle of fresh air.

The whine of machinery began to seep through his consciousness. Opening his eyes, he forced himself back to reality.

"Miguel!" Benj Begay called. The Advisor/Observer came striding across the landing field. The man wore a freshly pressed suit. Something obviously retrieved from one of the crates of personal possessions that had been locked away in cargo. Begay might have just stepped out of an office on Transluna. The professional cut of the clothing, shining a metallic blue in the light, looked oddly out of place against the background of dirt, shipping crates, and the high fence surrounding the domes.

"Benj. Good to see you."

"What's the word on the ship?" Begay stepped close, shaking Galluzzi's hand as if it had been years instead of days since they'd seen each other.

"Got Deck Three cleaned out. I wouldn't leave until that had been taken care of."

Benj's expression soured. "I can't imagine the kind of . . . Well, was it bad?"

"Call it macabre, grisly, insane . . . Hey, words don't convey the kind of things . . ." He shook his head. "Forget it. The whole deck's sterilized. Stripped down to the hull." He looked around at where forklifts were whining and moaning as they lifted shipping containers. "What's happening here?"

"Getting the first loads out of *Ashanti* now that Corporate Mine has been taken care of and the Maritime Unit has been happily dropped out on their reef. Figure that if you're done with Deck Three, with the additional crew to help, we can have the Cargo Deck emptied within another couple of weeks. Most of what you see here is ready to be shipped up. Loaded and sent back to Solar System."

"Given what the Supervisor's got floating up in orbit, and the number of containers I see here, we're not even going to come close to taking it all."

If I can even stomach the thought of spacing again.

"I've got a manifest of what goes first. Miguel, you're not going to believe it."

"Believe what?"

"The wealth." Begay took his arm. "Come on. I've got the manifest on my tablet. Let me take you on a stroll through town. Buy you a drink and the finest meal you've ever eaten. Then I'll brief you on what's at stake."

Galluzzi let Benj take the lead, followed him through a huge gate just before a giant hauler wallowed its way past, cloaking him with a light coating of dust. To his amazement, a man dressed in quetzal hide and coarse cloth stood guard with a rifle. And, yeah, he'd heard. Seeing it, however, was shocking.

"What's that?" Galluzzi hooked a thumb at the departing hauler.

"Clay," Benj told him. "Makes the finest sialon in the galaxy. As if that means shit. Most of those containers out there are full of it. Enough cubic kilometers to fabricate a dozen *Freelander*-sized ships. But forget the clay. It's inconsequential."

"What? That's why they founded Port Authority here in the first place."

"Those containers up in orbit? They're full of beryllium, rhodium, cerium, terbiums, ruthenium. All being kept pristine in vacuum. And then there's the gems, like nothing Earth has ever produced. After that, the gold, silver, platinum, and the like are almost boring."

Looking around at the central avenue just past the admin dome, Galluzzi asked, "When do we get to the good part of town?"

"You're here." Benj spread his arms to take in the entirety of the graveled north-south thoroughfare. "I give you the Transluna of Capella III."

Galluzzi's brain stumbled at that. He saw weathered domes interspersed with buildings made of stone, timbers, and some sort of plaster. Barrels, pieces of equipment, drying racks, little gardens, hand-painted signs, everything was a jumble, right down to the mismatched light poles that lined the street.

The people ambling past were just as bizarre. The colors, the outlandish cut and style of the clothes, the rainbow-effect quetzal hide, the wild and unkempt hair styles. Most men were bearded. Not to mention the big floppy hats and guns. So many guns. Hard to think that they hadn't all murdered each other upon the outbreak of the first discord. Even the women looked like cutthroats.

"This is the richest planet in the galaxy?" Galluzzi asked.

"Sum and total," Benj told him. "Me, I can't wait to get out of here. Even if it means shipping back aboard *Ashanti*, but I'll get to that in a bit. Want to see the worse parts of town?"

"I think I'm fine with first impressions."

A loud bang made him jump. Turning, he realized it came from the building with GUNSMITH burned into the curious wood sign over the door.

"They build and fix firearms. Sell them to anyone, can you imagine? I mean, you could just walk in there and buy a rifle. No questions asked, no one watching."

"Insane!"

"The whole place is, Miguel." Benj shook his head. "It's

one thing to hear that they're a bunch of libertarians. But once you set foot down here? Realize that, no shit, there really isn't any government to speak of? I mean seriously. No one takes care of these people. They're completely on their own. What kind of insanity is that?"

"Sounds scary."

"Yeah." Benj motioned. "Come on. After years of rations, I promised you a meal the likes of which you've never eaten. They might be a bunch of lunatics, but, by damn, can they cook!"

"What's the Supervisor say about all this?" Galluzzi tried to take in a whole new order of shabby as he walked beside Benj. "Why hasn't she restored order here?"

"According to the story, she tried. Quickly figured out it would be open warfare, and she'd have to kill them all to reestablish Corporate control. Now, that said, Aguila herself is off the rails if you ask me. She and her Corporate Mine are little better than the local savages."

"You been down there?"

"I have. They might call themselves Corporate, but it's in name only. You ask me, it's a sort of co-op. But one that's corrupted by Port Authority's cash economy. Miguel, there's no redistribution here. Even Aguila's people, they're rich in their own wealth. What they call plunder. And they're a clannish bunch. You say anything critical of Aguila, they're ready to reach down your throat and pull your lungs out through your mouth."

"What's Dek say about all this?"

"Dek?" Benj laughed almost hysterically. "I never knew that insanity was infectious, but he's gone as crazy as the rest of them. Figured that as a Taglioni, he should have come uncorked at first sight of this place. Instead, he's out in the bush, like he's fallen headlong into the absurdity that is Donovan."

Benj led him to a dome with benches out front. "This is Inga's. The local drinking and eating establishment. Well, there's the cafeteria, but the name pretty much says it. Down the street, The Jewel is a casino and whorehouse. One of two brothels if you can believe it, but that's a story for another time."

Galluzzi stepped inside to find the floor in need of

sweeping and followed Benj down into a subterranean room with a stone floor and long tables crowded by benches.

Benj found a spot in the back, off to the side, and told the young man who walked over, "Two of the lunch specials and two glasses of the amber ale."

The waiter said, "Uh, you're Skulls. You got cash or plunder?"

With careful fingers, Benj placed a coin on the table. "That's a ten. That enough?"

"You got it," the lanky twentysomething told him, turning to bellow, "Two specials, two amber ales." Then he was off to a table full of hatted, cloak-wearing, pistol-packing locals up front.

Galluzzi just stared at the coin, having never seen the like. Finally asked, "Why didn't we just stand up and shout?"

"Some of us try to cling to the illusion of gentlemanly conduct."

Galluzzi threw his head back, laughing with gusto for the first time in how long? "Hard to believe this place is for real."

"Oh, it is."

"What do you hear about the Unreconciled?"

"Guess they're out in some distant research station. The latest news is that the Prophets got turned into raving morons because they ate other people's brains. Some sort of protein malfunction that eats holes in gray matter. Spongiform encephalitis." Benj barely suppressed a shiver. "Damn, but I'm glad to be rid of them."

Galluzzi grunted.

Benj fixed him with a hard stare. "Miguel, I need to know. Once the cargo is loaded, how soon do you expect to space?"

Galluzzi leaned back, experienced a quivering in his heart. "I don't know, Benj. It's going to depend."

"On what?"

"The condition of the ship and crew. What the Supervisor orders. I don't know. Just how we all feel."

"How we *feel*? You heard anything I've said? This place is a lunatic's asylum. The closest thing to Corporate order is Aguila's mine. And *there's nothing there.* Just a mine, barracks, and a cafeteria. *This*"—he waved around—"is the best this shithole has to offer."

"Benj, take a breath. Listen to me. You were there. You know what kind of condition my people are in. It's been ten years. We almost died. Most of them are out of contract. If I post an order that we're spacing as soon as we're loaded, half of them will refuse. The half that I order aboard will hate me for cutting their shore leave. . . . And it's not like murder hasn't been committed on *Ashanti* before."

Benj rubbed his face with the flats of his hands. The old gesture of frustration having grown so aching familiar over the years. "Miguel, do you understand? We're talking about the kind of wealth that will make us all famous. Look back in history. The Spanish treasure fleets of galleons? The Venetian merchants of the Renaissance? They are *nothing* compared to the splash *Ashanti* will make when she's unloaded. Your photo will be holoed from one side of Solar System to the other."

Right. They'll have a face to put to the name. "So that's what a monster looks like. He's the one who left the cannibals to die."

Galluzzi asked, "And you, my friend?"

Benj's lips twitched before he said, "Who knows? Supervisor of Transluna? It wouldn't be out of the question."

"What if Aguila wants to go back? Take her own wealth. Put herself at the forefront of the discovery."

Benj's expression went tight. "I guess we'll just have to wait." A beat. "As the locals say, 'Welcome to Donovan.'"

"Meaning?"

"Meaning anything can happen."

Not that it mattered to Miguel Galluzzi. What did was the question that bounced around inside his head: *Can I space again? Do I even want to?*

33

The last time Shaka Mantu had walked under the stars, he'd been nine. Memory of that night, of the warm and moist air, and the South African sky, had clung to him during the long and terrible eternity of Deck Three. When the horror and hopelessness had grown too much to bear, he'd tuck himself away in his bunk and remember. Go back to his life as a boy before he'd traveled off to Academy.

Those hours he would spend with his mother and brothers, reliving life when there was a sky, home, and a future without death, pain, and misery.

On this night, he finally walked free under the stars. Different, it was true. Here no Southern Cross, no Magellanic Clouds, no Coal Sack were visible. And the Milky Way was brighter, wider, and stunningly different.

"But I am finally free," he said, raising his hands as he strode out beyond the northernmost dome.

His way wound through the scrubby trees; he let the curious sound of the night chime bathe him in its subtle music. If he thought about it, he could almost call the intonations tribal.

Warm air caressed his skin.

"God, I have longed for this." Inhaling, he filled his lungs and savored the perfumed scents. Tried to catalog them. Sort of a saffron? Maybe mixed with cilantro? A hint of tang similar to steeping honeybush tea?

Movement under his foot surprised him. He skipped sideways, startled. Then laughed. Yes, it was the roots. He'd heard that they moved. To experience it was a marvel. He tried to tread lightly, wearing his soft leather boots as the Messiah had ordered.

Odd that. It flew in the face of tradition.

"We are no longer like a fetus in the womb!" the Messiah had declared. *"As newly born infants, we must now learn to dress for our new world. Shoes will be worn at all*

times while outside. Just as children must learn to wear clothing."

Seven years barefoot. Now he had shoes again. It felt oddly restraining.

Call it a happy tradeoff for the ability to stroll under an open night sky. He tried to mince his steps, to mitigate the disturbance to the roots. Even in the darkness, with a sliver of moon to light the sky, he could see the trees shifting their branches, as if the leaves were watching him.

"Mama? I made it. I'm standing on a distant world. Tough times to get here. I did things. Things I hope you never have to know. But I lived."

Funny thought that she might be looking up at the night sky outside of Johannesburg, perhaps looking right at him, as he might be looking at her. And it would take thirty years for the light to travel between them.

How did the human brain synthesize that?

His path had taken him to the edge of the cliff. He sniffed, catching the faint odor of vinegar mixing with perfumed scents on the wind. The vista overwhelmed, and he marveled, looking out at the humped confusion of treetops that vanished into an indistinct horizon marked with stars.

What a miracle. This was an alien forest.

And he, Shaka Mantu, was seeing it firsthand.

Not bad for a Zulu boy. That day he'd received his first scholarship, who would have guessed that he'd . . .

The boulder he was walking around jumped. Something lanced through his left shoulder, the impact of it shearing through his scapula, upper ribs, and clavicle. Knocked him back. He would have fallen, but the spear took his weight. Dangled him.

Pain—like nothing he'd known—stunned him. Before he could draw breath, his body was grabbed. In the darkness, he barely saw the two tentacles that drew him close against the boulder . . . that was no longer a boulder.

He tried to draw breath.

To scream.

But his chest, fiery with pain, was frozen.

As his mouth worked soundlessly, the *thing* that held him pressed close. Warm tissue spread along his bare thighs, over his wrap, and onto his stomach. Like a jelly bath, it began to surround him.

And then the burning began.

He finally managed to draw breath.

Was about to scream, when the spear through his upper chest jerked sideways. Stunned with pain, he didn't realize one of the tentacles had shifted. He barely felt it seize the back of his head. Then he was pulled down, bent double, and his face was shoved into the warmth as the *thing* engulfed his head . . .

34

Not for the first time did Dan Wirth wonder if he was a moron, deluded, or just plain crazy. Right. *So, stop with the psychopath jokes, already.*

He'd swung the safe door open and was staring at the packed shelves. This was the second safe. The first—hulking in its place in the corner—he didn't bother to open anymore. It was packed with stacked ingots of gold, platinum, something called rhodium, and bars of ruthenium. Hell, he'd never heard of such stuff as that last. Now he had safes so full of it the legs had buckled.

He scowled, taking in the contents of safe two. The thing was a five-foot tall by four-foot steel box that Tyrell Lawson had welded together. This time Dan hadn't bothered to bolt it to the floor. By the time it was full, it would take a heavy-lift shuttle to pack the thing off. And where was he going to find a thief on Donovan dumb enough to chance stealing from him?

"Oh, Father, if you could see me now, you worthless piece of walking garbage."

But the old pedophile couldn't. And Dan hoped the cocksucker never would. The old man was the only living being in the galaxy who knew who Dan Wirth really was. And if there were any justice—real or imaginary—dear old Dad was either dead before his time or brain-wiped for the sick shit that he was.

"So, what the hell do I do when this one's full?" Dan wondered. Wasn't going to take much. Maybe another couple of months. He stuffed the bag of rubies in the right-hand side. How many damn rubies could a single planet produce?

Allison had suggested using some of the gems to inlay the bar, and then covering the whole thing with glass. Sure as hell, that would be a crowd pleaser. The richest bar in the universe. After all, he already had a dozen fifty-to-sixty-carat "pigeon-blood-red" rubies, not to mention all those thirty-to-forty-carat rocks that constantly trickled in. And then there were the emeralds, the diamonds, sapphires, and all the rest.

"Fucking pain in the ass." He slammed the door shut and wrenched the locking lugs closed.

As he stood, Kalen Tompzen—dressed in a black shirt and wearing tight chamois pants—knocked and leaned in the office door.

"Uh, boss? Got something you might want to keep an eye on."

Dan walked over to his big desk, ensured the ledger book was up to date. Bless Ali for a good girl—it was. He raised his eyes. "What sort of something?"

"Guy's winning a lot of hands, boss. Dalia gave me the high sign. I've had Vik watching. Shin, too. Can't see how he's cheating."

"What's his take?"

"He came in with nine SDR. He's up to about three fifty now."

"Nine to three fifty? Now there, by God's ugly ass, is a man after my own heart." Dan stepped over to the mirror, adjusted the fine white silk scarf tied at his throat. Real silk. The only one on Donovan. He'd obtained it from Amal Oshanti, one of the local housewives. The slit had traded a bedroom addition on her house for the scarf. She'd brought it all the way from Solar System back on sixth ship.

Traded, for fart-sucking sake!

Here he was, a man with two safes full of plunder, and he couldn't *buy* a scarf. No, he had to *trade*. But so be it. He now owned and wore the *one-and-only* silk scarf on the whole toilet-sucking planet.

He slipped his form-fitting quetzal-hide vest over his shoulders, looped the gold and rhodium chains into place, and strode for the door.

In the hallway he could hear the rhythmic thumping of the bed as Angelina provided some john with horizontal glee. Ali's door was closed, but then, she was supposed to be down at admin, dealing with Muley Mitchman's deed. Nice that she'd been seeing to the nitty shitty little details needed to manage property. And it kept him from getting frustrated, cutting throats, and making more trouble for himself.

Stepping into the casino, it was to see a new guy seated at the back table playing poker with Step Allenovich and Lee Halston. Obviously soft meat from *Ashanti,* the guy was nevertheless dressed like a farmer. Quetzal boots, local-fabric shirt, canvas pants.

He might have been in his thirties, sandy hair, and those eyes . . . ah, custom. Genetically designed. The pistol on the guy's belt was like nothing Dan had ever seen. Looked like a presentation piece, all wood, gold, and inlaid. Electronic no less. Fancy.

Had to be Taglioni, the one that slit Aguila had warned Ali not to exploit. All of which brought Dan's curiosity to full boil.

"Why, I do declare. A new face. What a welcome relief after the butt-ugly mugs I've been staring at for all of these last long months." Dan thrust out a hand. "Dan Wirth, owner, proprietor, and lord and master of The Jewel. Most pleased to be at your service."

"Derek Taglioni," the Skull replied, his handshake firm, and to Dan's surprise, a confidence lay behind the man's designer eyes. Something that reeked of power and influence. Be just Dan's pus-sucking luck if this guy turned out to be another fucking Tamarland Benteen.

"Mind if I sit in?" Dan asked, swinging a chair around from the next table. "Been a while since I've played a few hands."

Step Allenovich carefully swept his remaining SDRs into his pocket, saying, "Me, I've bled enough. I'll leave it up to you to get my siddars back from Dek here."

"Makes two of us," Halston muttered as he picked up his plunder. "I want enough left to cover my meals until the Supervisor pays me for that last load of timber I cut for her."

Dan took the deck, cutting and shuffling. The entire time Taglioni was watching him through those unsettling eyes. No change of expression, just taking his measure.

"What's your pleasure?" Dan asked.

"Anything you like. We were playing five-card draw."

"Works for me."

Taglioni tossed out an SDR.

As Dan shuffled again and dealt, he asked, "So what tempted a man of your obvious good sense to entrust his life and sanity to a long space voyage? Not that anyone would expect a ten-year transit, but I was half-crazed after a mere two years in *Turalon*."

"A small family disagreement," Taglioni told him without inflection. "I found myself in need of new opportunities, new challenges."

"You may have come to the right place. Anything I can help with? Property? Perhaps offer my services when it comes to making the right introductions? Not that a man of your means would be short on capital, but Corporate credit isn't negotiable in Port Authority. Our libertarian brethren insist on hard cash or plunder. Wouldn't be the first time I funded a promising venture when the right person was at the helm."

A faint smile played at Taglioni's lips. "What if I wanted to open a casino in that nice stone building across the street?"

Dan experienced that cold slowing in his chest, the keening of incipient combat. "I would wish you good luck. In the first place, Sheyela Smith is our local electrical wizard. Considered a non-replaceable asset, and she likes her building just fine, thank you. In the second, being the bustling metropolis that Port Authority is with its four hundred thriving souls, the traffic really wouldn't support two such specialized institutions." A beat. "Not even if they were clear across town."

Taglioni answered with a knowing nod. "Yeah, not really my sort of thing. How about I leave any such dealings to you and Allison?" He checked.

That little spear of relief made Dan chuckle. The guy was good. He'd dangled the bait and studied the reaction.

"So, what are you after?" Dan asked, folding to give the mark a false sense of security.

Taglioni took the cards. His shuffle was good. Almost professional. Dan was dealt two fours, took three cards. Was stuck with his pair.

God, he wished Art Manikin was still alive. Tompzen

was too new, didn't know the game. Wasn't trained to give the signals. No telling what Taglioni had in hand.

Dan bid it up to ten, lost to three sixes.

"Word is that people come to Donovan to leave, to find themselves, or to die." Taglioni gave him a grim smile. "Me? I'm not leaving, so it's one of those last two."

"Let's hope it turns out to be the former and not the latter," Wirth told him with a placid smile. At that moment, Allison entered, shot him a victorious smile, and tapped a slim index finger to the corner of her jaw. Her signal that the Mitchman deed was taken care of.

Dan laid his hand on the table, two queens. He was surprised to see Taglioni lay down three twos. What the hell?

For a moment Dan stared at the cards, then shot a glance at Taglioni's yellow-green eyes, noted the challenging curl at the corner of the man's lips.

Oh, so that's the game, is it?

Outside thunder crashed and boomed. Rain began to hammer on the roof. For the next two hours Dan played poker like he hadn't in years. Every bit of his concentration, skill, the benefits of his implants and fancy tricks. He barely broke even.

Playing Derek Taglioni, he might have been playing a chunk of granite. The guy had no tells. Not so much as the flicker of an eye, not a tick, nor even a slight shift of posture. A robot couldn't have played it better.

And through it all, Taglioni kept up a constant stream of small talk. Told of the cannibals, his hopes to get out in the bush, even asking about Dan and his background. Might have been the kind of meaningless chatter to be shared over a cup of tea.

By then The Jewel was starting to fill with locals, some calling for drinks, others catching on that a new guy was playing Dan at poker. As a crowd started to build, Dan thumped the table. "As enjoyable as this is, I've got to go to work."

He stood, saying, "Come back with me, and I'll exchange those chips."

Taglioni rose, following Dan into the back hall and to his office. Shutting the door behind them, Dan asked, "Whiskey?"

"Sure."

Dan poured, studying Taglioni as the guy took in Dan's big and ornately carved chabacho-wood desk, the two safes and the mismatched furnishings. "Where did you learn to play poker like that?"

"Implants backed by a program that monitors data." Taglioni didn't even deny it. "That and I've been raised since I was a kid to study strategy, negotiation, statistical analysis of risk. Everything a budding Corporate cutthroat might need to succeed in the deadly world of high-stakes politics." A faint smile. "Works for poker, too. Though I admire your ability when it comes to sleight of hand. That had to take years to perfect."

Dan handed him the glass of whiskey. Shit, the fucker had seen the bottom deals, the hustle. "Let's keep that last as our own little personal secret."

Seating himself behind his desk, Dan asked, "So, as one card shark to another, what can I help you to accomplish? That is, aside from setting up a running game in my establishment? I don't want the chuckleheads to figure out just how easily they can be skinned at the tables."

"They haven't figured out that the house always wins?"

"Oh, to be sure, they've heard the words before." Dan tapped the side of his head. "It's just the comprehension where they're a little slow on the uptake."

Taglioni pulled the big stuffed chair around in front of the desk, settled himself comfortably across from Dan, and stared thoughtfully at his whiskey. "So fill me in. I've heard the chitchat. You run the games and sex trade, have fingers in most of the local pies, loan money, investment. People who cross you end up dead of mysterious, and, yes, not-so-mysterious causes. Shig, Yvette, and Talina run what government there is, but you're always there. Sort of in the background. Something needs doing for the community, you see that it gets funded. In the old days, the word was gangster, mafia don, or maybe *capitan*. Some say the Supervisor is the most powerful person on the planet. Others say it's you. Which is correct?"

Dan rubbed the links of his vest chain between two fingers. "Aguila and I came to an unspoken agreement a couple of years back that we would never try and answer that question. But the fact that you asked it, well that makes you even more interesting. The last major player who showed up here was Benteen. Got a lot of people killed. Precipitated a disaster. He ended up as a science experiment up on *Freelander*. I would hope you're not entertaining similar delusions."

"Not even close." He studied Dan with those peculiar and evaluative eyes. "All I can figure is that you had leverage on someone in personnel to get a posting on *Turalon*. Some last-minute substitution for the real Dan Wirth. Which means he's dead, and you can never go back to Transluna."

Dan felt the cool calm seeping through his guts. His heart slowing. That clarity of purpose was taking possession of his brain and body. His pistol hung in its rack just below the top of the desk. He need only . . .

Taglioni waved it away. "Relax. I could give a rat's ass."

"Really?" Dan asked, trying to keep the emotionless tone from his voice.

"Mr. Wirth, how about we come to an agreement?"

"You have my undivided attention."

"Good. But first, answer me a question. Answer it honestly. What do you intend on doing with all that wealth? Word is that both of those safes are full to bursting. Are you eventually thinking about shipping it back to Solar System? Maybe going back as a rich and powerful man one of these days?"

"Maybe."

"Okay, so here's the agreement: You leave me alone. Stay out of my hair, don't cause me any problems. For my part, I'll do my absolute level best to stay out of yours. In return, if and when *Ashanti* spaces back, you can be on her. With all of your plunder. I'll use my connections to ensure you get to spend that wealth. No questions asked."

"Just like that? Out of the goodness of your heart?"

Taglioni grinned. "Well, all right. There might be a fifteen percent service fee tacked on."

"Ten."

"Ten . . . with the provision that you pay all additional expenses for bribes, fees, gifts, entertainments, and the associated graft that will be an unavoidable necessity when it comes to the Corporate Board."

Dan arched an eyebrow, the subtle feeling of satisfaction rising within. There might actually be a way out of this.

"So, Mr. Taglioni—"

"Call me Dek."

"So, Dek, outside of ten percent and expenses, what do you get out of this? Seems to me, you could get the plunder back to Solar System, turn me in for a reward, and claim a lot more than your ten percent."

Taglioni took a full sip of the whiskey, ran it over his tongue as real whiskey drinkers did, and held it. After he'd finally swallowed and savored the finish, he said, "The Derek Taglioni who boarded *Ashanti* off Neptune would have done exactly that. The one who scrubbed toilets and mucked the hydroponics tanks for the last seven years in a bid to stay alive discovered different priorities."

"Such as?"

"I'm not sure that a man with your form of narcissistic and antisocial psychopathy can understand. It's more attuned to Shig Mosadek's kind of world view, but for me, there's now a need to measure myself against my soul."

"You're right. Only Shig could understand shit like that."

Taglioni laughed. "So, there it is. Laid out. I've no designs on your operation here. If, in the future, for whatever reason, we come into conflict, I'd prefer that we figure it out over a glass of whiskey before we go to cutting each other's throats."

Outside, lightning flashed and thunder boomed. Rain came down in earnest.

"Yeah, I can live with that." *But why the hell is it that I don't really trust you?*

The sense of despair was hardly an unknown companion as Miguel Galluzzi ambled his way down the main avenue. After parting with Benj, he'd taken the opportunity to stroll the length and breadth of Port Authority. Not that there was a whole lot of either before running headlong into that impossible soaring conglomeration of fence.

This is the height of human achievement on Donovan? This miserable collection of disabled vehicles, ramshackle housing, junk, clotheslines, toys in the dirt, and makeshift warehouses?

His feet hurt. His back ached, and his limbs were tuckered from the gravity. The yawning sense of despair just wouldn't turn loose from him.

Didn't matter that people had been friendly, had greeted him with a smile, and almost to the last, had introduced themselves. Hadn't even recoiled when he told them who he was. All had been most cordial—a fact that surprised him given that even the women had been armed.

Galluzzi had never been too taken with airs, but the fact remained: He was a captain. Here, even the children treated him with a most unsettling familiarity. What irked was that he was *not* one of them. Never would be.

Nevertheless, he'd been polite, done his best not to offend. After all, it was their town. Their world and ways. Not to mention that good manners seemed particularly prudent when talking to an armed man or woman—even if they were of menial status.

Glancing up at the clouding sky, Galluzzi sighed. How damn forlorn could a man be? He hadn't expected much of Port Authority. What he'd discovered, however, made him want to drop his head into his hands and weep.

He passed The Jewel. Considered entering, having not been in a casino since Macao some twenty years ago. But after laying eyes on the brown-haired man in a quetzal vest who was watching him from the doorway, he'd had second thoughts. Benj had already given him fair warning, and besides, after the glory, color, dash, and excitement of Macao, what depths of disappointment could a Port Authority casino plumb?

So he had forced his tired feet to carry him past, headed back . . . Where?

He stopped short in front of the admin dome, could see the hospital marking the south end of the avenue. Was about to turn and follow the side street to the shuttle field, when Shig Mosadek stepped out of the admin dome's double doors.

The short Indian was clad in a quetzal-hide cloak, his embroidered fabrics looking rumpled. The man squinted at Galluzzi, then smiled and waved. He shot a look at the sky, and called, "Just a moment. I shall be right back."

Then he vanished back inside for all of twenty seconds before emerging with a second hat and another of the quetzal-hide cloaks. These he presented to Galluzzi, saying, "I heard that you were in town, Captain. Forgive me for not finding you sooner. We had to work out a title dispute on a couple of claims out west. The previous owner was killed by a rogue quetzal we call Whitey. Old Mao had left his claim to Muley Mitchman but owed a gambling debt to The Jewel."

Even as Shig spoke, a most remarkable blonde woman, tall, dressed in a suggestive form-fitting sheath crafted from some local fabric, emerged from the admin dome.

Galluzzi instinctively straightened, squared his shoulders, as he reminded himself not to stare. What the hell was wrong with him? Damn, he hadn't been locked up in a ship for so long that he'd gape like a drooling idiot.

If the woman noticed, she didn't let it show, but stepped up next to Shig, dwarfing the Indian as she fixed enchanting blue eyes on Miguel.

"Don't let me interrupt," she told him in a melodious voice.

"No interruption," Shig told her. "In fact, I'd like to introduce Captain Miguel Galluzzi, master of the *Ashanti*. Captain, this is Allison Chomko, one of the partners in The Jewel."

"My pleasure," he told her, taking her offered hand. The touch sent an electric pulse through him. In that instant, he could have lost himself in her smile and those wondrous eyes. His heart began to hammer in his breast.

To Shig, the woman said, "Thanks for your help in there. I'll give Dan the rundown. I think Muley is happy with the settlement. If not, we'll work something out."

"He's young. If he can stay alive out there long enough, it could be the turning point for him. Mao had high hopes for that new diggings of his."

Again she fixed that miracle-blue gaze on Miguel, adding, "My honor to meet you, Captain. Do come by. I'd find it a pleasure to buy you a drink, and you'll find me a rapt audience if you'd be kind enough to share your experiences."

"I . . . well, of course. I'd be delighted." What in hell was it about her? She'd turned him into a stammering idiot.

He remained mesmerized as she gave him a radiant smile, turned, and strode away in a walk that hinted of almost feline grace. She seemed to float, the sway of her hips, the straight back, the way the light was shining in her . . .

Galluzzi blinked, tried to shake it off.

Shig, an amused smile on his lips, glanced up at the sky. "Might want to get indoors. This one's going to come down hard. I don't have Ali's allure, but I'd stand you a drink. Perhaps we could talk about your plans. Have you a place to stay?"

"I, uh, assumed there would be Corporate housing somewhere around the shuttle port."

"Ah, well, even when we were Corporate they never quite got around to such basic facilities as spacers' quarters, let alone an officers' lounge. As Dek has recently relocated to a dome of his own, you'd be more than welcome to use my study. My futon has a reputation for remarkable comfort. I've passed many a pleasant night on it myself."

"I couldn't—"

"Oh, no inconvenience. I assure you. It's a separate building. I won't even know you're there." Shig smiled. "Come. This hat and cloak are for you. By the time the night's over, you'll be thankful to have them."

"Where to?"

"Inga's of course. There really is no other place except

the cafeteria, and though Millicent's cooking is filling, it's rather uninviting for extended conversation."

Back to the tavern?

The first drops of rain began to fall as they made it to the tavern door. Galluzzi fingered the thick quetzal leather, amazed at the patterns of rainbow light that ran under his thumb. Had to be the crystalline scales on the hide.

Inside, and down the stairs, Shig led the way to the right side of the bar, propped himself up on one of the stools, and indicated the second from the end for Miguel, saying, "We keep that last one for Tal. Not that we're much for status and ceremony around here, but she's earned it the hard way."

"That woman, Allison. She's a partner in The Jewel? I mean, I've heard rather unsavory things about it." He couldn't shake the image of her. Figured she'd be haunting his dreams for a while.

"Owns forty-nine percent of The Jewel; and she's branched out into various real estate, mining, and development ventures. Let's just say that her start was a little rocky. Various tragedies left her ill-used and wounded. A fact that she realized and corrected. Once she took the bit in her teeth, she's made a rather impressive turnaround."

"I see." Wasn't the place also a brothel?

Shig lifted his hand in Inga's direction, asking, "What will you have?"

"I would kill for a cup of coffee or hot chocolate."

"Wouldn't we all? The coffee trees are supposed to produce beans this year. Meanwhile, we have a variety of teas, all of which, to our horror, are herbal and without caffeine."

"The amber ale was good."

After Inga had taken the order, Shig asked, "So, what are your plans? How can we be of service here?"

Galluzzi turned, looked over his shoulder at the people trickling down the stairs and into the tavern, water shining on their cloaks. "I haven't a clue." He laughed. "It's odd to admit, but I figured after what I'd done to the transportees—and if I ever lived long enough to make it here—I'd be arrested, tried, and executed." A beat. "Looked forward to it, actually."

"Might have happened that way, once upon a time," Shig agreed. "*Freelander,* up there in orbit, however, has taught us all an interesting moral lesson: Sometimes the universe leaves us with nothing but bad decisions."

"Sounds remarkably like situational ethics."

"Welcome to Donovan."

IMPOTENCE

*T*wo people are missing. Mauree Baktihar and Shaka Mantu. Third Will Tikal has been out searching with his team. Shaka told one of the women that he was going for a walk last night. Tikal said he tried to track him. That there wasn't even a scuff in the dirt.

Mauree Baktihar, mother of two, was last seen on the south end of the garden. The young men working in the field with her said that one minute she was there, the next she was gone. They wondered if maybe she'd stepped into the bushes to relieve herself.

Again, not a sign can be found.

As if my people would know what to look for.

I don't know what to do. Call everyone into the admin dome? Bar the doors? Tell my people that we're going to have to live like we did on Deck Three? Locked away? And that if we travel outside, we must do so in large parties for mutual protection?

Around me, the cafeteria is silent but for a humming from the air system and the rattling of the refrigeration back in the kitchen. On their tables, the Prophets are still for the most part. Occasionally one of them will twitch, jerk a leg, or utter a rasping snore. I envy them their peace as they fall ever deeper into the universe.

As for me, I cannot sleep, cannot rest.

I think I have been played by Kalico Aguila. Led here to a sort of trap. Vartan, however, has found something in his search of the sheds. Something that, if we play it right, will give me Kalico Aguila. Assuming I can allay her suspicion and lure her back here, I look forward to adding her to my collection. I want to feel her soul as it winds its way toward immortality.

That might turn out to be my lone victory.

Vartan—who knows these things—also tells me that Tyson Station might not have walls, fences, or cell blocks, but *that we're as incarcerated here as we were on Deck Three. He told me that privately, just before retiring for bed. I suspect he's with Svetlana tonight. They seem to favor each other.*

I find myself somewhat jealous.

Instead of wrapping myself in a woman's arms and celebrating the act of procreation, I sit here, alone, and in fear.

What can the universe's purpose be? What are we supposed to learn here? Am I too stupid to figure it out? Am I so blind with my three eyes that I cannot see?

The universe might not make mistakes.

But humans do.

36

As the supper crowd chattered on with raucous volume, the sound echoed off Inga's high dome. To Miguel Galluzzi's mind, it almost gave the place that hollow echo he'd heard in great cathedrals back on Earth. Above it all, the occasional bang of thunder and the soft pattering of rain made a most remarkable backdrop.

Now he placed a hand to his overstuffed stomach and shot Shig Mosadek a sidelong appraisal where the small man perched on his bar stool, the untouched half-glass of wine before him. "Is it always this loud?"

"New people in town. This is the first time some of your crew members have been here. We're a curious bunch. And visitors, especially after three years, are a novelty. Not to mention the, shall we say, unique events you've survived getting here. Makes you and your people the center of attention."

Galluzzi stared into his glass of beer. Fought the urge to belch. How long since he'd had a full belly? Let alone the enjoyment of tastes so long forgotten? He had forced himself to eat slowly, drink with moderation, and savor each bite. After what ration had become on *Ashanti*, he'd have sold his soul to the devil if it meant gustatory satisfaction the likes of which poured with such little fanfare from Inga's kitchen.

Except that Satan already owns my soul.

"That was a rather rapid transition from a look of bliss to one of misery," the observant Shig noted.

"You are a scholar of comparative religion?"

"I am."

"Do you believe in damnation? In a form of higher justice? That we are condemned to be judged for our actions?"

Shig's dark eyes fixed on his. "I do. But not in the way

that concerns you at the moment. Parsing religious philosophies down to the grossest of blunt fundamentals, the Eastern traditions assume that existence is a struggle to rise out of the chaos of creation to attain the sublime state of nirvana. The essence of the Western traditions is that divine good and evil are in conflict, and the goal is to act in the service of good in such a manner whereby the soul is granted salvation.

"Your, torment, Captain, is whether your decision to save your ship and crew came at the expense of your humanity and soul."

Galluzzi rolled his glass of beer on its base. "I thought by scouring out Deck Three, it would make it easier. I wish there was a way to scour the soul."

"The Western faiths provide the penitent with paths to forgiveness, some as easy as simply declaring yourself to be a believer. In a single stroke—or a dunking—your sins are washed away. All is forgiven. In other traditions, it's a little more difficult."

"That sounds remarkably like a cheat."

Shig chuckled to himself. Smiled. "Indulge me in a little experiment. A mind game. Looking back with the God-like clarity of hindsight, let's put the 'you' of today—knowing what you do now—back in that place. In that terrible moment of decision, what would you change? What would you decide differently?"

"I don't know, Shig. I chose my ship and crew, and in the process, condemned three hundred and forty-two people to starvation, murder, and madness. That was a crime against humanity. Those people were under my care, my responsibility. Given what they suffered? Well, someone has to pay."

"Thought you'd be arrested upon arrival, didn't you say?"

Galluzzi's right hand began to twitch. "And here I sit, with a full stomach and a tasty beer. Where's the justice in that? I feel . . . disgusted with myself."

"You haven't answered my question: With the benefit of hindsight, what would you do differently?"

"That question tortures me every night. Lurks down under my every waking moment. Those were innocent, good, and amiable men, women, and children. They were decent human beings guilty of nothing. They were deserving of the best."

"Having thought it all through, you still can't find a better solution than the one you made?"

He shook his head, a leaden emptiness in his gut. "If there is justice, why am I still alive and so many of those good people dead? I turned the ones who survived into monsters. And in the process, became one myself. God, karma, the universe, even the quanta should see me blasted and burned for eternity."

He tried to keep his voice from breaking. Damn it. He jammed his spastic right hand behind his belt.

Before Shig could reply, he said, "But if I'm not to be held responsible? If the Supervisor isn't going to arrest me, try me, punish me? There's part of me that urges me to walk down to the shuttle deck, key in the override, and cycle the lock. Let it blow my body out into vacuum." Galluzzi smiled wistfully. "I find a certain solace in the notion that for the rest of eternity, my body will tumble through the frozen and empty black. Staring sightlessly, limbs fixed, the moment of horror caught forever on my face. That out there, like that, I can finally atone."

Shig sat for a moment, head cocked, frown lines deepening on his forehead. "Tomorrow morning, will you take a ride with me? There's something I want to show you."

Galluzzi snorted his displeasure with himself. "What have I got to lose?"

37

Out on the aircar field, Talina Perez walked up and slapped a hand against the hull of Kalico's heavy airtruck. The vehicle had been unloaded from *Ashanti*'s hold the day before. Had spent all night with its powerpack on charge from Port Authority's grid.

Kalico had been living the high life back in Transluna when the last airtruck on Donovan had failed, stranding its cargo and passengers atop a ridge out in the Blood Mountains. The hull, stripped of anything useful, still sat there as a lonely beacon of dying dreams.

"You really think this is a good idea?" Talina asked, squinting in Capella's reflected light where it beamed off the polished duraplast bodywork.

Kalico turned as a wagon was trundled up to the tailgate and Terry Miska began handing crates of produce up to his wife Sasha. They'd had a bumper crop of okra and broccoli. Not to mention that they'd managed a good harvest from the wheat and rye crop. All staples that didn't grow at Tyson Station.

"They're still technically Corporate," Kalico told her. "Legally, they remain my responsibility." She indicated the containers of wheat being loaded into the back of the airtruck. "After the food offering they gave us last time, maybe this will soften the blow. No telling how they're going to react when I tell them that their prophets are victims of dementia."

"Why don't you wait? Give it a couple of days. At least until I get back. Then I'll go along."

"I'll be fine. They didn't even raise a finger last time Talbot was out there. If we have to eat another meal of Tyson green beans, I'm going to puke. Privates Carson and Muldare will be backup. They'll handle security."

"They going along in combat armor? With tech?"

"Thought about it. But after Talbot's last trip, I think

the Unreconciled have figured out how much they need us. Besides, I can handle it." She tapped the butt of the pistol on her hip. "Compared to mobbers, *Freelander*, and Tam Benteen, what are some whacked-out cannibals?"

"It's a cult."

"They're unarmed. Mostly malnourished women and children. It's just a hop out to drop off a load of food and to let them know what we discovered about the prophets. Give them a heads up that the people susceptible to kuru, the ones who are infected? Well, there's nothing we can do for them."

"So, why can't you do that with Carson and Muldare wearing armor?"

"Like that woman, Svetlana, told Talbot: Someone has to start treating them like human beings. By now it's sinking in that they're really going to make it, and they have to be asking questions: What's the future? How are we going to be treated? Are we abandoned out here? Cut off like pariahs? Are we condemned to be monsters?"

"Uh, yeah."

"Oh, come on, Tal. You, of all people, should know what it's like when everyone is looking at you like you're some sort of freak. Or have you forgotten why you ran off to Rork Springs?"

"My point is that they're not going to break down and sob over the future if your marines are in armor."

"Maybe, but it's a symbol that they're not trusted."

"Damn straight."

"If they were going to cause trouble, they'd have tried something with Talbot."

"So why you taking this?" Talina thumbed the side of the airtruck. "I'd be a hell of a lot happier if you rode out there in the shuttle."

"The A-7's up in orbit for repairs. Makarov's got the *Ashanti* shuttle techs doing a refit. Hell, we were only about four hundred hours overdue for maintenance on that bird. It'll be about a week, and she'll be back to as close to pristine as we can get without a space dock. This has the battery capacity to fly me out and back without a recharge."

"So you're placing your faith in an untested airtruck to meet with a bunch of cannibals, tell them their holy men are demented, and your marines aren't wearing armor when you do it."

"You make it sound insane."

"No shit."

At that junction Mark Talbot—pack and rifle slung over his shoulder—rounded the airtruck; his wife, Dya Simonov walked at his side. "We ready?"

Talina called, "Dya, tell me you're not part of this insanity."

"Hey, Tal. I'm the biologist and geneticist tagging along to answer any technical questions about the prion. Besides, they radioed in that they've got a couple of sick kids. I'm going to take a look at them. Decide if we need to bring them back to Raya for treatment."

"And where are you headed to?" Kalico asked, obviously happy to change the direction of the conversation.

"Taking Taglioni out to the Briggs' place. He wants to meet Wild Ones."

"And you call me crazy? You know what'll happen to you if that guy gets so much as a scratch? Let alone parasitized by a slug? Or worse, eaten?"

Talina arched a suggestive eyebrow. "The terrible Taglionis don't worry me."

"Well, they should." Kalico gave her a humorless grin. "I was in bed with Miko. Literally. When I got here, discovered *Ashanti* was missing and Derek with it, I breathed a huge sigh of relief."

"He may not be such a bad guy," Talina said.

"The scum-sucker I met a couple of times back on Transluna? A real piece of work. Maybe he's changed. Maybe, down under all that Taglioni cunning, he hasn't. He's a quetzal, Tal. And you think I'm crazy?" Kalico turned. "Come on, folks. Let's saddle up, as they say. Carson? Muldare? You aboard?"

"Here, Supervisor!" Carson's dark face appeared in the doorway.

A slam from the rear tailgate was accompanied by Terry Miska's call, "You're loaded, Supervisor. Thanks for the business."

Kalico put a foot in the step and swung up to the cab. "See you when I get back."

"Hey." Talina slapped the airtruck again. "This thing starts giving you trouble, remember, the Briggs homestead is your closest refuge. If you're down on charge, don't even think of flying it all the way back here."

"Got it." Kalico took a place in the front where she could see.

As she waved at Tal, she reassured herself. It would just be out and back.

38

Beyond the shuttle view ports, Donovan's sky darkened above the curved haze of atmosphere. Capella hung low over the eastern horizon as the shuttle arched its way into the indigo reaches that gave way to star-frosted space.

Miguel Galluzzi glanced to the side where Shig sat at the window seat, his eyes wide, rapt at the sight as the planet seemed to drop away below them.

"I'd think you'd never spaced before," Galluzzi noted.

"It remains a miracle, you know." Shig's voice was filled with awe. "This experience should never be commonplace. Should never be taken for granted."

"It's just a shuttle ride."

"Is it?" Shig turned thoughtful eyes his way. "Think, Captain. For at least a couple of million years as human imagination evolved on Earth, endless generations of proto-humans and then humans dreamed of the ability to defy the bonds of gravity, first to fly, and then to tread among the stars. What we do today is magical, and I revel in it. Not just for myself, but for all those millions upon millions of dreamers who lived out their lives craving."

"Never thought of it that way."

"No. But then my hope for today is to open your mind. To expose you to a broader understanding. I want you to learn to see from outside yourself."

"My eyes only see from one direction."

"And that, my friend, is the root of the problem."

Galluzzi laughed. But then, that was the thing about Shig. The little brown man said the most confusing things with such absolute surety.

And now, here he was. Headed, who knew where? *Ashanti, Vixen*, perhaps some view of Donovan from orbit? It seemed a bit extravagant. But Shig had been insistent.

The light patter of rain on the dome had brought Miguel

Galluzzi awake at dawn. He had been lying on his side, in his underwear, on a much-too-hard mattress. A moment of terror had seized him. Gray light was pouring in a small square window to illuminate a desk, bookshelves filled with old-fashioned books, a small but neat room.

Where the hell am I?

He had sat up in panic, having no clue as to why he wasn't in his cabin, surrounded by his . . .

Another patter of rain sounded on the dome roof.

The dome roof . . .

Donovan. You're on Donovan.

It all had come rushing back to him. An evening of drinking and eating with Shig Mosadek. Well, he'd drank. Shig, somehow, had managed to make a half-glass of red wine last him the entire night.

Shig had tapped on the door as Galluzzi was dressing. With two pails containing breakfast, the short scholar had led Galluzzi out through the misty rain, through the fence to the PA shuttle where the pilot was already spooling up the thrusters.

Throughout the liftoff, Shig had resolutely refused to declare their destination.

If anything, the mystery deepened as the shuttle climbed higher into orbit.

"Coming up," the pilot, a man dressed in quetzal hide and named Bateman, declared.

"From the off side, if you don't mind," Shig added. "I'd like the captain here to get the full effect of our arrival without bias."

"Shig," Bateman announced, "sometimes you don't make any sense."

"If sense could be made," Shig riposted amiably, "they'd sell it by the gallon bucket, and at a premium."

Galluzzi, from long experience, felt the shift in attitude, estimated that Bateman was making a 1.2-g burn to change delta-v. Then came careful maneuvering, the starfield wheeling beyond the shuttle's windows.

It came as a surprise as the sialon walls of a shuttle bay appeared outside, and Bateman neatly dropped them onto grapples. The resulting thunks could be felt through the deck.

"Hard dock," Bateman announced. "Powering the hatch, and . . . yes, we have hard seal."

"*Vixen*," Galluzzi declared. If it had been *Ashanti*, the ship would have announced itself, asked to bring the shuttle in. Odd, however, that Captain Torgussen didn't have the same protocol for his ship.

Shig unbuckled, stood, and extended a hand. "After you, Captain."

Galluzzi noticed that the short scholar had picked up a pack, was slinging it over his shoulder. "So, Shig, you think a little heart-to-heart with Torgussen's going to make me see myself from the outside? As I understand it, it was his crew who voted to stay here. *Vixen*'s circumstances are entirely different from *Ashanti*'s."

"They are indeed." Shig paused long enough to cycle the hatch. As the sialon door slid to the side, he said, "Be my guest."

Galluzzi strode forward, relieved at the feel of angular acceleration as compared to gravity. He walked right into . . .

What the hell?

The room was poorly lit by a couple of flickering overhead panels. To one side, rows of chairs stood in the gloom. Trash, not to mention marks on the floor, gave the place an abandoned look.

And then there was the air! What was it? A musty and thick odor. Something that smacked of an ancient tomb.

And then he felt the first . . . What the hell did he call it? A smearing of reality, as if time and normalcy wavered? Whatever it was, for an instant the effect was as if he'd viewed the room from underwater. Felt himself shifted sideways through time and space.

The hair on his head lifted, gooseflesh rising on his arms, and a shiver twisted its way down his back.

"Where the hell . . . ?"

"Welcome to *Freelander*," Shig said softly. "Come. I have something to show you."

Galluzzi—a quiver of fear like a sprite in his guts— stood rooted as Shig walked past, paused at the dark corridor beyond, and looked back. "Come, Captain. I know you're frightened. To date, however, none of the ghosts have proved malicious to the living. Though they are hard to ignore."

"Ghosts? You talk about them like . . ." Galluzzi winced, owl-eyed enough to believe in ghosts for once.

"Yes. I do," Shig told him amiably. "Do come."

It took all of Galluzzi's will not to turn and dash full out for the shuttle's lock.

Instead, throat stuck, nerves electric, he forced himself to follow the short scholar into the corridor, the way illuminated only by Shig's handheld light.

And then something reached out from the blackness and touched the back of Galluzzi's neck.

39

The comparison was hard to avoid. The last time Talina had flown this route with soft meat it had been with Cap Taggart sitting in the passenger's seat. That time, as this, she'd been headed to Briggs' place. Then it had been to ensure that Madison was transported to town. This time it was to allow Dek Taglioni the opportunity to visit one-on-one with Wild Ones.

And why the hell was she risking her butt flying a privileged member of the aristocracy anywhere?

Because Shig had asked her to.

Sure. And quetzals could fly.

At the thought, Demon shifted in her stomach. Other quetzal images played in the back of her mind. Scenes from Kylee's childhood with Rocket, the little quetzal and Kylee playing fetch with a knotted rag. For an instant she was Rocket, feeling the joy as he charged out, his third eye keeping track of the tumbling knot of rag, air rushing through his . . .

She blinked it away.

Pay attention, or you're going to get yourself killed.

She was entering Mainway Canyon. This was the easiest route through the towering Wind Mountains. A gigantic crack in the high range, Mainway Canyon's massive vertical walls of faulted stone rose to either side. Metals gleamed where veins crisscrossed the black, green, and red-brown rock. Overhead, the canyon rim made a silhouette a couple hundred meters up. And beyond it, snow-capped and soaring peaks shot up into the sky.

"Now that's stunning," Dek said, rising from his seat to stare in awe at the bent and folded geology. Not only were the colors vivid where the strata were exposed, but the sheer walls, the deep and ink-black depths of the canyon, were some of the most awe-inspiring on the planet.

She kept a careful hand on the wheel as the always-vicious winds batted them back and forth. If there was any good news, it was that no sign of airtruck wreckage was visible splattered on the walls, so Kalico's vehicle hopefully made the passage without incident.

When they crested the summit of Best Pass, they hit the winds head on. Bucked up and down. Talina fought the controls. Dek went pale, grabbing the support bar for all he was worth. Then they were through. Tal gave her geological lecture as they crossed the exposed deep-crustal rock, then skimmed over the two-billion-year-old ocean bottom.

As they picked up the head of the Grand River, it hit her that unlike Cap, Dek Taglioni sat listening intently, his questions short and to the point. His eyes might be alight, but they gave off the intensity of a student trying to absorb all he could. As if his life depended upon it.

On Donovan that was never just an academic concern.

"See that distant knob? Closest to the right on the southern horizon? That was our refuge when Cap and I went down in the forest . . . just about . . . there." She pointed to the approximate spot in the dense tangle of trees.

"Once you were down, how did you orient yourself?"

She pointed to her wrist unit. "Compass. The trick, as I'm sure you've heard, is to keep moving. In deep forest like this, if you stop, the roots will get you. My task was to get us to that knob. On Donovan, roots can't penetrate rock. Not enough to grab onto if another tree wants to topple them."

"The trees topple each other? Why?"

"We're not sure yet. Might be that they're some form of sentient life we haven't figured out. Maybe it's just instinct. Iji wonders if perhaps a tree gets sick, and the surrounding trees uproot it, cast it down as a means of keeping the illness from spreading. On the other hand, maybe it's like children on a playground: One just pisses the others off."

She expected some snide reply. Instead, he nodded as if storing that tidbit. Then asked, "And if there's no bedrock around?"

"Climb. Lower branches are the best. You can sleep in the axial joint where the flat on the triangular branch juts out from the trunk. Nine times out of ten nothing will show up to eat you."

"And that tenth time?"

"Welcome to Donovan."

"So, tell me about this nightmare I've been hearing about? Are they around here?"

"We've never found one this far north. Or in any kind of tree except a mundo. Nightmares live up in the branches. Dangle wispy looking tentacles down to ensnare their prey. You'll know a mundo tree by the big leaves. And I mean big, like a blanket."

"So nightmares don't prowl?"

"Seem to be solitary and sedentary. What this country is, however, is mobber territory. We see a flight of them headed our way, we run for it. They top out at a little over a hundred kph, and can't hold that for long."

"And who was the lucky bastard who found that out?"

She gave him a wink. "You're looking at her. Kylee and me. Outran a flock of the nasty shits back down at Mundo Base."

"Then I guess I couldn't have a better guide."

"Yeah, you could. Kylee for one. Mark Talbot. Tip Briggs. Listen, I'm going to introduce you to Kylee and Tip. Doesn't matter that they're little more than children. If you've got a lick of sense, you'll listen to every word they say. Those kids have been living in the wild since they were born. And they're still alive. You follow what I'm saying?"

"I do. And just in case I haven't said it enough, thank you."

"Just hope I'm not making a mistake." She shot him a look. "You know, I'm crazy for taking a Taglioni out into the bush. Something goes wrong? Eventually I'm going to end up in a pile of shit."

He chuckled, eyes fixed on the vastness of forest as they followed the Grand River west. "If I could have any wish, it would be that I could ditch the name. Just be Dek Smith. Or Dek Garcia. Being a Taglioni's a pain in the ass."

"You're kind of a puzzle."

"So are you, which makes us even."

She ignored his riposte, saying, "Okay, so you're a rich guy. Corporate royalty who wants to be like the common everyday kind of Joe. Wants to turn himself into just another nameless cog in the giant wheels of life. Happens every day. Why should I be surprised?"

"Let's just say I'm here to find myself, and you're free to attribute the reasons behind the quest to a peculiar idiosyncrasy on my part."

"That's nebulous enough. How am I a puzzle?"

"You're the most capable and competent woman on Donovan. A third of the Port Authority triumvirate. Head of Security and the living legend who wants to be rid of her quetzals. Given the advantage that gives you on this planet, why would you want to be rid of such an asset?"

She uttered a bitter laugh. "It's like having strangers inside my head. I get images from the past. Unrelated memories of quetzals long dead. Visions of times and creatures I can't comprehend. Understanding of things I don't have a conceptual framework for. Screws with my sleep. And there's times they butt in at just the wrong moment."

"My point, exactly. There, see? Now we understand each other."

She wheeled the aircar, turning north to follow the Briggs River where it cut down through the basalt, remembering the overland trip she and Cap had made. Ahead, broken hills beckoned where an upthrust fault had exposed metamorphic rock rich in metals. And atop the cliff next to the waterfall where the Briggs River thundered down into its chasm, Chaco and Madison Briggs had established their claim and farmstead.

Talina took a turn around the place and settled the aircar on the farmstead flat just back from the canyon's edge. The landing pad was on open ground next to the utility shed with its plug in. The garden looked lush where it stretched to the south, tall corn, beans, peppers, heads of cabbage and tangles of squash vines all mixed together. A trellis supported flowering hops vines. The wheat and barley were turning amber, almost ready for harvest.

"Welcome to the bush," Talina told Dek as the fans spooled down. She picked up the handset for the radio, keying the mic. "Two Spot? This is Talina. Made it to Briggs safe and sound."

"Roger that, Tal. Be careful out there."

"Any word from Kalico?"

"Roger that. She set down at Tyson an hour ago."

"Let me know if you hear from her."

"Roger that. Give Chaco my regards. Tell him I haven't forgotten I owe him that twenty."

"You got it."

Talina pulled her rifle from the rack on the dash and grabbed the pack she'd laid in the rear. Taglioni lifted his war bag and gun case, then followed her over the rail. She paused only long enough to plug the aircar into the Briggs' grid to recharge.

The Briggs farmstead consisted of a collection of drying and storing sheds, the workshop, and the solar collection array. A radio mast rose above the workshop roof to provide their link to the outside world.

Chaco, an oily rag in hand, emerged from the shop, a wide grin on his face. He was third ship, had grown up on Donovan. Now edging forty, his broad face was tanned to a perpetual brown. Sandy hair hung down to his collar and contrasted with the gleaming black beard. The man wore chamois and quetzal, with a fabric shirt from town hanging on his muscular torso.

"Hey, Tal! Always glad when you make it here on the first try."

"How you doing, Chaco?"

He lifted the oil-blackened rag. "Rebuilding the bearings in the main pump. We'd be fart-sucking up the creek if ol' Tyrell Lawson hadn't found some salvage bearings the right size. Just got the thing back together."

He walked over, offering an oil-stained hand. "Chaco Briggs. Glad to meet you."

"Dek Taglioni."

They shook like equals, and to Talina's surprise, Taglioni didn't immediately wipe his hand. Didn't even so much as glance at the smudges left on his skin.

"Madison's got crest and cabbage cooking." Chaco glanced her way. "You eaten yet?"

"Not since chili this morning. Brought your shopping list. Got everything except the pipe-elbow-thing. It's all in the crate on the back seat."

Chaco was giving her his infectious grin. "Think I fixed the pipe-elbow-thing. Made a mold and cast it out of gold. It's not like we don't have gold running out of our ears around here, and it's a soft metal. Squishes under pressure, so it makes its own seal. Don't need a gasket. And being soft, it takes vibration well. It's only a day since I put it in, but we've got water back to the house."

Taglioni had been listening intently. "Gold melts at over a thousand degrees centigrade. How do you get it that hot?"

"Used to be tougher to do. Chabacho doesn't burn as hot as hardwood on Earth. Lot easier now that Ollie Throlson's got those wells producing hydrocarbons. As it is, I had to trade the guy ten chamois hides for the cylinder of gas."

"I love it," Taglioni said with genuine amusement.

Tal added, "Two Spot says he owes you twenty."

"Yeah, I made him a knife. Used quetzal bone for the scales in the handle. Did you know that when it's buffed right, quetzal bone almost looks like mother-of-pearl?"

"And how do you know what mother-of-pearl looks like?" Tal asked.

"Madison has a brooch. Belonged to her mother back on Earth. Come on. Let's eat."

Tal followed Chaco to the stairs, descending the fifty feet to where the main house was built into a cavern in the side of the canyon.

"Wow," Taglioni drawled as he stopped at the railing, looking up the canyon to where the Briggs River plunged some two hundred meters in a magnificent waterfall. Layers of mist shimmered in rainbow streamers. Here the canyon was narrow, not more than one hundred meters across. Sunlight sparkled in the mica, quartz, and veins of metal exposed in the bent and faulted strata below the layer of basalt.

And in a dazzling display below them, the Briggs River tumbled over boulders and gravel banks as it roared its way south toward the Grand.

"Not bad, huh?" Talina asked, stopping to share the view.

"Back on Earth this would all be a Corporate-owned tourist attraction."

"Hey, Tal!" Madison Briggs called, stepping out on the deck to give her a hug. She stood tall and straight, just over six feet; her smooth dark skin had a satin tone. The high cheekbones and the unusual slant of her almond eyes made her one of the most beautiful women Tal had ever seen.

"And you must be Derek Taglioni," she greeted, taking Dek's hand. "Welcome. Come. We'll eat."

Madison had set a table just inside by the large window overlooking the falls.

Taglioni was seated—as the guest—with the best view. For a time the man sat motionless, staring out the window. Chaco noticed, grinned. That window was his pride and joy. Just getting it here had been a feat. Then it had to be carefully lowered by ropes from above before it could be framed and set.

"I understand," Taglioni said, as if from a distance.

"How's that?" Madison asked as she set a plate of steaming meat and cabbage on the colorful aquajade table.

"I see why you're here. Why you'll always be here. You have found what humanity has forgotten. You have made a dream."

Tal caught the look of shared communication between Chaco and Madison. Some sort of approval.

"There's worse places to be." Chaco dug into the food with a big serving spoon. Splashed some on Tal's plate. Then Taglioni's before he saw to Madison and himself.

"Where are the kids?" Talina asked.

"Tip, Kylee, and Flute are out checking on a rogue quetzal. Youngster, maybe ten or so. Probably just passing through, but if it's trouble for the local lineage, we want to know. They were going to try and make it back before you got here." Madison gave her that irritated-mother look. "As to Maria and Skip, girls who don't get their chores done don't get to enjoy company until all the laundry is folded."

"Tip is your son," Taglioni noted. "Kylee is Dya Simonov's, but who is Flute?"

"That's their quetzal," Chaco noted, an unaccustomed reserve in his eyes.

Taglioni took a bite. Closed his eyes. Chewed as if in bliss and finally swallowed. "What *is* this taste? I've never known such a . . . an interesting, mellow, what? How do I describe this?"

Tal tried hers. This wasn't just meat and cabbage. It had

a sort of anise saffron mixed with . . . No, there was simply no Earthly comparison to the delicate taste.

Chaco looked triumphant. "Cool, huh? Made barrels from aquajade, then charred them on the inside, right? For Inga's whiskey. But that raised the question: What if we fermented cabbage in one of the barrels. Shazam! That's the taste."

"Inga will buy all you can produce."

"If I could sell this in Transluna," Taglioni declared, "we could all retire."

"I like this guy," Chaco said with a smile.

Taglioni gave him a companionly wink.

"So, what's the trouble with Flute?" Talina asked. "Something going on there?"

Chaco leaned forward on his elbows and used a napkin to clean the grease from under his fingernails. If Taglioni noticed, he didn't so much as blink. Another point for Taglioni.

"Tal, it's like they're a threesome. The good news is that we don't worry nearly so much about the wildlife. Haven't seen a skewer, a bem, or a sidewinder around the shops for more than three years now. Makes it a lot safer for Maria and Skip. On the other hand, it's like the three of them are more of a family than we are."

Madison added, "Getting harder to get Kylee and Tip to make it through their lessons. And it's weird, they seem to share thoughts. Like telepathy."

"Molecules," Tal said, knowing intuitively. "TriNA reads our memories through transferRNA. Encodes them. Then, when the molecule is handed off to another person, it uses tRNA to code the memory to another brain. I have flashes from Kylee's youth all the time. Memories of her and Rocket and Mundo Base. All from when we shared molecules."

"Worries me about what else they might be sharing out there," Chaco muttered. "You know what starts to happen between boys and girls when they turn thirteen?"

"Sometimes it's funny to call them children," Madison said. "They're a lot more mature than I was when I was thirteen. Kylee in particular. Sometimes I think I'm talking to a grown woman."

Talina gestured with her fork. "Kid's had the crap kicked out of her by life. Don't know what would have happened if you hadn't taken her in."

"Got her language mostly straightened out. Took two years to keep her from cussing like a marine. Where'd she learn that foul mouth, anyway?"

Talina winced, made a face, and raised a guilty hand. "Uh, I was under duress at the same time she had the misfortune to think of me as a role model."

Taglioni, though wolfing food, and having gone back for more, was watching with rapt attention. Seemed to be hanging on every word. What was it about the guy? He might have been studying for his comps.

"She still hate people?" Talina asked.

"Not as badly. I think it helps that Dya and Talbot fly out every couple of weeks. I don't know what to think of her. She's different. But so is Tip." Madison took another helping.

"So, Dek," Chaco turned his attention. "Heard you had a pretty rough transit from Solar System."

"Some damn fool once said that wisdom comes through adversity. Looking back on it, now that I'm so wise, I'd have been a whole lot happier to have remained arrogant, dumb, and unenlightened."

"Taglionis," Madison noted. "As I remember they were pretty high up in The Corporation."

"Yeah," Dek agreed. "Most of the time when I went to family gatherings, we had to be on oxygen."

"So what brings you to us?" Chaco asked.

"I guess I'm like a pilgrim from the old stories: a man in search of some illumination or understanding. The part of me that I lost on the way here? I need to replace it with something else."

"You any good with tools?" Chaco asked. "Want to help me put that pump I just fixed back in the water system?"

Slugs in the mud! Chaco had just asked a fricking Taglioni to . . .

Instead of the rude response or explosion Talina expected, the man said, "Sure. Be my pleasure."

Well, what the hell other surprises lurked inside that unassuming shell?

40

I t hit him like an explosion. The scintillating pleasure shot through Dan Wirth's pelvis, up his backbone, and tingled the bottoms of his feet. He gasped, crying out as Allison's practiced muscles tightened and she rocked her hips. Rode his orgasm for every delicious instant of it.

Panting, Wirth rolled off of her, leaving his arm to drape over Allison's chest. "Wow," he rasped as the tingle faded. He blinked up at the ceiling. He'd had Hofer's best man hand-plaster the bedroom. Like Allison, there was nothing to match it on the entire planet.

"No complaints?" Allison asked, reaching for a cloth to mop up.

"You do that for all of the marks?"

"Of course. But you're the only one that gets it on demand and for free."

"Lucky me, eh?"

She was watching him with those calculating eyes. He missed the old Allison. The innocent one with the wounded-bird expression and hesitant, almost desperate approach toward life.

"You've been preoccupied." She tossed the cloth to the side.

"What's your take on Taglioni?"

"Not sure. He's different. I've given him the eye, he just nods. Has that strange smile like he knows and understands, is actually appreciative, but not interested."

"Think he's into men?"

"No. Definitely heterosexual, just not into a casual fuck." She shifted. "You remember, don't you, that we promised Aguila we wouldn't take him down."

"He says he can fix it. Make it so that I can go back. Live like a fucking Boardmember and lord it among all those high and mighty cocksucking assholes in Transluna. The slate wiped clean. A whole new life for Dan Wirth."

He waggled a cautionary finger. "All for ten percent and expenses. You know, the unsavory bribes for the Board and the rest of the ass-fucking bureaucrats. Now, why do I smell a quetzal in the bushes? What's wrong with this picture?"

"He say why he'd do it?"

"As a fuck-you to his cousin who's on the Board. And I'm supposed to believe that?"

Allison raised a pale shoulder in a shrug. "What else did he say?"

"That he's staying here. That he's not going back. And I'm supposed to believe that a child of that kind of wealth and privilege just lets it all go?"

"Depends on what happened on *Ashanti*. From the crew I heard that he scrubbed toilets. Lived with them, worked with them, no job too tough. Their story is that he changed when they all thought they were going to die. Maybe he doesn't want to chance that again. Aguila didn't. Not after *Freelander* showed up."

"So I trust the fancy prick?"

Allison reached out, turned his head to face hers. "You've been getting moody. You've got an anger building inside. Then, after you talked to Taglioni, you've been more like the old Dan. Like you're plotting and planning again. So tell me. The truth. What do you want?"

"I'm the richest man on the fucking planet."

"You are."

"I had to trade a bedroom addition for a toilet-sucking scarf. Those two safes. They're bursting. That's real wealth. Not on paper, or a line of credit. The triumvirate or Aguila need something, they come to me. I own half of this miserable planet. So, what's the point?"

She considered, the ghost of a smile molding her lips. "Wondered if that wasn't the trouble."

"Hmm?"

"He dangled the carrot, and you can't help but bite at it, hoping it's for real." A beat. "Might be. If it is, you'd go back?"

"To play in the big game? Baby cakes, I'd go in a second."

"So, he's offered you the chance to go back on *Ashanti*?

Is that the fool's play? Or is it the lucky draw? How do you tell if it's real, or a sucker's bet on red twenty-two?"

"Oh, I don't trust the fucker for an instant. I think he's playing me. Wants to use my wealth to bitch-slap that cousin of his. Now, knowing that, am I smart enough to sidestep the landmines before they blow my fucking foot off?"

"Are you?"

He made a face. "See, that's the gamble. Those Corporate cocksuckers play a rigged game. But tell me, who knows more about rigged games than me, huh?"

"You got any insurance that good old Dek won't have you arrested the moment you step off *Ashanti*? Then he gets all the plunder, and you're fucked."

"Oh, angel, you have no idea how that very thought rolls around inside my head. But, no. Sometimes you've got to go with instincts. Rather than making a fast fortune, I think he's playing a long game. Wants to use me as a pawn on the Corporate chessboard."

"Pawns get sacrificed."

"Uh-huh. And if they make it all the way across the board, they get turned into queens who can really kick ass."

She shifted, stared at him with an uncommon intensity. "You're seriously thinking about going, aren't you? Even knowing the risks."

He smiled, slapped a hand to her toned stomach. "What about you? Want to go with me?"

"Not for the time being."

"Oh?"

"Like you, I'm willing to play the long game." A pause. "What happens with The Jewel? This house? Your interests here?"

He gave her his coldest, threatening look. "You asked for forty-nine percent once. I'll give you half of everything. Anything you establish from here on out, that's yours. But don't fuck with my half."

"What about the house here?"

"Yours. But in return, you fucking damn well better be sending plunder back in my name. You see, Dek's right about one thing: If *Ashanti* makes it back to Solar System, they *will* be sending more ships. If my share of the plunder isn't on board, I'll still be rich enough to hire some nasty shit-sucker to pay you a visit."

"I'm smarter than that."

"Yeah. I think you are. You got the balls to do what has to be done?"

She gave him a taunting smile. "Only one possible problem."

"What's that?"

"Your good Mister Taglioni? He's out in the bush at the Briggs place. Odds are better than forty to one the silly son of a bitch is going to get himself killed before he can do either one of us any good."

TRAP

I *live in a state of confusion that I cannot confide to any-one. To do so would be a sign of weakness. If there is anything the Irredenta do not need at this point, it's even the suggestion that I am not in complete control. That I doubt—in any way—the Will of the universe.*

That's on the surface. The façade I present. The persona that I adopt.

Inside, I wish I could drop to my knees, raise my hands and implore the universe: Did I not sacrifice everything for you? I murdered my fellows, ate their flesh and organs in an act of holy sacrament. I committed myself, without res-ervation, to your Truths. I followed, without question, the wisdom of the Prophets. Endured the hideous agony of scarification as I sliced my skin and repeated the process time after time. Used a cleaver to amputate the soft flesh of my nose. Made my body a repository for the dead and de-stroyed relationships to ensure the dead I harbored would be reborn in the next available female.

How is my faith and sacrifice repaid?

Fatima continues to suffer. Three more people are miss-ing, two of them children.

And still another child, young Pho, is dead. This time, we know what happened. Manram saw the plant reach down, wind itself around the screaming child. The little boy was lifted off the ground and the plant began eating him. Manram ran forward, tried to pull little Pho away, and was grabbed up herself. She barely managed to tear free; large chunks of her arms, the flesh of her hands, a large patch of her shoulder are missing.

Another, Renzo Demopolis, age six, was found at the edge of the escarpment. He was in convulsions. Something blue staining his mouth. He's now laid out in the cafeteria in hopes the Prophets will, through some utterance, tell us how to cure the boy.

The impact is devastating. The children are the reborn souls of the dead. Purified. The universe promised they'd be immortal. That the Irredenta were the way—the vehicle through which all of humanity, the universe itself, would be purified.

I am achingly, painfully, aware that each of these children who dies at the hands of Donovan will be lost. For them, death is once again eternal and absolute. Renzo and the slug-infested Fatima, we can save. We can consume their remains again and insure their eventual reincarnation.

At least, I hope so.

I need the Prophets! I need their counsel. But to my absolute frustration, Irdan is mute this morning. Won't eat. His breathing is shallow, his limbs barely twitch. Callista and Guan Shi are mumbling so softly I can't hear, seem to be fading just as fast. I really look at them now, realize how wasted their bodies are. Living skeletons draped with sallow and loose skin. Their eyes have sunken so deeply into the sockets, they remind me of those Mexican Day of the Dead masks.

And what happens when they die?

With people bustling around the cafeteria, I dare not show despair. I cannot drop my head in my hands.

Cannot weep.

I am the Messiah.

I am contemplating the uncomfortable realization that I am the loneliest man alive when Shyanne Veda hurries in from the hallway, stops before me, and bows.

"Messiah," she says, avoiding my eyes. "There's a call on the radio. Supervisor Aguila is flying in. Says they're bringing provisions and want to give us some information. Should I answer?"

I give this consideration.

Is this the universe coming to my aid? And so much faster than Petre, the Chosen, and Vartan had anticipated?

That old and innate sense of opportunity fills me. "Tell the Supervisor we are delighted to accommodate her." Raising my voice, I call, "Someone! Find Petre! Call the Chosen. The Corporation is coming! You know the plan. It's time to spring our trap."

And in that instant, relief pours through me like a cool and refreshing wave.

I chuckle like a gleeful child.

I finally understand.

Of course we're suffering. Once again, the universe is teaching us a lesson: Just because we're in a new place doesn't mean we forget the holy Truths.

In this case, the Truth is that there is no progress without sacrifice, pain, and purification.

We need a new sacrament, and Kalico Aguila shall be our first. But we must play it perfectly. Petre and Svetlana have worked this out, planned every aspect of how to lure Aguila and her people to the right place. As The Corporation is the epitome of deceit, we must be even more cunning. As long as they are not wearing armor, if we play this correctly, it will make no difference.

41

Donovan's immense and endless forest gave way to the escarpment upon which Tyson Station perched. The day had gone from uncomfortably warm to downright hot. Kalico shifted her quetzal-leather hat where it hung down her back, the strap tight at her throat. Anything to get a little air. She wished she'd worn something lighter.

She stood beside Mark Talbot as the ex-marine kept the airtruck skimming a good two hundred meters above the highest treetops. Thickly packed forest stretched off to the irregular horizons—a lumpy mass composed of aqua-jade, various species of chabacho, stonewood, broadvine, and the curiously turquoise trees she'd never heard a name for.

And then, here and there, they would overfly an open spot, something she'd never seen except around Tyson. Usually it was a round hole in the forest, maybe a couple hundred meters in diameter and surrounded by towering trees. In the center, all alone, stood a most unique tree. Another uncatalogued species. This one a bright lime green with branches that ended in oversized round-shaped flat spatulate structures—could you really call them leaves? They reminded her of supersized ping-pong paddles on flexible stems. The tall tree occupied the exact center of the opening; apparently the rest of the forest wouldn't dare to intrude. Given the way Donovanian forest jostled, shoved, fought, and crowded, that made the plant, tree, or whatever it was, more than a little ominous.

Talbot pulled back on the wheel, and the airtruck climbed as it approached the dark basalt cliff upon which Tyson Station had been built. He crested the caprock and hovered while Kalico, Dya, and the two marines studied the research base. A couple of people were out, watching, hands to their brows to shade them as they squinted against Capella's bright rays.

"Try them again," Kalico said to Dya.

The woman lifted the mic, saying, "Tyson Base, this is the Supervisor. We're inbound with a load of provisions. We have issues we need to discuss. Please respond."

"We see you. You are free to park. Look forward to serving you."

"Serving us? Hope that isn't a cannibal joke." Private Muldare observed where she stared thoughtfully out at the five domes. They looked out of place—white and round as they were against the green, blue, and gray background. The sheds, made of chabacho wood, had more or less faded into the scenery as they weathered.

"Park? What is it with these people?" Kalico muttered under her breath. "All right, set us down in the landing field, Mark. But be ready to fly if they make a run for the airtruck. Carson, Muldare, be ready. Weapons on safety, but chambered."

She heard "yes ma'ams" all the way around.

Kalico braced a hand on the grabrail as Talbot swung the airtruck in a wide circle, settling onto the landing pad with the lightest of touches.

Kalico waited, counting the seconds. The people standing out before the domes just watched. A couple were talking back and forth, obviously about the airtruck's arrival. Nothing, however, indicated the slightest apprehension, not the least bit of concern. People didn't look off toward any of the sheds or other domes like they would if an armed party were hidden there and were expected to issue forth at any moment.

"Nothing," Talbot said through an exhale. "That's a relief."

"Very well," Kalico said. "Let's get those crates of food offloaded. Carson, Muldare, you're on guard so keep your eyes open."

Talbot lowered the tailgate, jumped down, and started offloading the crates that Dya and Kalico handed him.

Can you believe this? Kalico asked herself as she manhandled another crate to the tailgate. *I'm a pus-rotted Supervisor, working like a dockhand.*

Kalico muscled another of the heavy crates around. Imagine what Miko Taglioni would have said. Perhaps something like: "My, how the mighty have fallen."

It took them all of fifteen minutes to stack the crates off to one side. In that time, another three people appeared to watch the proceedings.

Finishing, Kalico wiped the sweat from her forehead and ordered, "Carson, you stay here. No one gets access to the airtruck."

"Yes, ma'am." Carson snapped a saluting hand to his brow.

"Why is my gut doing flip-flops?" Dya asked as Kalico led the way toward the large dome that housed admin, the cafeteria, and the offices.

Kalico nodded to the watching people as she approached, asking, "Where's Batuhan? Um . . . the first and last? Your leader."

"In there," one of the young men told her, averting his eyes in the process of pointing toward the admin dome. Then he scuttled away, as if afraid he'd be tainted just by her presence.

"Something's happened," Talbot half growled. "Last time, it was all a happy parade."

"Wish we were in armor." Muldare tightened her grip on her rifle.

"On your toes, people," Kalico muttered, her hand on her pistol. She led the way, pushed open the double doors, and strode down the hallway. Glancing in doors as she passed, it was to see the rooms vacant. Arriving in the cafeteria, she recognized a couple of the throne-bearers huddled around a little boy who'd been laid on one of the tables in the rear.

One looked up and started before saying, "Oh, it's you. What are you doing here?"

"Don't you listen to your radio? We've brought a load of groceries, things that don't grow here. It's all stacked out on the landing pad. Where's your boss?"

"Our boss—as you say—is the universe."

"Batuhan. Where is he? We need to talk."

"Then, let us talk, Supervisor," Batuhan announced, stepping out from one of the side doors. The big weird blue eye painted on his forehead and the amputated nose were always disconcerting. He carried his human-thigh-bone scepter in his right hand. The man was dressed in a breechcloth; his skin—apparently unwashed—still showed evidence of the white stuff he'd been plastered with aboard *Ashanti*. He walked over to the throne, seated himself, and crossed his legs as he studied first Kalico, and then Dya, before shifting his gaze to Briah Muldare, who stood at attention. Talbot, he ignored.

"Nice," he murmured. "Three beautiful, strong, and healthy females of breeding age. Such a change. But then, as the fetus, upon exiting the womb, transitions from the umbilical to its first solid sustenance, so to do we metaphorically make the change during our own birth."

"Right," Kalico told him. "And you'd damn well better stick to your metaphors. We're not your acolytes. But tell me. What's with the scars? Why the mazes on your cheeks? What's that all about?"

He raised a finger to the corner of his mouth, flat black gaze on hers. The blue eye on his forehead sent a quiver through her. Seemed to look right through her. She noticed that his fingernail was long, stained black with something that looked like dirty axle grease.

"I am the way," he said. "The beginning and the end. Only through me will you find salvation. But the body and soul are different, a duality of existences. Upon a person's death, through the sacrament of consumption, the body begins its transition to purification."

"Yeah, I got that part," Kalico told him.

Dya was looking at the guy like he was her worst nightmare. Talbot was fingering his pistol. Muldare's expression hinted that Batuhan was the most disgusting human she'd ever seen.

Call it unanimous in Kalico's eyes. "You left five butchered skeletons on *Ashanti*. They do something to piss you off, or just have an unlucky day?"

"At the last moment, their faith wavered. Salvation depends upon unity of spirit."

"And they didn't live up to your expectations, huh? So, what's with the patterns of scars? How does cutting designs into living skin purify the soul?"

Batuhan adopted the same tone he would use when talking to a child. "When we consume the body, it follows the path past the lips, over the tongue, and down the throat.

In the stomach it begins its assimilation, passing through the guts until finally only the profane—the summation of darkness, foul, and refused of salvation—is voided from the anus."

"No need to elaborate on that," Dya muttered.

Batuhan didn't even bat an eye. "The rest of the body, the pure portion, has begun its journey toward salvation. It is assimilated into our living flesh, made part of the whole. In the receptacle of my body, it lives on.

"But not being physical the soul releases itself from the flesh. It enters here"—he tapped the side of his mouth at the opening to the maze—"separating from the body at the time of consumption. Keep in mind that the soul is light, airy. Adrift without the flesh that once anchored it. Seeking any path, it enters the maze. A receptacle. A place into which the soul must lose itself. It must try this direction and that, slowly working out its way. Learning. Experiencing the twists and turns, feeling out the dead ends."

"Screw me in vacuum," Talbot whispered just loud enough for Kalico to hear.

Batuhan closed his eyes, leaned his head back. The big blue eye in the middle of his forehead stared mockingly as he played his long black fingernail through the various paths in the maze scarring his right cheek. The expression on the man's face was rapturous.

Dya looked sick. Muldare's face had gone pale.

Through a long exhale, Batuhan said, "Only when the soul has matured in the maze and found its way does it locate the exit." His black nail had wound through the twists and turns to the opening just in front of his ear. "From here it follows the path."

Batuhan's black nail traced the long line of scar tissue down the side of his neck, then forward to the suprasternal notch. From there the scar tissue split into three lines: the left into one pectoral spiral, the center ran straight down the man's belly, and the right into the right pectoral spiral.

Batuhan tapped fingers against his chest, saying, "The paths, one on the right, one on the left, lead to the spirals." The black fingernail traced the routes. "There, the souls that have not yet reached illumination are led in an ever-decreasing radius to the nipples. There they reside until a woman suckles them into her own body."

"Excuse me?" Dya snapped. "Did you say suckles?"

Batuhan fixed on her with dark and intense eyes. "Of course. In the same way a woman provides an infant with milk, I provide a supplicant woman with one of the souls that has lodged in my right or left nipple. She produces physical sustenance when an infant sucks from her breast. I produce a spiritual essence when she sucks from mine."

Kalico couldn't stop the shiver from running down her spine.

Fixed on Dya, Batuhan smiled. "I have the feeling that you are empty, a void that longs to be filled. Would you like to partake?" He shifted and offered his right breast in Dya's direction.

Kalico shot out a restraining hand as Talbot started forward.

"Not on your life," Dya managed through gritted teeth.

"And the center line?" Kalico asked, desperate to get off the subject of Batuhan's breasts.

"Ah, that is the route chosen by those souls that have achieved true purity." Batuhan shifted his dark-eyed gaze to hers. The black fingernail traced down the line of scar tissue to the separation around his navel, and then down under his breechcloth.

Kalico remembered the scars ending at the root of his penis. "Where, along with your semen, they can be deposited into a fertile female," she finished.

"Quite so." Again he leaned his head back, eyes closed, and took a deep breath. "I am the beginning and the end. I am the purification of the body and the soul's route to immortality."

"Then," Dya asked, "what's with the eye cut into your forehead?"

"It was a gift from the Prophets, who know the universe's will."

Kalico ground her teeth, feeling ill. Pus and ions, but she wanted to be shut of this place. Maybe nuke it from space. "Yeah, about your Prophets. We've got some information about them. Have you ever heard of prions? Or something called kuru? Spongiform encephalitis?"

"No."

"It's a protein disease, one communicable to people with a homozygous recessive genetic predisposition. It's called kuru, though it hasn't been seen since the early twenty-first century. It comes from eating another human being's brain, spinal fluid, or infected—"

"Stop it! Of course you'd manufacture such foolishness. Not only do we have no desire to hear, but we anticipated your heresy. The universe told us in no uncertain terms that you would do anything in your power—corrupt and tainted as you are—to mislead us."

Dya said, "It's not misleading, don't you understand? Your prophets are going to die. Their brains are already riddled with lesions. And you have other people—"

"Enough!" he barked, straining upright. "You are the mouths of deceit. Lies incarnate sent to tempt the pure back into perdition. By your very declarations, you betray yourselves. And in the end, we will finally rid you of your pollution. You will come to understand." He paused. Smiled to himself. "Soon."

Yeah, right. But Kalico gestured for silence on Dya's part as the woman drew breath to object. Saw the almost pleading look the woman gave her.

Batuhan studied his scepter as if something fascinating were to be found in the intricate carvings. "I need you to tell me what's wrong with two children. And then I need you to leave. And when you do, I want you to never come back. Our people don't need your kind of duplicity."

Kalico fought to keep her expression under control.

"Is that one of the children?" Dya asked, indicating the boy on the back table.

"It is. The other is a little girl. We think something is inside her body, so we put her in a back room where, if the creatures get loose, we can contain them."

"What's with the boy?" Kalico asked, stepping close to the kid. She looked down to see a half-wasted little urchin, his skin puckered in patterns of scars. That they were already white indicated he couldn't have been more than three or four when the boy had been scarified.

"Don't know," the first man said. "Found him like this at the edge of the cliff."

Dya leaned over, squinted at the faint blue stain on his swollen lips. "He ate berries off one of the bluelinda vines. They're pretty, almost a crystal blue, and deadly." She sighed, stepped back. "If you could see inside his mouth, you'd discover it's already blistered. Blood vessels are breaking in his tongue, the back of his throat, clear into his brain. The same in his stomach, and as soon as the enzymes eat through, his liver and kidneys will be riddled."

"What's bluelinda?" the third man asked. "How do we know which of the native plants to keep the children away from?"

"Keep them away from *all of them*!" Dya almost shrilled. "What part of 'all the native plants are dangerous' don't you get?"

"Hey," Kalico said, "easy. Now, what's with this little girl?"

"She's in the back," the first man told her, his eyes a flat brown, as if no emotion remained there. "Something's wiggling in her leg. Like a moving knot."

"Want to bet it's a slug?" Talbot managed to say through gritted teeth.

"Take us," Dya snapped. "If it's a slug maybe we can still save her."

"Might cost her the leg," Mark noted as they followed the man toward the door in the rear. "Was she barefoot?"

"To be barefoot is a sign of humility." Their guide had a prim, superior tone in his voice.

Dya turned to where Batuhan still sat in his throne. She snapped out, "This is Donovan, do you get it? There is nothing, *nothing* on this planet that won't kill you. Now, round your people up, get them dressed, and keep the kids out of trouble."

Before following the man down the hall, Kalico turned one last time to Batuhan. "Did you hear what she said? Otherwise, you're not going to have any children, let alone people."

Dya was almost vibrating with rage as she stomped along behind their guide. "They just let children wander? Are they mad?"

"Just ignorant," Talbot said in a calming voice.

Private Muldare had kept quiet, her hazel eyes shifting

this way and that, clearly uncomfortable. Her hand remained on the action of her slung rifle as they followed a hallway to the rear.

"Why'd you put her clear back here?" Talbot asked, a wary tone in his voice.

"Thought that if something was alive in her, and it got loose, we could catch it here in the back room." Their guide shot them a sidelong look. "You still don't get it, do you?"

"Get what?" Kalico asked.

"These children really aren't dying. The universe might be killing their bodies for the moment, but they're going to be purified and reborn. There is no such thing as permanent death among the universe's chosen."

Kalico made a desist gesture in Dya's direction to keep the woman from leaping for the guy's throat.

They had laid the little girl on a table in one of the storage rooms at the back of the dome. She lay naked on the duraplast surface, and Kalico winced. She could see three lumps moving slowly under the little girl's scarred skin. One on her upper thigh, two more slipping along under the delicate skin of her stomach.

"Shit!" Dya hissed, coming to a stop.

The little girl was writhing, her arms flexing, hands knotting, while whimpers broke from her throat. Behind the delicate lids, her eyeballs were flicking back and forth. The kid looked to be in agony as the slugs slithered through her guts.

"That's two we can't help," Talbot said. "Not with the slugs in her belly already."

"*Supervisor!*" came the cry in her earbud. "*Carson here. They're making a try for the airtruck. I'm . . .*"

Kalico was turning for the door when the distant bang of a rifle sounded. The throne-bearer whirled, leaped from the room, and slammed the heavy door shut behind him.

"Carson! Carson! Stat report! Carson!"

Even before Talbot could get a hand on the knob, the sound of the lock clicking home could be heard.

"The only way Carson wouldn't be responding is if he's dead," Talbot said laconically, a finger to his earbud as he glared at the locked door.

"Lot of good that's going to do them," Muldare noted

dryly as she unslung her service rifle. "Mark, step back. I've got an explosive round chambered. I'll blow the damned door straight off its hinges."

As Talbot leaped back, Batuhan's voice sounded through the room speaker overhead. *"If you attempt to shoot your way out, we will detonate the magtex charge in the ceiling. Most likely, so my people tell me, it won't kill you outright. They assure me, however, that you will be sufficiently stunned that we can disarm you and secure you without issue."*

Magtex? Where did they find the magtex?

But then, it was a mining colony. Could have been in any of the boxes out in the sheds.

"What about this little girl?" Kalico demanded, stepping forward. "You going to blow her up, too?"

"Fatima is already dying. Her body will become one with us, purified, and she shall be reborn into a better existence."

"Sick son of a bitch," Dya hissed, hands clenched.

"So?" Batuhan's voice asked reasonably. *"What will it be? Will you lay down your weapons? Or shall my people simply remove them from your stunned and disoriented bodies? For our purposes, it matters not if you are a little bruised and tenderized. Purification is a painful business either way."*

Talbot leaned close to whisper, "I don't see a camera. He can't see us, just hear us."

"Got something in mind?" Kalico mouthed the words.

"Plan B." And so saying, Talbot shoved a crate against the door knob to block it. Then he pulled his knife, stepped over to the BoPET polyethylene terephthalate wall, and with all his might, drove the blade into the plastic.

42

For this to work, everything must happen exactly as planned. That thought kept rolling around in Vartan's head as he paused behind a rusty piece of mothballed equipment at the edge of the landing field. The rear of the airtruck lay no more than thirty meters from his hiding place.

Capella's hard light burned down on his bare head, scorched his already sunburned shoulders. The heat waves rising off the hard basalt and low vegetation amazed him. Sort of like looking across the top of a hot stove. He'd never seen such a thing, even when he'd been on Earth those few days.

Being out in the open was still too new, the light, the moving air, the endless sky, all that musical sound from the wildlife. It scared him. Way down deep. Not to mention that he might be dead in a matter of moments.

The plan had made so much sense when he pitched it to Petre. But it was one thing to propose such an absurd idea while sitting in the cafeteria over a cup of delicious mint tea. Quite another to be creeping up to the airtruck, knowing that if the marine guarding it peered over the side, he'd be shot within an instant.

His heart hammered in his breast. A sheen of nerve-sweat had broken out on his face, neck, and chest. He felt sick to his stomach, muscles quivering.

Step by step, he made his way closer, and yes, right on cue, here came Svetlana, five of the children in tow as they emerged from the garden. The children—having been coached—caught sight of the airtruck, and at a whispered command, charged forward, shouting, laughing.

Perfect!

For the first time, Vartan entertained the faint hope that he might survive this after all.

Sure, the Messiah always promised that anyone who

died would be reborn. That through the Irredenta, they were all immortal. It came across as such a reassuring thought: His flesh would be consumed, purified, and his immortal soul would travel the maze, find its way into a woman's womb during intercourse. That he would be born again.

He licked dry lips and wondered if he really and truly believed.

The children were almost to the airtruck. The guard would have his attention focused solely on them.

Vartan sprinted for the airtruck. Reached the side. He flattened himself. Panting, he tightened his grip on the tape-wrapped stave of flexible steel.

It had come to him: If the Supervisor had left them defenseless, they'd have to craft their own weapons. Rail guns and rifles were too complicated. But humans had been building weapons for all of their existence. Bows were still used in sporting competitions back in Solar System.

He'd found the length of steel, tested its flex, and fashioned the bowstring from thin cable. The arrow, he had crafted from a dowel. To create fletching, he cut plastic to shape.

Not only that, but in practice, he could hit a man-shaped target dead center from ten paces.

"Hey, back away!" the guard bellowed from the cab door.

"They're just children!" Svetlana's voice protested.

"I said, get away!"

Vartan's heart had turned manic. Sweat was trickling down the side of his face. Fright bunched in his throat.

He crept around the front of the vehicle, saw Svetlana's subtle gesture to wait. She shooed the children away, stepping close to the airtruck. "What would you do? Shoot me? An unarmed woman?"

"Listen, we don't want trouble."

Vartan crouched, Svetlana at the edge of his vision as she walked up to the airtruck. "Step down here. Let me see you. Been a lot of years since I've seen another man."

"Can't ma'am."

Svetlana looked around. "Hey, uh, there's only you and

me. The kids are gone. I mean it. I want to look at you. Surely an undernourished and naked woman isn't a threat to a big man with a rifle."

The guard laughed, clearly uncomfortable.

"It's the scars, isn't it?" she said after a pause. "That's what fascinates you. They all mean something. It's for the souls of the dead. Oh, come on. You're not going to be able to see from up there."

Vartan heard the man step down from the cab. Svetlana backed away, giving him room. Asked, "Is it the spirals on my breasts? That's for the souls to follow when an infant suckles."

"Clap-trap in buckets, but that had to hurt."

Svetlana had maneuvered him so that the guard's back was fully exposed. Vartan stepped out from the airtruck, nocked his arrow, and pulled it to full draw. It was all his muscles could take. The arrow wobbled as he centered the tip in the middle of the man's back.

The seemingly broad expanse of the guard's dark shirt became Vartan's universe. Time seemed to slow. In that instant he felt Capella's heat, the sweat beading on his skin. Heard the rising and falling of the chime. Was aware of Svetlana's dark gaze holding the guard's, willing the man's attention into her own.

Vartan's fingers slipped off the bowstring. The stave shivered in his hand as the aluminum arrow leapt forward, caught the man just to the right of the spine, punched through the chest.

For a moment, the guard staggered, glanced down, as if in shock.

Svetlana wheeled on her heel, sprinting for all that her thin legs could carry her.

The guard managed to shout: "Supervisor. Carson here. They're making a try for the airtruck."

Then he lurched sideways, crashed into the side of the cab. Tried to prop himself. The rifle discharged with a booming concussion. Dirt exploded as the bullet tore a divot from the ground.

Vartan watched the rifle drop from the guard's hands to thud into the dirt. Then the man sagged, seemed to wilt. When he coughed, it was to blow a spray of blood across the side of the airtruck. A moment later he was down, gasping as frothy lung blood gushed from his lips.

"I'll be . . ."

Any revelry was cut short by the bang, muffled as it was from the inside of the admin dome. Scratch one Supervisor. Though it would break Shyanne's heart that Fatima's life had been the price.

Vartan, wiped his hot face. Stepped warily forward. He reached down, snagged the rifle away, awed by how heavy it was. Then he jerked the pistol from the man's belt.

He caught a momentary glimpse of the man's wide and straining eyes. Gaped at the blood, so much blood, gurgling up from his throat.

Then Svetlana was there, grinning. "Worked! Good shot!"

"Feast tonight, huh?" he mumbled, still too amazed at what he'd done to think straight.

The sound of gunshots could be heard from inside the dome. What the hell?

She clapped him on the shoulder. "Sounds like trouble in the admin dome. Now, you do know how to work that rifle, right?"

"Oh, yeah." He performed a chamber check, finding a round loaded. "Guess I better go make sure the Messiah and Prophets are all right."

He was panting by the time he arrived at the dome. People were crowded into the cafeteria, pressing around bleeding bodies who'd been laid onto the long tables.

The Chosen. Three of them. Looked like Burht, Shyute, and Wamonga.

Hurrying down the hall, he found Petre and the members of the Will huddled at the junction of two hallways.

"Got the airtruck," he told them. "What's happening here?"

"They slipped out of the trap. Shot three of the Chosen." Petre spared him a worried glance. "They're holed up in a stairwell at the far end of the hall. There's no way to rush them without being shot."

"Don't be a fool. They're in the basement, headed for another stairwell, figuring to get out behind us. Make a try for the airtruck. Quick. The rest of you! There're three more stairways. Block them. Seal them any way you can. Pile whatever, but be sure they can't get out."

He turned, seeing Tikal. Tossed him the marine's pistol. "Get to the airtruck. Keep it safe. Shoot any of the Supervisor's party who try to take it."

People seemed to explode into action, flying off in all directions.

"Should have thought of the other stairwells," Petre said sheepishly.

"If they break out, I can still stop them with this." Vartan slapped the side of the automatic rifle. "Military grade. I can disable that airtruck if they try and lift off. Assuming they get that far. And if they don't shoot me before I can finish the job."

"Just see that they don't, huh?"

43

Cutting a hole in the plastic wall took all of Talbot's strength. Good thing it wasn't a load-bearing wall like the one on the other side of the room.

Talbot muscled the flap back. Dya, Kalico, and Muldare scrambled past a couple of crates. They slipped through the slit and into the darkness of the adjoining room. As a sensor picked up their movement the light panel flickered to life. The way the ceiling curved meant they were in the rear of the dome. One of the axial hallways would be just beyond the closed door.

"This way," Talbot whispered, hearing Batuhan's demands for a response issuing through the hole behind them.

"Shoot our way out?" Muldare asked, flipping her safety off.

"It'll mean killing a lot of people," Kalico ground her teeth.

"What part of 'them or us' don't you get?" Muldare hissed back.

"Is there another way out of here?" Dya whispered. "One that doesn't leave dead bodies all over?"

"Yeah," Talbot said. "But you're not going to like how we're going to have to do it."

Kalico said, "Get us to the airtruck without turning this into a bloodbath. There's women and kids out there."

Talbot nodded. "Fenn Bogarten and I were all through this installation. We've got a way out, but it's down, through the basement, into an old lava tube in the basalt. While Fenn and I didn't check it out, it should take us into the forest. From there we can circle. Get to the airtruck from behind."

Kalico gave him a slap on the shoulder. "Lead forth."

Talbot unslung his service rifle, opened the door a crack, and leaned out. Seeing no one, he led the way into the hall. Lights flashed on as the sensor detected their motion.

The air seemed to pulse, suck, and blow; the dome shook as concussion literally blew Muldare through the doorway and into the hall.

"Briah?" Kalico asked the disheveled marine, "you all right?"

Muldare shook her head, worked her jaw back and forth to clear her ears. "Good to go, Supervisor."

"Hey!" someone shouted from down the hall.

Talbot didn't hesitate, but wheeled on his heel, lifted the rifle, and sent a shot in the direction of the young man who'd stepped into the hallway.

"There went our period of grace," Talbot growled. "Beat feet, people. Follow me."

He shoved past, heading for where the hall dead-ended against the dome. At the last door, he wrenched it open, tapped the light pad, and told the women, "Stairway. When you hit the bottom, we can't get through the walls down there. They're all load-bearing, so we've got to go back to the center. When you get there follow the first radial hallway to the left. Take it all the way back to the circumference. I'll be right behind you."

As the others started down the stairs, Talbot watched the hallway, took the time to thumb a replacement round into the rifle's magazine.

Shouts sounded, and yes, here they came—a knot of men led by the throne bearers and carrying what looked like clubs and spears.

Talbot took his time, braced his rifle, and shot the leader through the chest. As the leader fell, Talbot's second shot took the next man in the left shoulder. His last shot hit the third man center of mass. As they tumbled, howled, and screamed, those behind turned and ran.

Talbot bellowed, "That's just the start! Next man to come down this hall, I'm popping out this door and shooting the dumb pus-sucker."

He dropped back, eased the door closed, and pulled a screwdriver from his belt. This he hammered into the jamb with the rifle butt. Wouldn't hold them for long, but it might slow them down.

In the hallway, shrieks and mayhem told him that the Unreconciled were too busy retrieving their dead and dying to follow for the moment.

Scrambling down the stairs, Talbot hit the hallway, running full-out for the center. At the hub, he took the left in time to see Muldare at the far end, bringing up the rear. The light panels, being old, flickered, but illuminated the way.

Talbot pounded down the hallway after them.

"Now what?" Kalico asked as he arrived, panting, his rifle at the ready.

"Forget the doors to either side. It's just unfinished storerooms. They excavated this, figuring the base was going to grow. The assumption was that it would eventually house more than a thousand colonists."

He stepped past to the big cabinet that blocked the end of the hall. Handed his rifle to Dya. "Briah, give me hand here."

Together they grabbed the cabinet, muscled it to the side to expose a sialon door set in the basalt. Talbot clapped the dust from his hands, saying, "Bogarten and I didn't figure the Unreconciled needed to know this was here. It would have just gotten them into trouble."

"What the hell did they need that big a lock for?" Kalico asked as she gaped at the oversized bolt on the door.

"Maybe we don't want to know what they were trying to keep locked on the other side."

Talbot slid the heavy bolt back and opened the door, looking into the black maw beyond. "Briah, tell me you've got a light in that utility belt of yours."

"Sure."

"Inside. Now," Talbot ordered. After the women hurried in, he slid the cabinet back as far as he could to block the door, then closed it behind him.

"You were right." Dya eyed the darkness, running nervous hands up and down the backs of her arms. "I'm not liking this at all."

Muldare was shining her light around the irregular sides of the old lava tube. "What is this place?"

"Volcanic eruption," Talbot told her. "As a result of the meteor impact. There are places where the lava runs hotter than the surrounding rock, and when it drains out it leaves these tunnels behind."

"What now?" Kalico asked. "Where does this go?"

"Supposedly all the way to the base of the escarpment," Talbot told her. "But no one's been down this since the base was built."

"I can't do this," Dya whispered.

"Sure, you can," Talbot told her, hugging her close.

"There's something in here with us. You can feel it, can't you?"

Kalico turned to the woman. "Hey, it's either this, or you can go back. Batuhan will kill you, chop you up, and eat you. Then as your flesh is purified by digestion, your soul can figure out the maze, avoid getting sucked out his nipples, or finally ejaculated into a fertile female."

Dya made the most horrible face Talbot had ever seen his wife make. "You're right. There're worse things than dying in terror. In the dark."

He kissed her fondly on the lips, saying, "I'll be right here with you, wife."

DISBELIEF

I stand over the bodies of the Chosen. Petre and his members of the Will have carried the bodies of my dead friends to the cafeteria, have laid them out one by one on the tables. Blood drains from the holes blown in their chests. Their eyes are half-lidded, lips parted, the bodies limp in death.

Three friends, three believers. The repositories of so many of our dead. They were my priests. They helped me bear the burden.

Jon Burht was the first to declare his faith. I stare down at his face, remembering those terrible days during the Harrowing and Cleansing when he stood at my side.

Then came Felix Shyte. I step over, take his hand. It is cold and limp as I run my thumb over the scars running back in thin ridges from the tops of his fingers.

Will Wamonga was the third to join me. Now he lies shot clear through and bleeding, taken far too soon.

For the moment all I can do is stare down at them. At the terrible wounds that heartless bullets have torn through their flesh, bones, and organs.

Only Ctein Zhoa is left of the Chosen. He stands to the side, expression traumatized, as if he cannot come to grips with the horror. He is wringing his hands. Tears streak down, losing themselves in the maze of scars carved on his cheeks.

The Chosen must be processed, of that there is no doubt. We must attend to them first thing, before the dead they host can dissipate.

Or so I hope.

We are in uncharted waters here. What are the spiritual ramifications of so many living hosts all dying at once? How do we save the dead they contain, as well as themselves?

I glance over at the Prophets where they have been reinstalled in the cafeteria. Irdan isn't moving. For the moment

I wonder if he, too, is dead, and then I see his chest spasm. Callista and Guan Shi are staring out with empty eyes, but only Guan Shi still flexes her fingers as if she's playing an imaginary piano.

Petre, a pistol in his hand, rushes in from the back, saying, "They're in a stairwell, Messiah. I've got Vartan covering the doorway with that rifle we took from the marine guard. I've had the other stairwells sealed off. They can't get out."

He is looking at my dead Chosen, a barely suppressed horror in his eyes. Like me, he has to be wondering how this could have gone so terribly wrong. We are supposed to have the Supervisor and her people on the tables, to be preparing their bodies for sacrament.

Instead, my Chosen are murdered, and we have a single dead marine to show for it. He's still outside and unclaimed, given as busy as we have been here.

"How did they escape the explosion?" I ask.

"Cut a hole in the wall, Messiah," Petre says, swallowing hard.

"So we have armed and deadly intruders in our basement. How do we determine their whereabouts? How do we deal with them?"

"Vartan says we need a drone. I remember seeing some in the science dome. They'll need charging—that is, if the batteries are still any good."

"See to it. And have Vartan arm one with explosives. I want a flying bomb I can use to kill those people without additional casualties." I close my eyes and let the rage build. As if the universe is staring over my shoulder, watching, waiting to see if I am capable of solving the crisis.

"No matter what the cost," I mumble through gritted teeth, "I will see them dead."

Nothing else is acceptable.

44

Night had fallen. The roar of the waterfall generated its own music—a kind of background that made sitting out on the Briggses' deck in the warm damp air, drink in hand, a most special event. Overhead, in the narrow band of sky visible from the canyon, the Milky Way painted the Donovanian heavens in glowing swirls of light.

Talina sat in the back, having surrendered the seats closest to the crackling fire to Dek and Chaco. Chaco had built the blaze in his homemade steel fireplace. It perched atop its tripod out on the corner of the deck. The smell of burning aquajade and chabacho lent the air a familiar and reassuring perfume. One Talina had never quite been able to get enough of.

Kylee, who'd appeared just at sunset, sat off to the side, partially obscured by the night. She'd shared that special hug with Talina, given her a knowing look from those almost sagacious and oversized blue eyes. Definitely not the eyes a thirteen-year-old girl should have.

"Kip and Flute are keeping an eye on the rogue," she said. "I think he's got the message. No new opportunities here. Looked like he was moving on."

Which meant the Briggs quetzals wouldn't be hunting it down and killing it for invading their territory. Maybe. One never really knew with quetzals.

Kylee had been circumspect during her introduction to Dek Taglioni; she had been the minimum of polite and very much wild-thing suspicious. Now Kylee sat back in the shadows beside the railing, listening to the conversation as Chaco and Dek drank their beer.

The irony of it fascinated Talina: Derek Taglioni—one of the most privileged scions in The Corporation—side-by-side with Chaco Briggs, the ultimate do-it-yourself stand-on-your-own-two-feet self-made man.

Briggs was one of the original Wild Ones. He'd fled here

after killing a man who'd had the ill grace to pester Madison with his attentions when, clearly, she wasn't interested. Briggs had come from nothing in Argentina. But to listen to him and Derek swapping thoughts about the pump they'd fixed, about the work it had taken to get the water system back to perfect, Talina was witness to the ultimate in male bonding.

Talina tossed off the last of her beer, rose silently, and stepped into the house. At the crude tap, she refilled her glass with home-brew amber ale. Madison had Maria and Skip industriously employed at the sink, finishing the last of the supper dishes.

"How they doing out there?" Madison asked, glancing up.

"You'd think they'd been replacing pumps and getting sprayed by broken water pipes their entire lives. Prince and pauper, a match made in heaven. Who'd have thought?"

"Chaco had one of the best days he's had in years." Madison dried her hands with a towel as she walked over. "Pour me one. I'm ready." To the kids she said, "You two get them dishes put away, and it's off to bed."

"But there's a fire," Maria complained with a little girl's pique at cosmic injustice.

"Bed." Madison accented her will with a pointed finger.

As the kids shuffled off, Talina grinned and poured Madison's beer.

The tall woman lifted it to her lips, sipped, and sighed. "I needed that." Then she gave Talina a thoughtful look. "So, what's with Taglioni? Really?"

"Shig's taken with him. Hell, half the town is."

"And you?"

"Me?"

"He watches you with the eyes of a man who knows what he wants in a woman. For the time being, he's learning, figuring out what it will take to get it."

"And you think I'm 'it'?" Talina leaned her butt back against the counter beside the sink. "He's soft meat, Madison. And me, I'm not sure I want his kind of trouble."

"It's almost four years since Cap died. Three now that you've been learning to live with the quetzals inside. What are you saving yourself for? To be a holy relic in the name of chastity?"

"I don't know. Guess I'm a little scared. I'm not sure that I'm not part crazy. I don't have clue if I could carry on an intimate relationship with anyone. I sure as hell don't know if Dek Taglioni, of all people, would be that man."

"You watch him with a woman's eyes."

"Most people think my eyes are too filled with quetzal."

"I mean a *woman's* eyes. The ones she uses when she's interested in a man. He keeps doing the right things, doesn't he? And he's not half bad to look at. He's been tested, this one. And better, he knows he is ignorant, that there are things he has to learn, but he is not afraid to take chances learning them."

"He's also got another side. The guy crossed swords with Kalico back in Solar System. When I asked her about it, she said, that when they met that last time in Transluna, Dek was scuzzier than toilet water."

"Maybe he was." Madison took a swig of her beer, bracing her butt next to Talina's. "That was how many years ago? We all have heard how close *Ashanti* came to being another *Freelander*. People change when they are living with the knowledge that each breath might be their last." A beat. "You still the same woman who spaced from Transluna all them years ago?"

"Well, I guess he's got your vote."

Madison gave an offhanded shrug. "If he were still a spoiled Corporate candy ass, he'd have quit the first time a seal failed, and he and Chaco got drenched. He stuck it out. Stood there with a wrench on that fitting. Not only that, the guy not only enjoyed it, but he knew his shit. Pointed out a couple of things Chaco had never thought of. And more to the point, Chaco doesn't take to many men. Finds that most of them don't measure up. Don't have what it takes. And there he is, drinking beer like he's with a kindred soul."

"Okay, so the guy walks on water." Seeking to change the subject, Talina said, "If I were you, I'd be more worried about Tip not coming home. He's out there in the dark hunting a rogue quetzal. That would have my undershorts in a lot tighter knot than Dek Taglioni could ever tie them in."

Madison's expression strained the least bit. "Yeah, I worry. We've lost too many kids to Donovan over the years. Every time Tip and Kylee don't make it back for supper, the trepidation's there. Is this the time they don't come home? Is my child out there hurt and in agony? Maybe dying, and I can't do a thing about it? That's the worst. The not knowing."

"So?"

"So, it's who Tip and Kylee are going to be, Tal. That's the price I pay as a mother out here. Living is a dangerous—and often too-short—business. So you get on with it."

"Yeah, I guess."

She heard the laughter as Dek and Chaco shared some story out by the fire.

Madison gave her a pat on the shoulder. "You and Dek are in the back rooms. Neither you nor he are ready yet, but there's a connecting door should the day ever come."

Talina was giving Madison a "no way" look when Dek stepped in, a grin accenting the dimple in his chin. He had an empty glass in his hand.

"Chaco's out of beer. The good news: Kylee's taking me hunting in the morning. Chaco talked her into it."

Talina pointed with a no-nonsense finger. "I can't stop you, but if that girl gives you an order, even if it sounds crazy, you do what she tells you!"

"Yes, ma'am," Dek told her as he gave her a two-finger salute. "Way ahead of you."

He paused only long enough to refill the glass, give Madison a winning smile, and vanish back onto the deck, where the talk promptly turned to where chamois might be found in the morning.

Talina took a deep breath to still the sudden tension in her chest. Anything could happen out there. "I hope this isn't a mistake," she murmured.

Madison had a sliver of smile on her lips. "Yep. It's back."

"What is?"

"The way you look at him with a woman's eyes."

45

Every muscle and joint in Vartan's body ached; his brain had that fevered feeling of fatigue. His thoughts had gone muzzy in a head that felt stuffed with wool. When he blinked, the lids seemed to scrape over his eyeballs. The ability to carry a thought to its conclusion had congealed. He'd forgotten how much he hated exhaustion and fatigue. All he wanted to do was sleep.

The cave had been terrifying. Draining. First the descent filled with mind-numbing fear of being shot from the blackness, then the sapping ascent back to the door. Climbing the stairs from the basement took every bit of his concentration. His muscles screamed, his lower back ached under the weight of the rifle. Just those fifteen stairs—not to mention Donovan's gravity—had him winded by the time he reached the ground-level hallway.

The way his feet kept tripping over themselves it was as if they had become disconnected from his brain. His legs had a loose and rubbery feel.

Vartan plodded his weary way into the cafeteria where the Messiah slouched in his throne. The man sprawled more than sat, chin propped on his chest, dark eyes dully fixed on the wasted body lying prominently on the table just before the throne. The eye in the middle of The Messiah's forehead seemed to stare at infinity.

Vartan thankfully slipped the heavy rifle from his shoulders, let it clunk onto the nearest table. He pulled a chair out, slid it around, and dropped into it with a sigh.

Irdan. That's who lay upon the table.

Off to the side, Callista and Guan Shi were each being sponged by a couple of the children. Not that either of them looked more than half past the shade of death.

"What news, Second Will?" the Messiah asked softly.

"We followed the tunnel as far as a drop off, Messiah. By then the hand lights were failing, getting too feeble to see into the depths. We turned back. Blocked the door with enough heavy items they can't shoot their way back inside.

"Meanwhile, Tamil has discovered a blueprint of the admin dome. The tunnel apparently has an outlet down in the forest. That's where they'll come out. The cliff is pretty sheer immediately above the lava tube. The trails they'll need to climb back up are to the north and south. We have enough people to defend them if they try and return that way in an attempt to get the airtruck."

The Messiah kept his gaze fixed on Irdan's corpse, as if momentarily expecting the dead Prophet to utter some startling revelation.

"What of the armed drone?" The Messiah's words were barely a whisper.

"Petre has it on the charger again. It should have a full charge, or as much as it will take anyway, in another hour or two."

"Tell the First Will that my orders are as follows: He, you, and Tikal will each take a squad of fifteen people. He will descend the north trail. You and Tikal on the south. Once down the escarpment, you will have your teams fan out in three groups of five to comb the forest floor. You will sweep your way forward, closing on the vicinity of the cave exit. Where—"

"Messiah, I don't think—"

"What you think doesn't matter." The Messiah shifted his gaze, eyes like cold black stones in his head. The hollow created by his missing nose whistled as he inhaled.

The mad power of the Messiah's gaze and the intensity of his anger sent a shiver through Vartan. The painted blue eye in the middle of the man's forehead seemed to bore right through Vartan's soul.

Implacably, the Messiah said, "Each team of five will search. When they locate the Supervisor and her party, they will not engage. They will only alert you or Petre as to the Supervisor's location. You will then use the drone. Fly it right into the middle of the Supervisor's party. There, you will detonate the explosive. At that time, everyone will converge upon the location, recover the bodies, and bring them to me."

"Messiah, I—"

"My orders are not up for negotiation, Second Will."

Vartan chewed his lips. Blinked in the glare cast from the cafeteria lights and jerked a short nod. It took all of his effort to push himself up from the chair. Took three steps before he remembered the rifle and plodded back to retrieve it.

Ten years in Deck Three, doing nothing. Now he was planetside, malnourished, dealing with a heavier gravity. His physical endurance was spent.

Outside, he glanced up at the starry sky, wondering when night had fallen.

"You all right?" Shyanne asked as she appeared out of the dark.

"I just want to sleep for a week. Lay in the sun and eat steak before sleeping again. He's ordered us to put together teams, to go into the forest in search of the Supervisor." He hesitated. "You heard about Fatima?"

"She's dead. And they never even let me see her. For that . . . Well, never mind. It's all going to shit anyway."

"Be careful, Shyanne. I know how you're—"

"Vart, you don't have the first fucking notion about how I'm feeling." The anger and grief in her voice made him wince. To change the subject, she said, "You heard about the prions?"

"Something."

"Vart, everything that happened? The Prophets? It's a disease." She hooked her fingers in quotation as she said, "Divine revelation? Hardly. It's dementia from a physical source. From eating contaminated brain matter. We weren't *saving* the dead. They were poisoning us."

"Best not say anything about that where any of the Will could hear. You'll be sliced up, boiled, and put on the table next."

She chuckled humorlessly. "Look around. Okay, we're off the ship. But we're still on our own. And so what? Think back. Remember who we were when we first set foot on *Ashanti*? Remember those people? The things we believed in. The kind of human beings we were? We've given up so much of ourselves to madness. Justified . . . well, everything as the price of survival."

"Yeah." He hung his head, rubbed the back of his sore neck. "Used to be human."

"You were a security officer. I was a vet tech." She shook her head, curled her hands into desperate fists. "I look back to the woman I was, to the man I was in love with and married to, to all the dreams."

"Those were good days. Maybe . . ."

"Maybe would be a lie. We're monsters, Vart. That's what Batuhan and his supposed Prophets have made us. Look at the scars." She traced fingers along the lines that led to her breasts. "This is the mark of Cain. The visible proof that I participated in the sick murder of my friends, that I willingly seared their flesh and ate it. That I sold my humanity and self-respect to keep breathing, whored myself to that twisted Mongolian monster and his minions in order to bear their children. So I lived? To become . . . what kind of *thing*?"

"Hey, Shyanne, don't—"

"Vart, wake up. We'd have been better off dead. You, me, all the rest of us. Now we're, well . . . Let's just say we're a sort of human pollution."

The words stung. He'd loved her once. With all of his heart. Could remember how they'd delighted in each other. They'd been so young, so possessed of each other that they'd soared. Like two souls who'd fit like meshed gears . . . and lost it all.

"I've got work to do."

"Vart. There's a way, you know. An out. You know Batuhan's batshit crazy. This whole living graves and immortality sham is a lie to justify the most heinous crimes human beings can commit. But just 'cause we played along to save our worthless lives doesn't mean we still have to."

"Shyanne, don't. If the wrong people hear you—"

"You can fly the airtruck, can't you? It's a way out of the insanity. We can find a place. Somewhere—"

"I'm going to pretend I didn't hear that. Now, Shy, take my advice: Don't. Say. Another. Word. Not to anyone."

She stared at him in the dark. Nodded. Finally said, "You take these search parties down into that forest, most of those people are not coming back."

"Oh? Think they'll just wander off looking for Eden?"

"I've read the reports. The ones Batuhan says are all lies. I've tried to treat the ones Donovan's already claimed. You were a smart man once, be one again."

He yawned, wished the fatigue would let him clear his head. "Sorry, Shy, I've got to get ahead of this thing with the Supervisor."

"You really believe that Batuhan's a divine messiah?"

"You keep your head down, Shy. I know you're hurting. And I'm so sorry about Fatima. But promise me you won't do anything stupid, all right?"

Her laughter sounded heartless. "Oh, you know me, Vart. I don't have any stupid left in me."

He laid a gentle hand on her shoulder, took a deep breath, and forced his trembling and weary legs to leave her standing there as he plodded toward the dormitory to form his search parties.

What he would have given for a short, quick nap.

46

Time vanished in the cold black of the lava tube. Was it only hours, or a day? Kalico Aguila wasn't sure. And she had started to regret her once-flippant remarks that being in the tube was better than being eaten by Batuhan's cannibals. She'd been in some dark places before, especially her mine. But nothing as dark, cramped, and terrifying as this.

When Muldare had occasion to flip her light off, the blackness was complete. Total. Literally the stygian depths of the tomb.

And worse, there were things. Invertebrates that scuttled around in the black recesses, always running from the light.

"How you doing?" Talbot asked his wife.

"There's something in here. Watching us. Waiting," Dya told him, shivering. "Mark, promise me. If something happens, if it looks like we're trapped here, you'll shoot me. You will, won't you? You won't leave me to die in the dark."

Kalico swallowed hard. From the tone in the woman's voice, she was clap-trapping serious.

"We're going to make it, wife." Talbot told her in a voice dripping love.

What was that like? To be loved so completely? Kalico took the moment to wonder—not that she'd ever allowed herself such a fantasy. Still, here, in the evil blackness, she envied Dya Simonov that warm reassurance.

Up in the lead, Muldare took a deep breath, as if nerving herself as she crawled up and over a hump where the floor rose. "Got another drop ahead," she said before shining the light back so Kalico could slither across the clammy wet rock in the marine's wake. Only to find herself perched on a shallow ledge before the tube dropped off into inky depths.

Kalico reached back, took Dya's hands, and helped the

botanist negotiate the hump. The woman was trembling, her jaw quivering with fear as she swung her feet around to find purchase on the ledge. Then came Talbot, his rifle clattering on the unforgiving stone.

When Muldare shone her light into the depths, the invertebrates scattered like perverted lice. Skittering this way and that, they hid in cracks, huddled in shadow, and seemed to flow down into the depths.

"I hate this place." Briah Muldare's voice was a hoarse whisper.

Talbot was staring down into the hole. "Shit on a shoe, but that's a straight drop."

"So, what now?" Kalico asked—felt something drop onto her head. She panicked, clawed with frantic fingers to rip the skittering invertebrate out of her hair. The little beast, legs thrashing, sailed out into Muldare's light and vanished into the blackness below. Kalico willed every ounce of her courage to get her heartbeat back to normal.

Pus and ions, I'd give a kilo of rhodium for a drink of water. Give up the whole damn Number One mine to be out of here and back in Port Authority chowing down on Inga's chili and drinking whiskey.

Talbot took Muldare's light, flashed it around the walls of the shaft, and then leaned out, saying, "Bless you, yes!"

"What?" Kalico craned her neck, trying to see.

"Got a rope here." Talbot handed the light back to Muldare, dropped to his knees, and backed over the ledge, feeling his way with his feet.

"Mark, damn you, you be careful," Dya cried, leaning forward. "So help me, if you . . ." She couldn't finish.

"What makes you so brave?" Muldare asked, trying to hold the light for him.

Talbot grinned weakly. "I survived four months in the forest. Alone. Every time I figured I was dead, I wasn't. When I eventually do wind up dead, I'll know I've either just made a really dumb mistake, or that the odds finally caught up with me." A pause. "Ah, there. Little bit of a foothold here. Don't mind the invertebrates, they crunch under your boot."

"Did you *have* to say that?" Dya cried, on the verge of tears.

Talbot lowered himself, feeling for footholds. "Got another one. Ouch. *Shit!*"

"What?" Kalico's heart starting to hammer again.

"Don't put your fingers in the crushed invertebrate." Talbot wiped his hand on his coveralls. "Their guts really burn."

We're all going to die in here.

Talbot eased himself over the edge. "Okay, got the rope. So, the good news is that someone passed this way before. And better yet, left us the rope. Best of all, the invertebrates haven't eaten it. The bad news is that while it's knotted, it's still just a rope. Means we each have to climb down, one by one."

Kalico—seeing Dya shaking and on the verge of tears, and Muldare looking pretty rocky herself—said, "You go first, Mark. Then Dya, Muldare, and I'll be last."

"You'll have to do it in almost total darkness," Muldare told her, a worried look in her hazel eyes.

"So?" Kalico shrugged. "I'll manage."

God, can I lie to myself, or what?

Screw this being strong for everyone shit. She wanted to drop to her knees and throw up.

Talbot was already descending the rope. She could hear his clothing rubbing against the stone, the occasional clunk as his rifle butt hit rock. The man's breath kept coming loud in the cavern. How long? Ten seconds? Twenty?

"I'm down," Mark called. "Come on, Dya. Feel with your feet as you lower yourself over the lip. If it feels like a step, it is. Once you grab hold of the rope, use both of your feet to grip the knots."

In the flashlight's glow, Dya's face was a mask of terror. She tried to swallow. Couldn't. Tears glistened at the corners of her eyes. Who would have thought that rock-solid Dya, woman of steel, would have been afraid of the dark?

"I can't." It came as faint whisper.

Kalico bent down, placed a hand on the woman's shoulder. Forced a kindly confidence she didn't feel into her voice. "You going to let a Corporate bitch like me show you up? Besides, down that rope is the only way back to Su and Damien, Tweet, Tuska, and the rest of the family. Nothing you couldn't do in the light of day. The only difference is that now you do it in a tunnel."

"It's okay," Talbot called from the bottom. "Not more than five meters."

"I don't want to die in the dark," Dya whispered. Her entire body shook, but somehow, looking numb, she swung her feet over the edge. "Something's here. Feel it? Watching us."

Kalico couldn't help herself, a shiver playing down her arms as she stared at the surrounding black, and damned if she didn't feel some presence. Cold. Heartless. And malevolent.

Muldare took Kalico's hand for stability, leaned out to shine the light as far down as she could to help Dya see.

Foothold by foothold, the trembling Dya lowered herself, tears streaking down her face. She was below the lip, said, "Got the rope." Then added, "Fuck me. Here goes."

For a moment there was silence, then a yip of fear echoed in the shaft.

"Dya!" Kalico and Talbot cried in unison.

"It's . . . It's . . . I'm okay. Just . . . Just . . ."

"Take your time," Talbot called. "Feel your way."

"Shut up!" Dya shrieked. "I've been on a rope before."

At the terror in the woman's voice, Kalico closed her eyes.

She's going to lose it. She'll freeze. Won't be able to move. When her fingers cramp, she's going to fall.

And what? Land full on Mark? Leave them both crippled here in the terrible black?

She glanced sidelong at Muldare, wanted to shout down to Talbot to stay out of the way.

Oh, sure, and that would really seal Dya's fate, wouldn't it?

"How you doing, wife?" Talbot called up.

"Okay," Dya squeaked. "I found the rope. Got my feet on the knot."

Kalico sucked her lips, her heart hammering. *Come on. You can do it.*

Then came the sound of clothing sliding on rock. The softer sounds were Dya sobbing, struggling. But the sliding on rock continued, getting ever more faint.

Then, "I . . . I'm slipping! I can't hold on any . . ." It ended with a shriek. Then a muffled thump.

"Mark? Dya?" Kalico called, hanging out as far as she could over the edge. All she could hear was whimpering, the sound of someone broken.

47

Kalen Tompzen's words, "Boss, I could handle this," kept repeating in Dan Wirth's head as he stalked through the main gate that opened out onto the shuttle field. Fact was, he never liked going out beyond the fence. Somehow, leaving the protective barrier behind with nothing between him and Donovan was like walking down the central avenue buck-assed naked with his prick and balls wagging in the wind.

Not that being inside Port Authority was all that safe. Since landing on Donovan, he'd spent how many nights huddled in The Jewel while search teams scoured every square inch of town for a man-eating monster? Good old Dube Dushku had been torn in two and swallowed by a quetzal just on the other side of the wall where Dan hid in his office.

Yet, here he was, Tompzen's assurances echoing in his head. Sure, the ex-marine could have hunted Windman down. Made the appropriate example of him. Beat the guy to a pulp, broke an arm, or dislocated a shoulder. Got the message across that a mark didn't waltz out, leaving The Jewel holding the bag. Not when said mark lost more than five hundred at roulette. The guy wouldn't have had the chance to skip if Vik Schemenski hadn't been so busy at the table.

But Windman had, and now the situation must be dealt with.

Dan squinted, staring across the shuttle pad. The place where the PA shuttle usually sat lay vacant; the clay was baking under Capella's hot glare. To the right, just before the seven-tall wall of shipping containers sat an A-7 shuttle from *Ashanti*. That had to be where Windman, a copilot, would be found.

In fact, wasn't that him? The guy lounging on the open loading ramp where it was lowered in the rear?

Dan took a deep breath and started across the hard red soil. In places hot exhaust had melted it to a glassy texture. In the distance the chime kept rising, almost finding harmony, and falling into that awful discordant and atonal fugue before rising again.

I could be gone from here.

Dek Taglioni's offer hung in his imagination like a desert mirage: alluring, and just out of reach. If only Dan could trust the guy. The opportunity was just too good to be true, but what if it was real? On Donovan, at least he was safe, secure, and alive. But that was where it ended.

The conundrum just added to Dan's foul mood: knowing that he wasn't trapped. That this wasn't the end of the road. That if he'd just keep his wits, he could be off this rock, back in the game. The *real* game, where it wasn't just pissing around with a bunch of broke-dick colonists on a backwater world, but Transluna! Where absolute power awaited anyone with the cunning and moxie to seize it.

All of which had caused him to give Kalen Tompzen a wink and say, "I'll take care of the guy."

Dan *needed* to get the hell out of The Jewel, away from the wary gazes his people kept giving him. Damn it, he was desperate for action, any kind of action. And thumping the shit out of copilot Windman was going to be a relief, a way to vent the growing frustration.

"Don't kill him," Allison had warned as Dan had settled his hat on his head and checked his knife.

Of course I won't kill him. He's Ashanti crew.

But that was part of it, the whole frustrating thing. It was the pissant little rules. Like having to trade a fucking bedroom addition for a scarf. By God's ugly ass, he was tired of placating a bunch of candy-dicked and self-righteous bastards.

He grinned, a swell of anticipation rising within as he walked up to the shuttle ramp and called, "Ensign Windman in the flesh! Why, of all the people to encounter. Luck is with me for sure."

Windman, who'd been doodling on his tablet looked up. The guy was spacer pale to start with. Now he went two shades whiter. Swallowed hard.

"Oh, no need to fret," Dan reassured the rabbit-eyed Windman. "You and I just need to talk."

Dan glanced around. "But not here. I mean, anyone could walk by, and you do have a reputation to maintain. So, how about we both saunter over past that shipping container and enjoy a bit of privacy while we figure out our little dilemma."

"Uh, I'm not an ensign. Just a copilot." Windman wobbled unsurely to his feet.

"Either's good enough for me." Dan placed a reassuring hand on the spacer's bony shoulder. He could feel the guy flinch down to his toes.

Windman nerved himself. "Listen, I know how it looks. Me slipping out like that. But, uh, hey, you've got this reputation. Like, I know I screwed it, shouldn't have made that last bet. But you need to know that I'll make it—"

"Sure you will. That's what we're going to discuss. How to make it right. 'Cause I suspect you really don't have any five hundred siddars hidden away up in that ship, am I right?"

"Well, no. But when I get back to Solar System, after *Ashanti*'s been this long in space? I mean, with bonus and time, and being over contract, I'll have more than enough—"

"But that's then. Not to mention in way far off Solar System. We have to talk about now."

Dan propelled copilot Windman past the last of the stacked shipping containers. Caught a glance of Pamlico Jones where he ran one of the forklifts toward the *Ashanti* shuttle. Jones was smart enough to leave matters be that didn't concern him.

Behind the towering crates, a couple of big transparent plexiglass boxes—some sort of shipping crates—stood in a haphazard line. No telling what they had been used for. Given the rows of air holes in the tops, whatever had been in them must have been organic.

Beyond them, it was no more than fifty meters across the ferngrass to the bush. There a low line of aquajade, sucking shrub, claw shrub, and scrubby chabacho trees shimmered in opalescent greens and turquoise. A flock of scarlet fliers fluttered in aerial dance among the branches. The chime grew, louder, wavering in the heat.

Dan stopped Windman before the transparent crates, the guy's escape blocked from behind by a low hillock covered by ferngrass.

"Listen, Mr. Wirth, I really am sorry." Windman was craning his head, eyes searching for any possible route of escape. It had to be dawning on him that for whatever was about to happen, there would be no witnesses.

"Sorry is a good word, but it doesn't have any value. Get my point? I could say, 'I forgive you' but it wouldn't mean anything either. Now, let's say you have five hundred SDRs in that pouch on your belt. You hand that over, and we're all square. Even. The accounts balance. But you don't have five hundred, and sorry's just a word. No more than an exhalation of air."

Windman's mouth must have gone dry because it took him three tries to swallow. A growing terror turned his quivering eyes glassy. "Wha . . . What's going to happen to me?"

"Well, that's a problem isn't it? How do I get any value out of a broke spacer who can't cover his debts? I guess the only thing I can figure that would make you of any worth to me is as an example."

"Huh? What kind of example?"

Dan put the whole weight of his body behind the swing, drove his fist deep into Windman's gut. The spacer, malnourished and skin-and-bones as he was, didn't have a chance. Air whooshed from his mouth as he bent double. Stumbled back three paces and dropped hard on his butt.

"So, this is going to hurt," Dan promised, taking a step forward. "Sorry, but it's the only way you can . . ."

The hump of ferngrass behind Windman shifted, seemed to liquify and flow. Rising, the ground was swelling and expanding, beginning to take shape. The three eyes that blinked open on the great triangular head were fixed on Windman's back.

The spacer sat hunched on his ass, legs out straight, had both hands on his gut. His eyes were bugged, mouth open, expression that of a man in pain.

Dan froze. Stared in disbelief as the huge creature formed behind the clueless Windman. Large. Easily two meters at the shoulders as it seemed to materialize out of thin air. But what the . . .

Quetzal.

Dan had seen enough of them. Dead, of course. Never in the flesh. Never this close.

Tears were streaking down Windman's now-red face. He gasped for air. Started to throw up. Never got the chance to finish.

The quetzal struck, remarkably fast for so big a beast. The movement was a blur, the head twisting sideways. Mighty serrated jaws snapped shut on Windman's torso, crushing his shoulders, chest, and gut. The beast twisted Windman sideways and lifted as it straightened its head. With a claw, it ripped most of the shirt off the man's body. The spacer's head, forearms, and hips protruded from the jaws like doll parts.

Like some grotesquely oversized terrier, the quetzal shook Windman, his limbs flopping loosely. Where the serrated jaws clamped tight, they severed Windman's neck, an action that pitched the man's head like a volleyball to bounce and roll just short of Dan's feet.

The quetzal's hide now flickered in crimson and black patterns. Dan heard the crackling and snapping of Windman's bones, watched the thing gulp the man's upper body down. Straightening its neck, the great quetzal reached out with its claw-sharp foreleg and ripped Windman's pants from his legs. The cloth sailed out to flutter to the ground.

With another shake and gulp, the hips and arms vanished.

Dan stumbled back, gaping in horror as the quetzal stripped off Windman's boots and choked the rest of him down.

The big plexiglass box stopped any further retreat when Dan's back slammed against it.

The last of spacer Windman was an oversized lump traveling down the quetzal's throat. The three eyes fixed on Dan. Opening its mouth, the creature sucked air, venting a low harmony from the vents back by its tail.

Dan shot a quick look, as desperate for an escape as Windman had been such a short time earlier. Backed against the transparent container as he was, his fingers slipped off the latch.

Faster than a heartbeat, Dan flung the door open, darted inside, and closed it. A millisecond later, the quetzal hit the thick plastic with enough force to rock it back precariously.

Desperately, Dan studied the latch, figured it out, and shot the bolt home that would lock it. As he did, the giant quetzal charged again, hit the plastic hard, and toppled it backward. The impact jarred Dan down to his bones. Then the quetzal leaped full onto the box, its weight flexing the plexiglass as it twisted its head this way and that, biting at the box.

Fuck me, but if that latch breaks . . .

Through the transparency, Dan had a close-up and mind-numbing view of the creature's blade-like and bloody teeth, the red gullet, and swelling throat tissues.

For what seemed an eternity, he and the quetzal stared at each other. The thing's bloody jaws now pressed against the clear plastic, leaving crimson smears.

That's when Dan noticed the crippled left front leg, the bullet scars along the beast's muscular hide.

"Whitey," he whispered.

48

The shape in the sucking shrub thirty meters away might have been a small boulder. The bulk of Dek's body was hidden behind the bole of an aquajade tree. In the early morning light he squinted, shifted his focus slightly to one side. As if . . . yes.

"See it?" Kylee Simonov asked from where she hunched beside him. She was peering out from the other side of the tree. She'd been the one to spot the thing, having picked it out through a mere gap in the dense growth. That she'd seen it at all amazed him.

"Kind of that rounded shape," Dek told her.

"That's it. Now, on the left, you see that pointed part? Sort of blends into the branches? Notice how it's not moving like the rest of the plant?"

"I do."

"You want to put your bullet back where that pointed part merges into the rest of the body. That's actually the back of the head and neck."

Dek carefully eased his Holland & Holland hunting rifle up to his shoulder. Braced it against the trunk of the aquajade to steady his aim and sighted through the optic. Sure enough, the IR gave him a complete rendering of the fastbreak. Dek placed his point-of-impact dot on the thing's . . . well, neck. As the dot settled, he caressed the trigger.

The pop of the bullet leaving the rails at fifteen hundred feet per second was surprisingly mild. But then he'd dialed down the velocity for such a close shot. The Holland & Holland could accelerate a bullet as fast as eighteen thousand feet per second. Assuming one really wanted to blow a hole in something. The downside was horrendous shoulder-pounding recoil, and the powerpack would have to be ejected and replaced after three such hyper shots.

At the impact, he watched the fastbreak explode from

the bush, make a fantastic leap, and collapse on the ground. As it did, the shrub thrashed its branches, irritated by the disturbance.

"Good shot," Kylee told him. "But you've got to hurry. See how it's over by that claw shrub? The roots will have your fastbreak in another thirty seconds. And once they do, you don't want to try and wrestle it back. You'll end up being sliced clear to the bone."

Dek cycled another bullet into battery, rose, and trotted out to the fastbreak. Yep, the roots were squirming in the thing's direction. He picked it up, awed by the weight, by the warm limpness of the body.

My God. I just killed something.

The sense of elation faded into a feeling of unease. He stared thoughtfully at the beautiful creature. The soft hide was covered with a sort of feathery pelage that now took on a sheen of color—like oil made rainbow patterns on water. How did it do that? What passed for blood was leaking from the bullet wound, splattering red-brown on the soil. The three eyes in the triangular head were already sightless, growing dim.

This creature, this living thing, had been happily going about its business. Had thought itself hidden, without a care. And from out of nowhere its life was suddenly blown out of its body by a carnivorous monster from a planet thirty light-years away. Where was the justice in that?

Kylee propped callused hands on her young hips. She was giving him a thoughtful appraisal. The kid was supposedly thirteen, just entering that period of transition from a girl to a young woman. The changes in her body were evident. If she continued the way she was, she'd be stunning. Except for her alien-blue eyes, the almost triangular cheekbones. And her legs—maybe because of a growth spurt—appeared a bit too long for the rest of her body.

Not exactly an everyday blonde blue-eyed northern European kind of girl, she exuded a sense of danger, of otherness. From the moment he'd made her acquaintance the night before, he'd wondered if she wasn't as likely to stick a knife in his guts as give him a smile.

"It's called hunter's remorse," she told him. "Instead of

torturing yourself for taking a life, blame it on the universe. It's how being alive works. Something has to die for something else to eat. Same on Donovan as it is on Earth. Maybe more so here."

"Why's that?"

"Because on Donovan, it's how information as well as sustenance is transmitted. TriNA is ingested, passes through the gut wall, and is incorporated into another organism. Pretty tidy actually. But that means if you want access to information, as well as nutrients, you have to eat it. Take quetzals. Among them cannibalism is an expected part of the life cycle. You want to know how to hunt chamois? Eat one of your elders who excels at hunting chamois."

"That's . . . um, unsettling." And hewed too closely to the clap-trap the Unreconciled claimed to believe. He studied the fastbreak, noticed how the stripes and shadows on its hide were fading to brown. So amazing that everything on Donovan changed colors.

"Come on," she told him. "We need to get your kill back and cut it up. It will be lunch." With that she turned her steps down the trail toward the farmstead.

Dek followed, careful—as he'd been instructed—to put his feet where she did, to pay attention.

"I really appreciate you taking me out hunting this morning. I've never done this before."

She gave him the slightest twitch of the shoulders. "I wanted to see how stupid you were."

"I . . . see." Which, of course, he didn't.

"Talina's my friend."

The way she said it, Talina was a lot more than that.

"I really appreciate her bringing me out here."

"Yeah, I know you do."

"Oh?"

She shot him a knowing look over her shoulder. "You're way more interested in her than just as a friend."

"I am?"

"You give her more eye contact, heartbeat changes, pupils dilate. Your smell goes more musky. Sexual interest. Male attraction. The hormones are working."

"Oh, come on."

"Yeah, you're probably only partially aware. That over-civilized part of you has spent most of your life trying to keep the limbic system under control."

"Listen, I don't know where you get all this, but I—"

"Watch out for that blue nasty. Step wide."

He did, realizing his attention had wandered. Amazed at the same time that she'd known he'd strayed from her path even though he was behind.

"What about me being stupid?" he asked. "I didn't understand that."

"The last time I got stuck with soft meat, it was Dortmund Short Mind. He was a professor and about the most stupid man alive. Letting him live was a mistake. He ended up killing Trish through gross incompetence, and that broke Talina's heart. If I had let the quetzals eat him, the world would have been a lot better place." A beat. "Though it might have been an act of malicious injustice to the Rork quetzals."

The way she said it, so matter of fact, sent a shiver down Dek's back. "Remind me not to be stupid."

"You pay attention. That's more than I expected. I can see what Talina likes about you."

That caught his interest. "She likes me? She seems kind of standoffish."

"She's waiting to be disappointed."

"She tell you that?"

"Didn't need to." Kylee pointed to her head. "Part of her is in here. I've got a lot of her memories. Her thoughts."

"You've shared molecules," Dek guessed, shifting the fastbreak to his other shoulder. The damn thing was heavy. His muscles were still adapting. He didn't want to start panting. Not in front of Kylee. The need to make a good impression had become a great deal more important.

"Yeah." She fixed her attention on one of the aquajades, slowed. "Changes the way you think."

She held up a hand, head cocking as she stopped in the trail. Around them, the chime was rising and falling, the music slightly different than what he'd grown used to outside Port Authority.

"Something's wrong," she told him. "We need to make time. Hand me the fastbreak."

He did, unsure of what might be wrong. All he could hear was the background of chime, the faint whisper of the morning breeze in the aquajade and chabacho leaves.

"Got to hurry now." She flipped the fastbreak's body over her shoulder like it was a sack of cloth. "Concentrate, Dek. Do as I do. Follow me. Footprint for footprint. If I veer wide, so do you."

"Got it."

"That will be an uncommon change from the usual soft meat."

And then she was off, seeming to float as she trotted effortlessly along the winding path.

Concentrate. Don't be stupid.

Within a hundred meters, he was panting and staggering. His Holland & Holland, not weighing more than four kilos, had started to feel more like a bar of lead.

Under his breath, he whispered, "Oh, Dek, what have you gotten yourself into?"

That's when the sound of the approaching airtruck finally penetrated his thoughts.

49

The dark corridor reeked of something more than just a dead ship. A presence filled it. Something Galluzzi couldn't quite manage to comprehend—a quality that seemed to slip off at a ninety-degree axis from reality. That it did so at the very instant Galluzzi began to grasp its essence made it even crazier.

"Where are the lights?" Galluzzi tried to keep the panic from his voice.

"The *Turalon* crewmen supposedly fixed them. Not up to their usual standards."

When Shig shone his light down the corridor, Galluzzi would have sworn that something devoured the photons. As bright as the beam was, it should have penetrated more than just a mere ten or fifteen meters. Light didn't disappear that way; that it did here was plain unnatural.

Shig added, "I don't think their hearts were in any of the repairs. Hard to concentrate when you're constantly looking over your shoulder. I suspect only fear of Supervisor Aguila's wrath enabled them to patch up the few systems they did. Get the ship stabilized . . . and get the hell off. Workmanship wasn't a priority when things were sneaking in at the edges of their vision."

"I'm creep-freaked enough to understand where they were coming from," Galluzzi said through an exhale. "Next time something touches me, I'm out of here."

He kept wanting to ask the ship for light, for air, for an explanation as he would aboard *Ashanti*.

They chopped the ship's AI out with cutting torches, he reminded himself.

Shig continued to plod forward, his light a truncated cone of reality in the dark insanity that was *Freelander*.

"I saw her," Galluzzi whispered. "*Freelander*. In the yards outside Transluna. They were fitting her structural members. Just the rude skeleton that would become this ship. I remember how amazed we all were. Knowing that we were on the leading edge of ever bigger and better ships."

And now she has come to this.

Shig stopped at a hatch. Then he turned, shining his light past Galluzzi and back the way they'd come. "Consider this: We're looking at the transportees' deck. All this black and empty space. They voided this deck. Five hundred people suffocated here, most of them in their bunks. Then they turned off the heat. Let them all freeze. Think of that. Five hundred corpses, frozen solid. An entire deck as a deep freeze."

Given the difficulty with which Galluzzi managed to swallow, someone might have jammed a knotted cloth into the bottom of his throat. He stared back into the depths, tried to imagine the frozen corpses, eyes frosted white, lips pulled back from teeth that glinted with icy crystals.

The voice beside Galluzzi's ear whispered, *". . . wasn't but two days ago when Melanie . . ."*

Galluzzi whirled, threw up his arm, crying out. "Get away!"

Shig flashed his light back. "Hear something?"

"A woman. Whispered something about two days ago. Melanie something."

"If you want, you can look her up on the transportee manifest. That, or search long enough, you'll find her name on the wall."

"What wall?" Galluzzi put a hand to his heart, trying to still it as the shadows closed in around him. He could *feel* them. Kept turning his head, trying to see behind him, fearful of another touch like the one he'd felt outside the shuttle bay.

"You'll see. This way." Shig cycled the hatch manually, opened it to a corridor where the lights flickered on. The panels glowed in what Galluzzi would have called malaria yellow and cast a urine-colored tone on the corridor that led to the Crew Deck.

But the walls . . . Galluzzi tried to understand. Dark, as if poorly covered with...what? Scribbling? Scrawling?

"That's writing." He bent to peer at the looping script. Layers and layers of it. Sentences written over sentences.

Thousands upon thousands, until the original meaning was hidden in a mass of looping black ink.

"We've never bothered to scry them all out, given the overwriting, but one of the most frequent is 'The exhalation of death is the breath of life. Draw it fully into your lungs.' My personal favorite is: 'The fingers of the dead wind through our bodies, stroke our hearts, and caress our bowels.' I've always wondered if it was metaphor or factually derived."

Galluzzi stepped warily along the corridor, awed by meter after square meter, the countless layers of overwriting covering walls, ceiling, and floor. He finally saw a legible line that read: "I am vacuum. A cloud of emptiness. I am vacuum. A cloud of emptiness. I am vacuum . . ." and then it was submerged in a tangled chaos of overwritten lines.

"How many days . . . No, how many *years* did they dedicate to this?"

I am reading the ravings of the long dead.

His hair was on end again, a tremble in his muscles. Every fiber of his body wanted to turn, chase pell-mell back through the dark corridor and to the shuttle. To be rid of this . . .

He jerked to the side, sure that something had just passed him. A faint image of a human. It vanished as quickly as it had appeared.

"Did you see that?"

"No." Shig told him. "But I don't believe you've glimpsed the bits of movement I have, either. One seemed to appear out of your right side, only to evaporate. Your only response at that instant was a slight flinch."

"They *lived* in here for one hundred and twenty-nine years?"

"Correct." Shig ran his fingers over the black mass of scrawl, as though it were braille. "They are writing to the dead. This hallway was the only one they left unsealed. Through this door, they brought the bodies, one by one, over the years. Carried them right through here before dropping them into the hydroponics."

Galluzzi endured a flashback. Saw again the stripped and broken human bones sent down the chute from Deck

Three to find their ignominious end in *Ashanti*'s hydroponics.

"We are all monsters," he whispered.

"Perhaps. Among other things. All of which makes the study of humanity so engrossing, if not particularly illuminating."

Shig fought off a shiver, turning his steps forward. Took a companionway up, having to turn his flash on again.

Then they stepped out on the Command Deck where again the lights came on with that off-putting urine-yellow glow.

"It's the light in this place," Galluzzi growled. "Like it's sick."

"Captain Torgussen has a theory. When *Vixen* puts her sensors on *Freelander*, it's as if the ship is still tied to wherever it went on the 'other side.' They think it's leaking particles, photons, energy and what have you, back into that universe."

"That's . . ." But no, apparently it wasn't impossible. "My God, Shig, what happened to these people?"

"Mass murder. What they believed was an eternity trapped aboard *Freelander*. And, well, I want you to see this."

"Crew's mess, isn't it?" He stepped through the hatch as Shig shone his light into the room's center.

For a long moment, Galluzzi squinted, trying to make sense of the dome-like structure in the exact center. Some sort of yurt, or cupola. Rounded on the top, perhaps two meters across, two-and-a-half tall at the peak. But what was the lattice-like dome made of? He couldn't place the rickety looking materials.

Shig slapped a palm to the wall, and dim lights flooded the two-story room with a faint glow that cast eerie shadows across the scraped and dirty floor.

"Holy shit." Galluzzi fought for breath.

Bones. The whole damn thing is made of bones.

It put Batuhan's carved throne to shame as a mere pipsqueak's mockery.

Galluzzi felt himself pulled, almost staggered his way to the front of the thing. Stared in disbelief at the incredible artistry. Vertical femora held up the walls. Then came the lines of columnar shin and arm bones, the rows of staring skulls. Thousands and thousands of bones.

"Where did they get so many? My God, there must be hundreds of people here."

"All of them." Shig stopped beside him, rubbing the backs of his arms. "Even the last one."

Galluzzi followed the nod of Shig's head to where the wasted skeleton lay in the doorway. "How come they left that one lying there?"

"Because she was the last. There was no one to wire her bones into the temple."

50

Talbot clutched Dya's body close to his chest as she wrapped her arms around him. Whimpering and sobbing, she buried her head in his neck. The surrounding cavern was blotted with shadow where the weak light of the flash high above didn't penetrate.

"Hey, it's all right," he crooned, petting her hair.

"Damn it! What's happening down there?" Aguila's voice thundered from above.

"We're all right," Talbot called back. "I caught her. Dya's fine. But, hey, you guys might get down here. It's pitch fucking black."

He lowered his wife to her feet, saying, "Keep a hand on my belt. The footing's a little treacherous." Then he fingered around for the rope, felt an invertebrate scuttle its way across the back of his hand.

I really hate this place.

"I thought I was going to die," Dya whispered behind him. "God, Mark. I've never been so scared."

"You were almost to the bottom. It was only about a meter. I could see your silhouette as you fell. Told you I'd be here for you."

"Do you know how much I love you?" she whispered. "If I don't make it . . ."

"We're going home to Su, Kylee, and the kids. You'll see."

He felt it when Muldare's feet found the rope. "That's it, Briah. Just like basic training."

"Fuck you, Talbot," she called down. "I was always your beat on a fast rope."

He held it for her, watching the flashlight beam darting this way and that as she descended, the light obviously held in her teeth. As she reached the bottom, he could see the gallery they were in. Sickly pale invertebrates kept fleeing like a receding wave before the light. The floor continued to slant down, a second tube coming in from the side to join theirs.

"Supervisor?" Muldare asked, shining her light up.

"Damn, it's dark up here," Aguila's voice called down. "Okay, there's a little light refracted. Hold the flash steady. Right there. That's good." And then, "I'm coming down."

Mark got hold of the rope, thankful that Muldare's light was shining up. At least he'd have warning if the Supervisor's body came plummeting down.

"I should have been last," Muldare noted. "I'm trained for this."

"Yeah? Fleeing through lava tubes on a planet thirty light-years from Solar System? Pursued by twenty-second-century space cannibals who are going to save the universe by dismembering and eating people? All the while knowing that if nothing in here kills us, we still have to survive virgin forest full of things that want to make a meal of us? What part of training did I miss?"

Muldare gave him a wry twist of the lips as she said, "Asshole."

Aguila found the rope. He felt it whip as the woman clamped her feet on the first knot.

Talbot grinned to himself as the rope snapped back and forth in his grip. Not that he needed to worry about Kalico. After the three of them had descended, no way the Supervisor wasn't going to make it to the bottom. Didn't matter that her heart was going to be in her throat, Kalico Aguila was going to hit bottom looking like she'd never even broken a sweat.

And she did, almost stumbling for footing, as she stared around at the sloping tunnel.

"How far do you think?" she asked.

"No telling," Talbot told her, taking the lead and feeling his way down the slope.

"Any of the rest of you as thirsty as I am?" Muldare asked.

"Dryer than the desert," Dya agreed, seeming to pull courage from somewhere deep inside.

"Turn the light this way. PA should be scrambling. We're way overdue." Aguila held up her wrist monitor in the flash's glow. "Shit. It's been ten hours since we started down this tunnel. How far does this go?"

That's when Muldare said, "Maybe you haven't been noticing, but as the bearer of the light, I have. Eyes adjust to illumination so it's hard to keep track. When we started, my beam was good for close to a hundred meters of tunnel. Now we're down to maybe thirty. My advice, people, is that we make time while we've still got light."

Talbot glanced at the beam. Realized it didn't hurt his eyes as badly.

"Yep. Move it. Muldare, you're right behind me lighting my way. Supervisor, Dya, you stay hard on her heels. Let's go."

And he hurried down the sloping surface.

Problem was, he had to have Muldare's light tucked close behind him. He dared not step into a shadow—since on more than one occasion it was a hole that dropped away into unknown depths. Nor did he trust the occasional huge invertebrate that skittered from their path. The things were supposed to be bug-sized, right? So what was with the big ones—the size of lobsters—that fled this way and that? The things looked lethal with barbs, claws, and spikes sticking out of their bodies.

Anyone who'd lived on Donovan knew that when it came to critters, anything that looked like a weapon was. They also knew that while Donovanian wildlife was deadly to humans, in many cases, a person's only safety lay in the fact that said wildlife had never seen a human before, and usually didn't know they were edible.

But if so much as one of the big bugs figured that out?

As the light began to dwindle, Talbot had to ask himself: *Shit on a shoe, where's the end of this thing?*

With the others crowded close, he edged around a vertical stone column, scattering a chittering horde of clicking and scurrying creatures. Here the tube divided. So, which way?

"There!" Muldare pointed with the dying light.

A faint arrow was scratched in the basalt pointing to the left-hand tunnel.

"At least it's not an A.S.," Muldare noted.

"A what?" Dya asked.

"Arne Saknussemm." Muldare glanced back and forth. "Didn't any of you read Jules Verne?"

"Who?" Aguila asked.

Talbot hurried into the tube, stumbled, and almost fell headlong into a dark hole that dropped away on the left side of the cavern.

"Dya?" Talbot called as his heart tried to hammer its way out of his chest. "How you doing?"

"Okay, Mark." But her voice was shaky, on the edge of panic.

"Supervisor?"

"You forget, Marine. I run a mine." Aguila's voice had a forced joviality. "I'm used to holes. And these don't have explosives drilled into the rock at the end."

Yeah, but you also have elevators that you can ride out into the sunlight.

Talbot shinnied past on the lip of the hole as Muldare's fading light illuminated the way. Ahead, he could see nothing in the depths but an eternal blackness.

Under his breath, Talbot whispered, "Get me out of here, God, and I'll live the rest of my life in the out of doors under an open sky."

But the slanting tunnel just kept winding ever deeper into Donovan's depth. They made their way, step by step, clambering over humps of rock, squeezing through tight spots, avoiding bottomless drops, for another three hours.

As the light flickered out, they found the end of the line: a door set into the basalt. Wouldn't have been a problem, but the damn thing was locked.

From the outside.

And then Muldare's beam went dead, leaving them in the pitch black.

51

When did a nightmare end and mind-numbing terror begin? Where was the line? Nothing had prepared Vartan for the things he'd just survived. Nothing. Not even the Harrowing and Cleansing.

During those terrible days people had been ritually murdered, their bodies carefully cut into pieces, cooked, and reverently consumed. If it was truly the universe's will, it made sense.

What he had just witnessed? Just survived?

Incomprehensible.

Vartan staggered back, away from the last of the trees and onto bedrock, making sure he kept his feet moving. That the thin roots here couldn't take hold. Twisting, he turned the rifle to cover every approach; the fear-shakes finally took possession of his muscles.

Tried to swallow.

Couldn't.

That slimy feeling down in his guts urged him to stop. To void his now-liquid bowels of their fear. Breath chattered in his panic-spasming lungs.

Nothing made sense.

Stop. Think. What happened?

Fifteen people had accompanied him down into the forest. Per orders, he'd broken them into three teams. Given each a direction to search. His team had consisted of Mars Hangdong, Hap Chi, Sima Moskva, Will Bet, and Tuac Sao. With Tikal's teams, they had made the long climb down the south trail, the slow and awkward descent from the heights evidence of the poor physical condition they were in. They'd reached the bottom, exhausted. Were resting on a stone outcrop, away from the roots, when the airtruck had roared off overhead.

Vartan had seen a body fall from the side. Thought it was a female. Tried to make sense as to who would be thrown out of the vehicle so wantonly, let alone why the thing was in the air. Svetlana and Hakil were supposed to be guarding the vehicle.

Leaving that for later—once his party had caught their second wind—he had waved farewell as Tikal's parties had spread out from the base of the trail.

For him and his team it had been magical; the journey north along the basalt had been a revelation: the sights, the realization of life in every direction, and most of all, the colors, smells, and sounds. After so many years locked in the prison of Deck Three, here, spinning all around them in a tapestry of blues, greens, cerulean, and yellows and reds, the forest was like a dream come true. Just inhale and pull the perfume into the lungs. Listen to the rising and falling chime.

Magic.

They'd laughed, leaped from stone to stone, marveled at the roots that squirmed under their feet. Stared up at the brilliant blue of the sky and the beams of light cast through the branches by Capella.

They'd located the door that marked the tunnel exit. Chained and locked, it meant either the Supervisor's party had found it open, chained it to keep pursuit from following, or they were still locked inside. He'd studied the ground. Could see no tracks, but that didn't mean anything. Vartan was a city person who wouldn't know a track unless it was glaring.

If his quarry was locked inside, well and good. He had them. If not, he needed to know. Leaving Mars Hangdong to guard the door, he'd taken Sima, Will, Tuac, and Hap Chi to run a quick sweep into the forest as insurance that Aguila wasn't ahead of them.

Nothing big, just check a couple of hundred yards into the deep forest. Besides, he wanted to see. To walk under the towering giants and marvel at the sights and miracle of the place.

At the edge of the basalt flow, some weird plant had grabbed Will Bet as he stepped beneath it. What looked like giant yellow-black-and-red-striped flowers had fastened onto Will's neck and arm. Jerked him up high and out of reach. The flowers had proceeded to bite down on the screaming Will. Damn thing wasn't fazed when Vartan shot a couple of rounds through the thick stalk. The only reaction came from the plant's roots as they slithered out of the ground in his direction, cutting off retreat back the way they'd come.

In horror, they'd fled down the tumbled basalt and into the darkness of the forest. Scrambled across a tangle of giant roots. Realized the damn things were twisting! Slowly, but surely.

Sima Moskva, mother of two, was next. Something resembling knee-high stalks, pale on the bottom and dark brown on the tips, exploded in some kind of spores that puffed into Sima's face. Sent her into convulsions on the spot. She had fallen, bucking, gagging, her eyes protruding from her head.

. . . And died within moments as the roots she lay on began to writhe and wind around her body. Trying to resuscitate her, Tuac Sao was seized by the same convulsions, having caught a whiff of the spores.

With the roots slipping around their feet, Vartan and Hap had fought a battle to pull away. Barely managed to jerk their way free. Each got a grip on Tuac, tried to hoist the choking, gagging man from the encircling roots. Couldn't.

They'd stumbled back, watched in awed horror as the roots wound around the dead Sima and dying Tuac. Didn't take more than ten minutes total before the thick bunching of squirming root mass had totally engulfed both bodies.

"Vart?" Hap had said. "We've got to get out of here."

"Yeah," he'd panted, consumed by fear.

But trying to get back?

Which way? He was all turned around.

The faintest of screams carried through the chime. Had to be Mars. Vartan hurried off across the roots, realized that the ones that were squirming marked his back trail.

Hadn't gone more than ten meters before he heard the hollow impact. A sodden thud. Like someone dropping a melon from a height onto a duraplast floor. Vart had scrambled the rest of the way down the root mat. Turned, figuring that Hap had fallen, and he would help him back to his feet.

Nothing.

Hap was gone.

Vanished.

Looking up, Vart thought he saw movement up in the trees. Couldn't be sure.

Again, a scream from the direction of the basalt flow.

Somehow Vartan had staggered up onto the basalt flow, panting, falling, tripping over his own feet. He'd kept the rifle, hadn't lost it in his panic. He'd veered wide around where the flower-thing was chewing on Will's head and arm.

The door remained chained.

"Mars!"

Nothing but a slight variation in the chime answered him.

Vartan paced before the door, looking for any sign. Blood. Scuffed dirt. Something dropped.

But he found nothing. The only thing moving was the thin layer of roots that quivered and extended in sinuous patterns across the shallow soil.

"Mars? Where are you?"

Only the endless chime filled his hearing.

Vartan came raggedly to his senses. Realized he was sobbing. Had been for some time.

Terrified down to the marrow in his bones, he wiped tears from his eyes and turned his steps back for the trail. They'd been what, no more than fifteen or twenty minutes here? And he was the only one left?

Veering wide around the gaudily colored plants—shivers wracking his muscles—Vartan tried to cover everything with the rifle. Not that shooting the monster-flower plant had saved Will.

At the trail up, he flopped onto the exposed stone, panted for breath. Tried to find some sort of sanity down in his reeling and tumbling thoughts.

I'm supposed to be the strong one. Trained in security.

And all he had left was consuming terror.

A scream. Barely audible, carried from out in the forest.

Vartan turned to stare out at the vast expanse of green, blue, and turquoise. Was it human? It had been so faint, almost drowned by the chime.

Tikal's parties were supposed to be out there. They'd

been sweeping the forest behind Vart's group. Had fanned out from the bottom of the trail.

Scarlet birds burst from the forest canopy, started flying his way.

Vartan cried out, remembering the stories of some flying creature that sliced a man's flesh from his bones.

He pulled up the rifle, fired a burst. Missed. Nevertheless, the flying things veered off and dove into the trees.

Got to get out of here.

Some deep well of terror gave life to his exhausted muscles. Whimpering, sometimes sobbing, he scrambled up the steep trail. He climbed until exhausted. Flopped onto the unyielding basalt, unable to go farther. Panting, spent, he gave up. Closed his eyes, waiting for . . . what? Surrender?

Death?

Nothingness?

He came to. A sound, a shadow, a hint of movement at the edge of his vision sent him scrambling in panic. Breath tearing at his lungs, he swung the rifle around. Couldn't place the threat. Climbed. His feet kept slipping and sliding for purchase given his slick-soled city shoes.

And he made it. Fell weeping on the basalt caprock atop the mesa. The sight of the domes and fields just past the solar collectors was like a miracle of salvation.

After gathering his wits, he struggled to his feet; the heavy rifle hung from his trembling hands. Thirsty. So thirsty. Exhausted like he'd never been.

He managed to stumble his way to the admin dome. Stared at the mangled remains of a woman laid beside the door.

Her face was a bloody wreck; the limbs were broken, rudely askew. The oddly short and contorted torso didn't make sense—at least until he realized her back and hips had to be broken and compressed. Like a human who'd been crushed five inches shorter by a macabre hammer blow. Which explained why her left leg was dislocated so high up on her hip, as if growing out of her waistband. And then there was the bruising and blood.

The scars. So familiar.

Svetlana?

He wavered on his feet, blinked. Kept trying to understand the impossibility of what he was seeing.

This broken bone and meat wasn't Svetlana. She was his lover. His friend.

"She fell from the airtruck," Marta's soft voice said from behind him. "Shyanne and Tamil stole it. Flew it away. Svetlana and Hakil tried to stop them . . . were clinging to the outside. Svetlana landed in the garden. Hakil fell into the forest off to the east."

Svetlana?

Could this cold and brutalized pile of maimed flesh be the woman he'd come to . . .

The world turned glassy in Vartan's vision: He saw it waver, fade, and slide slowly to the side. Thought he heard the distant chatter of automatic weapons fire from somewhere below the rim. Then a singing and ringing sound drowned it out.

The last thing he remembered was his body hitting the ground. Even that faded into a gray haze.

52

As Kalico watched—hands clamped hard to her ears—muzzle flash worked to illuminate the door. Even so, the sound deafened in the confines of the lava tube. Talbot adjusted his aim. Fired another burst. Without hearing protection, the guy had to be in physical pain, given the way Kalico's ears rang.

Holes, shining light could be seen in the door.

Talbot threw his weight against the door, slamming the thing open. Daylight spilled in and Kalico, holding Dya's hand, stumbled out into Capella's blinding glare. Here, near the base of the cliff, scrubby aquajade and stonewood—stunted by the thin topsoil—poked up through some curious species of ferngrass. It had a paler blue tint than what she was used to at Port Authority.

"They're going to have heard that," Briah Muldare said as she turned, staring up the steep slope that rose behind them. They had to be at the bottom of the Tyson escarpment, though nothing could be made out at the top a couple hundred meters above them.

So had PA sent in the cavalry?

Muldare indicated the bullet-severed chain that had secured the duraplast door. "Makes you wonder what used to live in that tunnel that they'd have brought a door down here and chained it shut."

Talbot slammed the portal, fiddled with the broken chain, and gave it up as a bad idea. He rolled an angular chunk of basalt over and used it to prop the door closed.

They all looked disheveled, hair in tangles, clothes filthy, smudged, stained, and scuffed. Kalico assumed that her face, too, was smeared with, well, who knew what that greasy-looking stuff might be? Invertebrate shit?

Her mocking internal voice chided: *You look like you've been locked in a cave for a day.*

Kalico took in the surroundings. The lava tube had

opened onto a flat that stuck out on the west side of the Tyson escarpment. Sheer basalt, tumbled boulders, and the aforementioned trees that could find enough soil to cling to rose to the rim where it loomed above them.

From the angle of the sun, partially hidden by trees, and according to her wrist unit, they'd emerged in late afternoon. Crap. Night would be falling in a couple of hours; they were all suffering from thirst and hunger. And they were heading out into the forest without a lick of shelter in any direction.

Talbot pulled his radio from its belt pouch. "I'm resetting the broadcast frequency so the Unreconciled won't monitor us." He hit the mic, and said, "Port Authority, this is Mark Talbot. Do you copy?"

The only answer was static.

"They have to know we're overdue," Muldare groused as she fingered her rifle.

Talbot asked, "Does anyone read? Hello. Can anyone hear me?"

Kalico tried her personal com, knowing it would only link as far as the airtruck, assuming it was still up top. "This is Supervisor Aguila. Does anyone copy?"

Nothing.

Muldare was trying her own radio.

"Sure wish *Vixen* was still in orbit," Kalico groused. "With their survey array, they'd have a chance of picking up our signal."

"Too far out for the handhelds," Talbot agreed, reholstering the unit on his belt. "Where the hell are our people? Two Spot should have half the town here to look for us."

"What now?" Muldare asked.

Around them lay nothing but forest. A flock of scarlet fliers had appeared, perhaps drawn by the unusual sound of gunfire. The chime was rising and falling, adapting in the invertebrates' eternal quest for a symphony.

"Whatever we do, we've got to move," Talbot warned, his eyes on the roots and ferngrass they'd walked out onto. Several of the sucking shrub plants were swiveling branches in their direction.

Kalico turned her attention to the escarpment. The

cracked basalt, much of it columnar, would be an impossible climb. "Where are the trails up?"

"Back to the north," Talbot told her. "And another one down on the point at the southern end. We going back up? They'll be waiting if we do. It's easy to monitor those trails. Lay an ambush."

Kalico squinted. "The airtruck is up there. We've got two service rifles, three pistols. Assuming they got Carson, they've got his rifle with forty rounds and his pistol with twelve."

Dya arched an eyebrow. "You want to go to war with the Unreconciled? You're going to have to shoot down a lot of people to get that airtruck. Thought that avoiding that scenario was why we took to the tunnel in the first place."

"We're overdue by a whole day," Talbot reminded. "What the hell is wrong? Where's Step, Talina, and the posse?"

"And what kind of reception will they be flying into?" Muldare wondered as she fingered her rifle.

"Batuhan had fifty-seven adults to start with," Kalico mused. "Mark shot three. Carson might have taken one down with that gunshot. Given the number of children it's killed, Donovan might have taken out a couple of adults by now, maybe more."

Dya stuffed her fingers in her back pockets as she eased her weight off the shifting roots. "The radio and the airtruck are up top. That's where rescue is going to head first. That's where we've got to be."

"And that's where Batuhan and his cannibals are going to expect us." Muldare, too, was staring up at the high rim, as if expecting to see people staring down from above.

Talbot re-slung his rifle. "Doesn't matter. We've got to move. I've got point. Dya, second. Supervisor, you're third, and Muldare, you've got the six. Walk carefully, people. Try not to disturb the roots."

"Which way?" Kalico asked.

"West off this point, then north through the forest, skirting the base of the basalt to where the slope isn't as steep and rocky," Talbot said. "Even if we can't take the trails, there should be an easier climb leading up into the high ground. We can circle and come around from the north. But be careful, this kind of terrain is just made for bems and skewers. And God alone knows what else might live in the cracks and crevices. Things we've never seen."

When it came to wilderness, Kalico did as she was told. No one—except maybe Talina and Kylee Simonov—knew the backcountry better than Talbot. If there was a chance they could make it, it would be because of his and Dya's forest skills.

Assuming this section of forest had the same threats and followed the same rules they were familiar with.

Dya's skills had been honed in the south, outside Mundo Base. As had Talbot's. That was nearly a thousand kilometers away, in a different ecosystem. Who knew what sorts of deadly creatures lurked in these forests? Especially given that of the last five occupants of Tyson Station, only three had been found, and they'd been skeletonized.

Kalico fell into step behind Dya. The change in the woman was like night to day. A literal analogy. Dya Simonov was once again herself: calm, in control, capable. As if stepping out from that black hole, she'd shed her mind-numbing fear like an old coat.

Well, everyone had his or her weakness.

"There's your bluelinda," Talbot noted, pointing with his rifle as he entered the trees. The thing was indeed beautiful; the little berries, like a string of royal-blue glass pearls, hung from the undersides of the branches where the plant climbed up the side of an aquajade.

The aquajade here were smaller, more widely spaced. Biteya bush, thorncactus, and sucking shrub hung on as understory, and the numerous gotcha vines reminded her of spiderwebs strung between the trees.

Talbot led the way carefully, rifle up, eyes scanning.

Overhead, tree clingers—the first Kalico had ever seen in the flesh—leaped from branch to branch, staring down with their three curious eyes.

The chime seemed to change as they walked farther out onto the point.

"Hold up," Dya called. "Got a bem. Smell it?"

Talbot sniffed, trying to sample the morning breeze.

"Your nose is always better than mine. But, yeah. It's there."

Kalico realized the roots were reaching for her feet.

Step by step, she followed Dya forward until Talbot called, "Got it. On the right. About ten meters ahead. By the base of that aquajade."

Kalico followed where he pointed, seeing what looked like a tumbled basalt boulder. Scenting the breeze herself, she thought she picked up the slightest scent of vinegar. Took a long gander at the bem. "Damn, they're good. Even knowing what to look for, I'd have thought it was a rock."

Talbot cut wide, leaving plenty of distance between them. Bems weren't fast, depended on their perfect camouflage for success in hunting.

They had reached the edge of the flat, the ground dropping away on either side into deeper forest. Kalico was wishing she had eyes in the back of her head, trying to see everything in this deadly world of greens and blue. The leaves were all either moving on their own accord or stirred by the slight breeze.

The chime covered any forest sound. Movement on the branches was caused by the vines, invertebrates, or the shifting of the trees.

She almost ran into Dya's back, so quickly did the woman stop.

"Damn," Talbot, up in the lead, cursed.

Kalico craned her neck, looking around Dya to see a body. Well, okay, most of a body. Naked, obviously male, the thing was suspended a good two meters off the ground, having been wrapped up in dark green vines that wound around the legs, the torso, and single remaining arm. Other vines were woven into the chabacho and neighboring aquajade to support both plant and victim.

The main stem of the plant looked as thick as a man's thigh, the upper part engorged. Two stalks ending in . . . well, hard to call them flowers, were expanding and contracting, taking slow bites out of what remained of one shoulder and the bloody neck. Didn't matter that an arm and the head had already been devoured; the scar patterns identified the remains as one of the Unreconciled.

Below where the body hung, a flock of invertebrates scuttled around and through the man's scanty clothing as they snapped up any bits and drops that fell from above.

"What the hell?" Muldare asked through a horrified exhale.

"Tooth flower," Dya said woodenly. "One of the biggest I've ever seen."

"It's eating . . ." Kalico couldn't finish. Could only stare.

"Come on," Talbot almost barked the command. "Poor bastard was probably searching for us. Keep an eye out, and let's get the hell off this point."

"To where?" Dya wondered. "It's going to be dark long before we can work out any trail back to the top."

"Don't know," Talbot said, cutting wide around the tooth flower and its feast. "Rock outcrop? Maybe a low crotch of a tree if we can find a chabacho big enough and without any of the carnivorous vines."

Kalico swallowed hard, wishing again that she had something to drink. Wishing she were away, back in Corporate Mine. Wishing she were anywhere but out here in the forest.

As she passed, she could hear one of the tooth flowers contracting; the sound was accompanied by the snapping of human bones as the teeth sheared through the man's clavicle, upper ribs, and vertebrae.

Dya whispered, "Judging from that poor bastard back there, I guess the Unreconciled aren't as pure in the eyes of the universe as Batuhan thought."

"Yeah," Muldare said in a tight voice. "Maybe the universe found Batuhan's methods wanting and decided to improve upon the process."

53

Talina watched the airtruck drop toward the Briggs pad to land beside her aircar. Dust swirled up, blowing out in curling clouds to dissipate as the vehicle settled onto its skids.

Capella's harsh light gleamed on the sialon and metal sides, glinted from the windshield up front. Airtrucks weren't masterpieces of elegance, being built strictly for utilitarian function.

As the fans spun down, a thin woman opened the door, climbed wearily down. She was naked but for a wrap around her waist; her ratty brown hair was confined with a tie at the back of her neck. Talina could see the lines of scars crisscrossing her pale flesh. Some sort of spirals—centered on the nipples—covered each of her small breasts.

"Pus-sucking hell," Chaco whispered where he stood beside Talina. "So that's a cannibal?"

A rail-thin man appeared in the door behind the woman and stepped carefully to the ground. He, too, only wore a breechcloth; his bare feet, like the woman's, looked so incongruous on the raw dirt. No one went barefoot on Donovan. At least not if they wanted to avoid a most hideous death as slugs slithered around their insides, eating their guts and muscles. The man was dark-skinned and the scars stood out—lines of them running down his torso, arms and legs, and around his face. They'd been patterned like triangles to accent his broad nose.

"Hello," the woman called, starting forward, a hand shielding her eyes from Capella's strong light. "I'm Shyanne Veda, and this is Tamil Kattan. Thank you for the beacon. We didn't know what to do."

Talina stepped forward, hand on her pistol, wary eyes on the airtruck. The thing could carry up to fifteen, maybe twenty people if they didn't mind being packed in like sardines. "How many of you are there?"

"We're all that's left. We started with six. Batuhan's First Will got the other four. Tamil, here, he was the important one, he could fly the airtruck."

"Where's Supervisor Aguila, Dr. Simonov, Talbot, and the marines?"

Shyanne had a panicked look on her face. Her lips parted, and she was panting. From the heat? From exertion? Or fear? "One of the marines, the one they left to guard the airtruck, he's dead. The others got away. At least I think they did. The Messiah had people searching everywhere. Even sent teams down into the forest. Batuhan sent so many after them, it gave me and Tamil our chance to break away. But damn him, he knew. Tried to stop us. We shook Hakil and Svetlana off as we were climbing from Tyson."

"Who are Hakil and Svetlana?" Talina asked.

"They're some of the Messiahs' 'Will.' That's what he calls them. Police. Enforcers. The ritual executioners. They ensure that what he wills is done."

Chaco made a wait-a-moment gesture with his hands. "Hey, I'm Chaco Briggs. This is my place. So relax, huh? Start at the beginning. You're not making a lick of sense."

Tamil had stopped a couple of steps behind Shyanne, dark eyes glancing uneasily from Talina to Chaco and back. The guy kept licking his lips. Couldn't quite figure out what to do with his hands, so he started wringing them.

Shyanne fought down what looked like a surge of panic. Swallowed hard. "Listen. I'm a veterinary tech Level I. There were six of us. With scientific backgrounds . . . or maybe just the kind of people who didn't buy the bullshit, you know? But it was survival. Who the hell wanted to have their throats cut and be eaten? The things we did to . . . to . . ."

When she couldn't finish, looked on the verge of breaking down, Talina snapped, "We know. What happened at Tyson?"

Tamil told her, "Shyanne was listening from the kitchen. Hoping to get back to see her daughter. Understood the moment the Supervisor said it was a prion that was giving the Prophets their visions. Shyanne explained it to us. Not that we'd bought the clap-trapping holy prophet shit. We'd already figured that once we got dirtside, we'd get away. Figured that out clear back on *Ashanti*. Then, seeing where we were? Surrounded by wilderness? It was like being crushed."

"Then Aguila shows up with the science." Shyanne had found her voice again. "There were six of us who thought we'd finally gotten our chance. Here was proof that would debunk the whole 'we're chosen by God and the universe' thing."

Tamil added, "But Batuhan had members of the Will in place, waiting. Tricked the marine guarding the airtruck. Killed him. Closed the doors to the dome, figured he had the Supervisor trapped, right? But they pulled guns. Shot some of the First Chosen. Those are the ones who carry the throne and attend the Messiah. The Supervisor and her people managed to get down into the basement."

Shyanne said, "Stalemate. Batuhan can't attack them head on. They've got enough firepower to kill everyone in that stairwell. Meanwhile, the rest of us, the disbelievers, we're waiting for rescue. Someone's going to come for the Supervisor. But it gets dark.

"So we plan. Come morning, with Tamil at the wheel, we'll fly out. Find help."

"But somehow Batuhan knows; he has the Will grab four of us." Tamil chuckled in what was clearly gallows humor. "Cuts Jilliam's and Cumber's throats right there. Starts butchering them for feast. Don't know what happened to Kleo and Troy."

"We play the game." Shyanne's eyes had gone dull. "But we're being watched. Then, at daybreak, there's a cry. Turns out that the Supervisor and her people have found a way into some tunnel. It takes a while to figure out, but this tunnel goes down somewhere on the west side. So maybe they've escaped into the forest."

Kylee—a fastbreak over her shoulder—with the panting and sweating Dek Taglioni stumbling behind her, rounded the workshop and pulled up. The way Kylee fixed on Shyanne and Tamil was like a mongoose on a cobra. Talina gave her a hand signal to wait and listen.

Shyanne might have been oblivious. "First thing this morning Batuhan sent search parties to hunt them down, and we made a break for the airtruck. Thought we had a chance. Barely got if off the ground. And that was with Hakil and Svetlana clinging to the side, swearing they'll kill us."

Tamil spread his hands like a supplicant. "If you hadn't heard us on the radio, sent us that beacon, we'd have never found this place."

"Get back to the Supervisor." Talina stepped close. "She, Dya, Talbot, and one marine escaped into the forest, right? So, they're still out there?"

"As of when we left." Shyanne nodded.

"There's about thirty of the chosen hunting them," Tamil added. "More than enough to chase four people down."

"Shit on a shoe," Chaco muttered.

Kylee stepped close, shooting the scarred woman and man a scathing glare. "So my mother and father, Kalico, and some marine are out in the forest? Being hunted?"

"Yeah, kid," Talina said softly, the quetzals in her blood having quickened. In her mind she was seeing forest trails, smelling the scent of prey, vision going keen in the infrared and ultraviolet.

"How much chance can they have?" Tamil asked, almost pleading. "There's only four of them. With the airtruck gone, Batuhan has nothing to keep him from sending everyone in pursuit."

"It's not the Unreconciled I'm worried about," Talina said.

"We've got to go get them." Kylee's gaze had gone vacant. Her eyes seeming to enlarge.

Yeah, she was sharing the same images Talina was.

"What about the rest of Batuhan's people?" Tamil asked, a look of desperation in his dark eyes.

Kylee—in a voice thinner than wire—said, "Sorry. They had their chance. Nothing we can do for them now."

"What does that mean?" Shyanne's gaze flicked from face to face.

"On Donovan, stupidity is a death sentence," Talina told her. "Let's tell Madison what's coming down and get packed."

"Not me," Shyanne cried, on the verge of tears. "I'll die before I go back there."

"Me, too," Tamil said in a hoarse whisper.

From the look in Kylee's eyes, she was more than ready to help them along.

"We'll take care of you until this is over," Chaco said.

"Let's beat feet." Talina turned, images of deep forest playing in her head. Four people, without armor, in unfamiliar territory. And just because they were among the best on the planet, this was still Donovan.

They didn't have much time.

54

When Dek appeared on the landing pad with his rifle and packed war bag Talina demanded, "What the hell do you think you're doing?"

"Packing my shit to go along. What do you think I'm doing?"

"Hey, soft meat, the last thing I need is a newbie Skull stumbling around in the forest and turning himself into supper for the nearest sidewinder."

"The last thing you need is to set down somewhere in the forest, only to have good old Batuhan stumble over the airtruck. Who guards it while you search? Or did I miss something?"

A sliver of smile bent Talina's lips. "Bound and determined to get your ass in a sling, huh? Okay, get your gear on board."

As Dek turned away, he heard Chaco say, "You sure that's a good idea? He's a solid guy, got potential, but you're going to get him killed."

Dek turned back. "You just keep an eye on Shyanne and Tamil. Maybe they're really refugees. Maybe not. But you figure that after what they've been through, what they've done, they're still Unreconciled. Probably not as soft and cuddly as they are trying to appear. Think: Broken goods."

"Gotcha." Chaco stuck out a hand. "Hey, Dek. You make it through this? You gotta place out here with us. You understand?"

"Thanks, Chaco."

He placed a foot in the step up to the airtruck and noticed Talina's evaluative stare. "What?"

She arched a slim eyebrow. "Must have been some day down in the canyon fixing that pump."

"Turned out to be a little more complicated than Chaco thought. We got it working, why?"

She rolled her lips between her teeth, her gaze going alien on him. "Nothing. Get aboard."

He slung his pack onto the deck, climbed in, and racked the Holland & Holland next to Talina's service rifle. He made sure he had his bullets and a spare powerpack for the gun in his web gear.

Kylee was fastening the straps on a backpack, glanced sidelong at him. "Told you she liked you."

"You see different things than I do."

"Yep." She didn't look up. "You might want to move out of the doorway."

"Huh? Why, I—"

Kylee reached out, grabbed him by the web gear, and jerked him sideways. Damn near yanked him off his feet.

As Dek struggled for balance, something huge, flashing yellow and black, scrambled through the space he'd occupied. The thing blocked the light, filled the doorway. The sound of claws could be heard as they sought purchase on the sialon deck.

Dek planted a foot, whirled to stare at the creature that now took up way too much of the compartment. Big, fully two meters at the shoulders, the beast swung its muzzle to within inches of Dek's nose.

A great triangular head filled Dek's vision, and he had to look from eye to eye to eye, so widely were they spaced across the top of the monster's head. Black, gleaming, they seemed to see right through to Dek's bones. Patterns of violet, mauve, and orange replaced the yellow and black designs running over the beast's hide.

"Wha . . . ? What?" Dek staggered backward, slammed into the duraplast wall. Knees gone weak, his heart now hammered so hard it might burst his chest. He fought to get a breath.

A yip of terror escaped his throat as a membrane, like an unfolding sail, ringed the creature's neck and began flashing colors so brilliant they almost hurt the eyes.

Dek opened his mouth in the attempt to cry out. A blur shot from the beast's mouth. Like a hard leather rod, it jetted past Dek's lips, flicked over his tongue and bumped off his molars. The force of his reaction banged the back of his head off the wall. As the leathery thing glanced off Dek's soft palate, his gag reflex tried to bend him double.

An overpowering taste—like concentrated peppermint extract—flooded his mouth. Saliva began to pump. Paralyzed, he stared across the great triangular head into the top eye. It seemed to have expanded, filling Derek Taglioni's entire universe.

"*Flute!*" Kylee's barked command barely penetrated Dek's fugue. "*Back off!* Leave him alone."

Just as quickly, the tongue was gone. Somehow Dek kept from collapsing, managed to lock his knees, back braced against the airtruck's cargo bay.

For long seconds he fought to fill his lungs, to keep from throwing up.

"They don't know how rude humans find that," Talina muttered from the wheel where she was checking the battery indicator and fans.

"What the hell?" Dek squeaked in terror as he gaped at the . . . the . . . what? Dinosaur? Dragon? Or . . .

"This is Flute," Kylee told him. "He's a quetzal. Don't mind the French kiss thing. It's how they say hello."

A quetzal? Here?

Dek gaped at the creature in rapt horror. Quetzals ate people. He could well imagine, looking as he was at that big mouth filled with wicked serrations that served as teeth. They ran from one side of the wide triangular jaw to the other.

He wanted to spit the terrible taste out. His mouth kept watering.

"You sure you want Flute along?" Talina asked. "This is last call for him to get off."

Kylee stepped over, placed a hand on the beast's . . . um, shoulder? With her other hand, she pointed toward the rear of the compartment. "You better go lie down. And don't look out the windows. When Rocket flew, he almost went catatonic."

Flute flashed a riot of orange and sky-blue; the intricate designs ran down his hide as if flowing. That sail-like collar had deflated flush with the beast's neck. Then, with remarkable agility for a creature that large, it curled itself along the floor, conforming to the back bench.

"Shit on a shoe," Dek wheezed. "It's going with us?"

Kylee fixed her alien-blue gaze on him. "That's my mom and dad out there in the forest being chased by cannibals. Get it? And Flute likes Mom."

Dek jumped as the fans spun up, Talina at the wheel. Still shaking—and as scared as he'd ever been—he stepped to the door, gave Chaco and the cannibals a farewell wave, and slammed it before anything else could leap in with him.

Talina was on the radio. "Two Spot? Got trouble at Tyson. If we can believe the source, Carson is dead, and Kalico, Dya, Talbot, and Muldare are hiding out in the forest. I'm heading that way from Briggs. I'll let you know what's up as we get closer."

"Roger that. But, Tal, we're on lockdown. Got a quetzal. At least one is in the compound. Got another five outside the fence trying to get in."

"Shit. Figures. I'll send an update as soon as I know anything."

"Roger that. We get this resolved, we'll come on the run."

It hit Dek that everything had happened so fast. Now, as they soared out over the forest, it was with the realization that he was flying out to confront the Irredenta, to attempt the rescue of Supervisor Aguila and her party, accompanied by a quetzal-infected teenager and Talina Perez. And he was locked in a small compartment with a man-eating monster. One that—of all things—had stuck its tongue into Dek's mouth. What part of this wasn't insane?

Oh, Derek. You were the one who wanted to get a feeling for the real Donovan.

Which left him shuddering. If this turned out wrong, if the quetzal didn't eat him, it would be the Irredenta who'd be picking his bones clean.

Hard to believe that he'd considered that nightmare safely left behind the day he'd shuttled out of *Ashanti*.

55

A quetzal in the compound? Five more trying to get in? The desire to wheel around, fly full-throttle for PA, tore at Talina's soul. She should be there. No one knew how to hunt quetzals like she did.

Down in her gut, Demon hissed, *"Got you, didn't we?"*

"Yeah? Bet there's going to be nothing but steaks and leather by nightfall, you creepy little shit."

Talina took her heading for Tyson. As much as she yearned to head for PA, Kalico, Dya, and Talbot needed her. First hand, she knew the sense of desperation that came from being lost in the forest.

"So, from Two Spot's report, it was six of them. Three on the Mine Gate, three from the shuttle field." Talina shot a glance at Kylee. "That's a whole new tactic. And in the middle of the day."

"Whitey really hates you, huh?" Kylee gave Talina an evaluative blue-eyed stare.

"Yeah, lucky me."

Demon tried to claw at her stomach, hissing in rage. *Piece of shit.*

Talina checked her compass and airspeed. Below her the wild Donovanian terrain unfolded and flowed. The airtruck responded instantly to the touch. The fans and gimbals were all tight, within tolerance. Ungainly as the airtruck looked, it handled like a dream, a reassuring feeling after all of these years. Hard to believe that the power indicator really meant what it said. Reliable. So good that she could partially ignore that constant and nagging worry about what to do if they went down. How damn long had it been since she could fly without fear?

Dek was scrunched in the corner of the cab, back to the door. He kept staring in disbelief at Flute. The look on his face was priceless: Like the guy just knew the terrified quetzal was going leap across the cargo box and eat him.

Not a chance given that Flute was flashing the bright yellow-and-black patterns of terror mixed with teal anxiety spots in addition to glowing way down in the infrared.

Quetzals really hated to fly. That he'd dared it at all was mark of the beast's affection for Kylee and perhaps Dya. Or—who knew?—it was some other quetzal experiment cooked up by his lineage.

Kylee stepped up to the dash beside Talina, her gaze fixed on the landscape. In a voice barely above a whisper, she said, "He's not ready, you know."

"Flute? Then why'd you insist he come along?"

"I mean Dek."

"He wanted a taste of Donovan. As long as he just stays in the airtruck, keeps it out of the cannibals' hands, he'll be all right."

"You're not setting us down at Tyson, so that means we're setting down in the forest. You've got a place in mind?"

"Ridgetop, a couple of kilometers north and above. Mostly basalt bedrock. If Dek locks the doors, shoots anything that tries to force its way in, he'll be all right. And I'll set the radio on the PA frequency before we go. If something happens, Shig can have Manny Bateman run the shuttle out to pick him up after they mop up this quetzal trouble."

Kylee shrugged.

Talina shot Kylee a questioning look. "Did he shoot that fastbreak this morning, or did you?"

"He did. He listens well, but he's still weak from being on that ship. I get what you see in him. With the right luck, he might make it. Really different than Cap, though. This one's more centered. If Donovan doesn't kill him, he could be a full partner."

"Got it all figured out, huh?"

"He's a world of improvement over Bucky Berkholtz."

"There's times I wish you didn't have so much of me in you."

"No, you don't."

"And why's that, kid?"

Kylee flipped her hair back, grinned. "Because every time I want to lose it, want to fucking scream, and cry, and beat the crap out of Tip, or unload all my frustrations on Madison, you're there. Down deep. It's like having a big sister inside my head. At first, I hated it. Really, really, hated it. Now I'm the most thankful girl on the planet."

"Glad to be of service. Having you inside me . . . well, it's a balance. Keeps me on track with all these asshole quetzals running around inside my skull."

Kylee nodded, her worried gaze fixing on the horizon. "Think Mom's okay?"

"Don't know, kid. Nobody in their right mind wants to take a chance on the forest, not without a full set of armor and tech. If it was anybody but your mom and dad, I'd say write it off. And as good as your mom is, Talbot's even better. Maybe as good as anyone on the planet when it comes to staying alive."

"He's not us," Kylee countered, referring to the quetzal in their blood. "And we've got Flute."

"Which is why we'll find them."

"You think this lockdown could be Whitey?"

"Bet on it. That snot-sucker's still ahead of me. Killed a prospector last month. Old Chin Hua Mao. As good a veteran Wild One as you'll find in the bush. Somehow Whitey, or of one of his lineage, got old Chin by surprise while he was working his claim in the Blood Mountains."

"There," Kylee pointed. Having spotted Tyson in the distance.

Talina keyed the radio. "Kalico? Mark? Dya? Do you read? Come in. Kalico? Mark? Dya? If you can—"

"*Got ya, Tal,*" Kalico's voice came faintly through the receiver. "*We're about a half klick west of Tyson, moving slowly. Where are you?*"

"Coming in from the east in the airtruck. Anyplace I can set down?"

"*Negative on that. We're on the floodplain below the basalt. Trees are four hundred meters tall if they're an inch. We'll have to find someplace open enough you can drop down.*"

"What's your situation? Who's with you?"

Beside her, Kylee went as tight as a coiled spring.

"*Me, Talbot, Dya, and Muldare are still out here. We think Carson's dead and the Unreconciled have his weapon.*"

Consider Tyson hostile. Repeat, Tyson is hostile. You copy that?"

"Roger that." Talina keyed the mic again, calling, "Two Spot, you get that relay?"

"Affirmative."

Talina circled wide of Tyson Station, peering down through the windscreen as she did. It was to see a handful of people watching from the domes, some waving her in. As the angle changed, she spotted a few more. Not more than seven visible in the whole compound.

"What do you think?" Kylee asked as they curled around to the west. A person need only look down on the vegetation to know where the deep forest lay and where shallow bedrock restricted the size of the trees.

Talina keyed the mic. "Supervisor? If my calculations are correct, we should be right above you. Trees are definitely too thick to attempt a descent here. Canopy looks like it's woven as tight as a blanket."

Talbot's voice came through. *"You find a safe place to put down. We'll beat feet to wherever you are."*

Talina drifted them north, searching. There had to be a hole, something with a rocky outcrop where the roots hadn't taken hold. The last thing they needed was to set down and have roots wind themselves around the fan blades.

And there, she saw it. An opening in the canopy. One of the weird lime-green trees with those monstrous paddle-shaped branches. It stood like an isolate out in the center, but if Talina could slide down along the margin of the branches, she could drop them at the edge of the root zone.

"Kalico?" Tal keyed the mic. "We're maybe a kilometer to the north and west. Got a hole. We're going to ground."

"Roger that. Got a reading on my signal?"

"Affirmative." Talina plotted the fix, glanced at her compass. "We're north, twenty-five degrees west. Figure that we'll meet you halfway. After we're all loaded, it'll be three hours to supper and beer at Briggs' place."

"Best news we've heard all day. Got any water? Repeat: We need water."

"We'll bring some." Talina smiled at that, gave Kylee a reassuring wink, and began her descent. She dropped the airtruck down just out of reach of the waving branches. As she did, the chabacho and aquajade leaves kept turning her way, pulling back from the downdraft created by the fans.

Even the vines retreated, and here and there, some forest creature vanished into the darkness, fleeing in panic as the airtruck roared past.

"Kylee, grab a couple of water bottles. Dek, you lock the door after the last of us is out. I'm putting us on the edge of the root mat. If you see them creeping toward the airtruck, you call me ASAP on the radio. I'll beat feet back and lift us off before they can latch hold of the frame or tangle in the fans."

"You sure you don't want me to just take the controls and hover?"

"You can fly this thing?"

Taglioni shrugged. "It's been a while. Looks like standard controls. Nothing different from my old Beta Falcon."

Talina grinned as she set them softly on the dark-gray soil just beyond the edge of the roots. "My, you're just one surprise after another, aren't you? Why didn't you say something?"

"You never asked." He was watching out the side window, staring at the weird lime-green tree where it stood maybe fifty meters away in the center of the clearing. "What is that thing? You got a name for it?"

Tal glanced, noticed the gigantic leaves—somehow reminding her of the woven handheld palm fans of her youth—had turned their way. Reacted to their descent.

"Nothing official," she replied. "Iji calls them lollipop trees. I heard Talbot call it a ping-pong-paddle tree. We've never had the time or people to fully study them, let alone a lot of Donovanian life. That's what Tyson Station was originally all about. If there were any notes about those trees, they never survived the evacuation."

Kylee unlatched the door to stare out thoughtfully, her nose working, as if she'd pick up anything beyond the stench of exhaust and hot motors.

"Let's go, people," Talina called, pulling her rifle from the rack. "We've only got a couple of hours before dark. Flute? We're here. You can open your eyes and turn blue and pink now. You survived your first flight."

An eye popped open on the top of the terrified quetzal's head. It focused on the open door. The beast damn near bowled Kylee off her feet as it rushed to make its escape.

"Hey! Don't be an asshole!" Kylee shouted at the departed quetzal, then slung her backpack with the extra water over one shoulder, grinned, and leaped out after Flute.

Talina handed Dek his rifle, saying, "Keep the door closed. Anything tries to get in that's not us? Shoot it."

"Yes, ma'am." Dek took his rifle.

"Talina!" Kylee's scream brought Talina to the door, her heart skipping a beat.

Kylee was standing at the edge of the root mat, staring up over the top of the airtruck. Flute, too, was fixed on whatever was up there, his panicked colors instantly gone, replaced by perfect camouflage as he hunched down and blended with the background. Only his three gleaming black eyes were visible.

Talina leaped to the ground, whirled, bringing her rifle up.

For a moment, she could only blink at the impossibility of it.

The ping-pong-paddle tree was moving, bending. The fifty or so giant paddle fans—each maybe ten to fifteen meters across—were glowing in eerie viridian as it leaned toward them, the bulk of it hidden by the airtruck.

"Dek!" she screamed. "Get out of there!"

As she did, the first of the big paddles slapped down on the top of the airtruck with a solid thump. Another pasted itself against the tailgate, shivering the truck. Dek, in the open door, was knocked free. Rifle in hand, he tumbled to the ground—barely kept himself from landing face-first.

"What the hell?" Talina barely whispered as the airtruck was shaken as if it were a toy. The huge paddles had conformed and latched onto the top and sides. And then the tree began to straighten, lifting the vehicle as if it were a feather.

Behind her right ear, Rocket's sibilant voice told her: *"Run!"*

56

When Talina Perez shouted *"Run!"* Dek was still stumbling forward. Using his rifle for balance, he staggered to a stop, tried to understand what had happened. One instant he'd been in the door, looking down at Talina, Kylee, and most astonishing of all, the way Flute had seemed to vanish before his eyes.

The next it was like the hand of God had pitched him out onto the ground.

As he caught himself, he turned to look. Couldn't believe what he was seeing: the airtruck was being lifted, something big and flat, glowing lime green, stuck to its top. More of the great pads had attached to the sides and front. And behind them, the rest of the giant fan-shaped green spatulas waved and fluttered, as if trying to get to the airtruck.

"What the hell?" He stood rooted.

A hard hand pulled him around. Talina glared hotly into his eyes. "I said *run*! Follow me. Now!"

She dragged him violently backward.

Kylee was already sprinting across the roots to disappear into the shadows under the trees.

"Flute!" the girl called as she vanished into the forest. "Come!"

The quetzal materialized out of apparent nothingness, seeming to just pop into existence. The beast moved like nothing Dek had ever seen. Literally a streak of yellow and black as it shot into the shadow of the trees.

Following on Talina's heels, Dek spared one last look over his shoulder. The lollipop tree had lifted the airtruck a good sixty or seventy meters into the air. He could hear the buckling of metal; the loud popping as sialon and duraplast ruptured and broke.

As pieces fell from the crushed vehicle, the lower leaves

caught them, fielding the wreckage like baseball mitts caught fly balls. The whole huge tree seemed preoccupied with the bits and pieces.

And then he was in twilight, heart hammering, a cold sweat like he'd never known turning his skin clammy.

Kylee had slowed, staring around. Flute, his colors still a riot, was making a weird tremolo from his tail vents.

"What the hell?" Talina asked, rubbing a hand on the back of her neck. "You ever seen that?"

"Nope." Kylee muttered. "I got nothing from quetzal memory, either. But my quetzals aren't from around here."

"Keep moving," Talina told Dek. "Don't let the roots grab hold of your feet. And you follow us. Do as we do."

All he wanted was drop to his knees and shake, but somehow, he nodded. Said, "Yes, ma'am. So . . . what do we do now?"

"Link up with Kalico," Talina muttered. She checked her wrist compass, said into her com, "Kalico? You there?"

Dek couldn't hear the response through Talina's earbud.

"Yeah, well, I've got bad news. One of those ping-pong trees just destroyed the airtruck. Crunched it up like it was made of paper."

A pause.

"No shit! And I'll add a fuck, cunt, damn, and hell, to boot!"

Talina's expression communicated distaste as she listened.

Then: "Yeah." A pause. "It's that or nothing." Another pause. "We're headed your way."

Talina took the lead, walking softly across the thickening mat of roots. "Wow. Turns out the Supervisor can really cuss when big trees eat her airtruck. Too bad you weren't listening in, kid. You could have learned some great new swear words."

"Never knew anyone could out-cuss you, Tal. So, what's next?" Kylee had one hand on Flute's side as they stepped over a thick root. To Dek's amazement the root was squirming, as if uncomfortable with the very soil in which it was embedded.

Talina told her, "We've got to link up with your folks and

Kalico. Find shelter for the night. Then, in the morning, we've got to get to high ground. That, or a radio where we can get back in touch with PA."

"That sucks toilet water," Kylee murmured, then pointed. "Dek, see that? That's called you're screwed vine. Don't get close to it."

"And don't touch *anything*," Talina warned.

"No shit." He took a real good look at the you're screwed vine, committing it to memory. Clutched his rifle close. As he followed, he kept staring down at his booted feet. Weird feeling how the roots squirmed underfoot.

Around him, in the dim shadows, the world seemed to close in. In places the roots crowded into great bundles that merged into the monstrous trunks of trees that in turn rose to impossible heights. Vines, their stems the diameter of oil drums, wound up into the overstory. Here and there he could see clumps of inter-knotted roots as if neighboring trees were wrestling and trying to strangle each other.

The sound! The chime here was louder than he'd ever heard. Rising, falling, shifting. And when he looked closely, he could see the invertebrates scrambling through the root mass. Keeping a wary distance from their passage.

Flute uttered a gurgling chitter, his hide flashing teal and sky blue. Kylee turned her attention to the quetzal, asking, "How so?"·

Flute, his colors going muted green, displayed in a riotous pattern followed by royal blue and a deep purple.

"Flute says there's something bad here. It's an old memory. Almost mythical. He thinks we should veer a little more to the east. He's just catching hints."

"Flute?" Talina called. "Take the lead. Your call. We just have to get to Dya. You understand?"

A harmonic sounded from the quetzal's vents, the color patterns turning sunset-orange as the beast hurried on ahead.

Talina must have had an incoming communication. Dek heard her answer, saying, "All I can see from here is roots and tree boles. Something's spooked Flute. We're headed a little more east before we veer south. Should have eyes on you sometime soon."

A pause as Talina listened.

"No," Talina told her com as she hurried along. "Can't hear a thing over this chime, but we'll be listening for your call."

"I wouldn't have believed it," Dek whispered, watching in awe. "Quetzals are intelligent? They can understand something as complicated as that?"

"Well, duh," Kylee muttered under her breath, gaze turned up as something shifted in the branches above.

The pace picked up with Flute in the lead. Dek found himself pushed to the edge of endurance, panting, trying desperately to keep up. When had his rifle grown so heavy? And the damn thing was always in the way.

"Flute?" Talina called. "Got to slow down some."

Dek grinned under his layer of sweat. "Sorry. Ship muscles."

"Yeah, and don't think forest travel is always this fast," Kylee added. "It's remarkable how many predators run for their holes when a quetzal's out front."

"But don't get cocky," Talina growled, gaze roving. "Tooth flower, biteya bush, brown caps, claw shrub, and the like couldn't care less. They'll still kill you."

Dek funneled all of his concentration into just keeping up. Putting one foot after another where Talina put hers. In the trees overhead, something screamed, the sound agonized and unearthly.

At a bundle of giant roots—all laced together like a nest of monster worms—Flute bounced gracefully to the top. Froze there.

Laboriously, Kylee, Talina, and finally Dek climbed up, scrambling from one massive root to the next, like ascending giants' stairs.

At the top, Flute remained motionless, his collar fully expanded, muzzle lifted, mouth open as he sucked in air and vented it behind his tail. For Dek the process was fascinating to watch.

"What's up?" Kylee asked, her own nose lifted and sniffing.

Talina, too, was scenting the air.

Something about the way they did reminded Dek of hunting dogs.

For the moment he was happy to crouch in the half light,

pant, and wipe the sweat from his face. Damn hot in here. Moist. Felt like a low-level steam bath.

Talina cupped her hands and bellowed *"Talbot? Kalico?"* at the top her lungs, then cocked her head to listen.

Up in the high branches, some creature tweeted, cackled, and cooed in an unearthly juxtaposition of sound. Might have been something from a bad dream, but none of the others seemed bothered by it.

He glanced around, wishing he had better light. Wondered at the smells of the place: all musty, damp, and curiously mindful of mold-slimy cilantro. When he concentrated on just one spot, he had the eerie realization that things were moving. Slowly, to be sure, but moving nevertheless. The roots, the vines, the shadows, all alive.

A distant scream was followed an instant later by the sound of gunshots.

And then silence.

Viscerally, Dek understood: That scream had been human.

57

What the hell was it? Talbot stared at the oddity. Some sort of seed? No, had to be a creature. Reminded him of a picture he'd seen of a sea urchin back on Earth—a big ink-black ball-like thing bristling with countless slender needles pointing out in all directions. But this wasn't under water, it rested on the forest floor. The beast was at least a meter in diameter, and clearly had three eyes. So, animal then. What sent a shiver down his back was the hundreds of gleaming needle spines, and each of them was quivering.

Kalico was still spouting the occasional colorful curse word. She'd started cussing upon receiving word of the airtruck's fate. Kept muttering the occasional acid-laced profanity.

Behind him, Dya said, "Never seen anything like that before. Looks like a . . . a . . ."

"Giant sea urchin?"

"Yeah. But this thing's bigger than an oversized beach-ball."

Talbot glanced around; the masses of roots piled and interlocked like a giant knot. Tough to go around.

The forest began to chime with a greater intensity, as if building to a crescendo. A few faint beams of light shown through the high canopy a couple hundred meters over-head. The vines swung as if in a breeze—though the muggy air pressed down, still, heavy, and damp.

Reaching into his pouch, Talbot dug around for an ob-sidian pebble he'd picked up during a geologic survey with Lea Shimodi. Squinting, he pulled his arm back and threw.

The pebble arched, hit the pincushion dead center.

Talbot figured the thing would threaten, wave the long needle-thin spines around. Instead, to his horror, a haze of them shot out from the round body. Deadly little arrows traveled five or six meters, sticking into the surrounding roots like wicked spears. The roots immediately began to writhe as if in great pain.

"Guess we don't want to go that way," Dya said dryly.

"Guess not," Talbot agreed, rising from his crouch. "All right, it's backtrack or nothing."

"Great," Kalico whispered. "What I'd give for a bottle of water."

"Wish it would rain," Talbot agreed. "That aquajade we tapped didn't have enough to more than wet our whistles." Not to mention the heavy metals that had to be in the sappy and thick liquid.

He turned back the way they had come, seeking to avoid stepping on the same roots they'd disturbed earlier. The chime seemed to mock them as the invertebrates played their rhythmless symphony.

Talbot retraced his way around the old chabacho with its five-meter-thick trunk, took his heading as best he could. North. They had to keep going north and a little west. Once they hooked up with Talina and Kylee, they could keep better track of Kalico and Muldare. When it came to forest, nothing beat Talina and Kylee's quetzal sense.

Face it, Mark, he told himself, *you've just been lucky so far.*

He'd avoided disaster by the merest hint of luck since leaving the cave. Just that innate sense of his, developed during all those months in the forest down south. But it was only a matter of time before the odds caught up to him.

Here, outside Tyson Station, the pincushion-sea-urchin thing was just the latest of the threats he'd barely recognized in time. So, too, had been the purple-burst flower, as they'd called it. The plant had just been too gorgeous: a riot of crimson, canary-yellow, and deep purple. He'd poked at with the extended barrel of his rifle and barely managed to keep his gun when it shot out and tried to eat the muzzle.

But so far, the only casualty was Muldare, who'd somehow gotten too close to the local variety of gotcha vine, which, it turned out, was significantly more mobile than the varieties Talbot and Dya were used to. Unexpectedly, it had leaped out far enough to brush the marine.

They'd had to pull sixteen of the wicked spines out of

Muldare's arm and shoulder. Briah, trying to be stoic, wasn't succeeding. Her face remained a mask of pain.

"Kylee?" Dya shouted as they started back around the big chabacho.

The chime mocked her in response. Overhead a flock of scarlet fliers swooped low from the branches, apparently drawn by the change in the chime. A few of them managed to snatch a couple of inattentive invertebrates, and then they were gone. Vanished back into the heights.

Again, Talbot took the lead, climbing over roots, lending a hand to Dya, who lent a hand to Kalico, and then to the grimacing Muldare as she brought up the rear.

"Do you know the difference between roots and a marine boot-camp obstacle course?" Muldare asked as she clambered over the latest pile of slowly writhing roots.

"Obstacle courses don't eat you?" Dya wiped at her sweaty brow.

"And they don't move," Kalico groused as she jerked her foot away from a closing gap where two roots pulled themselves tight.

"We can't be more than a couple hundred meters from them," Talbot insisted as he helped Dya down to what he assumed was ground level.

Kaliço tried her com, asked, "Talina? Where are you?"

A pause.

Kalico nodded, said, "Yeah, we're still headed north. But in this shit? We could miss you by fifty yards and never know it."

To the rest she said, "Talina says that all she can see is trees and roots."

"When we get home," Dya insisted, "Su's making us spaghetti with that red sauce and chamois meatballs."

"Damn, that sounds good," Kalico said between panting breaths. "Me, I'm pouring a bathtub full of water and drinking it dry."

"Watch it," Talbot told her. "Slug there."

The thing was stretched out on a rare bare patch of damp soil. Odd to see one just out in the open like that. They usually liked having a layer of dirt between them and their predators.

"Shit," Kalico skipped sideways. Her boots were probably thick enough to stop the creepy little beast, but why take chances?

"Yeah, I see it," Muldare declared as she leaped down. With a quick draw, she used her combat knife to slice the thing in two. It contracted, spilling goo onto the nearest root. Even as they watched, spindles of root began to suck up the fluids and entwine themselves in the twitching halves.

"Spaghetti, huh?" Kalico said longingly as Talbot started toward the next bundle of straining and bunched roots. They blocked the way between two of the towering broadvine trees, their trunks almost obscured by thick coils of vines.

"You're welcome to come," Dya told her. "We can always set an extra place."

"Do you know how long it's been since I've had spaghetti? Don't imagine it will be the same as Luigi's in Transluna, but I'm already salivating."

"What's Luigi's?" Talbot asked. "Never heard of it."

"You wouldn't of," Kalico told him. "It's a favorite hangout for white-assed soft-belly Corporate types. I'll bet Su's sauce is better. What about the noodles? Homemade or does she buy them from Millicent Graves?"

"Homemade," Dya told her. "The only thing this Luigi's might have on us is eggs for the noodles. As if any of us can remember what an egg noodle tastes like."

"Count me in," Kalico said through what was obviously a dry mouth. "I'll bring the wine."

"Deal," Dya told her.

From his position in the lead, Talbot grinned. Funny how their relationships had changed over the years since Kalico had tried to seize Mundo Base out from under Dya, Su, and Rebecca. But then that was Donovan for you.

Talbot clambered up, hoisting himself from one thick root to the next. It was maybe a three-meter climb to the top. There he stopped, staring ahead in the gloom, half expecting to spot Talina and Kylee struggling over the next root mass. Only to see nothing in the dim half-light but more roots. A vast expanse of them fading into the shadowed recesses.

"Crushed the airtruck?" Kalico wondered under her

breath as she grasped Dya's hand and let the woman pull her up the last of the climb. "What would have possessed Talina to set down next one of those damn lollipop trees?"

"It was close to where we were?" Talbot guessed. "Let me guess: No one's ever reported that lollipop trees can crush airtrucks? Sort of like no one's seen purple-burst flowers or sea urchin pincushions before, either."

"At least no one who lived through it," Muldare said wearily and winced as she climbed to the top of the roots. "How long was Tyson occupied?"

"Maybe four years," Kalico answered, dropping to sit on the top root and rest her feet on the one below. "Most of that time was spent building the base, establishing the garden, flying regional cadastral surveys."

Again Dya cupped hands and shouted, *"Kylee?"*

The forest seemed to scream back as the chime shifted up a notch and something screeched a mocking mimicry from above. No answer from the girl could be heard.

"Fire a shot?" Muldare suggested.

"Maybe. In a bit," Talbot said. "If we don't run into them soon. Sure as hell, we don't need to worry about the Unreconciled. Dressed the way they are, if they tried to make it this deep into the forest, they'd be a meal."

"They'd know where we are though," Kalico noted as she leaned her head forward and massaged the back of her neck.

"Think they wouldn't have seen the airtruck go down?" Muldare shifted her rifle and rolled her sore and swelling shoulder. "Surely they would have had someone watching from the cliffs."

"Get me out of this," Dya whispered to the empty air around her, "and I'll never leave PA again." She chuckled. "Funny, isn't it? I just want to hug the kids again. Sit on the couch and listen to Su complain. Hear the kids playing."

"I want a jug of water," Kalico whispered. "A big one. Like a couple of gallons."

Talbot nodded, shifted his rifle, and rubbed his shoulder. Damn, his empty belly was like a hole in his gut. He worked his mouth to stimulate enough saliva to swallow. Of everything, he hated being thirsty the most. Miserable as he was, he knew Dya and Kalico had to feel even worse.

Unlike him and Muldare, they'd never undergone this kind
of deprivation.

He glanced up at the trees on his right, in the direction
of Tyson Station. That was the closest food and water. Up
there. Right under the noses of the Unreconciled. With the
airtruck gone, that was the only choice left.

*So, what are we going to do? Shoot our way through the
middle of them?*

With Talina, that would give them three rifles, five pistols. Firepower enough to murder every last cannibal up
there.

Murder?

What else could he call it? Batuhan hadn't seemed like
the type who could be bluffed. The guy *believed* he was a
messiah who had a direct link to the divine universe. How
did anyone rational deal with that?

Fact was: They had to get back up to Tyson. Soon. Dehydration was taking its course. Not to mention lack of
sleep. It—along with hunger—was making them stupid.
Slowing their thoughts and reactions.

It had been pure dumb luck that no one had been killed
so far. It wouldn't hold.

He glanced down at Dya. Wished she wasn't here.
Wished, with all his heart, that she was still back home.

Dear God, I love her.

Yes, he loved Su, too, but Dya had always been special.
Not only had she been the first of the Mundo women to
become his lover, wife, mother of his first child, but more,
she fit the best. Together they'd shared the most. Been the
strength in the marriage after Rebecca's death.

If anything happens to her . . .

It would kill him.

And then there was Kalico Aguila, once the unassail-
able Supervisor who looked down on him from on high.
Still one of the most formidable women on the planet, here
she was—a dependent partner in the desperate bid for survival that was Donovan.

He cupped hands around his mouth, filled his lungs to
shout . . .

It came from the side. A blur. He'd barely started to
turn, to try and identify the movement, when a blast of

something ripped through his chest like a fountain of fire.
Lifted him bodily from the roots.

Stunned agony.

Pain like he'd never known.

He was being lifted. Could feel his legs jerking. Felt and
heard his ribs breaking. His chest torn in two.

The forest spun, his body flopping like a rag doll's.

He had the horrible realization of something big stuck
through his center. Bloody. Impossible to conceive.

A scream could be heard from somewhere far away.

As his consciousness began to fade, the distant sound of
shots could be heard.

And then he was rudely . . .

58

The weight of the room, the dark shadows, and most of all, that insidious dome of moldering human bones, pressed down. The air like a miasma. What kind of sick minds built a monument to the people they'd murdered? The light played weirdly over the skulls, the polished leg and arm bones seemed to dance in the shadows cast by the intricate rosettes made of vertebrae and phalanges.

The dead stared out from the dark recesses, peered between the cracks, and filtered through the myriad of wired femora, humeri, and jaws. Each empty eye socket glared with malicious intent.

In all of his life, Miguel Galluzzi had never known a sensation as disturbing as this. His soul felt besmirched and fouled.

He turned, fought the tickling wetness that preceded the urge to throw up. As if the mere act of puking his guts out would rid him of the pollution, filth, and contamination that now clung to his skin like a film.

In the corner of his eye, he caught a flash of a long-haired man in yellow overalls as he hurried past. Hardly enough to recognize. Just that fleeting impression.

The temple of bones might have been a malignancy. It loomed, seemed to expand. Began to suck at Galluzzi's soul. The sensation akin to the structure pulling a hazy thread of his spirit into its low-arched doorway, past the sprawled skeleton that lay like a broken doll.

"I have to get out of here," Galluzzi whispered hoarsely.

"I understand," Shig said reasonably and turned on his heel. As he passed the double doors, he slapped the wall panel. Darkness fell over the monstrosity of bones with a solidity that sent a quake down Galluzzi's back.

Though left behind in darkness, he could *feel* the dome of bones—its looming presence. That the thing was alive, sentient, watching him with the gaze of an inquisitor. In judgment of his life, soul, and sanity.

Galluzzi stumbled under the impact, braced himself against the hallway wall as he fought for breath. Tried to still the pounding.

The light smeared, slipped sideways, momentarily blurring Shig's concerned expression.

"Death is here," Galluzzi whispered. "It's all around us. Feeding on our souls."

Shig's features solidified again as the man said, "Curious that you'd use those words. It's one of the phrases in the hallway we passed through. You read that there?"

"No. Just . . . just came to me."

"You've gone pale."

Galluzzi blinked, finally able to get a full breath into his starved lungs. "I knew Jem Orten. Have I told you that?"

"No."

"Like so many of us, he was hopeful of getting *Freelander.* Would have sold his soul to sit in the captain's chair." He fought back tears. "Maybe that's what he did, huh? He just didn't know it when he spaced out of Solar System."

"Can you walk?"

Galluzzi managed a weak nod, pushed himself off the wall. It was like the surface didn't feel right. Sort of rubbery, not quite . . . well, real.

When Galluzzi looked down, his right hand was jumping around like a wounded songbird. The staccato clicking sound came from his chattering teeth.

Unseen *things* kept touching him. But when he looked, there was nothing there.

"I want out of here," he told Shig without the least bit of shame. "This place is hell, and I want no part of it."

"Just this way, and we'll be gone."

Following Shig through the half-light down the hall took all of Galluzzi's will. They passed the Captain's Lounge, the door ajar to expose a dark room. Unseen eyes peered out at their passing. Whispers and hisses, barely below the threshold of hearing, issued from within.

Before the door to the AC, Galluzzi started, sure that

he'd seen someone peering at him from the wall. Familiar dark eyes were watching him. The lips were in the process of forming words. When he fixed on the sialon, the woman's face wasn't there. Just. Blank. Fucking. Wall.

I saw her. Black hair. Asian features. Like I knew . . .

"Oh, shit. That was Tyne."

"Excuse me?" Shig had stopped before the duraplast and steel door that led to Astrogation Control.

"Tyne Sakihara," Galluzzi said, voice rasping. "Someone I knew back in Solar System. Spaced with me on a couple of my early runs. We were . . . well, intimate. I loved her." He choked on the memory. "Once upon a time." Galluzzi balled his fists, used them to scrub at his eyes. "What the hell is wrong with me? Why would I see her face? Like it was coming out of the fucking wall?"

Shig watched him with eyes that almost glowed. "You *saw* her?"

Galluzzi forced himself to breathe. Glanced back at the blank and featureless wall with its faint coating of grime. "Has to be my imagination. She's somewhere back in Solar System. Bet she's got her own ship by now."

"She's here." Shig's voice carried no emotion. "Behind that wall. In Astrogation Control. Or at least her skeleton is. She was locked in with Captain Orten. When it became apparent that there would be no exit, he shot her in the head before he turned the gun on himself. Her bones were still on the floor when Talina sealed Tamarland Benteen behind this door."

Shig reached out, reverently running the tips of his fingers over the battered surface of the AC's door.

As the words sank in, the hallway slipped sideways, seemed to spin around Galluzzi. Voices whispered in the air around him. He slumped against the far side, tried to steady himself.

"She's behind that door? Dead? With Jem?" He ground his teeth. Tried to understand. "Why the *hell* did you bring me here?"

"So that you would understand."

"And Tamarland Benteen is in there, too?" He could hear the panic in his voice, the incipient insanity. "Should we knock and announce ourselves?"

"No, we should not. If Benteen's alive in there, pounding on the door would be a cruel form of baiting. If he's dead, like Jem and Tyne, the action would be futile and without meaning."

"What the *fuck* are you saying?"

"I'm saying, Captain, that reality can be many things. That behind that door, Benteen may be alive, or he may be dead. You cannot know until you open the door."

Shig leaned close. "You, Captain, had a choice to make: You could save your ship and crew, or you could suffer the same fate as *Freelander*. Like knocking on the AC door, you could not know the outcome until you'd made the decision and observed the results. Your reality is illusion."

Something cold, like an icy finger, slipped along Galluzzi's ribs. Tyne had stroked him like that when they were lovers. The sensation was real enough that he yipped and leaped sideways. With a nervous hand he batted at his side.

Looked down to see . . . nothing.

"I want out of here. *Now*."

"After seeing all this," Shig gestured grandly at the ship, "do you still think that blowing yourself out an airlock would be in the interest of cosmic justice?"

Galluzzi stared woodenly at the battered and welded AC door. The last refuge of Jem Orten and Galluzzi's once-beloved Tyne Sakihara. The final internment for Tamarland Benteen.

"I don't know what to think anymore."

"Ah," Shig said through an exhale. "With that realization, you have just taken the first step on your new Tao."

"My what?"

"Your path. Only after you stop questioning will the answers come to you."

Galluzzi flinched as maniacal laughter echoed down the hallway, vanished.

As loud as it had been to Galluzzi's ears, Shig apparently hadn't heard it. Not even a hint.

59

Kalico Aguila was sitting wearily atop the highest root, staring out over the dim forest floor with its tangles of roots, vines, and immense tree trunks. Her only concern was how miserably thirsty, hungry, and exhausted she was.

Talbot stood beside her, Dya squatted at his side. Muldare, to Kalico's right, was scanning the surrounding forest through her rifle's optic in search of any sign of Talina's party.

Something tore through the air. Mark Talbot's body jerked under a mighty impact. Was flung forward and up off its perch. The man's rifle clattered down across the roots, torn from his hands by a force that catapulted him into the heights.

Kalico froze, gaped, unable to comprehend what she was seeing: Talbot's body—skewered through the chest—was being hauled skyward by some long tentacle. The man's arms, legs, and head jerked and swayed, limp like rubber. Then he was gone. Pulled into the high branches. Vanished.

It seemed impossible.

Couldn't be happening.

Dya's piercing scream shattered Kalico's dazed disbelief.

Briah Muldare—her instincts true to her training—pulled up her rifle. She didn't hesitate. The blasting racket of a burst hammered at Kalico's ears as bullets shredded the branches high above. Bits of detritus came floating down, but no body. No terrifying alien.

"Mark!" Dya screamed, her throat straining until the veins stood out. She leaped to her feet, almost tottering on the root. Her fists like rocks, muscles flexed as she stared up in absolute horror at where her husband had disappeared.

"What the hell?" Muldare whispered hoarsely, her rifle

at the ready, muzzle pointing toward the dark branches overhead.

Kalico scrambled down, recovered Talbot's rifle. She raised it, worked her mouth to try and swallow. Felt her heart hammering against her chest as if fit to burst.

Overhead, only the slow shifting of the branches—the apparently endless dance that was Donovan's forest—could be seen. The chime rose and fell as if nothing had happened.

"*Mark!*" Dya screamed again. She struggled to keep her balance on the high root as it slithered to one side.

"We've got to get off of here," Kalico said, shifting the heavy rifle as she scanned the heights.

"Come on, Dya," Muldare said as she started down, leaping from root to root. "There's nothing—"

"That's *my husband*!" Dya continued to stare up, tears leaking down her cheeks.

"Damn it, Dya," Kalico cried. "He's gone! You saw that same as I did. Whatever that thing was, it punched a spike, a tentacle—whatever the hell that was—right through his chest!"

"We can't lose him," Dya almost whimpered. "Not again."

"Dya, come on!" Muldare shouted, starting back up the roots to physically drag the woman down.

Dya began, "This will break Su's heart! Leave us . . ."

This time the spike came from behind. Unseen. Caught Dya Simonov between her shoulder blades. The point of it, black and sharp like polished horn, shot out between her breasts. It jerked her upward so hard and fast the weight of the woman's head could be heard snapping her neck.

Kalico, taken aback, stood paralyzed as Dya Simonov disappeared up into the high branches.

"Supervisor?" Briah Muldare scrambled down, grabbing her arm. "I need you to leave this place now!"

Talina's voice was yammering in Kalico's earbud, demanding to know what was wrong. What the shooting was.

Kalico nodded, struggled to think. Let Muldare pull her sideways, ahead. Somehow Kalico managed to run, to put one foot ahead of the other.

Lost track of the mad scramble as she climbed up over

masses of roots, half-leaped, half-fell down the far side, only to stagger onward. She couldn't think, couldn't answer Talina's frantic call for information through the com.

Panic. It was all panic.

Until something deep inside her screamed *Get a grip!*

"Wait!" she cried, pulling up, slowing, aware of what their mad flight was doing to the roots. Looking back, she saw a writhing trail. *"Think!"*

"Think what?" Muldare cried, the glaze of panic in her hazel eyes as she scanned the trees, shifting her rifle this way and that. "There's something up there!"

Kalico spun the woman around, glaring. "And there's things down here! You want worse than thorncactus to worry about? Now, think! We've got to go slow, go smart, or we're as dead as Dya and Mark. You hear me?"

"Yes." Muldare swallowed hard. Jerked a nod.

"Good." Kalico fought for breath. Thirst, hunger, exhaustion, and now horror. Could this get any worse?

Have to find Talina!

Signal shot.

Or would that draw the beast?

She pressed her com. "Talina? Where are you?"

"What the hell is going on?"

"Something in the trees. Something big, Tal. Like nothing we've ever seen. It took Mark and Dya. No warning. Just speared them through the chest and jerked them up into the trees!"

For a moment there was silence as Kalico tried to catch her breath, shifted the rifle, eyes on the darkening branches above.

"Mark and Dya?" Talina's voice came softly.

"It's in the trees! Something big!" The panic was building again.

"Roger that. In the trees. We'll keep an eye out."

"Talina, you don't understand. If it's hunting you, you won't have a chance. No warning. It's that fast. That deadly."

Again there was silence.

Say something, damn it!

Then, *"Kylee's coming. She's riding a quetzal, so don't shoot it."*

"Roger," Kalico said. "Kylee's riding a quetzal. Don't shoot it," she repeated for Muldare's benefit.

"Yeah," Kalico whispered to herself, desperately searching the high branches. "As if a quetzal would stand a chance against this thing."

And worse, it was getting dark.

60

Talina watched Kylee climb up on Flute's back. The sight never ceased to amaze her. As if the camouflage-mottled quetzal was a pet horse instead of an alpha predator.

"You be damned careful," Talina warned again. "Aguila sounds like she's on the edge of a breakdown. No telling about the marine she's with. They could shoot at anything that moves."

"What about Mom and Dad?"

"Nothing new there, kid. Kalico says whatever this thing is, it speared them and hauled them up into the trees. That's all I've got so far. *Pay attention!* First priority: Find Kalico. She'll tell you more."

"Someone's going to pay for this," Kylee vowed, tapping Flute and saying, "Let's go."

With Dek beside her, Talina watched Flute stretch out; the blonde kid on the beast's back bent low as the quetzal leaped to the next batch of roots and disappeared on the other side.

"Dek, you stay close now. We can't afford a mistake." Talina shifted her rifle, staring up at the darkening branches overhead.

"I don't get it," Dek said as he followed behind her. "Hauled them up into the trees? What can do that?"

"Nightmare hunts that way." Talina experienced that familiar crawling in her gut, and for once it wasn't Demon. "Maybe that's what this is."

But as she glanced up, it was to wonder what kind of nightmare could reach that far, lift that much weight that fast. Mostly they suspended their prey like dangling fruit as the tentacles wound down and into their victim's guts. It took days.

Spearing the victim's body? Jerking it up? It just didn't sound right.

Or it's something we haven't seen.

And worse, it had taken two of the most important people on Donovan. Dya Simonov had revolutionized their understanding of Donovanian genetics, was in the process of developing local plants that humans could actually digest in case anything happened to the terrestrial species upon which survival depended.

And if Talbot was dead, too? Another talented second in command at Port Authority security? A friend? Just gone like that? Poof? Hauled up into the high branches to be eaten?

"You look grim," Taglioni noted as he panted along behind her.

"Just thinking what it means to lose Mark and Dya. On the com Kalico said this thing speared them through the chest. Yanked them up into the branches. Said it took just a couple of seconds."

Taglioni shot a furtive look up at the darkening branches overhead. "That's what? Forty, fifty meters up? That's a lot of muscle to haul a body up that high."

"Now you're getting the idea." Talina shook her head as she climbed over a bundle of interlocked roots, reached back, and helped the struggling Taglioni as he clambered awkwardly over the mess.

"You know, it's starting to get dark." Stress thinned Taglioni's voice. "We going to be able to track down Kylee and the Supervisor in the dark?"

She tapped the side of her head. "Part of the curse of being infected is that I can see in the dark. We're fine. At least I am. You? If you can't see where you're putting your feet? If you blunder into a chokeya vine? Guess you'll be the main course for some lucky critter out here."

"And to think, I used to worry about being eaten on *Ashanti*. That was my night terror. That the Unreconciled would get loose in the night. Come slipping up from Deck Three. Sneak into my room, and I'd be helpless as they started carving on me." He chuckled hollowly, eyes on his feet as he tried to match her steps. "Why does it always come down to being eaten?"

"Stop. Take my hand. We're climbing this knot of roots. There's a tooth flower off to the side. I need you to follow my lead. Don't do anything dumb."

"You got it."

"Give me your rifle." She took it, slung it next to hers. "Okay, let's go."

She eased Dek over the tangle, ensuring he didn't accidently close the distance with the tooth flower. Damn, the thing was bigger than the ones she'd seen previously. And it was aware, watching them where it hung down from a thick vine that spanned the space between two aquajades.

On the other side, she took a quick look around. Noted a sidewinder that was easing out from a dark hole. The thing had probably hidden as Flute passed this way. The roots were still squirming but starting to relax after the quetzal's passage.

"How much farther do you think?" Dek asked.

She gave him a sidelong glance. Dark as it was getting, the guy probably figured she couldn't see the outright fear in his face.

In the branches high overhead, something uttered a whistling, almost hypersonic scream. Taglioni jumped half out of his skin.

"Don't know, Dek. Guess you'll just have to trust me."

She saw the flicker of amusement behind his fear as he said, "Oh . . . sure." A beat. "Gave myself up for dead back when the ping-pong tree crushed the airtruck."

61

To say that night fell like the flick of a switch wasn't quite right. But the analogy wasn't too far off the mark. At least, not as far as Kalico Aguila could tell.

For the moment, she had effectively been brought to a dead stop. Couldn't tell where to put her feet. Wasn't able to see more than a couple of feet in any direction. Go bumbling around? Stick her head into a cutthroat flower, or maybe a biteya bush? Offer a tempting leg to a sidewinder?

"We're fucked, aren't we?" Briah Muldare asked, stepping uneasily to the side as roots squirmed under her feet. The woman kept sweeping with her rifle, using the optic's IR to search for approaching danger.

"Kylee will be here." Kalico tried to say it with assured bravado. Fact was, she'd never been as sure that she was about to die. Terrified that some spearing thing was going to lance through her chest. And she'd never know it was coming.

The voice, from the darkness off to the right called, "It's us! Don't shoot!"

Kalico laid a hand on Muldare's rifle, just to be sure the woman understood.

Given all that had happened, the sight of a slim blonde girl riding up on a quetzal like it was a quarter horse didn't seem as incredulous as it should. Kalico figured her sense of reality had taken so many blows, nothing was beyond belief.

"Damn, we're glad to see you."

Kylee unhitched her backpack, slung it down. "There's water. Talina's right behind us. Which way to my parents? Back there? Follow the roots?"

"Kylee, listen. Whatever this thing is, you really don't want to—"

"We'll be back."

"—take any . . ."

The quetzal—Kylee on its back—wheeled, leaped to the top of the root mass Kalico and Muldare had just climbed over, and vanished into the encompassing darkness.

"Did I just see that?" Muldare asked hoarsely. "A kid riding a quetzal?"

The water was the finest Kalico ever drank. She and Muldare emptied the bottles, heedless of saving even a drop. The water hit her stomach like a gift from God. She was already feeling better.

Now she peered around in the almost charcoal black. Kept shifting her feet, wishing she could see what the roots were doing.

"Supervisor?" The rising stress in Muldare's voice couldn't be missed.

"Yeah, I know."

Got to do something.

They couldn't just stand there. The roots were going to be grabbing hold. Kalico could feel them underfoot, becoming more agitated, starting to cling.

"Here, take my hand." She reached out, got Muldare's hand.

Step by step. That was it. She thought she was headed north. The darkness pressed down around her, thick, almost solid.

"What do you see with your rifle sight?" Kalico asked, lifting Mark's rifle, trying to hold the heavy weapon one-handed, to see through the optic. The thing was too heavy, or she was too weak. It would take two hands, and she couldn't convince herself to turn loose of Muldare's hand.

"Root mass ahead," Muldare told her. "Maybe four meters."

It was foolish. A sure recipe for disaster. But so was standing still, letting the roots entangle their feet. Get stuck in them? Unable to pull free? They'd entomb a person. Surround her, crush her, and absorb the decomposing body.

At least this way I'm doing something.

Kalico wanted to throw her head back, to howl with insane laughter. She was going to die here. In the darkness. From something horrible. Like that tooth flower that had been eating that man's naked corpse. Why? Because she was running from a bunch of cannibals. In the twenty-second century? Shit, who'd believe it?

"This isn't going to end well, is it?" Muldare asked softly.

"Probably not." Kalico squeezed the woman's hand in a gesture of solidarity.

"For the record, ma'am. I want you to know that while I sided with Cap back during the *Turalon* days, it has been an honor and the finest privilege of my career to serve you these last four years."

"I appreciate that, Briah. But we're not gone yet. Kylee and that insane quetzal should be back at any moment."

"Maybe. Ma'am, whatever that *thing* was that got Mark and Dya, no child, and I daresay no quetzal, can stand up to that." A return squeeze and a tug stopped Kalico. "And that's why I'm taking the lead. If there's anything out here, I'm stumbling into it first."

"Can't do that. You're as blind as I am. If it were daylight, with your training, yes. You'd have a better chance of spotting the danger than I do. But here, in the black? I can't ask you to take a risk I'm not willing to take myself."

"You think I don't know that? That any of us don't know that? Besides, I can scan with my optic." Muldare shifted to the lead, took a step. Kalico thought she saw the woman sweep the night with her rifle sight. "Wonder if any of those assholes back in Transluna would have had a clue?"

Kalico pulled Muldare to a stop. "You hear that?"

"What?"

Kalico turned, let loose of Muldare's hand and raised her rifle. "To the right, Briah. I'd swear I heard something."

"Got to go," the marine said. "Roots are pulling on my foot."

Kalico cocked her head, allowed herself to be pulled another step forward, worried she was just antagonizing the roots Muldare had trod upon.

She was on the verge of taking another step when a voice off to the side said, "I wouldn't do that. You've got a couple of brown caps about three meters ahead of you. Step off to the right."

"Kylee? That you?" Kalico asked.

"Yep. We're going to hop down from these roots, Supervisor. Don't shoot us."

Kalico heard the thump as a heavy body landed on the root mat.

"Okay, walk toward my voice. We've got to get you out of this little bowl and into someplace where the roots aren't as pissed off."

"How the hell can you see?" Muldare asked.

"She has quetzal TriNA," Kalico answered when Kylee didn't bother to.

"Yeah," Kylee said shortly. "My weird eyes. They'd kill me back at Port Authority because of my infection. Call me a freak."

Kalico winced at the anger in the girl's voice. "What did you find back there? Any sign of the creature?"

Kylee's voice was like stone. "Tell me what happened, Kalico. All of it. Everything you remember about how my mom and dad died."

Kalico felt her way forward across the wiggling roots, step by step. "Mark was standing up high. Looking for any sign of you and Talina. It hit him from the side. Like a long black fire hose swinging down from the high branches. The tip was a black spike, like a horn. It speared clear through his chest and literally ripped him upward so hard it tore the rifle from his hands."

"Your mother wouldn't come down," Muldare added. "I was headed back up to drag her, and that black spike hit her from behind. Took maybe two, three seconds, to yank her up into the branches."

"Got a step now, Kalico," Kylee's voice was flat. "Don't trip over that bottom root. Sling your rifle and climb like a monkey. I'll tell you when you reach the top." A pause. "What did it look like? A nightmare?"

"No." Kalico felt her way up the roots. "That's the spooky thing. Private Muldare fired a burst at the branches after it took your dad. Nothing. We couldn't see a body, a shape, just the branches up there. If any of the rounds hit it, it didn't react."

"Mom wouldn't come down?"

"She just stood there, shouting for your father."

"That's the top, Kalico. Sling your leg over. Muldare? You're next. That's it. That's the root. Now climb."

Kalico felt her way over the root, eerily aware that one of those fire-hose-thick tentacles could shoot down from the black, could skewer her, and no one would even know. They'd just hear the falling rifle, and she'd be gone. Vanished into the blackness.

"It's something we've never seen," Kalico said as she felt her way down to the flat root mat. "Did you find any sign back there?"

"Nothing," Kylee said, voice clipped. "Neither did Flute. Just a couple of drops of blood. All spattered wide."

"I'm sorry, Kylee." Kalico stopped, staring around in the blackness, wondering where the girl could be, and even worse, where the hell was the damn quetzal? That monster could be right at her shoulder.

Kylee softly, bitterly, asked, "Why the hell were they out here to start with? What did those people up there want to do to you?"

"Going to cut our throats and eat us," Muldare growled. "And me, personally, I'm about to go explosive on the whole lot of them."

"You won't be doing it alone," Kylee said. "I think Flute and I are going to pay them a little visit. Sort of a remembrance of Mom and Dad."

"Kylee," Kalico said. "Don't start something—"

"'Bout time!" Kylee raised her voice and called. "What took you?"

Kalico turned, seeing the yellow haze of a handheld light as it shone through the roots.

Talina's voice carried: "Hey, I got soft meat with me. Didn't want him stepping into a you're screwed vine. Might have given the poor plant indigestion."

Kalico vented a sigh of relief. Felt her heart settle back where it belonged in her chest. She watched as Talina crested a batch of roots, shone her light back, and took a second gander as Derek Taglioni clambered woodenly over the roots, a long rifle swinging on his back.

"You brought *him* out into this mess?"

"Wasn't exactly my preferred plan," Talina told her, shining the light around. "Good to see you, Private."

"Ma'am," Muldare said respectfully.

"What's the plan?" Kalico asked.

"We're beating feet," Talina said. "If we don't get the hell off this floodplain, back on the basalt, we're dead."

"Yeah," Kalico agreed. "Someplace where the trees aren't as thick and tall. Where that *thing* can't hide and pick us off one by one."

"Where's Kylee and Flute?" Talina asked.

"They were . . ." Kalico glanced around, following Talina's flash as it searched the surroundings.

"Kylee?" Talina called.

Kalico felt that deadening of the heart. If she was headed up to Tyson, going to pay Batuhan and his people back for her parents, it would be a . . .

"Over here," Kylee called. "We've got a path out of here. And I think we need to go. Soonest."

"Go," Kalico ordered Muldare. "Then you, sir," she told Taglioni. "I'll bring up the rear."

"Middle of the night like this? That could get you killed," Talina told her wryly.

"Yeah? So what couldn't?"

62

Dek's feet might have turned to wood for all the feeling they had. His coordination was shot. For a time, all he prayed for was the opportunity to lay down on the soft root mat, close his eyes, and let the rhizomes entomb him in their gentle caress as he dropped off to sleep.

Have I ever been this exhausted?

And it seemed like there was no end to it. Endless forest. Endless toil. Danger on all sides.

You can do this. Gut it out.

He focused his entire universe down to the bobbing flashlight beam, its wavering shadows as they leaped and jerked on either side. His Holland & Holland might have been an ungainly bar of lead. The weight of the sling felt like it was sawing its way through his shoulder.

And he'd only what? Crossed a couple of kilometers of forest?

Panting, he kept forcing one foot ahead of the other, jaws clenched with determination. It was just walking, following in Talina's footsteps. Didn't matter that they were starting up, that the way was turning rocky.

"Watch out for the chokeya vine," Kylee called back. "I severed it just above the roots. It won't latch onto you now, but you really don't want to touch it or get any of the fluids on you."

Dek blinked, looked up into the flashlight glare to see Talina Perez, rifle extended to hold the deadly plant out of the way as it flipped and twisted in death.

Climb. One foot, then the other. And for God's sake, don't stumble when you're passing that damn stem.

"How you doing, Dek?" Talina asked as he staggered his way up the trail.

"Praying we have supper reservations at Three Spires," he murmured on the way past.

"What's Three Spires?" Talina asked.

Behind him he heard Aguila's musical laughter.

"It's a plush and tony restaurant on Transluna," Aguila explained to Perez as she ducked beneath the dying vine. "Not the kind of place anyone but a Taglioni would know."

Dek managed to gin up a bit of rage at the tone in her voice. Used it to power his flagging muscles. And, miracle of miracles, it got him to the top of the steep climb. Then, reaching the flat, he stepped to the side, bent double, and propped his hands on his knees as he sucked air into his hot and starved lungs.

"How you doing?" To Dek's surprise, the voice belonged to Aguila.

"I'm thinking that being dead takes a whole lot less effort than this does."

Kalico dropped down to a crouch beside him, calling, "We need to take a break, people. On the basalt like this, we're finally off the worst of the roots."

Dek gasped, lowered himself to the bare rock. Every muscle in his body was on fire. His joints screaming and gone to rubber.

Talina's voiced carried from where she had stopped in conversation with Kylee and Muldare. "We're calling it, people. This is about as safe as we can get. Bedrock, sparse canopy. Kylee, Flute, and I will keep watch. Dek? You, Muldare, and Kalico get some sleep if you can. I know it's rock, but it beats the living shit out of roots."

"And they know we're both about to fold," Kalico muttered. "God, I'm fucking exhausted."

"Me, too. Amazing what ten years in a starship will take out of you."

"Everything but the memory of Three Spires, I guess."

Between panting breaths, he told her, "It just came back to me. I remember now. That's the first place I ever met you. You were there, on Miko's arm. My God, dressed in that radiant blue gown. Same color as your eyes. You could have stepped straight from the spotlight at the Paris fashion show. This absolutely gorgeous woman, and so much more than Miko ever . . . Well, it doesn't matter."

Beside him, Aguila shifted. "Surprised you remember anything from that night. Let alone what I was wearing. That was what, ten years ago? Eleven?"

He tilted his head back as he gasped for air. Could see the stars between gaps in the trees. Felt so much freer to be out of the deep forest. A weight lifted off his chest.

"More like thirteen. I remember. Right down to the words I said." He made a tsking sound. "If I could go back, I'd punch that toilet-sucking silly little shit that I used to be clear into next week. Beat him to within a millimeter of his over-righteous life."

He glanced at her, saw her eyes like pits in the darkness. "I am so sorry for what I said to you." He chuckled dryly. "Sorry for so many things I did back then."

Aguila reached out. Clapped a hand on his shoulder. "If we live through this, maybe we can talk." A pause. "Assuming this humility jag isn't just a passing phase. That or some twisted strategy affected to gain you some advantage."

"Is it that difficult to trust someone?"

"Nope." She stood. "I trust a lot of people. Many of them with my life. Just not a Taglioni."

And then she rose, staggered wearily over to where Talina Perez and Kylee were talking. The big quetzal behind them was barely visible in the faint light of the hand torch. Amazing how the thing could blend into any environment.

She really was the most beautiful woman I'd ever seen.

Closing his eyes, he could remember every detail.

Right down to the loathing she'd tried so hard to hide when he opened his clap-trapping mouth and . . .

"Hell, Dek," he told himself. "If I were her, I wouldn't forgive you either."

63

When Dan Wirth had been a kid, his snot-sucking excuse of a father had periodically locked Dan in closets—and once in a storage box where he'd had to lie for three days, hungry, thirsty, and wallowing in his own urine.

This was worse.

Dan huddled in a corner of the plastic shipping box, shivering and looking up at the distant stars. To his right, the stack of shipping containers rose like an impossible wall. Through the side of the toppled box, he could see across the ferngrass to the bush. The moon was waxing gibbous and hung low in the west. The night chime was different than the day's and fit to drive him half mad.

And there, not more than a meter from the box, he could see Windman's head. The gruesome thing lay on its side facing Dan. As pale as Windman had been in life, his head was beginning to darken, the eyes having sunk dully into the skull. The worst part was the gaping mouth. Invertebrates had been crawling into it, apparently eating the tongue because they now crawled out through the severed neck as well.

Not that Dan had ever suffered a pang of guilt, but he wished he could kick the loathsome thing out of sight. Just get it the hell away.

The miracle was that he was still alive. Trapped inside a clear plastic box, in Capella's direct light throughout the long day, without water. The suffering had been encompassing. Enough to make death seem a blessing. The entire time, he'd been terrified. Nothing, absolutely nothing he had ever seen compared with watching the empty ground rise, turn itself into a quetzal, and devour copilot Windman.

Not even Dan's nightmares—and he had plenty—could compare. The abuse he'd had to endure at his father's hands? The degradation and shame of sucking his dad's prick? Hearing the man groan in delight? The mental and physical abuse? All the shit he'd had to take? Didn't hold so much as a feeble flicker of the horror of watching a man eaten alive.

He could still hear Windman's bones breaking as Whitey crushed him.

What the fuck was that? To feel one's bones snapping and splintering? It wasn't just the pain, but the unbridled horror of being eaten alive.

I hate this fucking planet.

Worse, he couldn't leave. The fart-sucking quetzals had him neatly trapped, and the shit-sucking bastards were keeping watch.

So far, he thought he'd counted three. They'd been coming and going. Whitey was easy given his wounds. The second had been smaller, had scratched gouges in the plastic trying to get to Dan. How fucking bone-rattling was that? Hearing the grating of claws in plastic, feeling it through the box? The worst part was watching, seeing the teeth, the claws, knowing that if the plastic failed, that color-flashing horror was going to tear you out of your hiding place and rip you into pieces while it ate you.

The third beast was bigger. Not Whitey's size, but close. It had tried for an hour or so to wiggle its claws into the crack of the door and spring it open. Then it had tried the air holes at the top. Actually managed to elongate a couple, but the thick plastic had held.

Off and on through the long afternoon, one or another of the quetzals had appeared, checked his box, and gone back to whatever they'd been about since the siren had gone off.

That had been no longer than fifteen minutes after Windman was eaten—just about the time Dan was realizing how much sweat a human body could make.

He had been waiting. Longing. But no all clear had sounded.

Port Authority was still on lockdown.

Until the quetzal problem was solved, no one was coming to find him.

I'm the richest and most powerful man on the planet.

What kind of fucking solace was that? Unless something changed, he was going to die of thirst or hyperthermia in a plastic box.

Or he could simply throw the door open and be eaten alive.

He was considering that very thought.

Wondered if the quetzals were even around, when movement caught his eye. Slinking low, one of the beasts appeared at the corner of the shipping containers, seemed to flow across the ground. Its hide, in a remarkable feat, mimicked the colors of the ground it crossed.

The thing jammed its nose against the now-scarred plexiglass.

Dan thought he knew this one. Didn't have to see the mangled left front leg.

Whitey.

"I really hate this planet," Dan rasped through his dry throat.

As if it understood, Whitey chittered before turning. With a kick, the big quetzal knocked Dan's box hard enough to launch it nearly a meter.

Slammed around the inside, Dan groaned, took a breath.

When he opened his eyes, the door had held. He was still safe. But, through the plastic, Windman's decomposing head was now mere inches from Dan's face.

64

Vartan blinked. His lids grated across his eyes, feeling like he had sand in them. He was laid out on his bunk in the dormitory. A fan was blowing cool air from the ceiling vent. Light reflected from the hallway. He was naked, a blanket covering his body.

Clap-trapping hell, but he was thirsty.

He smacked his lips. Pulled the blanket back and sat up. His head hurt, and he had to pee.

As he staggered to his feet, every muscle in his body screamed. His joints might have been soldered, or at least rusted, given the way they bent when he moved.

At the sink, he drank and drank. Hobbled to the lavatory and sighed with relief as he drained his water.

Back at his bunk, he found his wrap, tied it around his waist.

"You all right?" Marta asked as he walked wearily into the small lobby out front.

She was seated by the door, staring out through one of the windows at the yard beyond. The soft glow of overhead lights illuminated the stark ground, reflected off old pieces of machinery, and finally surrendered to the night.

"What the hell happened to me?"

"You came stumbling in a little after noon. Saw Svetlana's body and collapsed. Fodor, Ctein, and I carried you here. Sent word to the Messiah that you were wounded."

He remembered Svetlana's broken body. Had hoped it had been a bad dream.

Marta glanced at him, her hazel eyes lackluster. "What happened out there? Where's the rest of your team?"

He sank into one of the chairs, rubbed his eyes. "Dead. Eaten. Buried in roots. Mars and Hap? They just vanished." A beat. "What about Petre and Tikal's teams?"

Her stare fixed on some infinity out in the darkness beyond. "They haven't come back. Haven't radioed."

"Nothing?"

"There's been gunfire off to the west. Then the airtruck reappeared. No telling if it was Shyanne coming back or someone else. It went down in the trees. Heard some more gunfire just before dark. Got to be the Supervisor's party."

"The children?"

She inclined her head toward the rear. "Got them all asleep in the back. I'm 'on guard,' whatever that means."

"I've got to get something to eat. See the Messiah." He struggled to his feet, wondering when he'd ever felt this weak, this defeated.

"Vart?" Marta looked up, an anxious glitter behind her eyes. "It's all coming apart. Everything. The universe? Being chosen? The Prophets? It was all a lie. We're dying. And we're not coming back."

She ran the tips of her fingers along the spiral of scar tissue on her breast, following it to her nipple. "Nothing there, Vart. No soul to be suckled into a reborn life. Just . . . nothing." She raised her eyes. "And do you know what that makes us?"

"Maybe the Prophets will—"

"Irdan's dead. Callista might be, too. Couldn't tell last time I was in there."

He nodded, asked, "What did you do with the rifle?"

"Left it at the admin dome."

Vartan stepped to the door, looked back. Marta's gaze was once again fixed on some infinity that lay beyond the window.

He walked out into the night, aware of the perfumed air, of the feel of the night breeze. Donovan's moon was hanging over the distant western horizon; its weak light illuminated humped treetops, cast shadows as the forest stretched into the distance.

The growling hunger that chafed his belly, the pain in his abused muscles, the desolation in Marta's eyes, it all left him empty. A sucked-out husk.

To his absolute disgust, Svetlana's broken body still lay off to the side of the admin dome door. For a moment, in the muted glow of the yard lights, he thought she moved. Looked closer, and realized her body was swarming with invertebrates.

"For the love of God!" He bent down, got one of her wrists, and with his last reserves, started dragging her off to the . . .

He hardly had an instant to react to the tickle of little feet as several of the creatures skittered up his fingers. Like fire, they began taking bites out of his skin.

With a howl, he let go of Svetlana, manically flinging his hand back and forth to sling the little beasts off.

Damn, but that hurt!

Backing away, he stared impotently at Svetlana's crumpled corpse. The yawning hollow opened wider inside him. Seemed to swallow his heart.

Flashbacks of her laughter, that dancing joy in her eyes. He'd reveled in her clever wit, in the times they'd laid in bed, holding each other, talking about the dreams they'd shared. Svetlana had been a true believer. Really thought she was the mother of the future, that she was the vessel of eternal life. That through her, the dead were reborn.

Sucking at the bites on his hand, Vartan peered at Svetlana's shadowed corpse, watched the invertebrates as they scampered into holes chewed in her flesh.

So much for the repository of the dead, for being the living grave. The dead were now being consumed by alien bugs. To be purified into insect shit.

Did I ever really believe?

Or did I just sign on to the lie to justify staying alive?

Shyanne had never believed. She'd played the game and done it well enough to survive. He'd always known her participation—good enough to fool the rest of the Will, and the Messiah, too—was a sham.

Was the fact that he'd never turned her in due to his own apostasy? Or because of what he owed her for having once been his wife? They'd loved each other back then, before the Harrowing and Cleansing. Before participating in abomination had broken that beautiful relationship.

He turned his eyes to the heavens, star-matted and stunning as it was: a wealth of Milky Way glowing in patterns of light. Shyanne had been smart enough to get out.

Or had she? Marta said the airtruck had come back to get the Supervisor.

But it hadn't left.

"Deal with it later."

He gave Svetlana's remains a final, grieving, glance and opened the door to the admin dome.

The lights hurt his eyes.

Plodding wearily down to the cafeteria, he entered. Saw Batuhan sitting in the throne, eyes on Guan Shi's emaciated body where it lay on the rear table.

The Messiah didn't look up as Vartan crossed the room, entered the kitchen to see Irdan's body laid out on one of the stainless-steel counters. The Prophet's left arm and leg had been stripped down to the bones. Not that much meat had been on them in the first place. Callista, also dead, rested just beyond, still untouched.

Additionally, in the rear corner, the completely processed skeletons of three individuals were piled atop each other, the blood-smeared bones intertwined. Someone had seen to the First Chosen killed by the Supervisor.

As if anything made sense in this madness.

It's a prion. A misshapen protein that causes dementia. Not divine revelation.

He might have had all the sensitivity of wood as he picked up Petre's old cleaver. Used it to chop through the top of Irdan's skull. Heedless of the bone chips, he grabbed the man's hair. The sound of the keen edge biting into bone sent shivers through him.

But in the end, he yanked the skullcap loose. It parted from the brain with a sucking sound. Vartan considered the Prophet's brain. Used the cleaver edge to slice it open.

What should have been pale gray and white wasn't right. Looked . . . what? Spotted? Stippled? Bits of off-colored . . . Didn't matter. Fact was, he seen healthy brain often enough to know this was wrong.

It's a disease. Not the universe.

"What do I believe?"

Vartan grunted at the irony. Walked to the rear and used a skewer to fish boiled cabbage from one of the big pots. Back in Solar System he had never been a fan of cabbage. Cold and soggy as this was, he considered it some of the finest eating he'd ever enjoyed.

Hunger—and ten years of ration along with the occasional stewed human—could do that to a person.

Full, he passed the remains of the dead Prophets and walked out to where the Messiah sat motionless, the faint whistle of his breathing audible through the gaping hole of his nose. The man's eyes were fixed on Guan Shi, as if the comatose and limp Prophet was on the verge of uttering some stunning pronouncement.

"Messiah?"

The man remained mute.

"Have any of the other teams reported in? My team, Will, Tuac, Sima, they're confirmed dead. Mars and Hap, they just disappeared. Gone. Taken by the forest. I barely made it back."

The Messiah might have been cast of stone for all the awareness he showed.

"Outside the door the invertebrates are eating Svetlana. They'll bite you if you try to touch her. I could use something, a rake maybe. A rope with a loop. We need to drag her away from the door. I can't bring her inside with all those things eating her."

Nothing.

"Messiah?"

The man's eyes—including the eerie blue one carved into his forehead—remained fixed on emptiness.

Vartan ground his teeth. Took a deep breath. "I'll figure it out on my own."

He turned, had taken a step when the Messiah, in a disjointed voice, said, "We are being tested, Second Will. The universe is winnowing away the chaff. Those who have been taken, they have been judged and found wanting. Immortality is not granted lightly."

"Found wanting?" Vartan tried to keep the incredulous tones from his voice. "Svetlana fell to her death fighting to save the airtruck. Mars, Will, Sima, and the rest of my team? There was no testing, just luck of the draw as to which of us was taken."

The Messiah raised his bone scepter. "Beware of your words, Second Will. The universe is listening."

"Messiah, two of the Prophets are dead. The third is dying. Three of the First Chosen are dead. Petre and Tikal's teams haven't returned. It's all falling apart."

"You must have faith." The words were said with simple

conviction. "The universe has brought us this far. It will not let us down now."

"Messiah, have you heard anything I've said?"

"Vartan, you must trust. Believe that. Take it to your breast and hold tight."

"Messiah, we're dying like—"

"We *are* the immortal. Now, you have your duties, Second Will. You and the rest, bring me the Supervisor. I've heard that she's out there. Once we have the Supervisor, the rest of the people on Donovan, they'll fall into line."

Vartan placed a hand to his stomach, feeling the building ache. Damn it, he'd eaten too fast.

The Messiah was staring fixedly at Guan Shi.

Vartan stepped over, got a good look. Reached out and touched her half-slitted eyeball. No reaction.

"She's dead, Messiah."

Batuhan nodded slowly, sagaciously. "Then, so be it. The universe will provide. Just have faith."

Talina tilted her head back to better sniff the night breeze. Where Demon lurked behind her stomach, she could feel the piece of shit's tension. Rocket's presence perched on her shoulder, chittering his unease. Bits of memory, flashes of forest, glimpses of long-ago hunts played out in her imagination.

And something else. Something old and terrifying. Something *out there* in the dark. A looming danger.

She couldn't put her finger on it.

Quetzal memory.

"What is it?" she asked, concentrating on the thought. Wishing she had a direct link to the quetzal molecules instead of the hit or miss as transferRNA went through its rigmarole in search of the right information.

How the hell did that work, anyway? Too damn many pathways through the nervous system.

Dya had tried to explain it and . . .

Dya.

Dead.

That hurt. In a lot of ways.

Talina still owed the woman: On Clemenceau's orders, she'd shot Dya's first husband down in the street. Hardly seemed like she'd come close to making amends. Now Dya was dead. Smart, competent, resourceful Dya. And the loss wasn't just Kylee's, wasn't just Su's, and rest of her family's, but all of humanity's. Dya Simonov had known more about the botany, the genetics, the intricacies of TriNA. She'd been on the verge of a breakthrough with the native plants. Had barely begun to catalog her research.

Gone. Just like that.

Not to mention Mark Talbot. Steady as the stars in the sky. Talina ached for his amused smile, the wry sense of assurance the man possessed. Not to mention his skills when it came time to hunt rogue quetzals.

Where she sat off to the side, Muldare fought a whimper and cradled her arm. The thing was red, swollen. They'd hadn't been able to pull all the gotcha spines out. How the woman bore the pain and still managed to keep it together was a wonder.

Talina shifted her rifle, stepped over to where Kylee sat; the girl had her back propped against Flute's side. She looked up, eyes hot in Talina's IR vision. She'd been crying.

"How you doing, kid?"

"Really, really mad, Tal."

Behind her, Flute opened his left eye to study Talina. To say that quetzals didn't deal with death the same as humans did was an understatement. Especially given that they tended to eat their progenitors.

Talina dropped to a crouch, rifle across her knees as she listened to the night sounds. "You and Flute found where this thing got your mom and dad. Was there any clue as to what this is? Some scent? A track? Anything?"

Kylee worked her jaw. Knotted a fist. "A couple of spots of blood, and the roots were already absorbing them. Flute and I looked up. Couldn't see anything up in the branches. No thermal signature, no shape. Flute's sense of smell is a lot better than mine; he didn't catch of a hint of anything unusual. Maybe it had moved on."

Talina winced at the resentment and guilt in the girl's voice. Kylee's words echoed in Tal's memory: *"Everyone I love dies!"*

"We're going to find this thing," Talina promised. "The way Kalico and Briah described the tentacle, or whatever it was, the creature's got to be big. Something limited to deep forest where it can anchor among the high branches. And then there's the biomechanics of being able to lift a person that high that fast."

Kylee's lips were pursed, her face contorted. Now she said, "She shouldn't have been out there in the first place. *They* drove her out there. You know it just as well as I do."

At the venom in Kylee's voice, Talina took a deep breath. "You and Flute going to go on a rampage? Slicing and dicing your way through the Unreconciled? Murder every last one of them?"

"They *eat* people."

"So do quetzals. Flash killed and ate three people in the belief that he could synthesize their molecules. Learn who they were. The Unreconciled think that by eating people, they can purify them. Give them immortality. Where's the difference?"

Kylee's hot glare would have melted sialon. "I really hate you sometimes."

"Yeah, it's a pain in the ass when someone brings up all this rational, put-it-in-perspective stuff when all you want to do is go murder forty or fifty human beings. You gonna kill the kids, too?"

"Don't be an asshole, Talina."

"Right back at you, kid. Part of being a decent human being is thinking things through before you're hip-deep in the blood you've spilled." A pause. "And living with the guilt for the rest of your life."

Kylee leaned her head forward, buried her face in her hands. "There's so many things I needed to tell Mom. Tell Mark. Stuff I couldn't get myself to say. Like, I'm sorry. Like I let her down so many times. And I was there . . . stood there . . . like a fucking rock when Leaper and Diamond killed Rebecca and Shantaya. And I didn't care. I saw it! I just wanted everything and everyone to die."

"Your mother knew that. So does Su."

Talina dropped to a knee as her leg started to cramp. Carefully she scanned the surrounding trees, sorted the sounds of the night. That was the thing about having a quetzal in camp. None of the local wildlife was likely to sneak in for a snack.

"They also knew that you were different because you'd bonded with Rocket. That he's part of you, part of us." Talina tapped the side of her head. "Me, I'm a stopgap. You're the future. You, and probably Tip and others like you. Dya understood that. Yeah, she loved you, and it broke her heart that it had to be her beloved daughter who was chosen as the bridge to the future."

"I hurt her." Kylee sniffed, wiped her nose. "Really, really hurt her."

Talina shifted her butt. "You know why she left you out there when she could have talked Kalico into sending armed marines to bring you back? It's because she trusted you. The greatest gift you ever gave your mom was letting her and Mark come visit you out at Briggs."

"I'm tired of hurting, Talina."

"It sucks toilet water, but if you're going to really live, you're going to hurt. At least, if you're normal. Now, take Dan Wirth. He's a psychopath. Everything is all about him. No remorse. No guilt. No grief. On days like today, psychopathy sounds pretty good."

"I still want to kill cannibals."

"I hear you." Talina glared up at the high basalt escarpment where it blocked the eastern sky. "But here's the question: They were locked in a living hell, and the only path to survival led to a different kind of hell. If you or I had been there with the choices they had, what would we have chosen?"

"I don't get it."

"It's simple really: Would you have let them cut your throat and cook you? Become food for your fellow passengers? Or would you have chosen to live and cut someone else's throat, cooked, and eaten them? Choose."

"There had to be something else they could have—"

"Do you eat, or are you eaten? Pick."

Kylee glared at her. "It's never that simple."

"It was on *Ashanti*."

The girl crossed her arms, turning sullen. "Doesn't matter. When they drove Mom and Mark out into the forest, they weren't on any damn ship. Whole different rules."

Talina chuckled, her night-shifted gaze fixed on the heights above. "Yep. And before this is done, I'm going to settle with Messiah Batuhan."

"What about the rest of them?" Kylee asked.

Talina waved away a pesky night-flying invertebrate. "Well, if what we've seen so far is any indication, Donovan's slowly whittling the numbers down. And we gave them fair warning."

"And this thing out in the forest?"

"It'll have to wait its turn, but I promise you this: Its turn is coming."

"Good," Kylee whispered fiercely, "because I want to be there when we take it down."

66

Had it not been for Talina's quetzal-enhanced hearing, she wouldn't have known how long Kylee sobbed her grief. The girl had taken Flute, removed herself from the impromptu camp, and retreated up to the foot of the slope. Only then, out of sight, had she allowed herself to let go over the deaths of her mother and father.

That had been hours ago.

Talina, dozing off and on, had kept watch. The night creatures moved in the trees; night chime—so different from the sounds of the day—had risen and fallen in harmonic cadence. Briah Muldare had moaned in her sleep. Kalico, to Talina's amusement, snored. Taglioni slept with the sprawled and loose-limbed unconcern of the totally exhausted.

But nothing was as painful as Kylee's heart-wrenching grief.

The stars had wheeled most of the way across the sky when Talina stood, willing circulation back into her legs. That internal sense told her that morning was only an hour away.

Stepping gingerly, she slipped up the trail. Glanced around the bole of an aquajade. On the unyielding stone, Flute lay curled around himself like an oversized donut. The quetzal's vigilant right eye was fully fixed on Talina.

Took a moment for her to realize that deep in the curl, Kylee lay cradled. The girl's knees were drawn up to her chest, her hair splayed across the quetzal's foreleg. She might as well have been sleeping in one of those beanbag beds.

Flute's right eye regarded Talina with an unusual intensity. Seemed like nothing was getting by the quetzal on this night.

"How's she doing?" Talina asked softly.

Flute's hide flashed a deep-bruised purple, patterned

with black and infrared designs. Colors and patterns Talina had never seen.

Rocket's *Wayob*—perched on Talina's shoulder—whispered, *"This is grief. Something quetzals do not feel."*

Seemed she learned something new every day. "So, how come Flute's feeling it?"

Flute flashed the designs for *"Kylee hurt. Deep hurt. Makes eye-water. Do not tell."*

"Yeah, I wondered how she kept it together as long as she did."

Talina sighed, stared up at the stars. So the kid had buried her head in Flute's side and bawled herself empty?

"How are you doing, Flute?"

Again he flashed the bruised purple, then black and infrared. She swore that if only quetzals had tear ducts, Flute, too, would have shed a tear.

Didn't feel grief, huh? Flute did. Mark it up to humans changing quetzals as much as quetzals changed humans?

"Hurt with Kylee." The patterns were perfectly clear in the night.

"Yeah, buddy," Talina told the quetzal. "Me, too. Keep her safe."

The beast's hide shaded into orange, quetzal for "yes."

How much pain could a kid take in life?

Kylee's words: *Everyone I ever love dies.*

One of these days, the kid was going to explode. As it was, the only creature she could allow herself to be vulnerable with was a quetzal. How screwed was that?

Talina gave Flute a parting smile, then reshouldered her rifle. As she turned to go, a single whimper passed Kylee's lips. Even in dreams, her heart was breaking.

67

The day dawned hot and humid. Salmon pink colored the thin layer of high cirrus. Dek Taglioni roused himself, surprised that he'd slept straight through on the bare stone. But by damn and hell, he hurt. Every muscle felt like it had been torn from its mooring on his bones. His hips, knees, and shoulders were sore from the hard rock.

And he was thirsty. Hungry. His coveralls emitted the ripe odors of sweat and stink.

If any solace could be found, it was that where she lay beside him, Kalico Aguila looked worse. Her thick midnight hair was a filthy tangle, her clothes smudged and stained. Something black—looked like grease—smeared her right cheek, the side of her perfect nose, and left a streak across her forehead.

Even as he watched, she blinked awake. Looked around with almost tortured eyes. The woman's face was drawn tighter than old rope. Her left cheek was lined and wrinkled from where it had pressed into the fabric of her sleeve.

She sat up, smacking her lips, tongue sounding dry as she struggled to make enough saliva to swallow. Dek read the sudden distress as she placed a hand to her stomach.

"Here," Dek told her, reaching into his web gear for the energy bar Chaco had given him. "This will help."

She shot him an uncertain look, glanced at the bar, thick as it was with roasted grain, dried blueberries, and desiccated crest meat.

"How long since you've eaten?" Dek asked.

"Since we left PA," she said, closing her eyes. "God, I swear, I can smell that bar you're holding."

She took it with a hesitant hand, shot him a wary look, and carefully bit down.

He couldn't help but grin at the expression on her face. Worked his own mouth in an attempt to conjure saliva. Finally managed a swallow.

"Where's yours?" Kalico indicated the pocket in his web gear.

"In a bit," he told her.

Quick as she was, her eyes flashed that laser-blue intensity. "You don't have another, do you?"

"I ate yesterday," he told her. "If what I hear is correct, you were lost in a cave. Already hungry."

She handed what was left back. "Here. You're going to need it."

He declined to take it. Waved absently toward the rising bulk of the Tyson escarpment. "Once we get to the top, there'll be food. I'm fine. Ate an energy bar last night before I went to sleep."

That sharpness had faded into a thoughtful appraisal. "Liar," she said softly.

To avoid any additional complications, Dek staggered to his feet. Wobbled. Wondered if every cell in his body was being tortured. Then tried not to make a face as he took in the small camp.

Talina and Muldare, rifles across their laps, were seated on basalt boulders, talking softly. Even as Dek watched, Muldare uttered a stifled gasp, made a face as she shifted her wounded arm. The thing looked horrible. Had swollen to fill her sleeve. The hand was puffy and red. How the woman managed was a miracle.

Kylee and the quetzal were gone. Around him the aquajade and dwarf chabacho trees were turning their branches and leaves toward the morning, all focused on the top of the high basalt cliff where Capella's light would appear. The chime was involved in its just-slightly-off symphony.

As he walked carefully across the uneven stone, he could feel his calves, his thighs, his glutes, not to mention his back and shoulders. How long had it been since he'd hurt like this? University? When he was playing sports?

"Dek?" Talina called. "Where you going?"

"Behind these trees," he retorted over his shoulder. "And what I'm going to do is none of your business."

Looking back, here came Talina, stopping only long enough to scoop up his rifle from where he'd left it lying on the basalt.

She handed him the gun, a look of wry amusement glowing behind her alien eyes. "First, never leave your rifle out of hand while you're in the bush. Second, never step out of sight. Third, modesty has its place. But not here. Not now."

He glanced self-consciously to where Kalico Aguila was finishing the last of the energy bar and looking all the better for it. She was chuckling as she watched him squirm.

"Got it," he muttered. "So, how do I do this?"

"How about we both step around behind the trees. I'll glance around, make sure there're no slugs, no sidewinder, no gotcha vine or skewer, and that everything's copacetic. Then, while you attend to the realities of biology, I'll stand a couple of feet away and admire the surroundings. Take in a little bit of nature."

"You've got to be kidding."

"Not even slightly."

He took a deep breath. Laughed at himself. "Yes, ma'am."

As he squatted and attended to business, he glanced uncertainly at Talina. True to her word, she stood, rifle at port arms, her attention fixed on the surrounding forest.

After he'd finished, he stepped over, told her, "Thank you. Guess I've still got a whole lot to learn."

"Different world here." She gave him a wink. "Kylee's right. You've got the makings."

As he followed Talina back to the others he asked, "The makings? Of a disaster? Of a meal for a sidewinder?"

"Of a survivor," she told him. Then leaned close. "Thanks for giving that bar to Kalico. That might just get her through the day."

"Yeah. She's looking about all in."

"What about you?"

He made a face as he shifted his rifle on his sore shoulder. "Telling it straight? I feel like I've been pulled sideways through a singularity. Everything hurts."

"We can't take the easy trail up north. It'll be guarded. Too easy for them to roll rocks down on top of us, if nothing else. Assuming Kylee and Flute can find a way, we've got a hell of climb ahead of us."

"I know."

Talina stopped in front of Kalico, looked down. "You need to use the facilities?"

"No. I'm okay. Not enough water in me to run through."

Talina reached down, pulled Kalico to her feet. "You and Dek, you're the weak links. I need you two to keep an eye on each other. Help each other. Once we're up to the top, we'll get food and water one way or another. But we have to make it. All of us. Working together."

Kalico gave the woman a crooked grin. "You know, once upon a time, I was going to put you against a wall and shoot you."

Talina grinned back. "And if you had, where would you be today?"

Kalico reached out to slap palms with Talina as the security officer started toward the slope.

"Just got to get to the top," Dek told himself. "There'll be food and water up there."

"Yeah, that's the goal. Won't be too tough, just a little climb."

Kylee appeared from between the trees, trotting on her long legs. The girl's blonde hair was tied in a ponytail that bounced with each stride.

"Found a way up," she called to Talina. "Your instincts were good. Flute's up at the top, hunkered down and guarding the trail. There's some biteya and tooth flower to keep clear of, and I saw a sidewinder."

"All right, people," Talina called. "Let's get a little exercise. Muldare? You've got the six."

Dek tried to reshoulder his Holland & Holland, only to find the bruise was just as bad on his other shoulder.

Gut it out.

Three little words that he was really coming to hate.

Nevertheless he took his place, following Talina as she led the way through the scrubby aquajade and chabacho. Compared to what he'd seen back in the deep forest, these were really scrawny specimens. And he was just as happy to be able to look up and see patches of open sky on occasion.

Then they began the climb in earnest. In the beginning it meant scrambling from one toppled boulder to the next. Reaching back, giving a hand to the person following.

Within minutes, Dek was panting, a faint sheen of perspiration slicking his cheeks, neck, and chest. Water he couldn't afford to lose. The temperature had to be in the mid thirties, and the humidity left his sweat to pool.

"You were going to shoot Talina Perez?" Dek asked Kalico as Talina extended her lead on the cracked rock, climbing hot on Kylee's heels.

Kalico was already panting as she made her way around a toppled boulder and stared anxiously at the heights above. "You gotta remember, we didn't have a clue about Donovan. During those two years in transition on *Turalon* I had convinced myself the colony was in rebellion, that they'd seized the missing ships. Turned themselves into a bunch of pirates."

"I see." Dek reached down. Took Kalico's hand, and pulled her up, every muscle in his body complaining.

"No, you don't. Pirates are easy. You just shoot them. We ran into something worse: libertarians. I mean how do you deal with a bunch of lunatics who take it as an article of faith that they can govern themselves?"

"So what happened?" Dek shifted the rifle, anxious lest it might slip off his shoulder, hit the rocks, and mar the lustrous finish on the expensive wood with its beautiful inlay.

Kalico scrambled up next to him, anxiety in her eyes as she realized the magnitude of the climb she was about to attempt. "I put Talina, Shig, and Yvette on trial. When the locals figured out where it was going, Talina stopped the riot just before the Donovanians murdered us. I gave them Port Authority. Figured it was the easiest way to cut my losses."

He found toe-holds, got a grip, and forced himself to climb the next little bit. Turned, and again helped Kalico. Below them, Muldare—looking thirsty and hot herself— kept staring back the way they'd come, ensuring that nothing was following behind. She had her rifle slung, was somehow managing to climb in spite of her inflamed arm.

"So how'd you end up at Corporate Mine?"

Kalico staggered, almost lost her balance. Dek pulled her close. Kept her from falling.

"Thanks. Missed my step there." She wiped a sleeve over her forehead, smeared the smear more. "*Freelander* showed up. You've heard the story about that. What you haven't heard is that I saw myself in the temple of bones. Heard myself say, 'If you go back, you will die.'"

She chuckled, voice rasping with thirst. "Strange shit happens on that ship. Thing is: I said that, all right. More than a year in the future. Used those exact words with that pus fucker Benteen."

"Why didn't you space back on *Turalon*? From what I hear, they had a fortune on board. You'd have been a hero."

She blinked, wavered. "*Freelander* scared the shit out of me. All those lost ships. Vanished. I couldn't . . . couldn't . . ."

"Yeah, I guess I'd have done the same." He made sure she wouldn't fall, tackled the next climb, and reached back. Fought a slight dizzy spell. Had he ever been this thirsty before?

Come on, Dek. You can do this.

Somehow, he got Kalico up the next steep section.

"Why the hell am I telling you this?" she wondered under her breath. "You called me 'Miko's cerulean cunt' the last time I saw you. Asked Miko if I moaned while I was sucking his cock."

"It was outside the Boardroom, wasn't it?" He snorted derisively. "Wasn't even drunk that time. Just full of hatred."

"Of me?"

"God, no. Well . . . maybe a little. There you were, the most beautiful and capable woman in Solar System, with your perfect body pressed up against Miko's. I was so damn jealous." He blinked. Looked up at the next section. Saw the tooth flower off to the side that Talina pointed to.

"Mostly," he told her, "I was full of hatred for myself. For all of my failures, for all the frustrations that I blamed on everyone else."

He pointed. "Now, watch out for that toothy thing. We've got to climb wide."

She squinted, fixed on the tooth flower. "So, what are you now?"

"I don't have the first flipping clue. As a Taglioni, I should have hated myself the most while I was cleaning toilets on *Ashanti*. That's about as far as anyone in my family could fall. And yet, there I was, in the dark, scrubbing up other people's piss and excrement. Fixing the plumbing when the shit of menials plugged it up and stirring the septic in the hydroponics. And I was proud of myself for the first time in my life."

She was giving him that half-glazed look of disbelief. Her once-perfect lips were cracked, her smudged face fatigued and drawn. Nevertheless, she let him cup his hands for her foot, boost her up onto the next ledge. The effort took all of his energy, and he came close to dropping her.

"You ever get back to Transluna," she told him, "I wouldn't confide that to Miko. He'll rub your nose in it. Figure some way of humiliating you to the point that you'd rather be dead."

Dek licked dry lips. Tried to conjure spit . . . and failed. He could feel the building headache. Thirst, he decided, was the most agonizing of suffering. "Supervisor, there's nothing for me back in that hive of serpents and spiders."

The trembling in his muscles was evident as he levered himself up onto the narrow flat beside Kalico.

"Just going to farm? Maybe go live with Chaco Briggs?" she asked.

"Both good choices. But I think I want more. Shig says I'm more of a *rajasic* by nature. Means I'm predisposed to the hedonistic and active, the spice of life. According to Shig, while I was on *Ashanti* I managed to find harmony with the *tamas* in my soul. Sattva, he said, would probably elude me in this lifetime." A beat. "Sometimes I wonder if Shig delights in screwing with my head."

She laughed dryly as she tackled the next cracked section of rock. "I think the universe put Shig here because it's the only place left that he fits."

"What about you? If you could be guaranteed of getting back?"

She reached down, took his hand. Not that she had a lot left to pull with. Actually made it harder for Dek to clamber his way up.

She was panting, flipped her filth-matted hair out of her face as she told him, "Success on Donovan was supposed to be my catapult. Was going to shoot me right into a seat on the Board. Sure, I'd already won the golden plum: I'd fought my way into the position of Supervisor in charge of Transluna. That's always been a springboard. Only one place to go after that. And once I was on the Board, it would have been a matter of time before I was in the Chairman's seat."

"You still could, you know," Dek told her softly, seeing the longing in her eyes.

As quickly it was gone. "All I want at this moment is a tall glass of water and a meal. Not to mention anything that would kill this damned headache. Starting to feel like my skull is split." She paused, blinked. "Like I want to be sick. Slightly dizzy."

"Yeah." His entire body was hot. He'd have given anything for a canteen. Cool, wonderful, water.

The skepticism was back. As if it had finally occurred to her just who she'd been talking to. "So, really, why'd you give me that energy bar this morning? What was your goal in all that?"

"You needed it."

"Uh huh." She coughed hoarsely. "How about you stick to climbing, all right?"

"Sure," he agreed, wondering how he'd managed to pick a scab off such an unhealed wound. It hit him, of course, that he'd just reminded her of how badly she'd wanted that seat on the Board. What it must have cost her to make it so high up the echelon that it was dangling within her reach.

He took a deep breath, would have killed for a gulp of water.

And then the world began to whirl. A sick feeling tickled his gut with the urge to vomit.

"Whoa," he whispered. Blinked.

And started to topple . . .

THE DESERT

I was never trained in religion. My parents didn't believe in it. And Mongolia had its own history, placed as it was between the Buddhist, Taoist, Islamic, Russian Orthodox, and animistic spheres. A sort of crossroads for faiths of every kind. And through it all, the ancient magic of the steppes was constantly blowing.

I was raised to be agnostic, to look first for the laws of physics and science before any credence was given to the spiritual. That creed led me to electronics, gave me my trade.

Had taken me to the stars.

And Ashanti.

Where the universe found me. A blank canvas upon which it could compose, and finally paint. The rough sketch was, of course, the Harrowing and Cleansing, and with the gift of the Prophets, it colored between the lines, shaded, and added the subtle tones of composition that created the masterpiece that was the Irredenta.

The tool for the redemption and renovation of the universe, for its cleansing and rebirth into purity.

I do remember, however, that messiahs are always given one last test before they are granted the final revelations. For my ancestors out on the steppes, it was usually starvation and deprivation that preceded spirit visions, soul flying, and holy trance. For the Buddhists it was meditation. Fasting for the Muslims. Jesus was tempted by the devil while exiled in the desert.

Now I face my desert, my darkest moments.

I have half of the adults left who descended to Donovan from Ashanti. *Ten of the children are dead or missing. Shyanne and Tamil betrayed us and stole the airtruck.*

The universe tempts me to recant. Taunts me with the possibility that my people really are dying on Donovan, and doing so in a way that they cannot be reincarnated.

Worst of all, it has taken my Prophets from me. An act akin to stabbing out my eyes. Leaving me in a black haze of darkness where all I can do is reach out with feeble fingers in an attempt to find my way. But flail about as I might, my groping hands find only nothingness.

For all of its appearance as a lush forest full of life, spiritually Donovan is a desert. A parched waste devoid of reassurance. A land of thirst for those desperate to slake their longing for salvation.

What better place to test me?

I am panicked, frantic, and adrift.

Three of the First Chosen are murdered by that Corporate demon, their meat preserved in refrigeration in the kitchen. They await the sacrament of feasting, the moment they will be ingested, their souls to follow the path to regeneration.

My First and Third Will, along with their teams, are missing. Presumed dead. Which, I realize, is another test. I have no proof that they are really dead. The universe might produce them, like a rabbit from a hat, the moment I declare my lack of faith.

Svetlana, my second wife, has died from a fall. Perhaps it was the universe discarding her. That she'd fulfilled her duty, bringing as many of the dead back to life as she did. The children I sired from her will grow, become new vessels in which the dead can be reborn.

Vartan worries me. I've always been suspicious of his true commitment. More so since Shyanne and Tamil got away with the airtruck. I can't help but suspect Vartan allowed that to happen through omission if not direct knowledge.

In the end, I suspect that Vartan will have to be purified and reborn. But for the moment, I need him. He's the only person I have with any security training. He knows how to use a rifle.

If, somehow, the Supervisor is alive, she will come here. She must. She's the kind who does not leave unfinished business.

There is no telling why the airtruck hasn't flown up out of the forest. This morning we've not heard gunfire. Per-

haps Donovan has dealt with the Supervisor in its own way. Or something's wrong with the airtruck. The uncertainty is maddening.

Meanwhile, I must assume Aguila is alive. And she'll be coming for the radio.

But why take away my Prophets? Blind me like this? What's the point of leaving me to grope about? What am I supposed to learn?

I look up, state emphatically: "I have faith." I repeat: "I do not doubt!"

In my deepest soul, I believe it. Let the belief run through my veins with each beat of my heart. I will not waver. I am the repository of souls. The chosen one.

I stare at an empty cafeteria, seeing the bare tables where the Prophets once lay.

The place is so quiet. Only the hum of the air conditioning and refrigerators can be heard in the background.

The children are being kept safe in the barracks dome. I have people on watch to the north and south.

But I am not alone. I never am. The dead are with me. Living in my tissue. Waiting patiently in my loins. I am their repository.

Through me, they shall live forever.

I hear the steps, two people. One is having trouble. I can hear the sliding, half stagger.

When Marta pushes the door open, she has Shimal Kastakourias' arm over her shoulder. The woman is having trouble walking.

I wait, watch with ever growing excitement as Marta brings Shimal close, lowers her to one of the chairs at the table.

"What happened?" I ask.

Shimal stares up at me, her dark eyes panicked. "It's been getting worse, Messiah. At first, it was simple things. Dropping stuff. Stumbling."

I glance down, see Shimal's right hand. It trembles, twitches. My amazement and delight increase.

"Then, this morning"—Shimal swallowed hard—"I was having trouble. Kept slurring my words. It's better now. But I just fell over. Marta said I should come to you."

Shimal blinks, the wobble of her head barely visible.

Marta, gaze stony, says, "She thinks she's turning into a Prophet."

I close my eyes, lean my head back. A surge of relief spills through my breast, fills me with delight.

Of course.

That's the lesson.

What the universe takes, it will replace.

My soul rises on a wave of rapture.

68

The attack had been cunning, audacious, a whole new tactic. It might have worked but for Pamlico Jones. He'd been watching the corner of the shipping crates where Dan Wirth had disappeared with that *Ashanti* copilot, Windman.

While Jones wasn't about to stick his nose where it didn't belong, that didn't mean the man wasn't intensely curious, Dan being who and what he was. That Dan had been outside the fence was unusual enough. When he escorted Windman around the stacked containers and out of sight, Jones figured that Windman was about to suffer "an unfortunate accident."

So he'd seen the first of the quetzals that had poked its head around the shipping containers where Wirth and Windman had vanished.

Figuring that Dan Wirth and Paul Windman were already in transition to becoming quetzal shit, Jones had jumped on com and sounded the alert.

And just in time, Allison thought as she stared down at the "Quetzal Map" where it lay spread on the conference room table. At the sound of the siren, she'd dropped everything, run full out to the admin dome. Knowing that Talina was out at Briggs and Shig was up doing who knew what on *Freelander,* it had just been her and Yvette coordinating the search. That had been twenty-eight long hours ago.

"Still trying to absorb this," Yvette said softly as she ran her eyes across the map.

"They've never tried to rush two gates before. Let alone at the same time."

"No." Yvette placed a finger on the shuttle-field gate. "It's bad enough that one got through the Mine Gate. Wejee almost had it closed when that first quetzal darted through."

"He's just damn lucky," Allison agreed, her eyes on the

square that indicated Mine Gate's location. "If that first quetzal had stopped long enough to kill Wejee, the others could have made it through."

"Well, it didn't. It just streaked into town. Wejee managed to get the gate shut, got a couple of rounds into the second quetzal, and the third fled back to the bush."

"Three on the north, three on the east," Allison mused. "Charging the gates simultaneously." She tried to understand what that meant. Realized she was irritated with herself for leaving all of this for others over the years.

So, you alive or dead out there, Dan?

The best scenario would be if he were dead. For one thing, it would be a huge relief. She would no longer have to balance on the precarious teeter-totter of living with a violent psychopath. Sometimes the stress was unbearable. Especially over the last year as Dan had begun to realize he'd reached his zenith. If he was dead out there, The Jewel, the various properties, the claims, the house, all of it would be hers.

That being the case, Ali, how are you going to keep it?

She would have to move swiftly, mercilessly. While it had been serendipitous, Kalen Tompzen knew that she was the one who had brokered his escape from the shit-filled future Aguila had consigned him to. He'd back her, follow any order she gave him.

"Drone has a hit on the IR," came Step Allenovich's voice over com. *"Yeah, it's our quetzal. Got him in the box on one of the broken haulers."*

"Watch yourselves," Yvette called. "Don't take any chances."

"Screw chances. My call is to take him out with a drone. That haul box will contain the blast, won't even so much as mar the paint. Well, okay, old as that thing is, it won't mar the rust."

"Do it." Yvette exhaled wearily. "Tough hunt this time around."

"They cleared that area early last night," Allison said thoughtfully, staring at the map.

"Maybe it got around behind them? Maybe they just missed it? Doesn't matter. What does is that the thing was so harried it never managed to kill anyone."

"Guess that just leaves Dan and Windman."

Yvette turned pensive eyes on her. "You know the odds aren't good."

"I've been running that through my mind."

"Allison, why are you here? I mean, I appreciate the help. With Talina and Shig gone, you being here freed up Step for the hunt. But, seeing you walk through that door . . . ?"

"The last person you expected?"

"Uh . . . yeah."

Allison gave her a weary smile. "Let's say I've opened my eyes to entirely new possibilities. Some of which may change even as we discover what happened when Dan and Windman stepped out back of the shipping crates."

Yvette's cool green eyes didn't waver. "Bit brazen of you, don't you think?"

"Is it my business or my occupation that you object to? Or maybe my history?"

"Stow it," Yvette muttered. "The only saint in PA is Shig, and if he were here he'd just nod pleasantly and give us that maddening smile before he started spouting off on your karma."

A muffled bang sounded.

"Cap one quetzal," Step's voice came through com.

"Steaks and leather." Yvette accessed her personal com. "Sound the all clear, but send it out that we want everyone staying frosty, armed, and ready. They could try something else."

"Roger that," Two Spot's voice came through.

Yvette then asked, "Two Spot? Anything from Tal or Aguila?"

"Negative. Not a word since yesterday."

"Well, that sucks toilet water. Now we have to figure out what's become of Talina and the Supervisor. The shit never stops coming down."

Allison yawned, stretched. "Yeah, I need a couple of armed escorts. I want to see what happened out behind that container wall."

Because this was a watershed moment. If Dan was dead, fine and thank God. If, somehow, he'd managed to survive, it had become apparent to Allison that inevitably, it would be up to her to kill him herself.

69

"**T**al," Muldare called softly.

Talina turned, stared back down the steep escarpment. Muldare had her good hand on Taglioni, seemed to be pressing him into the rock to keep him from pitching off the slender ledge where the man was propped. Above him, Kalico was glancing down, looking none too steady herself. Bits of detritus were stuck in the Supervisor's already filthy hair. Something Talina had never seen.

Using cracks, Talina scaled her way back down and wide around Kalico. She got her fingers into a fissure and took a good look at Taglioni. The guy's eyes were unfocused, wavering. His muscles had that loose shiver that indicated a man on the edge.

"He's spent," Muldare said. "What the hell do we do now?"

"You're not looking any too good yourself. How's the arm?"

"Like a fucking fountain of fire. The only good news is that it keeps me from knowing how gagging thirsty, hot, and tired I am."

"Dizzy spells?"

"Not yet." Muldare gave her a suffering grin. "Marines don't quit. I'll make it."

But even marines had a point of no return.

Talina glanced up. Where was the top? Maybe another thirty or forty meters? Hard to tell from this angle.

"Kylee?" she called, hoping no one was at the summit to overhear. The girl turned, stared down, wild blonde hair framing her thin face. "You and Muldare, help Kalico."

Kylee immediately began to scramble down the rocks.

"What are you going to do?" Muldare asked, voice partly slurred by thirst. The marine winced as she hitched her swollen arm around.

"You and Kylee make sure Kalico gets to the top," Talina told her. "I've got Taglioni."

"Tal, he's about to pass out."

"Yeah. I know. So's Kalico. Too long without water and now heat stroke. So, hump your butt, Marine. Get the Supervisor up and out of here. Whatever it takes."

"Yes, ma'am," Muldare mumbled hoarsely, and taking a grip with her good hand, climbed past the sagging Taglioni.

Talina took hold of the guy, could feel his heart pounding like a triphammer. "How you doing, Dek?"

"Headache's fit to kill a horse. Everything just started spinning. Anything . . . Just want . . ." He wavered, and she pushed him back against the rock.

Talina filled her lungs. Looked up to where the others were slowly and clumsily working their way up the steep ascent. Kalico was going to fail next, and then painwracked Muldare. It'd be a miracle if the marine made it.

So, what to do about Taglioni?

Talina shifted her feet for the best purchase possible and swung the man onto her shoulders. Damn, his limp body jammed her rifle right into the middle of her back, bruising the spine.

"C'mon," she growled to herself as she took the weight. "All that quetzal strength better be worth something."

Demon hissed from down next to her liver.

She began to climb.

Handhold by handhold she made her way up. Felt the fingers of fatigue, her own lack of water. Quetzal visions kept spinning through her head: Bits of forest. A hot plain. Heat waves rising above the bush.

Talina imagined she had claws. Visualized how they'd look fixing themselves into the rock. Recognized the reality that she had hardly slept the night before. Had spent her time aching and grieving with Kylee over Dya and Talbot. About the "thing" out in the forest that had killed them.

And now?

Here she was, climbing with two rifles and seventy kilos of dead weight in an attempt to reach the summit where an unknown number of cannibals would love nothing better than to chop them all up and turn them into a sacred lunch.

"If that doesn't suck toilet water?" she asked between gasping breaths.

Sweat beaded, ran down into her eyes as she glanced up; Kylee tugged on Kalico's arm in an attempt to get the failing Supervisor over a vertical column of stone. Muldare had her feet braced and was pushing up on Kalico's butt with her good hand.

Kalico's butt? Really? And not a single protestation of outrage?

How was that for a measure of Aguila's failing state?

Talina grinned, hoisted herself up another half body length, and felt the burn in her muscles.

"Come on," she growled down at her stomach. "What's the point of having a piece of shit like you living inside me if you can't make me superwoman?"

"Weak!" Demon's voice taunted from her gut.

"Fuck you," Talina gritted through her teeth—and stared up at the near-vertical crack that led to the top of the next boulder. The basalt was in the signature columnar fractures; the only good news being that they'd been snapped into short segments. Sort of like climbing a stack of building blocks.

She puffed for breath, charged her muscles, and told Dek, "Hang on!"

Then she tackled the climb, shutting her mind off, simply willing herself to power up the slim fissure. Sucking air, heart hammering, she flopped herself and Taglioni across the flat surface atop one of the stones.

"That's it," she told herself. "Get your wind."

Where his head hung beside hers, Taglioni slurred, "She loathes me. Despicable walking shit that I am."

"I don't loathe you," Talina told him. "You've spent the last ten years in a ship is all. So far you've impressed the hell out of me, having made it this far."

"Kalico," he whispered muzzily. "Don't blame her. I was a real maggot."

She felt him fading, his hold growing limp. "Hey! Pay attention. Wake up. Concentrate. I need you to hang on to me. Just one more climb, okay?"

He worked his dry mouth. She felt him start, as if from

impending sleep. "Yeah. Awake. God, I'm thirsty. Fucking head's about to burst."

"Okay. Here we go."

She felt him tighten his grip, and with a cry she tackled the next vertical crack. Muscles burned, fingers ached as they sought a purchase; she gutted her way to the next ledge.

And the next.

Each time, it was supposed to be the last. Somehow, sag as he did, Taglioni held on. The man's weight on her rifle was like a knife-blade bearing into her back.

And then hands reached down. Got hold of Taglioni's shirt and rifle, pulled the man off Tal's back as she fought her way up and over a final ledge. Here ferngrass grew, a hollow marking the edge of the basalt flow.

With her quetzal vision she could discern Flute where he was flattened under the lip of stone, his camouflage melding with the rocks and vegetation.

Talina slipped her rifle off, flopped onto her back, and heaved for air as she stared up at the endless vault of sky. Capella's harsh light burned down, half blinding. Baking hot. Had to be forty if it was a degree.

"Screw vacuum," she gasped. "I don't want to do that again."

"We there yet?" Kalico rasped. "They can eat me. Anything to stop this headache."

"She hates me," Taglioni's voice was mumbling, and then he seemed to drift off.

"Who hates him?" Kylee asked where she lay on her belly at the top of the hollow, eyes on the approaches.

"Kalico." Talina tried to muster enough spit to swallow. Couldn't.

"Fucker . . . called me Miko's favorite slippery cunt," Kalico said through a dry whisper. "How far to water?"

"Doesn't matter"—Muldare's voice cracked—"I'll shoot any bastard tries to get in the way."

Kalico bent, tried to throw up, but only suffered from dry heaves. "Sucking snot," she whimpered. "That hurts."

Talina's heart had slowed to the point it was no longer trying to batter its way through her ribs. She smacked her dry lips, forced herself to sit up. Her fingers were torn and bloody from the climb when she picked up her rifle and crawled up next to Kylee and Flute.

People died of heat stroke. They were running out of time.

"What have we got, kid?"

Raising her head, it was to see the flat mesa top. Maybe fifty meters to the south, the first of the domes shimmered in the hot white light. A woman, wearing only a wrap around her hips, was standing in the shade of an old ramada this side of the dome.

Eat her, Demon hissed. *Moisture in her meat.*

"Go screw yourself," Talina muttered in return.

Demon chittered happily.

"There's just that one woman on guard." Kylee made a face. "What's with the scars these people have?"

Muldare, looking haggard, hitched her way up one-handed to take a look. "Marks a path for the souls of the people they eat. Or some such shit like that." The marine awkwardly unslung her rifle, laid it across the rock and tried to sight it. Hard to do one-handed on her weak side. "I could pot her from here. The way I feel? It'd be a pleasure."

"Yeah?" Talina asked, noticing how the marine's rifle wavered like a branch in the wind. Muldare'd be lucky if she could hit the dome on fully automatic, dehydrated and exhausted as she was. "And have the whole compound hear. Bet they'd come at a run. How many of them are there?"

"Maybe fifty adults? Maybe less. No telling." Muldare sucked at her dry lips, desperate eyes on the lone sentry. "If Batuhan sent all those people . . . down into the forest . . . to search for us? May only have a handful left. Look at us. Four of us got away . . . and Talbot and his wife . . . dead. That's half."

"I can handle it." Kylee reached down and pulled her long knife from its sheath. Sunlight glinted on the wicked blade's polished steel.

"Going to kill her?"

"Well, duh?" Kylee shot her a frost-blue look of disbelief. "My parents are *dead* because of these people. Mom and Mark came here to help them, and these fuckers drove them out into the forest."

Talina got a grip on Kylee's wrist. Squeezed. "No."

For a moment their gazes locked in a battle of wills. In the end, Kylee rolled her eyes, jerked her knife hand free, and asked, "So . . . what? We sing 'Coming Together Under the Bower' and make like best friends? I don't think so."

Talina glanced up at Capella. Figured the time at somewhere around eleven. The temperature, mixed with the humidity, was compounded now that they were in direct sun. Taglioni was already raving, Kalico at the stage of complete heat exhaustion. Dehydrated as they were, hyperthermia would kill them within the hour.

If that guard called out, brought twenty or thirty screaming Unreconciled soldiers charging down on top of them? What were any of their chances? Flute would unleash havoc among them. Tal'd open fire on full auto, mow them down to the last man, woman, or child.

So, what's a human life worth?

Talina slithered back down, picked up Taglioni's fancy hunting rifle with its waxed walnut, gleaming gold, and fancy inlay. She studied the thing, found the dial that controlled velocity in the pistol-grip's pommel. She set it to eleven hundred feet per second. Just subsonic.

Crawling up to her place again, she laid out prone, braced the rifle's forearm on a tuft of ferngrass.

As she got a sight picture, Muldare asked, "What are you doing?"

"Making the best of a shit-load of totally bad choices."

Talina settled the self-regulating sight on the woman's head, pressed the button on the sight that compensated for distance and trajectory, and took a breath. Letting it half out, she timed her heartbeat, and in midbeat, caressed the trigger.

The rifle barely uttered a *phfft*.

In the optic, the woman's head snapped back, her eyes gone wide. She dropped like a sack of potatoes. Kicked a couple of times and began to twitch.

"Why was that better than me knifing her?" Kylee demanded, her face in a pout.

"Because it's on my soul, not yours," Talina told her. "Muldare, you stay on guard. Flute, you make sure nothing happens to them. Kylee, you're with me."

Talina laid Taglioni's gleaming Holland & Holland to one side, took her service rifle, and not waiting to see if Kylee obeyed, sprinted for the curved side of the nearest dome.

She didn't bother to look at the woman she'd shot. Her peripheral vision was more than good enough to tell her the woman hadn't been killed outright.

With Kylee hot on her heels, Talina dared not take the time to finish the job. Instead she crept around the side of the dome, found the door, and unlatched it.

She slipped inside, closed it behind Kylee, and turned to cover the hallway with her rifle. Nothing. Just an empty corridor illuminated by a few flickering light panels.

"Where are we?" Kylee wondered under her breath.

"Science dome. Probably the last place Batuhan's maniacs would inhabit," Talina whispered. "Stay behind me."

She led the way down the hall, cleared the first two conference rooms, and then ducked into the lab. Looked to see that no one was hiding behind the counters. Even searched the hood and biocontainment room.

"Check the cabinets. We need clean jars. Jugs. Anything that will hold water." Talina ripped open the closest cabinets, finding empty shelves. In the next she found a couple bottles of alcohol, solvents, and a trio of one-gallon containers of nitric acid.

"Got it!" Kylee called, popping up from behind the counter with collapsible sample jars.

At the sink, Talina turned on the tap, cupped some and sniffed the water that trickled out. Kalico's techs had gone through the systems while under Bogarten's watchful eye. Smelled okay. She cupped it, sucking down handfuls. Waited while Kylee did the same. Now it would save the Supervisor's life.

"Come on. Come on," Talina groused as the slow flow began to fill the first jug. "Kylee. Go keep watch. Be just like our luck to have somebody stumble over that dead guard's body."

"What if they've overthrown Batuhan?"

"Then I just murdered a woman for no reason." *Yeah, right. Deal with that later.* "Now, go make sure the coast's still clear. Scoot."

Kylee vanished from the room.

What if they've overthrown Batuhan?

Talina ground her teeth. Tried not to think about it. The jugs filled with maddening slowness.

70

The soft sound of a fan finally penetrated the pounding headache. Next was a delightful and cooling mist that settled on Kalico's skin, followed immediately by a stirring of air that ran down her chest and belly, across the tops of her thighs, and all the way to her feet.

She swallowed hard, the action doubling the pain in her skull. She hadn't hurt this much since . . . since . . .

Her muzzy thoughts couldn't quite correlate the data.

"Here," a voice told her. "You need to drink again."

Kalico blinked as a hand lifted the back of her head. A glass was placed to her lips, and she sucked down the luke-warm water. Sighed as it hit her stomach. Then her head was lowered; a folded bundle of cloth served as a pillow. Overhead was a single light panel. Had to be daytime because Capella's beams were spilling in the window to her left. She lay on a low fold-out cot.

She gasped as the gentle mist settled on her skin again. Focusing, it was to see Kylee Simonov using a spray bottle to squirt Kalico's naked body.

Naked?

"Hey?" She tried to sit up. The blast of pain in her head caused her to whimper and ease her head back to the folded cloth.

"Stay put," Kylee told her. The kid had her head cocked, tangles of blonde hair falling around her shoulders. "Tal says you're going to feel like hammered shit for a while. But we've got to get you cooled down."

"Where's my clothes? Why the hell am I naked? What's going on?"

"You're in the science dome at Tyson Station. Stripping you down to the skin is the quickest way to lower your body temperature. No ice or cold water, so I get to squirt you and Dek down, then fan you to cool you off."

"Screw vacuum. What the hell happened to me?"

"Dehydration and heat," a weak voice told her from the side. She squinted against the headache, turned her head to the right to see Taglioni, his bone-thin and pale body as naked as hers where he lay on the adjoining bunk. The man looked positively miserable.

Kylee—positioned between them—turned and used her spray bottle, shooting him down from head to toe. Then she used a flat piece of plastic attached to what looked like a length of broom handle to waft air over his body.

"My head hasn't felt like this since I tried to empty a cask of Inga's whiskey all on my own," Kalico murmured. Then: "How the hell did we get here? Last I remember was on the cliff. Feeling sick. Ready to kill for a glass of water."

"Talina carried you both to the dome while Flute and I kept watch. Muldare made it on her own. She's asleep yonder."

Kalico followed Kylee's point to see Muldare. The marine was stripped down to her underwear, supine on what looked like a lab bench, a fan blowing across her body. Some kind of grease had been slathered over her swollen arm; from the angry-red color it must have hurt like a bastard.

"Drink." Kylee offered Taglioni her glass. The man finished it off. Set his head back on a small duraplast box that served him for a pillow. Then Kylee stepped over to a sink, set the empty glass under the dribbling tap, and returned with a full one.

Kalico was aware enough to suck it all down. Felt it seep through the empty hollow that was her stomach and into her aching limbs.

She asked, "If we're at Tyson, where are the Unreconciled?"

"Down at the admin dome," Kylee told her. "Tal and Flute are keeping an eye on them. Sooner or later they're going to figure out that the woman Tal shot is missing. When they do, it's really going to get complicated."

"What woman?" Taglioni asked.

Kylee turned, spared him one of her glacial-blue gazes. "They had a guard posted between us and this dome. Tal took her out with your rifle. I wanted to. She wouldn't let me."

"Took her out with my rifle?" Dek's expression indicated his confusion. "You mean, Talina shot her?"

Kylee tapped a finger to her forehead. "Pop! And down she went."

"Wasn't there some other way?" Dek asked.

"She was a cannibal. 'Cause of her, Mom and Mark are dead. What's to cry over?"

The cold tone in the girl's voice sent a shiver down Kalico's spine.

Meanwhile, Kylee shrugged, walked over, and started spraying Dek's body again. "Sure. We could have waited her out. Heat stroke being what it is, Tal, Flute, and I could have left your dead bodies down in that hollow. After dark we could have sneaked wherever we wanted. Stocked up on eats down at the garden, drank our fill from the cisterns. Slipped into the admin dome to get to the radio and sent an SOS to PA for a quick pickup down on the south end."

The girl switched her bottle for her fan, wafting it over Dek's body as she added, "So the guard is dead, and you, Kalico, and Briah are alive. Are you wishing Tal had played it the other way around?"

Dek's face had scrunched into an uncomfortable pinch. "Don't know. Hard to think rationally with this headache."

Kalico sighed as Kylee turned, sprayed her body again. She repeated, fitting the pieces together: "So, we're all in the science dome, and they're two domes away. Eventually someone's going find the dead guard's body. See that she's shot through the head. Realize where we are. This place got a back door?"

"Don't worry about the guard's body. It . . . went away. Let's just say that in the end, Donovan got her. Meanwhile we lay low. And yeah, there's a back door. But you're not ready to run. So, my advice? Go back to sleep. Tal and Flute are out there, keeping guard. We figure we're in the last place the cannibals would look for us."

"Flute is standing guard?" Kalico asked, delighted by the cool spray on her hot flesh. She felt beads of it running down the long lines of her scars. "What's he get out of all this?"

"Mostly he's fascinated," Kylee told her. "And a little worried."

"About Batuhan? This all goes sideways, Flute can fade into the forest, and they'll never find him."

"It's the forest that worries him." Kylee's face turned grim. "First, he'd be stranded here. If we don't take him, he's got no safe way back to his lineage. Normally that would be bad enough, because he'd be a rogue. The local lineages would hunt him down. Try and kill him."

"He didn't worry about that when he came here?"

"Sure. But it was only to pick up Mom and Dad and fly out. He wouldn't have been on the ground for more than a couple of hours at the most. When the airtruck was destroyed, Flute went on alert. Figured the local lineages would pick up his scent."

"Did they?"

Kylee waved the fan—cool breeze caressing Kalico's body. "That's the thing that's really got him worried. Not only did no local quetzals come after him, he didn't pick up their scent. Nothing. Not even old sign."

"I guess that's a relief." Kalico laid the back of her hand against her forehead. Wished it would ease the damn skull-splitting ache. Wished she had aspirin. She'd have given a fortune to cut the throbbing misery.

"Anything but," Kylee told her. "Flute thinks Tyson has been quetzal-free for years. Maybe all the way back to when this base was occupied."

"Flute thinks the people killed the quetzals?" Dek asked.

"In this mess of rocks and trees?" Kylee asked incredulously. "Humans wouldn't have a chance at exterminating an entire lineage. Forest is too thick. Hell, Tal's been hunting Whitey for three years in low bush, and he's still ahead of her."

"Then what's the explanation?" Kalico asked, head hurting too much to work out the intricacies.

"Flute thinks it's the thing that got Mom and Dad. Says he's got a memory. Something ancient. From the far west. He says the memory is only an image. A sort of black swinging spear shooting down from the sky."

"Sounds about right," Kalico whispered before Kylee put the glass to her lips. As she sucked down the water, her body seemed to give up.

She closed her eyes, laid her head back.

As she drifted into sleep, she heard Dek ask, "So, Flute thinks this thing's hunted all the quetzals? What can you do about it?"

"It took my parents," Kylee told him in a voice hinting at rage. "All I have to do is figure out how to kill it dead."

71

Vartan hurried down the hallway, burst through the doors into the cafeteria. He still felt weak, his muscles so sore that he limped. But his rising panic overwhelmed any physical discomforts.

People glanced up from where they sat at the tables. In a plush recliner brought in for her use, Shimal Kastakourias sat at the head of a long table immediately to the Messiah's right. On his left, Ctein Zhoa—the last of the First Chosen—served as a pitiful reminder of the Messiah's dying prestige.

For her part, Shimal shot Vartan a look fraught with worry. Her dark eyes were almost pleading, as if she were begging for anything but the honor of being the next Prophet. Vartan had always thought her a frail, mousy woman. Her training was as a solid-state board specialist capable of diagnosing and repairing sophisticated electronics, microscopes, computers, and the like.

Ignoring the plea in her eyes, Vartan went straight to the Messiah; the man had set his bone scepter aside to drink a cup of tea from the garden.

"Messiah, we've got trouble," Vartan said.

"Such as?"

"You remember all those crates we found while searching for the Supervisor down in the basement? One had a laser microphone for listening at long distances. I was down there to get a specimen pole to drag Svetlana's body away. Saw it. Thought it might be useful given our exposed location. Maybe give us a warning if the Supervisor's party and whoever was in that airtruck might be sneaking close."

"And?"

"And I charged it. Figured out where the best vantage point would be. Went up to the roof hatch. From up there I could see the whole compound. Figured I'd keep watch as the sun set. When I turned that mic on the science dome, it picked up conversations. There are people in the science dome."

"Perhaps some of our—"

"None of our people are called Supervisor, Dek, Muldare, or Kylee."

The Messiah's lips pursed, pulling down to elongate the hole that was his nose. "They are that close?"

"They are. From the conversation I overheard, something's wrong. The Supervisor, Dek, and Muldare are hurt, somehow disabled. Maybe wounded. But, more to the point, Talina Perez and someone called Flute are sneaking around the station, apparently keeping an eye on us. In the darkness out there, they could be anywhere."

The Messiah cocked his head slightly. "Perez and the others must have come on the airtruck. Where are Dya and Talbot?"

"Apparently dead. But I'm not positive. Might be that some creature in the forest got them. Something big. Maybe, for all I know, the same thing that got Mars and Hap. I can tell you this: They are hostile and planning some kind of action against us at first light."

The Messiah gave him a sloe-eyed glance. "How do you want to handle this?"

"They'll try for the radio. Any kind of action we might attempt against them, armed as they are, we'll have a lot of our people killed."

Ctein flinched. And well he might. He'd had to strip the flesh from the dead bodies of the First Chosen. His companions, friends, and fellows.

The Messiah set his tea down. "We have the armed drone."

"We do. And they have as many as three rifles. No telling how many more if Talina Perez was in that airtruck. And if we try to rush the science dome, she and this Flute person could decimate us with flanking fire. Especially on full auto."

One of those cold trickles of fear ran down Vartan's spine. "Messiah, if Perez has linked up with the Supervisor, she knows that we tried to kill Aguila. Given that she was in the airtruck, she's been in radio contact with the rest of

Donovan's people. You know what that means, don't you? They're going to be coming for us."

The Messiah inhaled sharply, the air whistling in his gaping nose. The black eyes seemed to flicker fearfully for an instant, then sharpened into that familiar cunning glint.

He turned to Shimal, who'd sat doe-eyed and uncertain through the entire conversation. "What do you think, Prophet?"

Vartan started. *Shimal? We are going to entrust our future to her?*

"These people?" Shimal asked. "They would attack us?"

Vartan sought some cue from the Messiah, got only a blank stare in return. The unblinking blue eye painted on the Messiah's forehead appeared fixed on eternity.

With nothing else to go on, Vartan said, "If they know we tried to kill the Supervisor and her party, attack would seem their most likely course of action. Think of how we'd feel if they'd tried to kill the Prophets, or even the Messiah, here?"

"And you say Supervisor Aguila is wounded?" the Messiah mused, his gaze going distant.

"She's being cared for. That's all I know."

"The science dome? That's just two domes away." Ctein's eyes shifted toward the north. "Not more than fifty meters from here. How did they get past Minette? She's supposed to be on guard up there."

"Maybe she never got the chance to warn us. Like so many, she's just gone. Vanished." Vartan drew a worried breath. "I'm really starting to hate this place."

"What about the armed drone?" the Messiah asked. "Second Will, can we use it against them? Kill them before they can strike us?"

"Not while they're in the dome. And don't forget, that Perez woman is out there somewhere. Probably waiting for reinforcements before she makes a try at us."

"How did this go so wrong?" Ctein asked under his breath. "Messiah, what do we do?"

Vartan caught a fleeting panic behind the Messiah's eyes, saw the man battle with himself, win the fight for calm. Ctein must have seen it, too, for he paled. Swallowed hard.

"Prophet?" the Messiah asked softly. "You have been touched by the universe, as were the others before you. What do you hear it say?"

Shimal's frantic gaze darted around the room, took in the people who sat at the cafeteria tables, riveted and listening. Had to see the fear reflected in their faces. The uncertainty.

The woman's voice broke as she said, "We need to be away from here. Gone. This place is death for us. Has been ever since that Supervisor brought us here."

Vartan would have laughed out loud. Be away? How? What did the woman expect? That they could just summon a shuttle? Fly off to . . . where? *Ashanti* wouldn't take them back. The Donovanians certainly didn't want them. And after they tried to kill and eat the Supervisor, she wasn't going to be in any kind of a forgiving mood.

The change, however, in the Messiah was immediate. The man smiled, a serenity in his expression. "The universe does not make mistakes. We shall leave."

He glanced Vartan's way. "Go back to your post, Second Will. Monitor our enemies. Take your rifle. It has a night optic as I remember. You should be able to see everything. If they try to break out of the science dome, shoot as many as you can. Keep them bottled up inside."

"Messiah?"

"In the meantime, we shall make our preparations."

"What preparations?" Vartan cried. "To go where? How?"

The Messiah raised a calming hand. "The universe has brought us this far. Place your trust in it, Second Will. This is just another test. One we shall pass as we have all the others. You must have faith. The universe will not let us down."

"But, don't you—"

"Have *faith,* Second Will. Now, you have your orders. I shall call on you when we're ready."

"Messiah, you can't—"

"*Faith!* Now go to your post."

Fighting his rising sense of dismay, Vartan bowed respectfully, backed away from the throne.

As he headed for the door, he glanced around. Took in

the watching Irredenta. Eighteen of them, mostly pregnant or nursing women. The rest, who were outside standing watch, numbered seven—including those guarding the children in the barracks—six if Minette was gone.

Leave? To where? They had already reached the end of the line.

"What do you believe, Vartan?" he whispered under his breath. That the universe would provide?

But his only answer was silence.

72

Miguel Galluzzi turned, hearing more of the maniacal laughter. *Freelander* seemed to be compressing the air, making it hard for him to breathe. He stared frantically up and down the poorly lit hallway, past Astrogation Control. Thought he saw a thin woman staring at him from the shadows. But for the long black hair, she might have been Tyne. Or, locked in the AC, had she let her hair grow?

"Captain?" Shig asked.

Galluzzi's heart began to pound, a foul taste on his tongue. A panic like he'd never known sent a tickle through his guts. Thoughts went dead in his head. He couldn't stand it. Had to get away. Miguel turned, ran, frantic to get away from that awful door, that eerie and haunted hallway.

Mindless, he pounded down the corridor. Powered by terror. A cry strangled in his throat.

"Captain? Miguel! Stop!" Shig's voice barely penetrated the heterodyne of fear.

Crazed, thoughtless, Galluzzi's feet hammered the deck. At the companionway, he instinctively turned: an animal in desperate flight, seeking only to hide.

Taking the stairs two at a time, he rounded the landing, charged out onto the Crew Deck, and fled pell-mell down the flickering corridor. Winded, he staggered to a stop, peering fearfully up and down the dimly lit passage. Nothing. Eerily empty, as if robbed of space itself. The effect was as if part of the very air, sialon, and light were missing. The reality he saw had the curious property of being incomplete.

Well, but for the endless lines of overwritten script.

Galluzzi tried to catch his breath, wheezed. His heart fought desperately to beat its way through his ribs.

Exhausted, Galluzzi slumped against the wall, felt his trembling legs give way. He slid down the smooth surface to curl into a ball. Across from him, barely legible in the looping script, he could scry out the words: *With each breath inhale the essence of the dead.*

Tears began to well, silvering his vision. Was that what he was doing? Inhaling the dead?

Tyne Sakihara, beautiful Tyne, with her soft dark eyes, petite nose, and charming smile. Dead. Up there. A moldering skeleton?

He'd loved her with a full and uninhibited passion. Figured that ultimately, after they'd exhausted their careers, in the end they'd be together. Married. The two of them had fit together that well. Soulmates. Of course they'd taken different berths, separated for the time being. That was mandatory. Part of the sacrifice officers made in Corporate spacing.

I saw her. He ground his teeth in grief and despair. He was as sure of that as he was of gravity.

Galluzzi scrubbed at his eyes with the heels of his palms. Tried to press the image of Tyne's face from his memory.

Her voice sounded so clear she might have been standing over him: "I saw the first of the bones, you know."

Galluzzi winced, tried to tuck himself into a smaller ball, to collapse his body until he could squeeze himself completely out of the universe.

Unbidden, the image formed in his mind: a jumbled pile of macerated human bones made a meter-tall mound on the floor. They had been dumped in a confused heap in the middle of the Crew's Mess, cleared as it was of tables and chairs. A brown-haired woman wearing a shift knelt in the center of the room. She held a string to the floor. A second woman, holding the other end of the string taut, walked in a slow arc. With a scribe she marked out a perfect circle.

"We were no longer in command," Tyne's voice explained. "The decision had been made that death and life were one. That only through death could life survive. Wherever *Freelander* had gone was eternal. Tried reversing the symmetry. Didn't work."

She paused, then added, "Jem and I made the decision to euthanize the transportees. It was our last act of kindness.

No one could explain why, but we were infertile. The women didn't conceive. Couldn't make *Freelander* a generation ship. So it was just us. Living off the dead."

Galluzzi clamped his eyes tight, pressed harder with his palms, but try as he might, he couldn't stop the vision. If anything, it clarified as if he were there in the Crew's Mess.

One of the women began using a vibrasaw to cut a shallow trench in the mess floor, following the scribed circle. The other began wiring the femora together, carefully choosing each for the proper length.

"Jem and I didn't want to end like that," Tyne told him. "It was crazy. The Chief Engineer used a cutting torch on the ship's AI. So we locked ourselves in the AC. Stayed there until it was clear that *Freelander* was lost. That we were going to be in that room forever."

"How could you?"

In his mind, Tyne smiled at him. Love, like he remembered so clearly, shone in her eyes. "In the end there is no right, no wrong. We are nothing more than chemical composites of carbon-based molecules that are directed by chemo-electrical impulses designed to allow the highest probability of replicating those same chemical composites. Billions and billions of us. Anything else, like ethics, morality, notions of deity, ultimate good or evil, are nothing more than abstractions. We need those delusions to mask the reality of what life is. They provide us with a sense of purpose."

The Crew's Mess was filling with people now. Crew in uniforms showing various states of repair. He watched as they began lifting the wired-together femora, raising them like a wall and fitting them into the trench excavated into the floor.

They're building that creep-freaked dome of bones!

"Do you know that I still love you?" he asked.

"Cling to whatever you have, Miguel. In the end, it's the only thing that makes existence worth enduring."

In the Crew's Mess, the *Freelander* crew were separating all of the arm bones from the jumbled pile.

73

Where she lay in the shadow of a defunct air compressor, Talina watched through her rifle's optic. She'd dialed the magnification up, which gave her a good look at the man. Maybe early forties, black hair, dark eyes. He was perched on the top of the admin dome. Every so often, he'd raise the rifle he held and use its optic to scan the compound. Most of his time he spent listening with a long-range microphone. He kept the laser fixed on the science dome window.

From the moment Talina had seen the thing, it was apparent that the Unreconciled knew exactly who was stalking around Tyson Station, and who was in the science dome.

Which meant what when it came to relative strengths and who might move on whom?

They knew Muldare, Taglioni, and Kalico had weapons. And might even know Muldare was wounded, and that Kalico was sick. If they'd heard that Talbot was dead, they'd know his weapons had been retrieved. Kylee—young though she might be—was half quetzal and enraged over the deaths of Mark and Dya. No telling what kind of havoc the kid might unleash on both the Unreconciled and herself in the process.

Talina pasted her cheek to the rifle's stock. Sighted through the optic. Took a series of deep breaths to oxygenate her blood, exhaled, and watched the dot settle on the watcher. All it would take was a couple of pounds of pressure on the trigger, and the dome-top rifleman's head would be jelly.

Maybe it was guilt over the woman she'd shot. Maybe it was the tortured expression on the man's face. The guy looked like he was wrestling with too many demons of his own. She slipped her finger back to the rest above the trigger.

The soft chittering came from behind.

Talina used her elbows to crawl back, rise to a seat, and glance at Flute. "Find anything useful?"

The quetzal flashed a pattern of infrared that read, "Young in half bubble. Three adults watch."

"Kids are in the barracks dome," she said to herself. "Not more than an hour ago, someone hurried from the admin dome to the barracks."

She ducked down as the door to the admin dome across the way opened. A handful of people, mostly women, hurried out and headed for the barracks. They were talking softly, shooting scared looks at the night as they went.

Talina heard the words, ". . . in the morning" and "Where will . . . go?" The rest was confused babble.

Talina checked the dome-top guard. His attention was fixed on the people beating feet to the barracks.

Using the distraction, Talina sprinted to the edge of the shop dome, out of the lookout's sight.

Flute, like a dark cloud, followed silently, his hide patterning the ground in perfect camouflage. Wouldn't work if the dome-top guard had his IR turned on.

At the rear of the science dome, Talina rapped three times. Waited. Rapped twice more.

Seconds later the lock clicked open, and the door swung out.

Talina sent Flute in first, then followed, locking the door behind her. The young quetzal, almost two meters at the hips, filled the hallway, claws clicking on the duraplast.

"So," Kylee asked from up front. "What did you—"

Talina put a finger to her lips.

After Flute had deposited himself in the conference room and was out of the way, Talina leaned close, whispering in Kylee's ear, "They've got a long-range microphone fixed on the lab window. They've been listening to everything we said."

Kylee's blue eyes widened as she mouthed the words, "They know we're here?"

Talina gave her a quick nod, whispered, "How're the others?"

"Sleeping." Kylee frowned, staring off toward the lab door. With a finger she beckoned Talina toward the conference room. This was on the science dome's north side, shielded from any eavesdropping by the snooper's laser mic. Closing the door, Kylee asked, "So, what are they planning?"

"Don't know. My guess? Something with explosives. They tried that on Kalico and your folks to start with. Given that we're armed, it's the best way to try and take us down." She glanced up at the ceiling. Just ordinary duraplast. Proof against wind, rain, and hail, it wouldn't stand a chance against magtex. "If they've got a demolition expert, he could crack this roof open like an eggshell."

"Eggs have shells? Thought they were just soft membranes the sperm had to get through."

"Not many chickens down at Mundo, huh?"

"Oh, you mean birds. I've seen pictures. For some reason Mom wasn't big on terrestrial ornithology."

At the mention of her mother, Kylee's eyes tightened, her jaw firming.

Talina knew that look. "Don't even think it. For the moment, we've got other responsibilities. First there's Kalico and Dek. I need you to keep them safe. Will you do that for me?"

"Those fucking cannibals killed Mom and Mark."

"How about you and I take it up with Messiah Batuhan when we get Kalico, Dek, and Muldare out of here. Deal?"

Kylee gave her that searching look. Finally said, "Deal."

"Good. Now, let's go sit next to the window where that guy on top of the dome can hear, and spin all kinds of stories about how we're attacking the dome with rifles, grenades, and seismic charges sometime in midmorning, shall we?"

"And what are we really doing?"

"Slipping out the back way about an hour before dawn. While they hit the science dome, we're flanking them at admin. At the same time they're busy blowing this place up, Flute and I are barging into the radio room to call the PA shuttle to come pick us up."

"Flute?"

"Can you think of a better way to terrorize a bunch of soft meat?"

"Wish you wouldn't use that term when you're talking about cannibals."

"Good point."

74

More than anything, Dan hated being afraid. He'd lived his entire childhood in fear. The consuming, soul-numbing kind. His pedophile father had used Dan's fear like a sharp blade to separate him from any thought of rebellion or betrayal. Wielded it masterfully to keep Dan compliant and an accomplice in the man's perverse sexual proclivities.

When, at sixteen, Dan had killed his first victim, the act washed through him like a revelation: he had power. A realization that reinforced itself like the rebar in a concrete wall when he'd stood over Asha Tan's dead body a mere year later. That he never suffered a moment's remorse was, he realized, a blessing. One that he could never fully comprehend but deeply appreciated.

Despite the bone-chilling fear in his youth, he'd never known it like he did in that plexiglass box: numbing, crushing, soul-devouring. And all the while, Windman's severed head was mashed against the plastic. The nose had been flattened against the transparency; the lips had pulled back, mouth gaping with the bugs crawling in and out and up the nostrils. Those eyes—drying, shrinking, turning gray—kept watching Dan with a haunting gaze. The damn head mocked him, belittled his impotence. A witness to Dan Wirth's total helplessness and terror.

All of it was compounded by the suffering heat, the thirst, and hopelessness.

Just when he could take no more, when he was on the verge of unlatching the door and throwing it wide, a quetzal would appear. The thing would gnaw on the box or attack it with those razor claws. Helpless and mesmerized, Dan would watch shavings of plastic curl away under the blade-like teeth or peel in strips as the claws carved off long curlicues of material.

By the time the first rays of dawn had lightened the eastern horizon, they'd chewed a hole in the corner just above Dan's head. The smell of quetzal breath had choked him.

He'd been delirious by then, fantasizing a thousand nightmarish images. In some he was back in his father's bed, hearing the old man's cooing voice as he forced Dan from one degrading act to another. Or in Hong Kong, ducking and running as Corporate security forces hunted him, chased him past piles of dead rioters, their bodies all interlaced.

Then had come the numb surrender into oblivion . . .

Windman's head was hanging in a gray haze, talking to him. The man's voice couldn't quite penetrate the plastic. Sounded muffled and indistinct.

Fucking prick. What a candy-dicked screw up. Couldn't make himself understood, even in death.

A piercing sting in Dan's arm shattered the image, caused him to start. To pay full attention.

"He's coming around." This was a woman's voice, not Windman's.

"Dan?"

He knew that voice: Allison. But how had she gotten into the box with him?

He tried to speak, heard a rasping.

"Dan? Wake up."

His head hurt. When he tried to swallow, it was with effort, and a terrible taste filled his mouth.

He got his eyes open, blinked his vision clear. Saw a ceiling. And then Ali leaned over, a reserve behind her blue eyes, tension in her lips. "Dan? Can you hear me?"

"Yeah," he croaked. The rasping? That was his voice? "What the fuck?"

Raya Turnienko leaned into his field of view. "You almost died. We have you stabilized, rehydrated, and you're on an electrolyte and sucrose drip. Your organs are rebounding. You'll be weak for a day or two, but there's no permanent damage."

"I was . . . in that fucking box. Quetzals."

Allison crossed her arms, studying him with an unnerving intensity. Disoriented as Dan was, he could see the change in her. Something dangerous and new. Predatory. Reminded him of the fucking quetzals that had been chewing on that shit-sucking box.

"You know," Allison observed, "it's a miracle that you got into that arbor box. As it was, another hour or two, and you would have shut down. We'd be digging a grave for you up at the cemetery. As it is, Fred Han Chou only needs a soil auger to dig a hole big enough for Windman's head."

Dan winced. That fart-sucking head. The fricking thing was going to fill his nightmares from here on out as it was. Maybe he'd go up and piss on the thing's final resting place.

"When can I get out of here?"

"Tomorrow . . . if there are no complications," Raya told him.

To Allison, he croaked, "What's happening at The Jewel?"

"Shin, Vik, and Kalen have it under control. Everyone's delighted that you're alive."

He heard the lie in that. Fought down a cold sliver of anger. Anger? Why? What the hell did he care?

The image of three deadly eyes in a huge triangular head filled his memory. He could feel the vibrations as teeth chewed away plastic. *The snot-sucking thing wanted to eat me.*

Now that he'd made it, his people couldn't have cared less.

I've got two big safes filled with plunder.

And what was he going to do with them?

"Did Taglioni come back?"

Allison's eyebrow quivered, as if in a question. "He's out with Talina at Tyson Station. Something's gone really wrong out there. There's been no contact."

So, the rich prick was probably quetzal shit, or maybe lunch for a bunch of cannibals.

"Figures. My fucking luck." *I could have gotten out.*

I think of the story of the garden near the brook of Kedron. I think about it often. That place where another messiah faced his darkest hours. Of all the messiahs, his story speaks the loudest in this particular moment of tribulation.

Am I forsaken?

Have I failed the universe?

Committed some unforgiveable sin?

It cannot be pride, for I have always doubted my worthiness. Wondered why the universe chose me, of all men, to shoulder the crushing responsibility. I have always lived in terror that I might fail.

Faith has been the unyielding pillar inside me, my shield and justification. Faith is a wonderful thing: Just believe, and it will carry you through.

It always has.

And now, in the midnight of my soul, when I am shaken with doubt, I have to ask: What more do you want of me? Haven't I given enough? Haven't my people?

We have sacrificed so much, suffered, endured, and prayed in desperation. Didn't we prove ourselves through trial and fire during our incarceration on Deck Three? Didn't Prophecy promise us that we would begin anew, grow, mature, and flourish on Capella III before venturing forth in service of the universe?

What we have found here is heartbreaking. In a matter of days, so many are irretrievably dead. In defiance of Prophecy, they are lost forever. I am bereft, crying, "Why?" as I stare up at the night sky.

What if it was all a lie?

I look at the faces of my people. They are so close to desolation and defeat. More so than even during the days of the Harrowing and Cleansing.

The human soul can only endure so much: close to eight years of suffering, with only a nebulous arrival at Capella

III to buoy their hopes. Like an intangible dream. But they clung to the seemingly impossible aspiration.

And then the miracle: Release from Deck Three into the light.

Only to be ultimately betrayed.

Hope, promises, anticipation.

Everything we believed.

All a deadly deception.

Was I the greatest of deceivers?

Those are the questions that haunt me. Now I am faced with a bone-numbing decision: Do I trust in the voice of an untried Prophet? Is Shimal truly the voice of the universe? She has said we need to leave.

To go . . . where?

The only avenue left that I can see is to set forth into the forest. To venture into the wilderness as the Prophets of ancient Earth did.

But, if I can believe the warnings given by Vartan, the forest is death.

What am I to do?

What do I trust?

Where is salvation for me and my people?

The universe does not make mistakes!

I must believe. I must believe!

75

Vartan fought to stay awake. Overhead, clouds had obscured the night sky. Lightning flashed off to the east, flickers of it illuminating tortured and twisting clouds. The heavens had turned angry, as if to express their rage against all things.

It had been so long since Vartan had seen lightning. Almost what? Two decades? Maybe more. He fixed his staggering attention on the distant flashes. Desperate to keep his eyes open.

Had he ever been this exhausted?

His head, falling forward, banged painfully off the rifle, brought him awake. Flashes strobed in wicked white that shaped the clouds into eerie lanterns. They bathed the humps of treetops, turned the forest into an impossible landscape.

As Vartan resettled himself, listening to the night chime, he felt the shudder of steps leading up to the hatch.

Ctein called, "It's me," before appearing below.

"Storm coming," Vartan told him through a yawn.

The first distant boom of thunder rolled over the forest. Ctein turned where he stood half out of the hatch. "We're leaving just before dawn."

"That's crazy. Following Shimal out into the forest?"

"Here's the plan," Ctein told him. "The Messiah, the women, and children will form up, march down to the southern end of the mesa. They're going to take the trail down to the trees. They'll wait there. Watch. When the Supervisor's people find the base abandoned, they will walk out in the open. When they do, we use the drone to swoop in close, and detonate it."

Vartan rubbed his eyes, tried to get circulation back into his arms and legs. Anything to recharge his flagged energy. Shit on a shoe, his head felt full of fuzz.

"Listen to me. Ctein, I know you were among the First

Chosen. But this is wrong. Batuhan is wrong. What worked on Deck Three isn't working here. Anyone who goes down that trail is going to die."

A flash of lightning betrayed the man's incredulous look. "Do you know what you're saying? The Messiah gave you an order."

More lightning flashed in arhythmical patterns in the east. The low rumbling of thunder was louder now.

"He did. And I'll do it." The gravity, the exertions, the endless hours since he'd slept last, it all came to weigh on his weary soul.

The only two women in his life—Shyanne, whom he'd married, and Svetlana whom he'd loved—were gone. One, grieving and heartbroken, had escaped to who knew what fate, the other a rotting corpse that he himself had tumbled over the edge of the cliff. He'd watched in horror as her body smacked off rocks on the way down, each impact shooting colorful specks of invertebrates and bodily fluids until the corpse came to rest on a ledge far below.

Am I really living this shit?

He chuckled hollowly. "Go on, Ctein. Tell the Messiah that I'm taking matters in hand. He's not to worry about a thing. Just follow the Prophet's instructions." A beat. "And yes, tell him I have faith in the universe."

Just not the same as he does.

76

Carrots, garlic, and cabbage weren't Dek's idea of the finest of meals, but given that A, they had taste, B, they were incredibly nutritious, and C, that he'd been half-starved, he considered it one of the finest meals he'd ever eaten.

Talina had boiled the haul in a pan over a Bunsen burner. Then she'd stood guard as he, Kalico, and Muldare had finished off the stew and guzzled water.

The headache was now at half-strength, his muscles still wobbly, but his blood sugar was climbing. All in all, one hell of an improvement over the wreck he'd been.

Talina and Kylee had saved his life—not to mention Kalico Aguila's and Briah Muldare's in the bargain. Had to admire a woman like that.

Having left the science dome via the back door, Dek followed along behind Talina as rain fell from a midnight-black sky and lightning—in shapes reminiscent of an old man's tortured and throbbing veins—streaked, banged, and boomed. Didn't matter that he was sick-puppy weak, his stomach rebellious from having overeaten. Fact was, he was alive. Lot to be said for that.

In a contrast as stark as night and day, where he'd been in danger of dying of heat prostration, cold rain now pelted him in a staccato of big drops. Lightning knotted and pulsed in momentary misery—to vanish into afterimages of blackness. He was on the verge of shivering, and his breath fogged white in the flashes of actinic light. Didn't seem fair.

With lightning illuminating the way; he stepped over a section of pipe, careful to keep his rifle covered with the tarp Talina had provided him as a sort of rain poncho. He had the thing draped over his head, held the seams together at his throat. Must have looked like a pious Roman seeking the counsel of the gods.

Behind him, Kalico splashed along in his tracks, a similar tarp keeping her from the downpour.

"Watch your step there," he told her. "Don't trip on the pipe."

"I see it," she returned in little better than a whisper.

"How you feeling? Let me know if—"

"I'm a world of better. Thought I was going to die. Never would have made it but for that energy bar you gave me. Thanks for that. I owe you."

"My pleasure."

"Shhh!" Talina turned back, irritated.

Yeah, right. Some sort of distance microphone. As if they'd be heard over the roar of the rain where it beat on domes, in puddles, and racketed on old equipment. Not to mention the banging thunder, the crashing of the skies.

"Careful," Talina hissed, pointed. "That's the cliff right there."

Dek squinted through the fold in his tarp, caught the contrast between rock and dark pre-dawn empty space. He stepped right, veering away from the edge. Wouldn't that be the shits? Travel all this way, survive *Ashanti*, the forest, and heat stroke, just to fall to his death because of a misstep?

They were edging along the eastern side of the mesa, slipping between occasional aquajade trees that clung to the precipice. The figuring was that the Unreconciled would be planning an assault on the science dome, would be expecting them to sneak down the western side of the escarpment where the line of sheds would provide cover.

Briah Muldare—arm in a sling—brought up the rear. Holding her weapon one-handed, she kept sweeping her IR-enhanced rifle sight back and forth to ensure they weren't being followed.

Kylee and the quetzal had vanished somewhere into the storm.

Dek stumbled over an irregularity, caught himself just shy of sprawling face-first, and wished mightily for night vision.

The looming side of a shipping container brought him up short.

Talina took him by the hand, led him forward and into

the dark interior. Then she collected Kalico and Briah, saying, "I want you to stay here. Out of the rain. We're opposite the admin dome. From the front of the container you've got an effective field of fire in all directions. They can't take you by surprise, and they'd be idiots to try and rush you."

"And if they do?" Briah asked.

"We shoot them down," Kalico growled.

Dek winced, realizing what a slaughter it would be given Muldare's and Kalico's fully automatic weapons. At least for as long as the ammo lasted. Not to mention if the right-handed Muldare could even control the recoil with her weak-side left hand. Then there was Kalico's pistol, his Holland & Holland, and finally his pistol.

"Dek," Talina said.

"Yes?"

"The only threat to your position here is that rifle they took from Carson. Your job is to shoot whomever wields it. Take your time, breathe, and barely touch the trigger. Yours is the most accurate weapon we have at distance."

He took a nervous breath. "Right."

Talina laid a hand on his shoulder, was staring him in the eyes—though in the darkness all he saw was two dark spots in her night-shadowed face. Her voice dropped. "You understand, don't you?"

"Understand?"

"That when they tried to blow up the Supervisor, Dya, Talbot, and Muldare, it was for keeps. Just like when they killed Carson. It's not academic. Not a game. You're going to have to kill people before they kill you."

"I understand." Just saying it sent a ripple through his soul.

"You're sure?" Muldare asked as she peered out into the night. "You're the weak link here. The rich boy who never had blood on his hands. You hesitate at the wrong moment, we all die as a result."

Kalico said, "I could take the H&H. I've become a pretty good shot with a rifle. Save you the—"

"I got it," Dek said through a hard exhale, feeling his heart begin to race. "I kill the person with Carson's rifle. Make sure they can't use it against us." He raised a hand to still any reply. "Listen, I lived for years with the knowledge of what the Unreconciled were doing down on Deck Three. Had nightmares about them sneaking up in the middle of the night. Cutting me open while I was alive. And eating my . . . Well, never mind. I got this, okay?"

Talina slapped him on the shoulder. "You're becoming my favorite Taglioni."

"And how many of us have you met?"

"Just you. Talk about having an unfair advantage, huh?"

"What's your plan, Tal?" Kalico asked.

"Link up with Kylee and Flute. They're out on the flank, keeping watch. Once the cannibals move on the science dome, we make our play for the radio." She smacked a hand to her rifle. "With this and a quetzal, I'm pretty sure that I can get in and out. Once Flute roars and flashes his collar, I may not even have to kill anyone."

"Assuming Carson's weapons are deployed against the science dome," Kalico finished. "If their shooter is in the admin hallway when you burst in, that would change the equation."

"There's that." Talina shifted, stepping out into the rain. "As long as we see each other at the same time, it all comes down to who's faster. Their shooter, or me."

"Good luck," Kalico said softly as the woman vanished into the night.

Dek slipped out of his tarp, laid it to the side.

Muldare had taken a position at the open door. With her sore arm braced, she squatted against one wall as she swept the area between them and the admin dome with her IR sight.

Dek slipped his Holland & Holland from his shoulder, checked the charge and the setting.

"And now we wait, huh?"

Muldare said, "I've just scanned that roof hatch Talina told us about. It's closed. From now till dawn, it's just a matter of me spotting him before he can spot us. But hopefully that shooter is preoccupied, preparing to blow the shit out of the science dome. They do that, and rush the ruins, we got them."

"How's the arm?"

"Fucking hurts. I tell you, after this, I can stand anything. Raya could pull my teeth and I wouldn't need an anesthetic."

Dek, his rifle across his lap, sank down, back to the wall beside Kalico. "We come all this way. Cross thirty light-years, survive by the skin of our teeth, and we're trying to kill each other?"

Muldare whispered, "We gave them every chance. Came here to help them. Sometimes you gotta stamp out rot where you find it." Under her breath, she added, "Come on, fuckers. Step out and give me an excuse to shoot, will you?"

Lightning strobed again, illuminating the admin dome across the way. In that instant, Dek saw someone emerge. "Got movement."

He pulled up his rifle. Used the sight's IR to watch a woman hunch against the rain and run toward the barracks dome next door.

"Wonder what that's all about?"

"That's where the children are," Muldare said. "Assuming our intelligence is right."

"Children," Dek whispered. "So, we kill all the adults? What are we going to do with the kids? Murder them, too? Hold them responsible for the accident of their birth?"

In the back, Kalico murmured, "Scarred like they are, they're branded for life. No matter where they go, what they do, they'll be known as man-eaters from here on out. Talk about outcasts, there's no coming back from that kind of stigma."

"I wouldn't want 'em around," Muldare muttered under her breath. "It'd give me the creep-freaks every time I saw them."

Lightning almost blinded him: Thunder cracked in a detonation that jarred him half out of his skin. Might have been a condemnation from the gods.

With careful fingers, Vartan inserted his hand-crafted detonator and pressed it into the square of magtex with gentle and even force. As he did, the storm roared; waves of rain kept pounding the dome overhead. He huddled in the radio room, squinting in the dim illumination provided by the last functioning light panel.

What was he forgetting? His fatigue-addled brain wasn't working. Be a miracle if he didn't blow himself up.

On the table sat the radio. The last link to the outside world. The place Aguila's people would ultimately try for.

He started as a violent crash of thunder shivered the dome around him. Rattled him clear to his bones. Left him panting, scared half out of his wits. Loud bangs that sent the heart skipping weren't a good combination when fooling around with explosives.

It was the Messiah's order. Vartan should have thought of booby-trapping the radio room. Should have been stone-cold obvious. That he hadn't was a sign of his exhaustion. His fear and despair.

The Messiah's latest orders were that they leave at first light. Just as soon as they could see. Ctein would lead the way, followed by the women and the children. Then the Prophet and Batuhan, with Vartan and the three remaining men in the rear. The supposition was that in that order, Shimal would be protected.

Shimal, for God's sake? She was the Prophet now? The universe's voice to humanity?

Prior to her first muscle spasms, her growing problems with coordination, she'd been notable only for her fertility, having borne the Messiah four children in the eight years of their captivity in *Ashanti*. What possible reason did the universe have for choosing a woman as meek and submissive as Shimal?

To look at her now that she'd been chosen was to see the

fear bright in her dark eyes, the quivering of her jaws, and disquiet on her thin face. From her expression, she was more prone to throwing up than imparting the universe's wisdom.

And she orders us to leave?

Under his breath, Vartan whispered, "Damn it, Messiah, why don't you listen to sense?"

Where would they find food? According to the reports, nothing but some of the local animals was edible. Not to mention descending the south trail to the forest.

The forest?

Vartan been there. Watched his team die and vanish before his eyes. Petre's team had taken the north trail. And disappeared without a trace. This wasn't symmetry inversion, not even null singularity physics. The math was simple: leave this place and die.

Now, based on Shimal's utterance in a moment of confusion and terror, the Unreconciled were going to trust themselves to that selfsame horror? They were going to believe that the universe would protect them?

Vartan blinked against the gritty feeling in his eyes. Wiped his hands on his loin wrapping, and carefully prepared a length of thin copper wire from a spool he'd found in one of the sheds. This he tied to the detonator. Stringing it out, he tied the other end to the chair leg.

Whoever pulled out the chair would topple the block of magtex. As it tilted, the battery would shift, closing the circuit. And bang!

Checking his handiwork, Vartan used a wad of wrapping paper to conceal his bomb where it sat in the corner.

Not that he was much of a demolitions man, but he figured the corner of the room would help to direct the force of the blast against whomever might pull out the chair.

He heard steps. Looked up. Marta, her expression as lined and worried as Vartan had ever seen, stood in the doorway. "You about ready? There's a graying in the east. We can see well enough to go."

"It's raining like hell out there."

"And we don't want to be here when the Supervisor's people attack. We've got maybe an hour before they charge out of the science dome and start shooting."

He sniffed, tried to rub the exhaustion from his eyes. Took two tries to stagger to his feet. "You ever wonder how we got to this point?"

"We are the chosen," she said, repeating the words as rote. "The forces of darkness are going to resist. They have no other recourse. Until we bring about the Annihilation and Purification, even the atoms will oppose us."

"Spoken like a true believer," he said as he lifted the heavy rifle from where he'd leaned it against the doorjamb. Outside in the hallway, he picked up the drone controls. Wondered if the thing could even fly in the storm. Damn it, if the drone was grounded, they'd lost their most potent defense.

Marta's hazel eyes barely flickered. "And what are you, Vartan? You're the only one of the Messiah's Will left. What else do we have but faith? Those people out there want us *dead*!"

"Not that we left them with much choice."

She indicated the drone controls. "That going to work?"

"Hope so. Outside of the booby traps, it's our only chance. I might shoot one or two, but they'll get me in the end."

In a voice like acid, she said, "So good to know that you're optimistic. Shall I go tell the Messiah we're ready?"

"I guess . . . Well, hell, why not?" Vartan winced, forced himself to plod wearily down the hallway to the double doors that opened out front.

Peering through the windows, he could barely make out the faint shapes of aquajade across the flat, the square outline of the old shipping container. From this angle, he couldn't see the low hump of the barracks where Bess Gutierrez and the other women should have been preparing the children.

The children. Eighteen of them left. The rest taken by Donovan. Some vanished, others dead in pain and suffering.

"They were supposed to be the future. Immortal."

The futility of it all, like lead in his heart, left him on the verge of weeping. He could see each and every one of those kids' faces. Thin little girls and boys, the ones who'd laughed and jumped their way down the steps as they left *Ashanti*. Who'd bounced and played in Capella's light. All that hope, about to be extinguished in Batuhan's mad dash to the forest.

So much for the Revelation of immortality.

Flashes of lightning, like a staccato, illuminated the yard outside. Thunder banged, rolled, and echoed in reply.

No one in their right mind would stumble out into a downpour like this.

Come dawn, the Supervisor's people were coming. They'd be toting rifles, and as he'd heard through the long-distance mic, they'd be coming for blood.

He remembered the look in Shyanne's eyes as she pleaded with him to leave. Not for the first time since she'd stolen the airtruck, he wondered if she hadn't been the smart one.

"Ah, Second Will!"

Vartan turned at the Messiah's enthusiastic call. The man came strolling down the hallway, his bone scepter in hand. Behind him came Ctein—the last of the First Chosen. Then Shimal, her arm interlocked with Marta's.

Time to go.

It hit home like a thrown rock: The Messiah was leaving the throne of bones behind. No one remained to carry it.

Vartan slung the rifle, retrieved a hooded poncho he'd hung by the door, and draped it over his shoulders. No way he could bring the rifle into action, covered as it was, but he'd be damned if he'd be soaked to the bone. And more to the point, he needed two hands for the drone control. He'd be last in line. Awaiting the moment the Supervisor's group charged the admin doors.

He had to time it just right. Dive the thing—kamikaze like—right into the middle of them before he hit the detonator switch. One shot. Damn it, he *had* to do this right.

Vartan led the way out into the deluge, rain battering at the hood. Barely able to see, he slopped his way to the barracks, praying that the Messiah would declare the weather too wretched for the evacuation.

78

"*Tal?*" Kalico's voice sounded in Talina's com bud. "*Batuhan, two men, and two women, just left the admin dome. They're headed south. Can't see Carson's rifle, but one of the men was holding something in two hands. Some kind of controls.*"

Talina wiggled into the lee of one of the sheds, partially sheltered from the downpour. Peering around the corner, she watched the cannibals splash their sodden way to the barracks, where one by one they ducked inside. Draped as he was in a poncho that shadowed his face, she couldn't be sure if the last one in line was the dark-haired shooter, or carried a weapon, but he did hold something in his hands.

Accessing her com, she said, "Sort of argues against them making a try for the science dome, doesn't it? Unless they've decided to relocate the Messiah out of harm's way."

"*Roger that. Makes us wonder where all the rest of them are. They had twenty-five men, right? Lost three to Talbot, and another fled to the Briggs' place. We saw one being eaten by a tooth flower.*"

"Yeah, and you'd figure that Donovan got a few more of them along the way." She made a face. "But how many?"

"*Maybe a lot, Tal. Think about it. They've only had women on guard. Is that because the men are missing or reassigned to some other task?*"

"Like preparing a hot welcome for us when we arrive outside the admin dome?"

"*Got me. Wish we had a drone.*"

"Yeah. Me, too. Listen, we're not in a hurry. I'm going to slip over to where Kylee's keeping watch. Maybe she and Flute know something."

"*Roger that.*"

It took Talina ten minutes to ghost her way around the sheds to the south side where Kylee was supposed to be. Even then, she almost missed the girl.

"Ta Li Na. You going somewhere? Or just enjoying the rain after being half cooked for a couple of days?"

Talina craned her neck, which let cold water run down into one of the last warm and dry places on her body. Kylee lay belly-down under a piece of duraplast sheeting. Stared up as a flash of lightning illuminated her stony blue eyes.

"What do you see, kid? According to our count we're suddenly short of a bunch of cannibal men. Like all the ones we expected to make an attack on the science dome."

Kylee shifted her duraplast, water sheeting down the back. "I've got nothing." She hooked a thumb. "Flute, however, is prowling the rim. He could give a fuck about a bunch of human-eating humans. Something out in the forest's got him creep-freaked."

Talina glanced out at the dark trees beyond the escarpment. "Our mystery beast?"

"I catch a whiff," Kylee told her. "Just every once in a while when the wind's right. Nothing I've ever smelled before. Nothing that triggers quetzal memory with an image. It's more of a scary feeling. The biochemical kind that says, 'Run!'"

"Yeah, I've smelled it, too. Like rotted blood mixed with old hunger."

The rain began to let up, easing from a head-beating downpour to a gentler soaking. Looking east, the first graying of dawn cast silhouettes across the station.

"How about one menace at a time? We're not out of this mess yet. Let's deal with—"

"Tal?" Kalico's voice interrupted. *"Got action. Batuhan and a bunch of women and kids are pouring out the doors of the barracks. Looks like twenty, maybe twenty-five of them. All lining out in the rain and headed south."*

"What about the men?"

"Muldare counts three in addition to the Messiah. Where are you?"

"South of the domes, just north of the farm."

"They should be in your sight any second now. We're making a try for the radio."

"Hey! Wait! We're still missing a bunch of—"

"There's three of us, Tal. Armed. Tired. And pissed off. Besides, they're not expecting us this early."

Talina's heart skipped. "Damn it, Kalico, wait for me."

"Too late, Tal. We're going. Fast. Before they can react."

"Kalico?"

Nothing.

"What's happening?" Kylee asked.

"Kalico's making a try for the radio. I just hope she—"

"Yeah, well you might want to get under cover. Here comes trouble."

Talina spun, staring north. Seeing the first woman leading the way past the geology dome. And behind her came a parade of children.

Talina had barely ducked behind a rusted evaporator when a hollow detonation—as distinct from thunder as could be—carried on the gently raining air.

79

The downpour had let up enough that Vartan could chance the drone. As the Messiah's column plodded south through the wet and mud, he activated the flying bomb.

Using thumbs, he directed it up, the camera penetrating the early-dawn gloom with ease.

After it rose above the admin dome, he sent it scooting north to the science dome. Studying the image, he let it circle the building. Peered into the windows, finding all of the rooms dark.

Didn't mean the foe wasn't still hidden inside, but somehow, he doubted it.

Damn it. They were spread too thin. The smart play would have been to have someone up in the admin dome hatch with the long-distance mic. Someone to keep watch.

Instead he'd been called down to make bombs.

So what to do? Somewhere the Supervisor's killers were loose in the compound, armed to the teeth, and prepared to unleash a blood bath.

Got to find them.

Vartan blinked against his fatigue as he sent the drone high, turned its camera down. He had to believe they'd try for the radio.

"Come on, think, damn it. Where would they be?"

What would have prompted them to leave the safety of the science dome, head out into the teeth of the storm?

What was the old adage? That the best time to attack was before the crack of dawn?

When else would the supposedly unsuspecting Unreconciled be as vulnerable? Their sentries dozing? Groggy with sleep? Most still in their beds?

He switched the flight path, taking the drone south to focus on the approaches to the admin dome. Saw the first furtive figure burst from the shipping container, making a run for the admin doors.

"Gotcha!" Vartan's thumbs sent the drone plummeting as two other figures charged out in the wake of the first. Now it was just a matter of timing.

As the camera angle zoomed, he fixed on the first figure in line. She ran with that swinging stride of a woman. Long black hair was soaked, matted to her back. Had to be the Supervisor.

A feeling of giddy glee filled him.

He was descending too fast, applied lift, and watched the drone shiver as it struggled to slow.

The trick was to get all three as they reached the doors.

As the image continued to zoom, Vartan applied more power to the fans in an effort to achieve a hover.

Wasn't working.

Too much weight with the magtex? The batteries too old? Some complication with the rain?

As Vartan fought the controls, the straining drone must have given itself away. In the camera, the Supervisor looked up. Must not have seen the dropping drone against the storm-dark sky. Seemed to be searching.

Desperate as he was to get them all, the drone was falling too fast. He set his index finger on the switch. Was about to press when the Supervisor threw herself face-first into the mud.

The image vanished an instant before the boom of the explosion echoed through the soft patter of the rain.

Vartan stared at his finger. Tried to remember if he'd pushed the button. Couldn't. God, he was so tired. So defeated.

I just want this all to end.

THE BETRAYAL OF KALKI

*A*t the sound of the explosion behind us, I turn to stare back through the falling rain. My warrior has prevailed. Not being versed in such things I wonder if the detonation was the drone or one of the booby traps we left in the admin dome.

Either way, the Supervisor, or someone in her party, has received the final comeuppance.

Everyone has halted, looking back across the farm field with its wealth of crops.

I stare up at the graying sky as raindrops patter on my head and face. How long has it been? Twenty? Thirty years? The last time I felt rain on my head was outside Ulaanbataar. And then it was but for a moment as I ran for cover.

Here, now, I tilt my head to the falling drops. Water runs down through my hair, trickles across my face. I can feel it trace down the scars, following the path of souls. A symbol of life and renewal.

I need to see this for what it is, not the disaster that I have been fearing it to be. I have a new Prophet, though she has yet to experience the depth of her gift. As with Irdan, Callista, and Guan Shi, she will learn and finally surrender herself to the universe.

I have the children. The immortal ones. How silly of me not to recognize that it is they who are of greatest importance. Not the adults. All of which causes me to ask if I have mistakenly interpreted the Revelation. But it seemed so simple: Adults who could reproduce would be the logical repositories for the souls and flesh of the dead.

Think, now. Be smart. Just because the universe has turned my attention to the children for the moment doesn't negate the value of the adults. Ctein and I remain. As do the women. Nine of them. And, though not among the Chosen,

*there are Vartan, Fodor Renz, and Marcus Santanna. The
five of us men would not remain if we were not to be
the vehicles through which the dead are inseminated into
the women.*

*Though how all but Ctein and I ended up as repositories
eludes me. Irdan's Prophecy back in the early days on
Deck Three made it clear that the First Chosen and I were
to be the breeders.*

*But if that been the case, wouldn't my First Chosen still
be alive? Has the universe been waiting to correct my mistake?*

"Come!" I cry. "Let us move on."

*As they start forward, many of the children are shivering
in the downpour, their hair plastered to their heads, arms
tight about their chests. I see that some are crying. The
women are burdened with the neonates and those too small
to walk. Many carry two in hastily contrived slings. All but
Marta; I have assigned her to assist Shimal.*

*The women look miserable, their hair streaming water
from locks that lay tight against their skin. Gooseflesh covers their arms, their nipples tight from the cold. Each is
wracked by shivers as they plod through the mud in clumsy
footwear.*

*In the rear come Marcus and Fodor, each bearing a pack
that contains food for the journey. I have no idea what the
universe will provide for us when we reach the forest floor.
All I know is that forests have always been rich in resources.
I have faith. The universe will provide.*

*As we pick our way past the five big solar collectors,
lightning traces a brilliant design across the roiling clouds.
The instant, bone-jarring bang of thunder scares the children into sobs and tears. One little girl drops to the mud,
screaming her terror as tears mix with rain on her face.*

*A woman pulls her up, fearful that one of the slugs will
get her.*

*I can only suspect that the girl will learn something from
this. Perhaps it is a wake-up call for her reborn soul. A way
to trigger some forgotten memory that will remind her of
who she was before the Cleansing.*

*Up ahead I can see Ctein in the lead. He has reached the
head of the trail that leads down the steep and rocky slope.*

There, he hesitates, looking back to ensure that we are all following.

I am about to wave him ahead when I hear a shout behind me.

Turning, I see Vartan coming at a trot. Everyone stops, staring back. The women are shivering, teeth chattering as they shift the children they carry.

"Yes, First Will?" I call back—realizing only at this moment that Vartan is the only one of the Will left.

"We can't do this," Vartan declares in a most insistent voice.

"Excuse me?"

The man has a tortured look on his weary face as he trots up, feet splashing in the puddles. He stares out at me from under a poncho patterned by droplets and trickling water. The ugly military rifle is in his hands. Vartan's dark eyes are like holes in his face. "I said we can't do this."

A tight sensation in my chest is like my heart crabbing sideways and constricting. "The Prophet has told us—"

"Fuck Prophecy!"

I blink, suddenly find it hard to breathe. Has he gone insane?

Vartan looks past me. "Go on! All of you. Back to the barracks! Get those kids inside, and get them warm and fed."

"They'll do no such thing!" I roar. "You are relieved! You are condemned. I declare you an apostate!"

In a shockingly mild voice, he says, "All right." Then, ignoring me, orders, "All of you! Turn about. Head back."

"No!" I scream so loudly the hole in my nose whistles. I look to Shimal. "Prophet? What does the universe decree?"

Shimal is looking terrified, her dark eyes pleading as she shifts them from Vartan to me. "I . . . I . . ."

"Speak!"

"I . . ."

Vartan bellows, "She's not a Prophet. None of them were. It's a disease. A protein that eats holes in a person's brain. Don't you get it?"

I thrust my bone scepter at him, declaring, "You are an abomination!"

"Fuck you! We're not the Chosen. It's all a pus-sucking

lie!" His face is tortured; tears, not rain streak down his cheeks.

"The universe does not make mistakes!" I roar back at him, stepping up to face him. To my growing horror, he doesn't so much as wince.

"The universe doesn't give a shit about us. It never did. That bastard Galluzzi trapped us on Deck Three. And we did what we had to in order to survive. It was a shitty deal, filled with shitty choices, and we're what's left."

"The universe—"

"Is fucked!" He steps forward, thumping the heavy rifle against my gut. "The Supervisor and the others, they told us the truth: This place is killing us. And if you go down that trail, into that forest, not a one of you will be alive by nightfall."

"You don't know—"

"I've been there! I've seen! Petre was the best of us. His team, Tikal's team, my team, are dead because they went down there. You get it?"

"Hand me that rifle." I reach for the weapon.

"I'll see you in hell first, Batuhan." He shoves me backward, retreating a step and bringing the rifle up. To the others, he shouts, "Now, turn around. Get the kids back to safety. Dry off and get warm."

"You . . ." I swallow, trying to muster words from a fear-clogged throat. "You . . ."

Vartan says through an emotion-tight voice, "You're delusional, don't you get it? You've convinced yourself it's real? That you're special? It's a lie, it's ugly, and it's finished."

"You defy the universe?" I cry, reeling, seeking the right words. Panic, like a paralytic wave, rolls through me.

"I'm right here," Vartan looks up at the storm-brooding sky and lifts a knotted fist. "You want me? I'm right here! Blast me down! I dare you!"

The women gasp, actually cowering back, fearful eyes going to the heavens.

I, too, stare up, but only see twisting and torn-looking low clouds scudding off toward the west. I pray, with all my heart, for lightning to strike, to char Vartan down to the blackened bones.

Instead a soft and misty rain settles on us like dew.

I gape, suffer a physical pain in my chest. The world seems to have gone oddly gray. A sick feeling, like I am going to throw up, turns my stomach sour.

Vartan's display of the rifle is all the authority he needs as he orders, "All of you, get those children back to the barracks. Get them warm. Then make them breakfast. That's an order."

"But I . . ."

My objection is silenced by a single thunderous shot from the rifle that hisses past my ear. I cannot move. Every muscle locked tight.

But the others do, all shuffling past me and Vartan. Fear burns bright in their eyes as they glance my way. Vartan's hot gaze they ignore.

To my surprise Ctein and Shimal remain, apparently as stunned as I am.

"When we get back," I manage to say, "You will pay for this."

Vartan shakes his head, lips pursed. "Not you. Or you, either, Ctein. You preach faith?" He gestures with the rifle. "Go on. Take the path. If I see either of you up here again, I'm putting a bullet right through you. And when I do, there's no immortality. Just rot and Donovan's invertebrates."

He points the muzzle at my chest. I stare into the dark bore, a crawly tingle deep inside where the bullet will strike.

I turn to go, my feet oddly leaden.

As Ctein and I step over the edge, Vartan hollers, "Remember? The universe doesn't make mistakes!"

80

Talina slipped out of sight behind the concrete foundation of one of the solar collectors as the Unreconciled hurried past, some on the verge of running. As they slopped their way through the mud, they kept looking fearfully over their shoulders, as if the furies of hell were going to be in hot pursuit.

Talina leaned her head back, considered.

Well, well, call it a spur-of-the-moment Reformation.

As the last of the women, almost stumbling from fatigue, trudged past with two children in slings on her shoulders, Talina stepped out. Walking carefully, she took in the poncho-clad man as he peeled back his hood. Dark hair. Yep, the shooter.

Before him stood a woman, a frail-looking thing. Hair black with rain, her thin, scarred face, pale. The woman's hands were twitching; either her jaw was spastic, or she was shivering so hard her teeth where chattering.

She caught sight of Talina, and terror glittered in her dark eyes. She gave a slight nod to the man; he turned, bringing his weapon up.

He froze at the sight of Talina's rifle, fixed as it was on his chest. The man instantly understood. The merest pressure on the trigger would blow him away.

"Put it down slowly," she told him. "I'm not in a forgiving mood, so don't fuck with me."

He swallowed hard, eased the rifle down to the damp ground.

"Now, back away. Both of you."

They did, the woman wavering, as if struggling for balance.

"You're Talina Perez," the man said.

"The same. You?"

"Vartan Omanian. I was . . . Well, I guess that doesn't matter anymore." He smiled wearily. "Go ahead. Shoot.

But I'd ask that you take care of Shimal, here. She's got the prion. Nothing's her fault. Same with the women and kids."

"The prion? So you understand it?"

"Shyanne told me it was the explanation." The empty smile was back. "You heard what I told Batuhan?"

"Yeah."

"There it is. Sum and total. The universe's ultimate sick joke at our expense. So pull the trigger. I'm tired of being played for a fucking fool."

Talina lowered the rifle to her hip. "So, you've exiled Batuhan. Once I shoot you, who's in charge?"

Vartan shrugged. Glanced sidelong at Shimal and said to the woman, "Not you. The time for ranting Prophets is over."

Turning back to Talina he said, "Doesn't matter. But don't take it out on the women and kids. Irdan, he was the first Prophet. The guy was an asshole even before his brain started to go. Formulated the revolt against Galluzzi when we first realized just how fucked we were. Was one of the ringleaders when it came to murdering people he didn't find worthy back at the beginning of the Cleansing. He laid the groundwork. Batuhan backed him up."

"Someone had to object."

"Sure. And Irdan and the First Chosen slipped up behind them and cut their throats. Someone had to provide the calories that kept us alive. I think the only skeptic left is Shyanne. Hope she made it."

"She did."

He raised his arms, let them slap his sides in defeat. "I'm tired. Whatever you're going to do, do it."

She stepped forward, snaked Carson's rifle back and safely out of Vartan's reach. Keeping Vartan covered, she picked it up, slung it. "Go on. March. And help this woman. She's looking like she's about to fall over."

As Vartan took the woman's arm and started toward the domes, he said, "Listen, I don't know what you've got planned, but I'm not up to anything long and drawn-out. I really want it over. Fast. Quick. Painless."

"While I consider that, what do you think we should do with the rest of your people? Shoot them, too?"

"Pus, no! Especially not the kids. Not their fault who

they are. And someone's got to deal with Batuhan—assuming he doesn't have the guts to follow his own Prophecy. The guy's a true believer. That's his power. He really thinks the universe chose him. Chose us. So if he comes back, shoot him, and be done with it."

"Anything else you want to tell me?"

"Yeah. There's a couple of booby traps in the admin dome. One in the kitchen in the freezer, another in the radio room."

"Yeah. I know."

"How?"

"Com." She tapped an ear. "Muldare tells me the bomb in the radio room didn't go off when she pulled out the chair. Said it was a clever device, but the battery was dead. Didn't have enough of a charge to set off the magtex."

"Huh! Should have thought of that. Too fucking tired to think straight."

"Wasn't a complete failure on your part," Talina told him. "Muldare says she's in need of a change of underwear."

81

Galluzzi watched through the port-side window as the A-7 shuttle dropped through Donovan's stratosphere. The first red glow was forming on the shuttle's nose and wings.

Beside him, in the middle seat, Shig was staring out like a boy on his first spacing. A look of absolute rapture filled the man's round face; his grin, under other circumstances, would have been infectious.

Two days? It only seemed like a couple of hours.

Galluzzi had been shocked when he and Shig had finally stepped through the lock and into the PA shuttle. But then, that was *Freelander* for you. It screwed with time. Bent it, warped it, and stretched it out of shape.

What the hell had happened to him in there?

"She came to me," he told Shig, finally having come to grips with the revelations in the script-filled corridor.

He hadn't said a word after Shig found him weeping softly on the corridor floor. In an almost dissociative state, he'd allowed Shig to help him to his feet. Leaning on the short Indian, he'd let Shig lead him through the dark corridors of the Transportees' Deck. The phantasms no longer frightened him. *Freelander* had its own physics, its own continuum. Call it proof that the theoretical physicists were right when they said that time was a human creation used to explain the changing relationship between subatomic particles.

"By she I assume you mean Tyne Sakihara?" Shig gave him a mild look.

Galluzzi stared absently at the clouds flashing by the window. "I watched them build the dome of bones. I was there, Shig. It was that clear. I mean it was a real out-of-body experience. And Tyne was talking to me the entire time. Am I crazy?"

"No more so than any of the rest of us." Shig had a benign smile on his lips. "*Freelander* remains a mystery, and I suspect it always will. It exists as an enigma in our universe, part us, part other, and tainted by a physics we can't comprehend."

"So, is Tyne dead? She told me that life is only carbon-based molecules interacting with other molecules. That what we call thought is chemical and electrical impulses. So, if that was just me, imagining her . . . ." He frowned, struggling for the words.

"Maybe she's alive and dead at the same time?" Shig arched a bushy eyebrow. "She is right, you know. The science is clear: We're biochemistry. The existence of the soul can neither be proved nor disproved through the scientific method."

"And ethics? Morality?"

"Anthropologists will tell you they are constructs that serve an adaptive purpose when it comes to social relations with one's fellows. That individual and group survival increases when there are rules and expected norms of behavior."

Galluzzi fingered his chin as they dropped down over the ocean. "When it came to ethics, her exact words were: 'Cling to whatever you have, Miguel. In the end, it's the only thing that makes existence worth enduring.'"

"Was she a student of epiphenomenolgy to begin with?"

"No. But who knows what all those years in *Freelander* might have done to her before Jem put that bullet . . . Well, never mind."

Shig's smile was reflective of a deeper amusement. "Then it appears that First Officer Sakihara's very appearance belies her epiphenomenal argument. But that said, I agree with her advice. No matter what one's philosophical or religious compass would indicate, believing makes existence worth enduring."

"She said that euthanizing the transportees was an act of kindness."

"Given the fate of *Freelander,* what do you think? You have a most unique insight, having been in Jem Orten's shoes."

"He turned his transportees into corpses, I turned mine into monsters."

"That assertion denies the Unreconciled any claim to free will. A power that, not being an omnipotent god, you do not have."

"No, I suppose I don't," Galluzzi admitted as the shuttle braked, slowed, and settled on the PA landing pad.

82

Dek hurt. The throbbing pain lay deep within—a sort of background to his jumbled thoughts.

What the hell?

Where was he?

He tried to shift. Hurt more.

"Hold still," a soothing voice ordered.

It took effort to pry his eyelids open. Seemed like they'd been glued. The pain localized—a burning sting just under his left eye. After a couple of blinks, the white haze solidified into a duraplast ceiling with a light panel overhead. The dark figure resolved into Kalico Aguila. She sat in a chair to one side, her clothing mud-splotched and filthy, hair a tangled and matted mess confined by a filthy string tied at the nape of her neck.

"What happened?"

"Seems you saved my life again. You don't remember?"

He blinked, started to reach up for the irritating pain under his eye, only to have Aguila grab his wrist. "You really don't want to touch that. You've got a shard of sialon stuck into your cheekbone. Another inch higher and it would have gone through your eye and into your brain."

"A piece of what?"

"You don't remember the drone? Shouting for me to drop flat? Standing there, sighting on the drone as it dropped down to kill me?"

Dek nodded, worked his dry lips. Oh, yeah. He'd heard the thing, how it made a fluttering sound with the rain in the fan blades. The way it had fallen, headed straight for Aguila, it sure wasn't after reconnaissance.

"Kalico! Down! Now! Drop flat!" His words echoed in his memory. He'd shouldered the Holland & Holland, the rifle having the same pull and drop as the shotgun he'd used for clays and birds back home. The shot had been instinctive.

The thing exploded as the bullet tore through it.

And what felt like the fist of God had knocked him flat. After that? Nothing.

"So, where am I?"

"Admin dome." Kalico stood. "Muldare called. The PA shuttle's on the way. They've been locked down over a quetzal scare, but Whitey's raid failed. They'll be here within the hour. We'll get you back to Raya's. Let her pry the sialon out of your cheekbone. Don't worry about the blood caked in your nostril. Seems there's some sort of sinus behind the bone and above the teeth that bled into your nose."

"Why does the rest of me hurt?"

"Muldare says the blast knocked you back a couple of meters. And you've got bits of shrapnel here and there that will need to be dug out. Beyond that, you're just bruised. Lucky it didn't burst your eardrums."

All right. Enough of this. He took a deep breath, swung his legs out, and sat up. Damn. The headache was as bad as that toilet-sucking hangover back in PA or maybe the one he'd barely gotten over from heat stroke. He figured, at this rate, he could make his fortune importing aspirin to Donovan.

Kalico offered him a hand. Pulled him to his feet.

Sure enough, Dek discovered a whole lot of hurt. His joints, arms, shoulders, but nothing like the searing in his cheek. He carefully prodded at the angular chunk of sialon. Could just see it at the edge of his vision when he lowered his eyes.

Weird.

"So, what's with the Unreconciled?"

"Don't know. Let's go find out." Kalico gave him a sober inspection. "You okay to walk? Not feeling dizzy or sick?"

"I'll let you know."

She took his arm, just to be sure, and led the way out into the hallway, down to the cafeteria. To one side, Batuhan's throne sat, empty, like a monstrous reminder.

Dek turned loose of Aguila, stepped over, this being the first time he'd seen the thing. At first it repulsed him. But as he looked closer, it was to realize the mind-boggling talent and artistry that had gone into the carving of it. It begged a magnifying glass to see the intricate detail.

"Tal?" Kalico asked her com. "Status?"

She listened to the reply, shot Dek a look. "Talina's in the barracks. She's got the women and children there. Only three men left. Batuhan and one other were last seen taking the trail down into the forest."

"Kylee and Flute?"

"Now there's a question. Talina just asked me the same."

"They'll show up." Dek finished his inspection of the throne. Realized he was more wobbly than he'd wanted to admit. He walked over and settled himself into a chair at one of the cafeteria tables.

Kalico was watching him, something unsettled in her laser-blue gaze. He asked, "What?"

"I think until you get back to Solar System, you're going to have a really nasty scar. Those perfect Taglioni features of yours are never going to be the same."

"Maybe it makes me look dashing. Like a knuckle-and-skull adventurer. The kind of tough man who takes life by the horns and—"

"Don't push your luck. The way you are right now I could knock you over with my little finger."

He liked the fact that she was grinning as she said it.

"Yeah, I suppose. Still, it makes a good story. But what about the Unreconciled? Think Talina's all right alone over there? I lived with these people just one deck down. They're not kind and loving at heart."

Kalico took a breath, picked at the mud flaking off of her clothing. "I'm not feeling particularly forgiving at the moment either. They've relentlessly tried to kill us. The loss of Talbot and Dya hasn't hit home yet. But it will. I'm angry, Dek. My inclination is to burn Tyson Station and everyone in it to ashes."

= THE DARK SHADE OF BLACK =

I am bereft.

My stumbling progress is mindless. I just force my legs to carry me. Climb down stones, leap from one purchase to the next as I flee toward . . . what?

Ctein is plodding ahead of me. His shoulders sag. His movements are clumsy, like a man whose soul has gone dead inside. I see defeat in his every movement.

I haven't a clue where I am, where I'm going. I just proceed. Panting. Howling in lonely silence.

This is a terrible place that I do not understand. I can't put a name to the green, blue, and turquoise leaves. Branches and stems turn in my direction. There is no sky. I clamp a hand to my ears to still the rising and falling harmony of the chime. It is like a madness that echoes inside my skull.

Beneath my feet green and brown roots squirm. The feeling of movement unnerves me, pushes me to the threshold of endurance.

At least I know enough to avoid the vines. Try not to touch anything.

I follow Ctein along the edge of the tumbled boulders. We've reached the bottom of the trail. Turned north, seeking to skirt the cliff. It's mostly flat here. The trees are small, barely twenty meters high. Water drips from the alien-shaped leaves.

The rain has tapered into a fine mist, sometimes ceasing altogether as patches open in the clouds and shafts of light shoot bars through the rainbow-patterned virga.

Ctein—soaked to the bone—is no more than four paces ahead. He stumbles over a stone. Walks with no more grace than if his feet were carved of wood. I hear the labored breathing as he fights the shivers. Nothing has prepared us for such arduous travel as we are engaged in. Struggling over boulders, leaping gaps, spanning roots.

The boulder has a black sheen, gray where the sides were sheltered from the downpour. Irregularities, cracks, a faint smattering of what looks like lichen.

Ctein puts his hand on it to brace his passage as he's done on countless other boulders.

Instantly, the stone is alive. Stabs some slender lance-shaped spike through Ctein's chest. As it does, two hose-like arms reach out to grab him. They pull him close upon the thorn-sharp spear until it shoots out of his back.

I see the expression on his face. The pain . . . the disbelief.

Ctein's mouth works the same way a fish's does when it is left on the bank after being pulled from the stream. His eyes have bugged wide, the scars on his cheeks sucking, hollow, and pale.

I freeze. Try to comprehend. Am stricken by a horror that locks my muscles. Starves my lungs of air.

And the boulder changes color. Morphs from an irregular-shaped rock to an amoeba kind of a thing that begins to conform to Ctein's thrashing body.

Standing there with all the will of a stump, I watch it begin to engulf Ctein's body. Stand there so long I barely manage to pull loose of the roots that are winding around my feet.

When panic overcomes my horror, I backpedal, run with all my might.

And now I am here, staggering through the dim half-light of the forest floor. I scramble over mats of roots, stare up at the distant canopy. I wonder if my mind and soul are broken.

DIVINE COMEDY

The emptiness is complete. From my head to my toes, I am as hollow as a bottle. Thoughtless. Terrified.

I can't trust anything.

Ctein taught me that.

The one word that repeats—like an echo through infinity—is "Why?"

Finally, shaking, weeping, I climb onto a meter-high knot of great roots. There, I stare up at the high branches. I raise my hands and cry, "I gave you everything!"

The chime seems to mock me.

"I bled for you!"

I point to the scars running across my skin. "Each cut stung like fire! I lived in agony in the days that followed."

I swallow against the tears.

I see constant movement up in the high canopy. The endless motion of the forest. But no illumination appears in the patterns above. No shaft of forgiving light. The universe ignores me.

"I gave everything to you!" I scream at the heedless heights. "Everything."

Yet the universe did nothing as Vartan betrayed me.

Should I have made him shoot me?

But if I had, what would have become of the dead? I carry these people. They live in my flesh. Their souls reside in the scars that line my body. I am their living grave.

That was the promise. The sacred bond. The reason the universe chose me. Chose us. We were the end, and the beginning.

"What happened?" I ask through the sobs that wrack me. "Why did you betray us? Was it me? Was I unworthy?"

I listen desperately, hoping to hear the universe answer. Surely there must be words, but I can decipher nothing in the maddening rising and falling of the chime.

I have to have faith.

If I do not, I have nothing.

"The universe does not make mistakes."

But I cannot conceive its purpose. My soul has gone dark. Black beyond blackness. Hopeless beyond hopelessness.

I rise wearily, start picking my way down the slowly flexing roots.

I am almost at the bottom when a voice calls, "You might not want to step down right there. A sidewinder will get you."

I freeze, look up.

She is a girl. Blonde. Early teens? Her blue eyes are hard, seem to be oddly intense. Inhuman in both size and color.

She wears some sort of leather pants and cloak. Her shirt is a kind of rough fabric I can't place a name to. She perches on a pile of knotted roots off to my left.

As I gape, she says, "Wow! I thought I knew the definition of butt ugly. Seeing you gives it a whole new twist."

"Who . . . who are you?" For a moment I reel, hoping beyond hope that this curious girl is the universe's answer to my prayers.

"Kylee Simonov." She cocks her head. "Dya was my mother. Talbot was my dad. You tried to blow them up." She gestures around. "Chased them out here."

"Why are you here?"

"Um, you might want to move that right foot. Another thirty seconds, and you're never taking another step for the rest of your life. Which won't be more than about three minutes from now."

I look down, tear my foot away from the grasping roots.

A warbling, whistling sound can be heard off to the right; she again cocks her head. Smiles grimly. "Come on. This way."

I do my best to keep up as she scampers across the roots headed in the direction of the sound. I wonder at the grace, the seemingly effortless way she moves. A wild creature at home in her element.

"So," she calls over her shoulder. "What's with that stupid eye painted on your forehead? That meant to creep-

*freak the congregation? Let you sleep through the sermons
when they think you're watching?"*

*"The eye allows me to see the purpose behind the
Prophets."*

*"Got it. Makes the poor saps think you see God when
the brain-damaged goons babble."*

"Do you know who I am?" I snap, beginning to anger.

"One stupid fuckhead if you ask me."

*I stop short. "Don't use that tone with me! I am the last
and the first, the Chosen, the Messiah who—"*

*"You're quetzal crap, fool. You let your buddy back
there walk right up to a skewer. Stood there like a lump
while it stuck him through the chest and started to eat him.
Would have stepped right on that sidewinder. Would have
been a root-mummy by now if I hadn't told you to move
your foot."*

I blink.

*She looks back. "So, you following? Or are you even
more stupid than I thought."*

*I start after her, hearing my labored breath whistling
through my nose hole. "You going to kill me?" I ask. "Because of what happened to your mother and father?"*

*"Nope. Not that I don't want to, but there's that part of
Talina inside me. You think you're the living repository for
the dead? You oughtta try quetzal molecules sometime.
Same effect, but you don't need the scars. And the way you
were wailing back there? All the pain and sacrifice shit? I'd
guess you'd think it was a bargain."*

"The universe doesn't make mistakes."

*"The universe doesn't give a shit. Don't you get it, butt
ugly? You were trapped on a starship. Not enough food.
And, yeah, I'd probably come down on the side of eating,
rather than being eaten. I'm a spoiled brat when it comes to
saving my skin. Been out here too long where life and death
are immediate kinds of problems."*

"Little girl, you—"

*"Watch that vine. That's gotcha. Not that the scars it
leaves behind would stand out against what you've already
got, but the spines burn like liquid fire."*

I weave wide of the hair-covered vine.

"You don't understand Revelation," I mutter. "To be

filled with the rapture of true knowledge. To feel the presence of the universe inside your body. My failing was that in the end I wasn't worthy. Believe—as I do—in the Revelation, and the only explanation is that I wasn't devoted enough. But why the universe chose me remains—"

"Piss poor picking on the universe's part," she interrupts. "You sacrificed. You had faith. You're the repository. You suffered. It's all about you, huh? You. You. You. You." She glances back from the top of the roots she's scaling. "And you drove my mom and dad out here to die."

As I crest the top of the roots, she's already down the other side. I am reaching the point where if I can get close enough, I am going to reach out, grab her by the neck, and watch her alien-strange eyes bug out as I strangle her.

That warbling whistle sounds. Closer now. Where she stands on the root mat below, she seems to be listening. She alters her course slightly as she starts off in the direction of the sound.

I wonder if I should follow. But looking around, I haven't a clue as to where I am. Which direction is which. Nor have I seen anything edible. Wherever the foul child is headed, there will be food there. Shelter.

Exhaustion saps my limbs. That trembling that comes from hunger and low blood sugar robs my muscles. How many hours has it been since I slept? I'm not used to the exertion. I've sat too long on my throne.

I still have faith. The universe doesn't make mistakes. The child is wrong when it comes to that.

I am out here to learn an important lesson. Whatever it is, it's not something this insolent forest urchin can teach.

We climb up over a particularly high knot of roots, many as thick around as oil drums. They are contorted around each other in a dense ball.

Kylee leaps down the other side in a remarkable display of agility. She spins around at the bottom, seems to stare at a shadowed hollow among the roots across the way, and turns back, saying, "Stop right there at the top. Catch your breath where you won't get caught by the roots."

Winded as I am, my heart thumping at the exertion, I gasp for breath. I'm delighted for a chance to rest. And here I can be assured that nothing is going to ensnare me.

"Thanks, I was running out of energy."

"Guess it doesn't take much to be a cannibal, huh? Especially when you don't have to work for it. Just set off an explosive and cut up the victims. Chuck them in the stewpot, and you're made."

"You really are a despicable child. Where are you taking me, anyway? Ah, you have that airtruck out here somewhere, don't you? Is that it? You think I can fly it for you?"

She is staring thoughtfully at me. Tilts her head back, gaze going higher as if she's seeking some answer from above. "Mom came out to Tyson to help you and your people. Dad was along to keep her and Aguila safe. You're a clap-trapping idiot. And on Donovan, stupidity's a death sentence."

I stare down at her. Glance around, lest this is some kind of trap. I'm not going to play this game any longer. Looking back over my shoulder, I realize I can take a line of sight across the clearing, and another, and another, and make my way back to the Tyson mesa.

At this, I smile. The universe has not forgotten me. It has brought me here to teach me the way home. A metaphor.

I need to let Vartan have his moment, and then I will return, wiser, better suited to do the universe's work.

The dark side of blackness begins to lift from my soul. As always, faith has carried me through.

"Go on about your business, little girl. The universe has taught me what I need to know. It has shown me the way to save the dead. What it means to be chosen. And despite what you think, the universe really doesn't make mistakes."

I catch the blur in the corner of my eye. Hear the rush of something ripping through the air. Just as I fix on the curving length, it hits me. The point spears through my chest, overwhelms even the pain of Initiation.

My vision smears sideways as my body is jerked heavenwards. I see Kylee's face dropping away. With punctured lungs I can't even scream.

I am lifted, rocketing into the branches. My vision fills with images of green, an interlacery of branches.

As I rush into them, I catch a curious odor, like rotten blood. Then the eyes appear, magically, as if forming from

*the leaves themselves. Huge, deep, and blue-black, like
holes into eternity.*

*My last coherent thought as a gaping, tooth-filled mouth
opens is that I am being eaten alive. And then . . . the universe . . .*

Kylee flinched at the violence of the attack. Watched Batuhan's body flop under the force as the black spear on the
end of the tentacle shot clear through the man's chest, right
out among the three lines tattooed between the spirals on
his breasts.

As the cannibal was lofted skyward, Kylee sniffed.
Caught the faint taint of rotten blood. The old memory
tripped, something monstrous and ancient.

Horrified, she watched as the cannibal was jerked high.
Saw the three great eyes appear, as if opening out of the
leaves and branches. Dark, powerful, and remorseless.

In but an instant, the retracting tentacle stuffed Batuhan into a black hole of a mouth. And as quickly it vanished, merging back into an image of branches, leaves, and
vines.

For a long moment, the terrible eyes fixed on Kylee.
Filled with cold promise, they seemed to drain her soul,
suck her life away into some numbing eternity.

An instant later, they were gone.

From where he'd hidden, Flute vented a harmonic of
fear. The sound brought Kylee back to this reality. She
shivered, tensed, half expecting that diving tentacle to stab
down from above.

But nothing. She might have been looking up at pristine
upper story.

"So much for happy endings, huh?" she said. "Guess
those only exist in fairy tales."

The soft tremolo sounded from the hollow beneath the
roots.

"Yeah." Kylee kept her eyes on the spot where Batuhan
disappeared into the high branches. "It's still in the same
place. Remarkable how well it blends in. Doesn't hardly
show up in the UV or IR either."

Flute's body seemed to emerge out of the background as

the quetzal dropped its camouflage; dull patterns flashed over its body, the ruff held flat to the neck. Time to go.

"I agree. But keep low. That thing's dangerous."

As the quetzal streaked out from the hollow, it paused only long enough for Kylee to leap onto its back. Flute skirted the root knot, leaped a low tangle, and raced east.

"Hope it doesn't have such good aim when it comes to moving targets."

83

Vartan straightened, reached his hand around, and pressed on the small of his back. Overhead, Capella burned down with a fierce intensity. Vartan's skin had begun to brown, a process they'd been warned about after the first bad sunburns. The basket before him was half full of green beans. That left him with another half an hour's worth of picking.

He caught a flash in distance to the northeast, high over the trees. Stepped out from the confusion of crops and walked to the edge of the landing pad.

As it came closer, Vartan made out the airtruck. Watched it circle, hover, and slowly settle. Fans still spun up, the occupants waited, as if for some sign.

Spreading his arms wide in a gesture of open-handed surrender, Vartan braved the outwash from the fans. Almost had the hat ripped off his head.

Only then did the fans spool down, and the cab door opened.

Shyanne climbed down, landing with a sprightly jump. She was dressed in some sort of handcrafted fabric that looked more like burlap than any kind of clothing Vartan could put name to. Behind her came Tamil Kattan. The Sri Lankan glanced warily about as Shyanne gave Vartan a cocky grin and walked forward.

"Didn't figure to see you again," Vartan told her.

"Or I you." She flipped her brown hair back to expose the Initiation scars on her face. Sorrow and defeat lay behind her umber-colored eyes. "Chaco and Madison were fair. Did their best actually. But you remember that day when Perez told us that we were no long Irredenta? That's not quite true."

"How's that? We're off the ship."

Her gaze went distant. "This is the only place left for us, Vart. What we did up there on *Ashanti*? There're things that forever set a group of people apart. A history that can't be bridged. Not in the eyes of others. It's a stigma we can't outrun, can't outlive."

"That bad, huh?"

"Hey, they tried." Shyanne gave a weary shrug. "But the revulsion? It's always in their eyes. You can see it in the unguarded moments. The hesitation. The lack of trust that—no matter how they try and hide it—can't be overcome."

He bit his lip. Nodded. Turned to look where the women were standing in the fields, waiting. Unwilling to come forward after years of domination by Batuhan.

Shyanne gave him that old brown-eyed scrutiny. "Hear that you're in charge now."

"Someone has to be."

"Tamil and I, we'd like to come back. Is that a possibility? I mean . . . there's Svetlana. What happened to her and Hakil. I know that you and she were . . ."

Vartan chuckled under his breath. "She believed. We all did to one extent or another. But here's the thing: If we can't find it in ourselves to forgive one another, how do we expect the Donovanians to? It's got to start somewhere."

She gave him a weary smile. Turned to Tamil and said, "Guess you can unload our luggage."

Vartan looked up, saw Talina Perez in the doorway, her hand resting on her pistol. "Hello, Security Officer. How's Dek Taglioni?"

"Looks like he'll get away with a juicy scar. How are things?"

"Little Tina Brooks lost a lower leg to a slug. We finally got the bleeding stopped after we amputated. Looks like she'll live."

"That's tough."

Shyanne asked, "Who did the amputation?"

"I did. Scared the hell out of me."

"Then, maybe you're glad to have me back after all. I'm the closest thing you've got to a doctor. Not much else a veterinary tech can do on a planet with no dogs, cats, cattle, or horses."

Tamil was at the rear of the airtruck, had opened the hatch and was laying out what looked like leather suitcases.

Talina said, "Just so you know, we're going to be flying out west. Whatever that thing is in the forest, the one that got Talbot and Dya, Kylee thinks she knows how to find it. Didn't want you thinking we were after you."

"After you?" Shyanne asked.

Vartan took a deep breath, that lingering unease in his gut. "Let's just say that when the Supervisor and her party took their leave of Tyson Station they weren't in a forgive-and-forget mood."

"No happy endings, huh?"

"Nope." Vartan looked up. "Officer Perez, I'm saying this now, and I'll continue to say it. As long as I am alive, any and all are welcome at Tyson. No one, under any circumstance, will be turned away. PA or Corporate. That includes you, Security Officer. You want to hunt that thing? You're welcome to use Tyson as a base."

Talina's curiously shaped face reflected hesitation. "Thanks. I'll pass the word. Meantime, I've got to be going."

"Sure you won't stay for lunch?"

Perez's alien-dark eyes narrowed. "Don't press your luck."

With that she stepped back inside, closed the cab door, and began to spool up the fans as Tamil battened the back hatch and lugged the leather cases away.

As the airtruck rose, circled, and headed back to the northwest, Shyanne cryptically asked, "Did you have to invite her for lunch?"

"It's only beans and cabbage."

He turned, leading the way toward the admin dome. Truth was, he was glad to have her back. He needed someone to remind the women that they'd been people before the Messiah's tyranny had turned them into breeding stock. Shyanne would be just the woman to do it.

84

As the shuttle settled into its berth, Derek Taglioni couldn't keep a smile from bending the corners of his lips. The feel of the ship comforted him. Hard as that was to believe.

"Hard dock. Hard seal," Ensign Naftali told him.

Ashanti's always-pleasant voice announced, *"Welcome aboard"* through the speakers.

"Good to be back," Dek called. "Missed you, old friend."

"We missed you as well, Dek. First Officer Turner has been appraised of your arrival and will meet you in the Captain's Lounge."

Dek unstrapped, glanced over at Dan Wirth, seeing devious wariness in the psychopath's clever eyes. "You sure you want to do this?"

"Hey, I almost died in a plastic box while a bunch of overgrown lizards chewed on it. Lead forth, and let us begin." Wirth rose and extended a hand that Dek precede him. "Whole lot better arrival than that last departure from *Turalon*. I barely got off that bucket with my balls intact."

"Woman trouble, I take it?" Dek acknowledged Naftali's salute and led the way to the hatch.

"Is there any other kind?" Wirth asked, pausing long enough to adjust his quetzal-hide vest and its garish chains.

"Oh, yeah. Cannibals hunting you, jealous relatives, Corporate regulations." A beat. "An illegally assumed identity to cover a murder."

"Don't get funny."

Dek gave the man a flippant raise of the eyebrows. "Come on. Let's get this started."

As Dek led the way past the hatch, it was into a different *Ashanti*. The sialon had been scrubbed, the air smelling slightly astringent. Taking the lift, it was like a homecoming. The feel of the ship, so familiar after all those years. And at the same time, she was different. Smelled more earthy? Green? Alive?

But when it came to different, so was he: tanned, muscular, with a glaring pink scar under his left eye. Dr. Turnienko had repaired the bone in what she'd called his left maxilla. A scar he'd indeed have, but not a dent.

As they stepped out of the lift on the Command Deck, Wirth muttered, "I'd hate to discover that armed security personnel with a warrant for my arrest waited behind one of the doors. If that happened, you know I wouldn't hesitate to blow a hole right through you before they killed me."

Wirth danced his fingers on the grip of the holstered pistol at his belt. And true, he was fast enough that Dek wouldn't stand a chance.

Reaching the Captain's Lounge hatch, Dek turned. "Here's what you need to know: My cousin, Miko, is a smart, crafty, clever, and cunning monster. A craftier and more clever monster than I. And believe me, when it came to being a plotting pit viper, I tried. He despised me, with good reason."

"Not exactly a scintillating recommendation of character that you're giving him, or yourself, is it?"

"And you have a right to talk?" Dek arched a questioning brow. "By now your container with all the plunder is being loaded in the cargo deck with a Taglioni seal prominently displayed on it. It will only be opened by Taglioni agents in Transluna, and its contents will be reported straight to Miko."

"Yeah, yeah, and from there—with your recommendation and Miko's blessing—your people can buy my safe return. That's a shitload of plunder. In terms of Solar System, it's worth billions. You get your ten percent. But that's just a pittance compared to what's to come."

"I get more than that. I slap Miko right across his perfectly sculpted face. And I do it with wealth the likes of which he's never seen. There is no way you can understand what that means to me." Dek saw the hesitation in Wirth's eyes, and added, "Come on, Dan. In your world it's all about you. Heartless, without remorse. The high and rarified circles of power that make up Transluna are just the place for you. So, in a sense, getting you back to Solar System is my way of paying them all back."

"And to think some would call you petty."

Dek opened the door, ushered Wirth into the small room, and shook hands with Ed Turner. "Hey, old friend. Good to see you again."

"My God! Your face. I'd heard you were wounded. That's . . . horrible!"

"It's healing. Ed, this is Dan Wirth. Dan, Ed Turner is the finest First Officer to space with in the entire universe."

Turner shook hands with Wirth, offered seats, and Dek dropped into his familiar spot. "Hear you're in the captain's chair to take *Ashanti* back to Solar System."

Turner settled into Galluzzi's chair. "I don't know what Miguel's doing. I think getting here was just too much. That it broke something in his spirit. He's been living down in PA. Keeping a low profile at Shig's place."

"Hope you don't have as interesting a ride getting back."

"I'll take my chances. I'm just not a dirtie. And besides, you should see Deck Three. We ripped out the bulkheads, put in light panels, hauled up dirt. Turned the whole thing into a farm to augment the hydroponics. And we're going back as a skeleton crew. About fifteen of our people, some of Aguila's people, another ten of Torgussen's when *Vixen* matches with us next week. If we get stranded somewhere, we can survive for decades."

"Naw. If you've planned for it, it won't happen. My bet? You're back off Neptune in two-and-a-half years." Dek reached into his pocket and handed Turner the data cube. "This is important. I'm entrusting it to you, and you alone. Seal it in the captain's pouch. Mark it urgent delivery to Boardmember Miko Taglioni or whoever his successor on the Board might be."

Turner's washed-out blue eyes held Dek's for a moment. Then he glanced at Wirth. Nodded. Took the data cube. "It will be done."

"And as I speak, there's a container being transferred from the shuttle to the cargo deck. It, too, bears the Taglioni seal. Make sure it is immediately delivered to my family's agents."

"Yes, sir."

"Happy spacing, Ed."

Turner frowned slightly. Studied the cube. "Dek? You sure you don't want to go with us? You almost died down there as it is."

"Positive. You'd be surprised at what I found down there."

"Like . . . what?"

"A whole new world." Dek stood.

Wirth followed, shaking Turner's hand. "Good to meet you. Before you space, drop by The Jewel. We'll set you up right. Have Angelina give your cock the milking of a lifetime. On the house, First Officer."

"Uh, yeah. Thanks."

Outside the hatch, Wirth jerked a thumb back at the lounge. "Maybe he didn't get it? Outside of Ali, Angelina's the best on the planet. And it's not like just anyone gets free tail from her."

"Well, Dan. Not everyone's a connoisseur." Dek slapped the man on the back. "Come on. Let's get out of here before Turner gets any ideas about warrants and men with guns."

85

The last shuttle left Port Authority on a cloudy morning, rising through rain squalls before bursting out into Capella's bright light and ascending from the puffy white mounds of cumulus. Within minutes it shot through the stratosphere and into the darkening threshold of vacuum.

In the copilot's seat, Miguel Galluzzi watched the familiar patterns of stars form in all of their swirling majesty, the nebulae, galaxies, and dark matter stretching across his view. Capella was a glaring orb to the left as the shuttle changed attitude.

Where was . . .? Ah, yes. There. *Freelander* hung just over Donovan's horizon. A small ball against the background of stars. Even from this distance, it didn't look right. Having seen orbiting ships his entire career, Galluzzi couldn't put his finger on the difference. As if the thing was eating light.

He wondered if, in the infinite eventuality of time, the leak would drain his universe away, siphon it slowly into whatever hellish existence *Freelander* had passed through. If it did, what would happen to the essence of his beloved Tyne Sakihara? It turned out that he had to believe that he was more than molecules and electrochemical stimuli. Indeed, he'd decided what he'd cling to.

In silent tribute, Galluzzi raised a hand and snapped off a salute just before the vessel passed out of sight.

After *Freelander* he would never again see the universe through jaded eyes. Was that redemption? Or revelation?

"Thank you, Shig," he whispered under his breath.

Memory of the little brown man with the round face and unruly hair would remain chiseled in Miguel Galluzzi's heart and soul until he took his last breath. How, in all of creation, could luck have placed him into such knowing, caring, and competent hands?

The shuttle rolled under Ensign Naftali's skilled command. *Ashanti* appeared in view. Dead ahead. *Vixen*'s shuttle was just departing, returning back to the survey ship. It would have just deposited those crew members who'd opted to ride *Ashanti* home.

Their return created an interesting dilemma for The Corporation. The *Vixen* crew were owed an absolute fortune: sixty to seventy years' wages, including mission bonus, including overtime for service beyond stated period of contract, and compounded interest. And they were still in the prime of their careers.

Leave that to the Board to figure out.

Galluzzi grinned.

Naftali turned down *Ashanti*'s routine request to assume control of the shuttle prior to docking.

To Galluzzi's supreme satisfaction, the ensign settled them into the bay without so much as a quiver. The familiar vibrations told him the shuttle was locked down.

"Hard dock, hard seal," Naftali told him, turning in the command seat. "Welcome home, sir."

Galluzzi gave the ensign a wink, stood, and made his way to the hatch. There, Dan Wirth waited, his quetzal vest buttoned, the priceless rhodium and gold chains gleaming in the light. The man was smiling, boyish, which accented the dimple in his chin. A curious reservation lay behind his brown eyes.

"I'll see that you are assigned to Dek's old quarters," Galluzzi told him. "Best in the ship, as befitted a Taglioni."

"What about when we get to Neptune?"

"You are to be delivered directly to Taglioni agents. No customs."

Wirth's smile beamed in triumph. "Should be quite a ride."

Galluzzi paused as the hatch was undogged. "I do hope that you know what you're doing. You have quite the unsavory reputation as a gambler, cutthroat, and con man. But you do understand what you're getting into, don't you?"

"Biggest game of my life, Cap." Wirth gave him a wink. "And, yeah, I promise. I won't so much as lift a card with any of the crew on the way back."

The hatch swung open. Turner, Smart, and AO Tuulikki

stood waiting in dress uniform. They saluted in unison, and Turner said, "Welcome aboard, sir."

"Good to be back." Galluzzi studied Turner's watery eyes. "I'm not here to bump you out of the captain's chair, Ed. I'm happy to let you take her back to Solar System."

Turner and others were watching him warily.

"You all right, sir?" Paul Smart asked.

"Oddly, Paul, never better."

"Thought, given the way you left, that we'd be lucky to ever see you again," Tuulikki told him. "What happened down there?"

Galluzzi clasped his hands behind him, rocking up on his toes. "The Unreconciled were right about one thing: The universe continually teaches us. Sometimes you have to lose yourself to find yourself."

Turner winced. "Not sure I understand."

"No, Captain Turner," Galluzzi told him, "I don't suppose you do. And that's the crying shame of it. Now, why don't you good people show Mr. Wirth here to his cabin and take us home?"

With that he strode past them, headed for the lift that would take him to Crew Deck.

86

Sitting behind the big chabacho-wood desk, Allison leaned back in Dan's chair. With a long fingernail she tapped at her incisor teeth and studied the empty corner where Dan's safes had stood. The room looked remarkably empty without them.

She glanced at the ledger book on the desk. Business was down fifteen percent since Dan's departure.

Dan's last words echoed in her memory: *"Taglioni's got a way to fix it for me. I'm going back before I'm inclined to cut that beautiful throat of yours, or worse, wake up with your knife sticking out of my heart. You, babe, are going to run my interests here. Fifty-fifty. And don't fuck with me, or I'll send someone back to slit you open from your ribs clear down to your cunt."*

All of which gave her hope. If plunder was what it took to get Dan back to Transluna in spite of his background, she'd be a shoo-in when the day came.

At a hesitant knock, she closed the ledger, calling, "Come in."

Dek Taglioni stepped through the door and hesitated, looking around the room. "It's just not the same without those brooding safes, is it?"

"I have Lawson welding me up a new one. Sturdier legs this time."

He walked over, glanced at the whiskey in its blown-glass decanter. "You mind?"

"Help yourself." She arched a trim eyebrow. "I assume your visit has some purpose beyond a free drink?"

"Just thought I'd drop in and see how things are." He poured two glasses, bringing her one. Then he seated himself across from her.

She gave him a smile as she met his yellow-green eyes. The healing scar on his cheek didn't spoil his good looks, if anything the blemish added to the allure. Lifting the whiskey in mock salute, she said, "So, spill it. What irresistible proposition have you come to dazzle me with?"

"Straight to business, I see."

"In my world, business is all there is. So, here you are. A rich Taglioni. Handsome as all get out, and with that cute dimple in your chin. Dan's gone. Thank you very much. So, what's your pitch?"

"I did you a favor." He spread his arms, palms up to indicate the room around them. "Must be a relief to sleep at night without having to tread on eggshells. There's easier ways to make a living than playing Russian roulette with a stone-cold psychopath."

"Living with Dan has been both terrifying and educational . . . and I survived four years of it. Trust me, once I figured out what he was, I never underestimated what he was capable of." She gave him a narrow smile. "Or any man, for that matter. All of which leaves me very wary of you."

"I was wondering if you might need any of my . . ."

Another knock at the door. This one insistent. Kalen Tompzen called, "I've got him, ma'am."

"Excuse me." She stood, calling, "Kalen, bring him in."

She stepped to the back table, dropped her hand to the shelf built into the wall.

Tompzen—his face like a mask—opened the door and straight-armed Pavel Tomashev into the room.

The part-time miner, hunter, and prospector had a reddening bruise under his right eye. The man's chamois-hide shirt and pants were filthy and scuffed, as if he'd been dragged for a distance in the street.

Pavel blinked, swallowed hard, and fixed his eyes on Allison. "Hey, listen. I'm sorry. I wasn't thinking when I shot off my mouth. So, like, Ali, I won't do it again."

Pavel's exact words had been, *"If sweet Ali thinks I give a shit, she can come suck my cock."*

Allison gave him a humorless smile. "No. You won't. But your stupid fucking mouth aside, you walked out on Shin Wong owing the house almost five hundred siddars. Four hundred, ninety-seven to be exact. Is that right Kalen?"

"Yes, ma'am. And another fifteen that he stiffed Vik for drinks."

Tomashev winced. "Yeah, yeah. Five twelve altogether.

Listen. I was drunk. Shit happens when I get drunk. I'll bring it around soon as I can round it up."

"Put your hand out on the table. That's it. Palm down. Perfect." She smiled, fingers curling around the handle where the pick hammer lay on the shelf. With a fluid move, she swung the geologist's hammer in an arc. Drove the sharp point through the back of his hand, through flesh, bone, and tendons, and into the wood beneath.

Pavel let out a blood-curdling scream, tried to jerk his hand away. Immediately gave that up as a bad idea. He stared at his impaled hand, wide-eyed and panting. Just as he drew breath to protest, Kalen laid the blade of his knife against the man's gulping Adam's apple.

Allison leaned close. "Pavel, you will pay us what you owe us. Immediately. Now, the talk around town is that with Dan gone, sweet little Ali's going to be an easy mark. Not nearly so scary as that psychopathic throat-cutting Dan Wirth was."

She paused, watching the fear-sweat bead on Pavel's face. "What do you think? Should I give Kalen that special nod of the head that says, 'Do it?' You know, just so people know that sweet Ali's not a fainthearted little flower that just anyone can pluck?"

The man's bugged eyes were fixed on the spiked hammer. Blood was beginning to seep out around the steel. "N—No. I got the plunder, Ali. Don't need no throat-cutting. I'm good for it."

"I figured you'd be. Not to mention that I know how it is to be a little drunk. I've done some foolish things myself when deep in the cups." She gave him a saucy wink. "So it's a good thing I'm sober, huh? If I'd been drunk—and pissed off like I am now—I'd be even more enraged when I sobered up tomorrow and had to clean up all of your stinking blood."

She worked the point of the hammer loose and pulled it free; Pavel clutched his bleeding hand to his chest.

"But, you're right about one thing: It's not the same as when Dan was in charge. He'd have thrown you out in the alley to bleed. I wouldn't do that."

"Y-Yes?"

She told Kalen, "Take Pavel over to Raya's. Have her set his bones, sew his tendons together, and what have you. We don't want him lamed up, not when that latest strike of his out in the Blood Mountains is showing color. And wait, seems to me that The Jewel has a half interest in the proceeds from that claim, right, Pavel?"

"Y—Yes, ma'am. It's in the papers. Dickered it with Dan."

"Nice to know your memory is good. Now, don't let anything else slip your mind."

She gave Kalen the nod, and he removed his knife, steered the weeping Pavel Tomashev out, and closed the door.

Allison, sighed, inspected the blood dripping from her pick hammer, and wiped it clean with a rag. Retreating to her desk, she laid the hammer on the ornate wood with a clunk and seated herself before retrieving her whiskey. "Sorry. Like I said. I only do business these days."

Taglioni had an amused twist to his perfect lips. "Good. Because, along with cadging a free drink, I'm here for business. Now that Dan's gone, would you have any objection to me running a game at your tables now and then?"

"House gets fifty percent of your take."

"Twenty-five. Not to mention that being the only Taglioni on the planet, my presence brings a certain cachet to the place."

"I think we can see our way clear for thirty-five. Same as the tables pay off. Any *other* interests?"

Here it came. How long before he wanted to bed her? Tonight? Or was he thinking to make a longer play of it? Try and convince her it was true love?

To her surprise, he said, "Nope. That will do. At least for now. Sometime, in the future, as things progress, however, I'd like to talk to you about some of the properties you hold." He stood, tossing off his whiskey. "But that is for another day."

At the door, he gave her a respectful salute with his index finger. "Good night, Allison."

And then he was gone.

"Oh, brave new world," she told herself, and drained the last of her whiskey.

87

Kalico Aguila strode down the avenue, gravel crunching under her feet. She'd just left the shuttle, coming through the gate in the forefront of her weekly rotation up from Corporate Mine. Things were going well. Thanks, in part, to the brand-new mucking machines that had been included in *Ashanti*'s cargo manifest.

Also, and most auspicious, were the cacao seeds that had been included along with the agricultural supplies. Of less value were the two heavy-duty gleaners. Giant machines built for harvesting grain fields. Neither of the monsters could manage a complete turn without exceeding the limits of a local Port Authority grain field.

But then, this was Donovan.

Toby Montoya was eyeing both of the beasts, a gleam in his eyes. He was just waiting for the next time something broke at Corporate Mine, something that required his skill to fix. When it did, he'd be rubbing his hands in anticipation of the chance to dicker the harvesters away from Kalico. No telling what he'd make out them. Dump trucks? Brush hogs? Or something even more outlandish?

When it came to imagination on Donovan, The Corporation could have learned a thing or two.

"There you are!"

Kalico turned in time to see Dek Taglioni step out of the gunsmith's shop. The scion of wealth and privilege wore a quetzal-hide cape, a claw-shrub-fiber shirt embroidered with colorful quetzals, and knee-high boots. Pouches hung from his belt, and the wooden grip of his fancy pistol was polished to a sheen.

"Derek Taglioni," she replied as he walked up, a grin bending the scar on his cheek. "Thought you were out at Briggs' place."

"Back in town. Wanted to be sure that Wirth got off without issue. Had some other business. Trip's a lot faster in an airplane. Made my life easier after Pamlico Jones finally got it unpacked."

"Making yourself right at home out there, I take it?" She shot him a sidelong glance. The scar would slowly whiten, adding to his rakish charm. His hair was longer, and he now wore it combed back.

"Been out with Kylee and Tip. Made a couple of passes over the forest out west of Tyson. Been dangling biosensors down into the trees. Took us a couple of times, but we've got it. We can find the damn thing."

"You're talking about the beast that killed Dya and Talbot?" Memory of that day still plagued her nightmares.

"Kylee pegged it. The day she and Flute lured Batuhan into its lair, she caught a faint whiff. Called it a 'rotten blood' smell. It's something we've never seen. Huge. Probably arboreal. The sensor indicates it's about fifty meters across, has some sort of adaptation that allows it to cling to branches."

"I was there. Looking right at where Dya's body vanished."

"And you know how good Donovanian life is at camouflage, right? This thing is different. And it's smart. Bems, skewers, they freeze in place. This thing moves. Like it knows when we're looking for it."

Big as it was supposed to be? Muldare's shots should have hit it somewhere.

"Buy you supper?" he asked as they came even with Inga's.

"Sure." She said it without thinking, only to be shocked when she realized how comfortable she felt with him.

He caught the look she was giving him as he held the door. "What?"

"Who the hell are you?"

Quick as he was, he caught her meaning and bit off a laugh. "Not really sure these days, but I'm working on it. Make you a deal?"

"Yeah?"

"If I ever find out, I'll let you know."

She took the lead, heels rapping as she led the way down the stairs. Passing tables, she called out greetings to people, answered their waves, surprised that Dek got his share of smiles and hellos.

She perched herself on her usual high stool, Dek climbing up beside her.

"Amber ale and a whiskey?" Inga asked, striding toward them.

"And a supper special," Dek called, "Plus whatever Kalico wants."

"Chili," Kalico called.

"You buying?" Inga asked.

Dek tossed a ten-SDR onto the bar. "Keep the change."

After Inga flipped her towel up over her shoulder and bellowed, "Special and a bowl of chili" at the top of her lungs, she lumbered back toward her taps.

"Keep the change? What are you doing for a living?"

"Hunting. A little prospecting. Spending time with Kylee, Tip, and Flute in the bush when they'll let me. It's the airplane that makes the difference. Locked away in its crate in cargo, I couldn't trade it off back when I thought we were all going to die. Don't know what I'm going to do with the exercise equipment and the entertainment center. I'd set up a theater, but stupid me, I can't access Corp-net for content."

"What could you have been thinking?"

"That Donovan would be a cruder sort of Solar System. The kind of place where a cruder sort of man could be top dog. I'll never be that naïve again. Which is why I'm so taken with the bush."

"It's a miracle that you're still alive, you know."

"Nothing is as sobering as being human on Donovan. But I'm learning. I suppose in the end the odds will get me."

"Talbot said the same thing," she said softly. "And they did."

Dek took his beer as Inga set the drinks on the battered chabacho bar. He clinked it to the rim of Kalico's glass. "To Mark Talbot. And living every day as if it's the last."

"What the hell were you thinking, getting Dan Wirth a berth on *Ashanti*?"

"He wanted to go back. I gave him the chance."

"Why?"

"He was getting bored, Supervisor. The man is no one's fool. He'd risen as high as he can rise on Donovan. He knows better than to fiddle with PA or Corporate Mine because the minutia of everyday operations would drive him to insanity. He was the king of his heap. But what's the point of being the richest man in the universe if he's stuck on Donovan where no one cares?"

She felt that old wariness begin to stir down inside. "And what's your angle?"

"Completely mercenary. I like it here. As we just determined, given my penchant for the bush, I'm a short-timer before a bem, a skewer, a flock of mobbers, a quetzal, or some other weirdness gets me. But when I come to town, I want to spend time with Shig, you, Talina, and enjoy the place. If PA is to have any long-term prospects, Wirth had to go."

"What made you think he'd screw it up?"

"Bored? Frustrated? Eventually he'd have gone sideways at the worst possible moment. Someone would have pissed him off on the wrong day. It would wound my soul if, in a fit of pique, he'd have killed Shig." He fixed his yellow-green eyes on hers. "Or you."

"Thought you didn't like me."

"People change. I did." He gave her a noncommittal shrug. "So the best way to avoid Wirth's kind of trouble was to get him off the planet. He's a sick fart sucker, and he thinks he can play the big game in Corporate politics. Maybe he can. I give him a ten-percent chance of living out his first year."

"How do you figure that?"

"Because I just shipped two entire safes full of his plunder off to Transluna under a Taglioni seal. Of course, I get my share. Miko and the family get theirs. Makes us the richest family in Solar System. And Dan still has tens of billions of SDRs to play with. He's out of contract. Makes him a pain in the ass for the Board, but they'll deal."

"Or have him suffer some unforeseen accident." She saw the brilliance of it. "Should have thought of that myself. There's no way they can hush up that kind of wealth. The story will get out that a petty criminal, out of contract, returned from Donovan as the wealthiest man in Solar System. That's going to shake the Board to its roots. If a scum like Wirth can accomplish what he has, what could a talented, educated, capable, and well-backed individual achieve?"

He was smiling, something smug about it.

"Ah!" Kalico smacked the bar. "Well played. Miko will be wondering exactly that about you. Derek Taglioni, with all the family advantages, is loose and ungoverned on Donovan. Given the way Miko's going to twist and fret about what you're doing out here, he won't get a good night's sleep until he can send a ship and find out."

"Hey, Miko can sleep in peace. Me? I'm just a local hunter and prospector."

For a moment, perplexed, she studied him. "For a newcomer, your acumen amazes me."

Dek shrugged, sipped his beer. "Like I said. I like it here. I don't want it ruined."

"And how do I fit into your calculus?"

"You're right where you need to be. You don't know it yet, but you've found your place, and it's found you."

"I still want to be Chairman of the Board."

The corners of his lips twitched in amusement. "Who wouldn't? At least for a week or two. Unfortunately, once Donovan sank its claws into you"—he ran a finger along the scar on the back of her hand—"the woman who would have been Chairman was forever altered into something greater."

She shivered, surprised by the daring of his touch. "Greater?"

"As Chairman you'd be a master when it came to the intrigue; you'd revel in the accolades. But your heart would remain unfulfilled, your triumphs oddly vacuous. Each victory somehow hollow and bland in aftertaste."

She shifted uncomfortably, took a swig of Inga's whiskey. Savored it. "Who the hell do you think you are? Shig?"

"I'll never be that insightful, but he'd agree."

"Okay, guru, where the hell is my perfect destiny?"

"Right here. Living. Totally and unabashedly. Not only does Donovan need you, but you're complete as a human being. Vibrant. If you ever gave it up to go back to Transluna, it would rip a hole in your soul."

"You a psychotherapist now?"

He smiled as the food was set before them. "I cheat. I come from your world. It's an unfair advantage."

"I cheat, too. You're a Taglioni. Leopards don't change their spots." She took a spoonful of chili.

"The fact that you let me buy you supper is a start."

"Let alone that you saved my life . . . how many times?"

"Only a toilet-sucking boor would bring that up in a craven attempt to curry favor. I have other qualities." He pulled out another ten-SDR coin. "I'm turning into a pretty good hunter as well. Look! Earned by my skill and hard labor."

"Miko'd scoff."

"That pus bucket can fuck a skewer."

"Excuse me?"

"Sorry. Too much time around Kylee." A twinkle filled his eye. "I have to fly back out to Briggs tomorrow. Got a job to do. Well, assuming the cannibals at Tyson don't eat us. Have supper with me when I get back? My treat?"

"Why should I make a habit of this?"

"Hey, I'm not just any soft meat. When I go hunting it's with a quetzal and two teenagers."

Kalico threw her head back and laughed in a way she hadn't in years. Dek Taglioni? Well, hell, who knew?

88

The forest had taken on an ominous feel. In the dim quarter-light of the forest floor, the air pressed on a person, hot, almost syrup-thick. Kylee swallowed hard. Experienced that prickle of anxiety running through her muscles as she climbed up onto the root tangle. Perched on high, she balanced. With her quetzal-enhanced vision, she searched the high canopy. Up there, in the tracery of branches. She could sense it: the old, dark memory.

If she closed her eyes, she could feel a cold and hollow hunger. Something ancient. A sentience so alien it tickled her soul with feathers of terror.

Didn't count that it was a matter of honor, that she owed this to Mom and Mark. Fact was, she'd rather be back at Briggs with Tip and Flute. Safe. Not here in the dim forest, knowing that she was being hunted.

Flute had been willing, would have endured another flight, taken a chance at being killed. That he knew the risks, would have done it for her, said something about quetzals.

Maybe, because she'd said no when every fiber of her being wanted him here with her, it said something about her, too.

The chime rose and fell, ending in its uniquely atonal harmony. She was learning. Each region of Donovan where she'd traveled had its own unique chime, always a composite of the different species. The Tyson chime was as much a signature as Mundo's.

A faint rime of perspiration dampened her cheeks, her neck and chest. Warily, she shifted, following the slow twist of the root mass beneath her feet. Something called out in the heights, the sound low and warbling. Tree clinger? Hopper? Some unknown creature?

She tensed her muscles, flexed her legs as she shifted her balance in time to the root's movements. Her heart was thumping, driving adrenaline-charged blood through her veins.

"Hey!" she shouted. "Fucker! You up there! Come get me, you piece of shit!"

Kylee could imagine Talina's reaction. The woman always cringed when Kylee cursed. As if she'd forgotten just who taught her those choice words to start with. Madison would be horrified. But then, Madison was tens of kilometers away.

And this was personal.

Cupping her hands around her mouth, Kylee thundered, "Asshole!"

There, was that movement? A shift in the IR, a change of pattern? She'd have sworn the branches wavered for an instant. Not the sort of thing a quetzal would notice, but human eyes, trained by eons of terrestrial evolution caught the wavering shift of image.

"There you are!" She pointed. "Right there. Ha! I see you! Got your ass now."

Even vigilant as she was, she almost missed it. Was looking at the body. Not down below. Not where the spike appeared out of nothingness, curling toward her with ferocious speed.

Fast as she was, the thing missed her by a bare finger's width as it ripped past. She barely caught herself, dropping to one hand to keep from losing her balance on the high root. Shot a look to follow the ropy black barb as it was pulled up high again.

"Got it?" Kylee called.

"Got it!" Talina's head popped up on the other side of a clump of roots no more than thirty meters away. She braced her rifle on the top, sighted, and released a cracking volley as she emptied a magazine.

Staring up, Kylee watched the IR shift as the rounds hit home, drove deep, and exploded.

The creature sucked up its wounded part, rolling it up inside a fold of hide. How damn big was that thing? Those rounds would have torn a quetzal in two.

Kylee tensed as the black tip of the tentacle came whipping down again. Instinctively, she dropped down in front of the top root. Timed it and skipped sideways.

The impact as the sharp spear drove into the barrel-thick root toppled her from her hold. She fell, bounced off a root, and threw herself backward onto the mat below.

The whole mass went crazy as quetzal shit. She scrambled backward in a crab walk, watching the massive root, impaled as it was. The tentacle kept tugging, trying to break free. Would have, but the root, like a giant rolling drum, twisted around itself. Acting like a capstan it wound the impaled tentacle tight, trapping it.

From overhead, a deafening shriek sounded.

Even as the roots under Kylee's hands and feet erupted in movement, a thrashing began shaking the branches above. The sound of snapping, the rattle of leaves, a whipping back and forth as branches cracked overwhelmed the chime.

Careening for balance, Kylee found her feet. Arms extended, she scampered across the now-writhing mess, barely avoided being trapped as she fled over a bundle of interwoven roots.

Over the tumult, she heard Talina's voice shouting into com: "Dek? Where are you?"

Kylee raced across an open space, vaulted another bundle of roots, and barely skipped out of the way as a sidewinder whipped out from a hollow.

Heart hammering, she beat feet for the next tangle—and somehow got across before they convulsed with the intensity of God pulling the Gordian knot tight.

Panting, she located Talina, saw the woman backpedaling, struggling for balance on the squirming footing as she kept her eyes skyward.

Kylee chanced a glance. Followed the trapped tentacle up to where the great beast clung among the whipping branches. How big? Maybe fifty meters across the body. The legs weren't legs but elongated tissue that ended in prehensile tentacles that wrapped around the high branches. Even in extremis, the creature tried to mimic its surroundings, but the patterns were off, almost random, like a riot of alternating shapes.

"Dek?" Talina screamed.

Even as she did, the sound of the airplane was faintly audible over the creature's ear-splitting screams and the thrashing forest.

Kylee bit her lip, fought for balance, then turned and ran again as the roots began to roil.

"Run!" she shouted at Talina. Saw her friend turn, bolting across the traumatized roots. Together they scrambled across a high tangle of trunk-thick roots.

"Come on, Dek!" Talina said between ragged pants. "Where the hell are you?"

"He'll . . ." Over her shoulder, Kylee caught a glimpse of the tentacle thinning under the tremendous strain. It broke. The meaty parting of tissue and tendon like a clap of thunder. With the power of severed elastic, the trapped length snapped down onto the bundled roots. Above, the remaining stump shot up into the creature's body, its path marked by spewing fluids.

Then movement. Something big. Indistinct and incredibly fast. Accompanied by crashing and tearing, branches were being whipped back only to lash angrily forward. The entire canopy seemed to erupt.

"What the hell?"

"Kylee!" Talina screamed. "Duck!"

The detonation blasted downward as the branches where the beast had been were torn asunder. In the deafening explosion's roar came a clutter of broken branches, shredded leaves, and cascading detritus.

"Fucking run!" Talina shouted. And turning, she sprinted, leaping roots, pounding her way up tangles.

Kylee was right with her, matching her step for step.

"That's for Mom and Dad, you piece of shit," Kylee averred, and then she put all of her efforts toward speed as agitation spread through the roots like a tsunami racing toward a distant shore.

A last thought was: *This whole thing might have been a mistake.*

Any second now, the roots were going to be too wild, the footing too precarious. All it would take was a single misstep . . .

89

Dek yanked back on the stick, worked the rudder, and pulled a couple of gs as he rolled back over the forest. He'd dropped the charge perfectly. Had taken the time to ensure it was right on the money.

He could see the exact spot the magtex had detonated and torn a hole in the canopy. Trees were shredded, leaves torn, the forest reacting like a stone had been dropped into a pond. The agitation spread out in a giant ring. A meteor impact into an ocean would look that way.

"Talina?" he called. "Did we get it?"

No answer.

Instead, he checked the instruments. Should have been organic material blasted all over the place. Chunks of torn tissue, given the mass they'd calculated for the creature. His readings showed some animal tissue, lots of tree organics, of course.

"But not enough creature guts and goo," he murmured as he banked around for another look.

It was the angle of the light. He saw it. Like a V just ahead of the expanding tsunami of tree agitation.

He straightened, settled the airplane's nose on the point of the vee, and dropped down. His remote sensors made the tag. Got the same readings as when he'd flown the survey that originally pinpointed the creature's location. The difference this time was a lot of heat. Something big, moving fast.

But what the hell?

How could something that big travel that fast? And yes, he was getting a trail of animal proteins. The monster was wounded. Bleeding. Leaking. Whatever.

He dropped his airspeed to just above stall speed to try and keep pace. Couldn't. Had to circle.

"Dek?"

"Tal? You all right?"

"Fucking crazy down here." She sounded out of breath. *"Remind us not to be on the ground underneath one of these things next time we bomb it."*

"Yeah, well, I've got some bad news for you."

"How's that?"

"It got away. It's wounded, headed almost due west through the treetops. And Tal? It's moving along at about thirty kph."

Silence.

Finally, Talina's voice, almost sounding defeated, replied, *"Shit! What the hell is this thing?"*

"I don't know. I've got the recordings, but Talina? My take? That thing knew the second I dropped that charge. Like it knew exactly when to cut its losses and run."

Silence.

Then, *"I just told Kylee. Is it still moving?"*

"Affirmative. Doesn't seem to be slowing in the slightest. Just headed west like it's on a mission. And moving in a hell of a hurry."

"Roger that. Maybe Vixen *can pick it up on the long-range sensors. How's your fuel?"*

"About sixty percent in the powerpack."

"Yeah. We've done all we can here. See you back in PA."

Dek ground his teeth, glared down at where the agitation in the trees marked the creature's path. "What the hell are you?"

And more to the point, where was it going?

And how could it have known it was being bombed from above?

EPILOGUE

Inga's tavern was running on full throttle that night. And regular as clockwork, it was Hofer who'd been too deep in his cups. While he'd give you the shirt off his back when he was sober, the guy had a tendency to let his mouth overload his ass when he was drunk.

Now it was some poor ship's tech who was catching it; out of contract on *Ashanti,* he'd stayed behind to try his luck.

"Hey!" Talina bellowed. She pulled her pistol, banged it on the chabacho-wood bar. "You stop that shit, Hofer, or I'm gonna smack your head into next week! Now, beat feet. Take your sorry chapped ass home and put it in bed! I see you out again tonight, and *maybe* Raya will be able to put the pieces back together!"

Inga's went quiet as a tomb. People staring.

Three tables away, Hofer, almost reeling on his feet, craned his head in Talina's direction. The man's eyes—glittering with drink—widened in an owlish manner. He swallowed hard. With careful fingers, he let loose of the Skull he'd jerked off the bench and was about to punch in the face.

"Yeah, yeah," he muttered. Paused to straighten the Skull's rumpled uniform shirt, and on unsteady feet, wobbled his way toward the door.

"You!" Talina barked, pointing with the pistol. "Soft meat, you're no better. Get your candy ass out of here, or you'll be carried. Got it?"

The Skull, maybe in his mid-thirties, gulped. Not knowing what else to do, he snapped off a salute and slurred, "Yes, ma'am."

Then he, too, started for the exit on unsteady feet. Made it only to the foot of the stairs, bent, and heaved his guts all over the stone floor. Groans and catcalls went up from around the room.

Fitzroy and one of the Hmongs grabbed him by the armpits, hustling him up the stairs.

Talina reholstered her pistol and turned back to her glass of stout. The poor sod would probably find himself atop the nearest shipping crate come morning. No one just pitched a drunk onto the ground. Not in PA. Too much chance of a slug, you know.

Talina sighed, rubbed her forehead.

She'd seen Kalico down the bar talking to Pamlico Jones. Probably something about the *Ashanti* cargo. It hadn't turned out to be the mother lode everyone had hoped for. But for some lights, the six airtrucks, a couple pieces of ludicrous farm equipment, and the cacao seeds, most of the inventory turned out to be in support of the Maritime Unit.

Boats, underwater vehicles, diving pods, and the like were all good and well for Michaela's team out in the ocean where they'd dropped their main pod. Not so good for PA and Corporate Mine.

"Hear you missed the beast that got Talbot and Dya." Kalico appeared at Talina's elbow and hitched herself up on her stool, a half-glass of whiskey already in hand.

"Dek and I went over the video. It *knew*. No doubt about it. The thing snapped its trapped tentacle off and fled the moment Dek dropped his charge. Oh, and there's this. Memo to Supervisor: Do *not* be standing below when you try to blow arboreal monsters out of the trees in deep forest."

"A little hairy?"

"That's the closest I've been to dead in a while. Kylee and I made it. Barely. That entire forest went apeshit. As fast as we were hauling ass, we'd have been dead a couple of times over if the tooth flowers, sidewinders, and gotcha vines hadn't been hanging on for dear life." Talina grunted. "How stupid can we be? And this far into the game?"

Kalico shook her head. "I keep seeing that huge black *thing*. How it stuck through their bodies. Jerked them like eiderdown into the air."

"Yeah, well it's still out there to creep-freak your dreams. *Vixen* wasn't in position to track it. Kylee's pissed."

"Knowing something's out there is half the battle."

Talina toyed with her stout glass. "Heard that *Ashanti* inverted symmetry today. Think they'll make it?"

"Don't know. But with each ship, the odds get better. Dek sent Wirth back as bait. If *Ashanti* pops back in Solar System's space, it will be the richest treasure ship in all of human history. But it's Wirth's plunder that will focus the Board. Donovan will be the center of their every thought and ambition."

Talina raised her glass. "To the lily-assed Board. Maybe they can send us chickens again. I miss eggs, and I think we're smart enough to keep the hens from eating the invertebrates this time around."

"How were the cannibals doing?"

"Passable. At least they didn't interfere with the monster hunt. I think they're starting to realize just what a rough row they have to hoe out there. That woman, Shyanne, I think we can deal with her."

Kalico fingered the scar that ran down her jaw. "It's a new calculus. We've got two new settlements. Michaela Hailwood wants me to see the Maritime Unit as soon as she gets it fully functional. Talking with her, I get the feeling that some of her people are already getting antsy. Like Corporate Mine, I'm going to have to set up a rotation for them."

"Sure." Talina smiled grimly. "Hey, with the cannibals, the Maritime Unit, and the *Ashanti* crew who stayed, we're back to a thousand people. Not to mention a real living Taglioni."

"Dek come back with you?"

"Nope. He stayed out at Briggs' place. I guess Chaco showed him a real promising vein in the next canyon. Dek said he wanted to get some ore samples for assay."

"Oh."

Talina arched a brow. "Heard you and he went for a long walk the other night."

"I don't know what to do with him." Kalico gave her an evaluative look. "What he did with Wirth? He's thinking five moves ahead. And don't for a minute buy this humble I-wanna-be-a-Wild-One shit. He's a Taglioni. He can't help himself. That's still hidden down there inside him somewhere."

"Maybe. My take? He belongs to Donovan now. Like the Unreconciled, he's never going back."

"How so?"

"He and Flute have exchanged blood."

"He tell you that?"

"Didn't have to. I saw the wound. And I know it was voluntary. Which leaves you with a question for yourself: You ever going back?"

Kalico's gaze went blank, staring into some infinity in her mind. "Dek tells me I can't."

"And?"

"Scares me right down to my bones."

"Welcome to Donovan."

Kathleen O'Neal Gear

THE ICE LION
Book One of the Rewilding Report

One thousand years in the future, the zyme, a thick blanket of luminous green slime, covers the oceans. Glaciers three miles high rise over the continents. The old stories say that when the Jemen, godlike beings from the past, realized their efforts to halt global warming had gone terribly wrong, they made a desperate gamble to save life on earth and recreated species that had survived the worst of the earth's Ice Ages.

Sixteen-summers-old Lynx and his best friend Quiller are members of the Sealion People—archaic humans known as Denisovans. They live in a world growing colder, a world filled with monstrous predators that hunt them for food. When they flee to a new land, they meet a strange old man who impossibly seems to be the last of the Jemen. He tells Lynx the only way he can save his world is by sacrificing himself to the last true god . . . a quantum computer named Quancee.

978-0-7564-1584-5

DAW 222